BACK

Watch Your BACK

LISA Y. WATSON

URBAN BOOKS
www.urbanbooks.net

URBAN SOUL is published by

Urban Books
10 Brennan Place
Deer Park, NY 11729

ISBN-13: 978-1-59983-097-1
ISBN-10: 1-59983-097-3

First Printing: September 2009
10 9 8 7 6 5 4 3

Printed in the United States of America

Watch Your
BACK

PROLOGUE

A tall, muscular man paced the floor of his study. Deep in thought, he wasn't aware that the glass brandy snifter in his hand threatened to spill its contents with each turn. When he heard the front door open, his head snapped up. The resounding slam of it closing echoed around the room. *Candace.* Setting his drink down on the dark cherrywood desk, he riveted his amber eyes to the entrance. As if on cue, a woman glided in with a whoosh. Throwing her mink wrap and designer purse on the closest chair, she stood waiting.

The man's eyes smoldered with passion. Striding purposefully across the room, he pulled her into his arms, kissing her with slow deliberation. "Baby, you're back. You can't imagine how much I've missed you." His gaze traveled the full length of her body before he continued. "How was your appointment?"

The statuesque beauty in the body-hugging red suit sat down on the leather couch. Candace Monroe crossed well-toned legs before reaching over to retrieve her purse. Pulling out a compact, she assessed the damage his embrace had caused her meticulously applied make-up. "How do you think? The test was right the first time I took it," she replied, pursing her lips in the mirror. "Now it's confirmed. I'm pregnant."

He rushed to her side. Kneeling, he placed his large hands on her thighs. "Candace, that's wonderful news. It's the miracle I've been waiting for. Do you want to tell Devon, or shall I?"

One of her perfectly waxed eyebrows arched. Smoothing thick reddish brown hair tighter into its French twist, she tilted her head. "Tell him what? That you and I slept together while he was out of town three months ago? That we've been seeing each other since, and now I'm pregnant—with your child?"

"That works for me."

"I'm certain Devon won't take too kindly to being duped by his girlfriend—or you."

Startled, he leaned back on his haunches, the surprise on his face as genuine as the sneer on hers. "You're kidding, right? We're going to confess the truth—that while he was traveling on business, we rediscovered each other. I've never stopped loving you, Candace. Once we're married, we'll be the family we should've been long ago, before we broke up and you started dating Devon."

The laughter escaping her lips echoed off every piece of furniture in the room. Getting up, she walked across the expansive space. He stood.

"Have you lost your mind? For goodness' sakes, it's an affair. Nothing more. We aren't breathing a word. I'm going to have this baby, and Devon will be none the wiser."

"Like hell you are." He strode across the room. "You're carrying my baby. Mine. I have no intention of letting you pass off my flesh and blood as another man's child. You can get that out of your head. You will marry me. *Our* baby will be legitimate."

Running her manicured fingers along his jawline, she tried a different approach. "Darling, listen to me. You're blowing this way out of proportion. We've had some good times in the past. It was wonderful being reminded of the passion we shared years ago, but I'm not in love with you. I love Devon, and I'm not about to ruin my chances of producing an heir to the Mitchell fortune."

"It's not going to happen."

Candace let out a frustrated sigh. "Can't you see how important this is to me? I've got the name and face recognition. All my peers in the fashion world vie for my attention. Still, I'm not good enough for Devon Mitchell's family."

"Why does that matter?"

"Are you serious? It means everything. I'll no longer be just another girl they can turn their noses up at. I'll be family." Her face lit up. "Can't you see how much that's worth? I can. Millions."

Recoiling from the greed in her eyes, he felt his stomach lurch as if he'd been dealt a sharp blow. "You can't do this. I love you. I've always loved you. I want you to be my wife and for us to raise our child—together."

Her good humor vanished. "I shouldn't have gone to your house that night. Look, I'm flattered you care enough about me to want to marry me, but I won't accept your proposal. It has to be this way. When you think about this, you'll see my plan is the best one for all of us."

His laugh contradicted the malice in his tone. "How can you claim to be so smart and yet be so incredibly stupid?"

"What are you talking about?"

"This isn't the same bait-and-switch job of your mother's era, sweetheart. Today we've got advanced paternity tests. It'll take exactly two seconds after you tell Devon you're pregnant for him to demand DNA proof that the baby's his. You two aren't exactly on stable terms, and your relationship was imploding before we had sex. Truthfully, I'd be surprised if Devon doesn't boot you out the minute he gets back. When was the last time he even slept with you? Hate to put a damper on the fantasy, sweetheart, but if you don't think he'll question your claim that he's the father, you're delusional."

Candace shrugged. "I'll cross that bridge when I come to it. Besides, the last thing his family will want is a scandal. If I say I'm pregnant and that it's a Mitchell to enough people, they won't drag me into a lab to prove it. At the very least, they'll try to buy me off, and to keep me out of Devon's life, it'll cost them—big-time."

He looked at her as if she'd lost her mind.

Angrily, she snarled, "Don't look at me like that. This will work. I'm going to come out on top. I don't care if you believe me or not." Candace sailed past him. She was almost to the couch when he grabbed her arm.

"What does Devon have that I don't? You think there's anything you need that I can't give you?"

Condescendingly, she smiled at him as if he were a child. "His family has connections. You don't. They're worth millions. You aren't. They're well known and revered in the social world. You're an outsider. I've always dreamed of being a socialite, with the backing of a powerful family. You don't even know who your father is."

His eyes narrowed. "I know who my father is."

"Don't get offended. The point is I can't model forever. Even with the money I make and my investments, it won't be enough to sustain my lifestyle."

"You should've thought of that before we slept together." He shut his eyes to get a handle on the pain. Once again, the only woman he'd ever loved was slipping from his grasp faster than a dollar could burn. Contempt for her darkened his tawny eyes. "How could I have been this blind? I should've realized you're a heartless opportunist, ignorant to what true love is."

"Careful, darling," Candace warned. "You stand to lose almost as much as I do."

Roughly, he yanked her within inches of his face. Anger distorted his handsome features. "You want to play, gold digger? Fine. We'll play, but it'll be my way. You want Devon? You can have him and his family. It doesn't include my child. You've got one week until Devon returns from his trip. I suggest you think things over. There's a party being given the night he gets back. I'll be there, and you'd better make sure you show up, too." He loosened his hold, and his smile sweetened. "I'll be waiting for you to tell me Devon knows the truth about us, and if you don't tell me what I want to hear, your life won't be worth living, I promise."

Her eyes flashed in defiance. "Is that a threat?"

"You'd better believe it, sweetheart. I'll drag your name so far through the mud, you won't be accepted by anybody you deem socially important. I'll dredge up all the dirt-covered skeletons in your closet, and if I can't find enough, I'll make them up, just like the Mitchells will do if you try to back Devon into a corner with this ridiculous scheme. Hell, I might even tell them the truth myself."

Stroking his chest, she purred, "You wouldn't. You can't do this to me. You love me, and I'm carrying your child."

Peeling her hand off his body, he dismissed her. "Go home, Candace. Don't call my bluff."

She saw the determined expression and realized she'd underestimated him. She'd pushed him too far. Furious, Candace grabbed her things and stomped out. After exiting the room, she did her best to slam the door and tear it off its hinges. Seconds later, the front door suffered the same fate.

Walking to his desk, he retrieved his watered-down drink. He stared at the brown liquid and the partially melted ice cubes. Curling his lips in distaste, he threw the snifter against the nearest wall. The dark splotches of liquid etched random patterns across the wall's surface, while shards of glass littered the carpeted floor. As he fought to restrain his emotions, his heart hammered loudly in his chest. Candace's betrayal had left pain in his heart that threatened to overwhelm him. Though he still loved her, he'd meant what he'd said to her— every painful, gut-wrenching word. Moments later the full extent of her declaration washed over him. *You're going to be a father.* Candace's machinations weren't going to keep him from experiencing being something he'd never had growing up—a father. He wasn't going to let anyone take that from him. "Damn you, Devon."

CHAPTER 1

Candace chose her outfit with care. Everything had to be perfect. After all, this would be the most important night of her life. "A *Mitchell*," Candace said dreamily. In less than three hours, she would be engaged to one of the most sought-after bachelors in town. "Mrs. Devon Mitchell," Candace whispered, trying the name on for size. "I'll be marrying into one of the most respected, well-known, and ridiculously wealthy families in Chicago."

Spinning around in front of the mirror, Candace slid her tongue automatically over her teeth before she allowed her lips to part into her dazzling runway smile. She studied her reflection critically. The ice blue sequined Vera Wang gown she'd chosen was stunning. Her hairstylist had swept soft curls atop her head in a style that accentuated her long neck and plunging back line. Her make-up artist had given her a look that was natural and ultrafeminine. *Devon won't be able to resist you*, her inner voice assured her. Blowing herself a kiss in the mirror, Candace smiled. "It's showtime."

* * *

The party was in full swing by the time Candace arrived. Excitedly, she looked around the crowded ballroom for any signs of her boyfriend. She'd told him to meet her there instead of coming home first. It had been weeks since he'd left on a business trip, and she missed him. Candace frowned slightly, recalling the heated argument they'd had before he left, and the trace of anger in his voice when she'd spoken with him earlier. He hadn't wanted to come to the party. He'd told her as much, but she'd ignored him. Her plans were too important to leave to chance. She wanted a room full of important people when she made her announcement. Suddenly she felt someone watching her. Looking over her shoulder, she saw a man, but it wasn't the one she was waiting for. It was the lover she'd argued with a week ago. His expression was sardonic as his gaze traveled slowly up her body before coming to rest on her eyes. He was there to make sure she told Devon the truth about the baby she was carrying. *He'll ruin everything.*

"Stay focused," she whispered. Eyeing all the beautiful people and the media in the room gave her the boost she needed. With a confident sway of her hips, she turned and walked in the opposite direction. Candace was halfway across the room when she spotted Devon entering. Her heart fluttered excitedly. When their eyes met, she flashed him her signature smile, which had gotten her into more parties and men's bedrooms than she could count.

The anger in his gray eyes gave her pause. Her breath hitched in her throat. Something was wrong—terribly wrong. Candace stood rooted to her spot as she watched Devon stride toward her with purposeful, determined steps to intercept her. "No," she whispered as her hand traveled to her stomach. *You still hold the ace. Use it!* her inner voice commanded.

Candace zeroed in on the hostess of the party and allowed herself a triumphant smile before turning to walk up to the woman. The music the band played was loud, so Candace leaned in and whispered into the elderly woman's ear. A surprise registered on the woman's features. Nodding vigorously, the hostess grasped Candace's arm and led her toward the band.

Retrieving the microphone from its holder, the woman placed it in Candace's hand and gave her arm a squeeze. The band took this as their cue and wrapped up their song.

"Hello, everyone, I'd like to personally thank our lovely hostess for allowing me to interrupt what is by far the best party this town has seen in quite a while," Candace said into the microphone.

Loud claps echoed around the room. Candace used the time to look for Devon. She spotted him through the crowd. He was staring at her with curiosity. *Good.* Emboldened, Candace placed the microphone to her mouth again. "I'm sure all of you know me by now, but in case some of you have never picked up a magazine or watched television, my name is Candace Monroe."

Everyone in the audience roared with laughter, except the two men watching her from opposite sides of the room. Each wore a similar expression of anger.

"I hope you all don't mind my brief interruption, but I have the most exciting news, and I can't contain myself any longer. You see I just found out my fiancé, Devon Mitchell, and I are expecting a baby! I'm just beside myself with joy," Candace cried, with tears pooling in her eyes.

The crowd went wild with applause and cheers. Across

the room stood Candace's shocked and disgusted lover. Ignoring the condemnation in his eyes, Candace focused on her boyfriend. He looked murderous.

"Everyone, don't forget to congratulate Devon," she added, laughing and pointing to where he stood. "Go easy on him, though. He's just found out this minute that he's going to be a daddy."

All eyes were on Devon. He looked completely out of his element. It was mere seconds before reporters descended on his position, grilling him with questions and snapping pictures. Candace was also flocked by reporters and well-wishers. *You win!* she said to herself, with smug happiness. *Devon is yours.*

She watched him advance. It took some time, but eventually, Devon made it to her side. They were the longest moments in her life. "Hello, darling," Candace gushed, wrapping her arms around his neck.

Devon Mitchell's voice was calm, his stance relaxed, when he said, "Hello yourself."

Years of practice kept Candace from yelping when Devon's arms snaked around her waist in a tight grip.

When he spoke again, it was a harsh whisper in her ear. "Outside. Now."

She started to protest aloud, but his grip tightened. "If you'll all excuse me, I'd like a few private moments with my fiancé," Candace informed the crowd before allowing Devon to lead her toward the entrance. Looking over her shoulder, Candace saw her lover advancing. He was furious. His handsome features were contorted with rage. Candace breathed a sigh of relief as the crowd of partygoers inadvertently blocked his path.

* * *

Devon's knuckles were white on his leather steering wheel. He almost redlined the engine before shifting gears again. The car effortlessly responded to the increased speed. "What were you thinking?"

"What?" Candace said calmly.

"So, we're engaged now, are we? Funny, I don't remember proposing to you, and why in the world didn't you tell me before now that you're pregnant?"

"Devon, it's almost an hour's drive back to the city. Are we going to argue the whole time?"

"You've got a lot of explaining to do, Candace, and as you said, we have an hour."

Silence permeated the car. After some time Devon spoke again.

"Don't get tongue-tied now, sweetheart. You were just dying to talk at the party. Now it's just you and me, and you having nothing to say?"

"Look, I know you didn't propose, but I was just so caught up in the moment, darling." Candace's voice softened. "I wanted to tell you the good news in a big way."

"That isn't exactly the kind of news a man wants to hear about in public, with a room full of strangers and a camera in his face."

"I told you. I was overcome with joy."

"Overcome? Candace. You lied and told everyone we were engaged."

"So? What's the big deal? We're having a baby, Devon. Aren't you happy? Your parents are going to be grandparents again. Of course, we are putting the cart before the horse, but there's still plenty of time to—"

"To what?" Devon snapped. "Have you manipulate the situation as it suits you?"

"Why are you getting so upset about this?"

"This is typical, Candace. You only see what you want

to see. You only concern yourself with your desires, and to hell with everyone else. I'm sorry, but that's not how this story is going to play out."

"What's that supposed to mean?"

"I'm not marrying you, Candace."

"If you think I'm having a baby on my own, you better think again."

"You won't be on your own. I have every intention of doing right by my child and providing for him or her," Devon informed her.

"You just don't want to marry the mother of your child? You think you can just discard me when you tire of me? I've given you two years of my life, and I'm carrying a Mitchell heir. I'm not about to be a single mother, raising a baby on my own. I can promise you I've come too far to just lie down and let you discard me like some old shoe. This was not the plan."

Devon's laugh was harsh. "So what *was* the plan, Candace? Not once have I heard you mention the word *love*, but then it's never been about love, has it? Not love for me, anyway. It's been all about simple math. You thought being pregnant with my child, plus taking advantage of a public opportunity to spread your lies and deceit, would equal me chained to you for life? Sorry to burst that bubble, but you picked the wrong guy. I don't care how many cameras are around and how many interviews you do. I won't be pressured into marrying someone I didn't even propose to and who doesn't love me. I'm just sorry I didn't break it off before it caused my family public embarrassment."

"Ha! I knew you'd mention them sooner or later. It's always been about your precious family," she said acidly. "They've never liked me, never accepted me. They've turned their nose up at me time and time again. You won't ever have a lasting relationship with a woman, because no one will ever be good enough!"

"Millions of women will be good enough, Candace. It'll just never be you."

"How dare you!" Candace raged, throwing herself at Devon. "I hate you!"

Taking his right arm off the wheel, Devon blocked Candace's attack. "Candace, stop it."

"No," she yelled and struck him again. "You self-righteous bastard! He told me you weren't good enough, and I didn't believe him, but it's true!"

"What are you talking about? Who?"

Before she could reply, Devon's car lurched violently in the middle of a turn.

"What are you doing? Why are you speeding?" Candace screamed.

"It's not me. The gas pedal's stuck."

The car skidded off the road and kept going. Devon tried to correct the wheel. The sound of the right tires coming in contact with the grooves on the shoulder was deafening.

"Don't just sit there! Do something," Candace shrieked. "Turn the car off!"

"If I do, we'll lose the power steering. I'm trying to slow us down. Just hold on," he yelled.

Without warning, there was a deafening pop as the rear right tire burst. Devon lost control of the car as it skidded to the right, over the shoulder, and down an embankment. The sound of metal bending, glass shattering, and Candace's screams echoed throughout the cabin as the car rolled over several times before coming to rest precariously on its side.

CHAPTER 2

"No. Oh God, no. Candace!" Devon yelled, bolting upright in bed. His eyes burned from unshed tears mingling with the sweat sliding off his forehead. Devon's lungs felt as if he'd been holding his breath for some time. It was a while before the pounding in his heart slowed. *Candace.*

He swung his legs slowly over the side, then, with unsteady hands, cradled his head. A thin film of sweat covered his shuddering body. The bright blue light from the nightstand clock announced the hour. It was just past four in the morning.

Heavy steps propelled him toward the bathroom. Devon splashed cold water on his face. The jolt that ensued sent shock waves throughout his exhausted body. The haggard, weary image reflected in the mirror had become commonplace. More sleep wasn't an option. It would only send him back to that fatal night. A horrifying night filled with lies, deceptions, and inescapable pain.

Devon grabbed a pair of well-worn jeans and put them on, passing up a shirt and shoes. It was a familiar routine.

Descending the old wooden steps, Devon was careful to avoid the spot that creaked.

He entered a comfortable kitchen. Hardwood floors that had darkened over time greeted him every morning. Worn wood cabinets hung along both walls in the U-shaped kitchen. Faded wallpaper with a fruit-laden pattern hinted at the home's age.

"Thought you could use this," his uncle Henry said, hovering over the coffeepot.

"Thanks."

Sitting down at a farm table built for six that had only two chairs, Devon waited for his uncle to break the silence.

"Same dream, huh?"

He didn't bother denying it. "I hope I didn't wake you."

Intelligent gray eyes sparkled as Henry grinned at his only nephew. "Nonsense. I had to get up soon, anyway. Got work to do."

Comforted, Devon couldn't help the smile that escaped. His father, Sterling Mitchell, and Sterling's younger brother, Henry, were as opposite as wine and beer nuts. Their work ethic was the only common bond. Wealthy in their own right, each sibling had walked a separate path to personal happiness.

Devon accepted the steaming cup of coffee his uncle had poured. Henry sat down across the table. Loosening his robe for comfort, he sighed. "So, you wanna talk about it?"

The younger man inhaled the pungent aroma of the coffee. "What's the point? It never goes away. I'm not sure I want it to."

"Now you're talking crazy. Those story-hungry vultures tried, but they couldn't make their accusations stick. Implying that you meant to cause that accident and that the Mitchell money had covered it up was nonsense. It was an injustice to this family. You did all you could to save her."

"If we hadn't been arguing, maybe I would've been paying more attention to the road. If—"

"You're just torturing yourself, and for what? You think your guilt is gonna bring that girl back?" Henry's voice lowered. "Or the baby?"

Henry's reference to Candace wasn't surprising. His uncle had disliked her the moment her manicured hand had shaken his callused one. Never one to hold his tongue, the old man had had no qualms about telling Devon what he thought. After that, Henry had referred to her only as "that girl."

"I know my guilt won't change anything, but I caused the crash that killed her and our unborn child. I'll live with that burden for the rest of my life."

Slamming down his coffee cup, Henry refuted the statement. "Bah! The police reconstruction crew deemed it an accident. It was a mechanical failure, Devon. The gas pedal got stuck, your tire blew, and you lost control of your car. It happens." His uncle was thoughtful for a minute. "Besides, what that girl did to you was shameful, and to make matters worse, she's still torturing you."

"Whatever Candace did pales in comparison to her losing her life, Henry. She didn't deserve to die." Devon struggled for composure.

"My boy, you know I've been happy to have your company these last few months, but enough is enough. You can't hide here forever, raking yourself over the coals." Henry slowly stood. Walking to the sink, he rinsed his cup, then faced his nephew. "You've got to go. You've been idling here far too long. You ain't doin' nothing but making yourself nuts."

Devon gave his uncle a quick look. "You're kicking me out?"

"That's right. It's been three months since the accident. The media has gone on to more newsworthy stories, and that girl is dead and buried, God rest her tortured soul. I can't bear to see you suffering anymore."

"I don't know if I'm ready to pick up where I left off."

"Sure you are. I spoke with fancy pants a few days ago. My brother thinks it's time you got back in the saddle. So do I." Before Devon could protest again, Henry retrieved a large brown envelope from a cupboard. Sitting, he slid the envelope across the table.

"What's this?"

"Everything you'll need to get back up to snuff."

Devon's stomach tightened when he saw his father's bold, pronounced writing on the envelope. The thought of resuming his old fast-paced lifestyle at his family's technical services company made him uneasy. That uncertainty was reflected in his expression.

"Just take your time and mull it over, son. I'm going to get dressed, then go milk my girl." Squeezing Devon's shoulder, he left the kitchen.

"Watch yourself," Devon warned.

"Always do."

Chuckling aloud, Devon played the familiar scene in his head. Abigail, the obstinate cow, would stand quietly while Henry got himself positioned. The moment he reached for her, she'd move. It was a battle of wills, and the winner of the skirmish changed daily.

A minute passed before Devon gave the envelope his attention. Turning it over, he ripped open the top and dumped its contents—a letter from his father, current earnings reports, and other pieces of mail. Putting his father's letter aside, he glanced at a note from the Wells Gallery, one of the companies his grandmother had bequeathed him, before reading the financials. After reading the note, his jaw dropped. "What the hell?" Tossing the note aside, Devon picked up the gallery's earnings statement. He read it twice. He bounded out of his chair and paced the floor. "How the devil could profits be off like this?"

Six years ago, before she died, his grandmother Cecilia Grayson Wells had bequeathed Devon her company Wells, Inc., and several business assets. The Wells Gallery was her pride and joy. The gesture had humbled him. He'd been surprised that Nana Wells hadn't left the company to his mother or his aunt. Voicing his concern, he'd asked why the shrewd businesswoman had entrusted him with her life's work. He recalled his mother's words. *Your nana wants you, her only grandson, to inherit her legacy—to have something of your own.*

Vowing never to jeopardize his grandmother's faith in him, Devon had solemnly accepted the responsibility. By any means necessary, her interests would continue to prosper.

His grandmother's friend and longtime director, Paolo Gambrini, handled the day-to-day operations of the gallery. Unlike his grandmother, Devon remained behind the scenes, but final decisions rested on his shoulders. Up until now the arrangement had worked out well—or so he'd thought. Within the envelope was the director's letter of resignation. Since Devon was out of touch, the second in command at Wells, Maxwell Shaw, had had no choice but to grant Paolo's request.

First, Candace's death, followed by the media frenzy that had descended on his family, and now the gallery was in jeopardy. Devon's need to avoid the public eye had been his only concern. He'd been selfish. The wall clock indicated it was 6:45 a.m. He was on central time. He strode to the counter and picked up the phone. Devon dialed Wells and waited. He was calling eastern standard time, so they were an hour ahead.

When the receptionist answered, he spoke. "It's Devon Mitchell. Put Maxwell on."

"Oh, Mr. Mitchell. I'm afraid Mr. Shaw is in a meeting. If you'd like to—"

"What he's in doesn't concern me. Why he isn't on the phone does."

"Yes, sir," the woman said quickly. "Just one moment, please."

Seconds later Maxwell Shaw's voice came over the line. "Devon? Where in the world have you been?"

"Long story. I'll tell you later. Bring me up to speed. You can start by telling me what the hell is going on at my gallery."

"Frankly, Devon, I'm at a loss myself. Over the last few months, the gallery has suffered setbacks of one kind or another. As I stated in my last report, late shipments, lost packages, and mishaps are causing a strain on our overhead. We're hardly bankrupt, but the gallery can't continue losing profits. It's not good business."

Devon remained silent for so long, Maxwell cleared this throat. "Devon? Are you still there?"

"Of course, I'm here," Devon snapped. "I take it Gambrini's gone?"

"Yes. He's moved back to Italy."

"Have we hired a replacement?"

"We're in the process. We have an acting director,

Jayde Seaton. She's been with us for quite some time. Devon, maybe you should consider—"

"I'm not closing the gallery," Devon interrupted. "That's not an option."

"I would never suggest that. I was going to say maybe you should promote Jayde to director. She's Paolo's intended replacement."

"I'm coming to D.C. for an extended stay to get the gallery back on track. Have the house opened up, and get everything ready by the time I arrive."

"Forgive me for being blunt, Devon, but are you sure this is going to work? Art isn't exactly your forte."

"It's time I took a hands-on approach. I've been remiss in handling my grandmother's affairs. I'll be at the gallery as long as it takes to get things back on track."

"What about Ms. Seaton? As I said . . . we already have the paperwork—"

"I'm sure you'll find a diplomatic way to break it to her. The gallery is my responsibility. I plan to find the problem and fix it. How long it takes is irrelevant. I'm not going back to work at the Mitchell Group until the gallery's on solid ground. Get the ball rolling, Max. You've got three days."

After he ended the call, Devon closed his eyes and ran a hand over his face. Guilt twisted his insides. *How could I have let this happen?* With a shake of his head, Devon headed to the barn.

Milking Abigail, Henry was singing loudly and slightly off-key.

"I'm leaving," Devon shouted over the ruckus.

"'Bout time," his uncle replied over his shoulder. "So, when you headed to Chicago?"

"I'm not. I've got some problems at the gallery that need my attention."

"The gallery? Can't someone else handle it?"

"No. I've been negligent in handling my responsibilities there for too long as it is. Besides, I made a promise to my grandmother, Henry, and it's one I intend to keep."

CHAPTER 3

Jayde Seaton closed her eyes, deeply inhaling the cool, crisp air. Spring in Washington, D.C., was her favorite time of the year. Three weeks ago the National Cherry Blossom Festival had proclaimed the new season's arrival. It was a time for new beginnings. For Jayde, it meant a new direction for her life, starting with a promotion. With conviction, she bade old feelings of doubt and uncertainty good-bye. This would be her year.

A horn blast snapped Jayde back to the present. Waving in the rearview mirror, she maneuvered her Jeep Wrangler through the throng of traffic. Spotting a parking space, she descended faster than her golden retriever, Boomer, dove for table scraps.

After parking, she riffled through her purse to find meter money. Tissues, candy wrappers, scattered make-up, and other junk hid the elusive change. Finally, she felt the coins, but not before pain shot through her finger, caused by a wayward safety pin. With a yelp, Jayde yanked her hand away immediately, then placed her finger in her mouth. "I need a bigger purse or smaller junk," she announced. This time she used her other hand. Victory washed over her when she grasped a bunch of quarters.

Task completed, she fell into step with the other pedestrians moving down the busy sidewalk. Determined to shop at Pentagon City for a new suit, she braved the evening rush hour. Traffic in Northern Virginia was horrendous at this hour, but well worth it.

Earlier, she'd received a message that one of the executives at Wells, Maxwell Shaw, had requested a meeting with her in two days. Jayde's heart had soared with excitement. She'd been waiting several months for this. "Finally, I'm being promoted to director. Just like Paolo promised," she said aloud, elated. Jayde was about to whoop with joy again just thinking about it. Giddy with anticipation, she felt the adrenaline pumping through her veins. Her mind wandered as she contemplated the changes she'd make to get the gallery on a solid footing. Whirling around the corner, Jayde slammed into an immovable object. Someone then grasped her by her shoulders before she could fall backward. The impact forced the breath from her mouth in a loud hiss.

"Geez, I'm sorry, miss," said the deep-voiced man. "I didn't see you."

Before she could utter a reply, dampness invaded her skin. She gazed down at the dark spot spreading rapidly across her chest. "My suit—it's ruined."

On the ground between them lay a battered cup; the remains of the beverage seeped into the concrete.

"So is my mocha chiller," the man replied, with a smile. When she didn't respond, his smile faded. He bent down to retrieve his cup. "Look, I feel terrible about this. I'd be happy to get it cleaned for you."

In the awkward moments that followed, Jayde studied the casually dressed man before her. His body was

seriously toned, but his jeans were faded, and the leather
jacket he wore over his plain T-shirt looked like it had
seen action in World War II. Her gaze traveled higher.
The perfectly etched dimple in his chin mesmerized her,
as did his startling gray eyes. His smooth brown complexion provided a stunning contrast to his eye color.

The heat that suddenly flowed through her body had
nothing to do with anger. She momentarily forgot what
she was going to say. A blush warmed her face, which
bothered her more than anything. Some random guy
had slammed into her, dousing her with cold coffee,
and she was staring at him, starry eyed and dumb-
struck. *How pathetic.*

"Forget it." Annoyance at her own girlish behavior
tinged her voice with unnecessary harshness. "This will
never come out."

Devon arched an eyebrow at her tone but smiled,
anyway. "Okay," he said, reaching into his back pocket
and pulling out a wallet. "Then allow me to reim-
burse you."

For some reason, his calm manner irritated Jayde
even more. "Forget it." Jayde pushed past him. "You
probably can't afford it."

Jayde heard him calling after her, but she refused to
turn around. She was almost around the corner when
his last remark stopped her in her tracks.

"Excuse me, miss? You forgot your broom!"

Two days later . . .

After a final once-over in the bathroom mirror, Jayde
smoothed nonexistent wrinkles from her suit. Slowly,
she expelled a breath. "I'm as ready as I'll ever be," she

said aloud. Confident, Jayde headed for the conference
room. Despite an unsteady hand, she knocked firmly on
the door. She took a deep breath. It wasn't every day she
met an employee from their parent company. Paolo
had attended most meetings involving gallery business
at Wells. Even though she'd been acting director, this
was the first time she'd meet any of the executive staff.

A man's voice bade her to enter.

Jayde opened the door and went in.

"Good morning, Ms. Seaton. I'm Maxwell Shaw."

She strode confidently toward him. "Good morning,
Mr. Shaw." She shook his hand. "Please, call me Jayde."

"Only if you'll call me Max."

"Will do," she agreed. Jayde caught a movement to
her right. She turned to see a man casually seated in a
chair, with his legs crossed at the ankle. "Oh, I didn't
know you had a meeting in progress." She backed
toward the door. "I can come back another time."

"No need. This concerns you as well. Jayde, I'd like
to introduce you to Devon Mitchell," said Maxwell.

Jayde turned. The man rose to his feet.

"You!" she blurted out. "What are you doing here?"

Surprise was evident on Devon's face as well. Recovering, he stood and extended his hand.

Too shocked to raise her hand in greeting, she stood
there, staring at him. After a few seconds, Devon returned his hand to his side.

Maxwell looked from one to the other in surprise.
"You two know each other?"

"Yes," Devon smirked while looking down at Jayde.
"We've shared a coffee."

Jayde's eyes narrowed.

"I've heard extraordinary things about you, Miss
Seaton," Devon continued.

"It appears you have me at a disadvantage, Mr. Mitchell. I haven't heard a thing about you," Jayde retorted.

"Why don't we all have a seat? Jayde, would you like some coffee?" Maxwell offered.

She eased into the closest chair. "Thanks," she replied, looking at Devon pointedly. "But I'm not fond of coffee."

"Well, I'm sure you're wondering why I asked for this meeting, so I won't keep you in suspense. Mr. Mitchell has just been hired at the gallery," Maxwell explained.

"Really? I wasn't informed we were hiring anyone," replied Jayde.

Jayde noticed that Maxwell looked ready to expire.

"No, you weren't, and for that I apologize. You see Devon actually—"

"This came about rather suddenly," Devon interrupted, with a silencing look toward Maxwell.

"I see." Jayde felt her palms grow moist. It was her body's indicator that the encounter wouldn't turn out well. "So, what exactly has Mr. Mitchell been hired to do?"

Maxwell shifted in his chair. "He'll be the new director."

Painful seconds passed before realization dawned. This wasn't the warm, fuzzy feeling she was expecting to flood her system. "Director?" Jayde said hoarsely. "Did I hear you correctly?"

Maxwell nodded. "You did. I told Mr. Mitchell you'd be his liaison until he learns the ropes. I'm sure this takes you totally unaware. For that, I deeply apologize."

This was the second time the older man had apologized in less than five minutes. Jayde didn't think she could handle another one. "Totally unaware would be an understatement, Mr. Shaw. I was under the impression that . . . I've been the acting director since Paolo returned to Italy a few months ago. Surely, I should've known of this decision before now."

Maxwell shrugged. "I just found out several days ago myself, Ms. Seaton. By then the decision had already been approved. There just wasn't time."

"Wasn't time? Mr. Shaw, my home phone number is listed in the gallery's employee directory," Jayde returned.

Maxwell nodded but remained silent. Slowly, Jayde stood. Her dazed stare traveled from the bearer of bad news to her new boss and back again. "Well, if there aren't any additional bombshells, I'll take my leave. Mr. Mitchell," she ground out, not bothering to look at him. "Welcome aboard."

"Thank you, Miss Seaton. I look forward to working with you," said Devon.

Whatever. Jayde stormed out of the office before he'd finished his last syllable.

When Jayde left, Devon reclaimed his vacated seat. Closing his eyes, he massaged his temples. This endeavor had quickly become more than he'd bargained for. He'd expected . . . Truthfully, he hadn't known what to expect, but it sure hadn't been some hostile woman's wrath. He pondered their collision on the sidewalk days earlier. He almost laughed aloud at the irony. The hostile woman with mega-attitude he'd spilled coffee on was his new employee, Jayde Seaton—broom and all.

Earlier, Maxwell had rattled on about this Seaton woman. At the time, she'd sounded like a paragon of virtue. In person she was an exceptionally tall, very attractive, and well-dressed woman, but all that virtuousness remained to be seen.

Embarrassed, Maxwell faced his boss. "I apologize for her outburst. I'll go talk to her immediately."

"So far not too impressive," Devon said aloud. "Forget it. We can discuss Ms. Seaton later. Right now I want to discuss Gambrini's resignation. I'm curious why my grandmother's longtime friend would suddenly up and quit. Did you have any idea Paolo's resignation was coming?"

"None at all. It was a complete surprise to us as well. Your grandmother hired him personally. He was very good at what he did. Cecilia always sang his praises. I can't imagine why the old codger would leave." Maxwell frowned, causing his eyebrows to furrow. "We all thought he'd retire here."

"The drop in revenue seems to coincide with his departure. What's your take on that?"

The older man shrugged. "I'm afraid it's as much a mystery to us as it is to you. We certainly don't want to accuse Paolo of any nefarious actions. His name within the art community is beyond reproach."

"I agree, but as the gallery's owner, I have to explore all the possibilities, even the ones I may find hard to swallow."

"Devon, why'd you let Jayde think you were hired on? Why didn't you just tell her it's your company?"

"At this point, nobody is above suspicion. Secondly, I don't want anyone from the media getting wind that I'm in town. As far as everyone's concerned, you and Wells, Inc., still run the show."

"Why?"

"I can't conduct an investigation if everyone is always on their good behavior around me. If they know I own the gallery, I'll never get to the bottom of who's behind this."

"Devon, the director will have to interact with the public at some point."

"I can't risk it. We'll have to make sure I don't get spotted by any reporters while I'm in town."

"If that's the case, wouldn't it be easier to leave things the way they are? Jayde has done an incredible job in the interim."

"And yet we're still losing profits."

Maxwell bristled. "I don't believe for a second any of this is Jayde's fault. She has some exciting programs in mind and has exceeded our expectations at every turn. Despite the mishaps, the gallery is flourishing under her management."

Frowning, Devon sat forward in his chair. "Has anything happened lately?"

"A painting fell, just missing a client," Maxwell admitted, "also our long-awaited shipment of sculptures by Roderick ended up being a crate full of Chinese lanterns. Eventually, we found the errant shipment. It had been delivered to a warehouse across town. Luckily, the company that received it called us. We barely got the sculptures here and set up in time for the opening."

Devon steepled his fingers in front of him.

Maxwell smiled fondly. "You're more like your grandmother than you know."

"Am I?"

"God rest her, she used to do the same thing when perplexed about something," the old man sighed. "I miss her."

"So do I. Max, you were my grandmother's closest business partner and confidant. She had the utmost respect and fondness for you. You've been connected with my family longer than I have. Like my grandmother, I trust you implicitly. Do you think these are random acts?"

Maxwell looked Devon in his eyes. "You're right. I've been here since the beginning. Your grandmother was also one of my closest friends and confidants. There wasn't anything I wouldn't do for Cecilia. She was like family to me for over fifty years. Not once have I ever seen anyone do one harmful thing to your grandmother or any of her businesses, so, no, I don't think these are random acts."

Devon nodded. "I appreciate your candor."

"Speaking of candor, how is your father taking the news that you're here? I'm sure Sterling can't be too thrilled you're not at the Mitchell Group."

"I'm sure he won't be thrilled about my decision, but it can't be helped. This is personal, Max. I want to handle this myself."

"I'll help you any way I can. Where would you like to start?"

"With Gambrini. He's the only person that's resigned lately."

"I just can't bring myself to think for a moment that Paolo has anything to do with this."

Devon was thoughtful. "Maybe not, but someone is adversely affecting the profits of my gallery. I'm here to find the culprit, and until I do, everyone is a suspect."

CHAPTER 4

Once Jayde was safely behind her office door, she collapsed. Tears of anger and frustration flowed rapidly down her face, soaking the front of her clothes. Jayde couldn't recall the last time she'd been this upset. The rug had been yanked from under her.

Floored didn't begin to describe how she felt about not being named the new director. Jayde felt like buying two voodoo dolls, one resembling Maxwell Shaw and the other her new boss, then jabbing them with needles. Before leaving, Paolo had given her every indication that the job of director would be hers. It was a done deal—or so she'd thought.

A red haze clouded her vision. "First, the clumsy oaf crashes into me, and now he steals my job." At that moment, Jayde almost laughed at the irony. *Devon Mitchell. Ha!* He was more like Devon the Destroyer. He had cut her swiftly, but it hadn't been painless. In less than fifteen minutes, he'd destroyed her dreams, her aspirations, and her outfit. Who was she kidding? Besides the job, it was all about the suit.

A light knock at the door halted her one-sided

conversation. Grabbing a tissue off her desk, Jayde dabbed at her eyes before running a shaky hand through her hair. Her voice was devoid of emotion. "Come in."

The door opened slowly. A white napkin appeared, waving rapidly, through the crack, followed by her adversary's head.

"What are you doing?" Jayde asked.

"I, uh, didn't have a flag or a handkerchief. This was the best I could do on short notice. May I come in?"

Jayde waved her arm in invitation.

"Are you sure it's safe?" asked Devon.

Jayde glared at him.

He walked in, closing the door behind him. When he wasn't offered a seat, he leaned against the door. Silence dripped heavily through the room like warmed candle wax.

A full, uncomfortable minute passed before Jayde broke the sound barrier. "You owe me a new suit."

His eyebrows rose. "I owe you a new suit? If you recall, I offered to buy you a new one. You refused my offer—rudely, I might add."

Unable to stand still, Jayde crossed the room. "That was before I knew you could afford it. That doesn't seem to be an issue now, considering you just stole my job."

Her heady perfume invaded Devon's nose and his peace of mind. He stepped back. "I stole your job?" He laughed loudly. "Wouldn't I have to know you in order to steal your job?"

Jayde's hands were fists at her sides. It didn't soothe her frazzled nerves one bit to see him looking oblivious of any wrongdoing. She tried to calm down and deal rationally with the interloper, refusing to be swayed by his innocent smile. That "innocent" had just got the corner office. When she spoke, her voice was brittle.

"You . . . Don't play mind games with me, Mr. Mitchell. You don't know me. I don't know you. Who cares? I was promised that job," she said, tapping her thumb on her chest. "And I intend to have it." Folding her arms, she regarded him from head to toe. At six feet tall, Jayde was only a few inches shorter than him. Pulling herself up to her full height, she fixed him with a frigid stare. "If I were you, I wouldn't get too comfortable or order business cards, because you aren't staying."

His jaw ticked. Jayde knew her attitude was getting under his skin. *Good.* She hoped it burned. Common sense caused her to ponder whether she should be so insubordinate to the man that could be her boss, but she didn't care. He annoyed her to no end, and the sooner he left, the better. At this point she had nothing to lose.

"Miss Seaton, I think it fair to inform you, Maxwell had no bearing on my being hired. The approval came straight from the head of Wells, Inc. In case you didn't know, that would be the company that owns this gallery."

"I know that," she practically yelled.

"Good. Then you also know that Mr. Shaw didn't have a choice in the matter. Neither do you."

"Oh, I have a choice," she said boldly, not caring that she could get fired—at least not at the moment.

Taking a deep breath, Devon pinched the bridge of his nose. "Jayde—"

"That's Miss Seaton."

"Jayde," he continued, "I'm sorry about the confusion. I assumed the new arrangement had been announced to the staff before I arrived. I see now that wasn't the case."

"Brilliant deduction."

* * *

The need to retaliate against her for her rude behavior was all consuming. This woman was a piece of work. The longer he stood there, the more he wanted to yank her off that broom of hers and hit her over the head with it. Still, alienating her wasn't wise. Firing her would feel heavenly, but then he'd never know if she was the culprit. He'd do what it took to keep her there—to watch her. If she was guilty, sooner or later she'd have to slip up. And when she did, he'd take great pleasure in showing her insubordinate butt the door.

He took another calming breath. "Could we start over? We haven't gotten off on the right foot."

"Actually, we didn't get off on the right suit."

"Fine," he conceded. "Suit yourself, but since we'll be working together—closely, I might add—it would make our relationship easier if we could get past our differences."

"Look, Darren—"

His eyes narrowed. "That's Devon."

"Uh-huh. I possess a BFA from the University of Virginia, with a major in business, and a master's degree in art history. That makes me more than qualified to do my job."

"I wouldn't doubt it," he said dryly, "but what's your point?"

"I'm not new to the art community. I've done internships abroad and in the States, and in all my travels, I've never heard of you—not once."

Devon was effectively cut off when he started to speak.

"If you think I'm going to just accept you stepping in and taking away something I've worked my butt off to get, you can think again." With as much composure as her shaking body would allow, Jayde strode past him. Opening her office door, she waited.

Incredulous, Devon strode past her. He'd barely cleared the entryway before the door slammed behind him.

Thrust out into the well-lit corridor, Devon blinked a few times. *No, she didn't just slam the door on me. Last time I checked, I was in charge.* Heading down the hall, he made himself dismiss all thoughts of Jayde Seaton. He'd deal with the termagant later.

Several minutes later, Devon was ensconced in his new office. He leaned back in his chair. With his made-to-order Crockett & Jones loafers up on the expansive mahogany desk, he willed himself to calm down long enough to ponder his next move. "My first day back in corporate America and I have to deal with a self-involved lunatic."

He tried to concentrate on business matters, but thoughts of Jayde resurfaced. When he'd bumped into her days ago, he had only scratched the surface of the bitchy, high-fashion runway model attitude lurking within her. His jaw clenched. He was more than familiar with her kind. Though cute, the discourteous stranger from the coffee incident paled in comparison to the shrieking harridan stomping through his gallery.

The phone rang, effectively interrupting his assessment of Miss Seaton. Sitting up, he answered before the second ring. "Mitchell."

"Thomas."

Hearing his twin sister's voice, Devon broke into a huge grin. "Mel?" he said, with surprise. "How in the world did you find me? How are you, kiddo?"

"From the sound of your voice a second ago, better

than you. You sound like you're ready to chew nails, big brother. What's up?"

"First, tell me how you found me."

"Oh, please. It wasn't hard. Uncle Henry said you were taking care of business, and wouldn't tell me where you'd gone. From Dad's grouchiness, I deduced you hadn't returned to Chicago."

"So you called Max?"

"Yep. I badgered him until he admitted your whereabouts. Hardly rocket science, Dev. Now, why the surly tone?"

With a sigh so heavy it rustled the papers on his desk, Devon leaned back in his chair. "Well, for starters, I just met my best and most capable employee, Jayde Seaton. Too bad I want to strangle her. Mel, she reamed me out for stealing her job. She's like a little Chihuahua. She barely left me enough behind to sit on." By the time he had recounted both his encounters with Jayde, his sister was in tears.

"I like her already."

"I'm glad one of us does," he said dryly. "Personally, I'd like to buy her that designer linen suit, wrap it around her pretty little neck, and strangle her with it."

"Pretty?" Melanie snickered.

"Melanie," Devon warned.

Over the next half hour, Devon brought his sister, Melanie Mitchell Thomas, DDS, up to speed on the gallery.

"That's a unique way of handling the situation. But if memory serves, you don't have a background in art, do you?" she asked.

He shrugged. "What difference does that make? It's still a business, and I've got more than enough experience in that arena."

"Please, don't rattle off the business awards and accolades again," she groaned. "Do Mom and Dad know what you're up to?"

"No, and that's the way I want to keep it. I don't need them trying to interfere. This gallery is my responsibility. I plan on doing what I think is best."

"Easy, Dev. You don't have to sell me. I'm on your side, remember?"

He softened. "I know. I just didn't expect to have to deal with this type of headache so soon. I've been used to slow-paced farm life of late. I was hoping to get back into the business slowly, not at a hundred miles per hour—and headfirst." Devon expelled a harsh breath. "Enough shoptalk. How are my favorite niece and nephew?"

Melanie chuckled. "Don't you mean your *only* niece and nephew?"

"Same thing. So, what are Mitchell and Jetta up to this week?"

"The normal things a six-year-old and nine-year-old do." She took delight in filling her brother in on her children's latest shenanigans.

The nagging ache in his chest ran deep. He'd been away from everyone who mattered most in his life for only a few months, but it felt like a lifetime. "I really miss them." His voice broke. "I miss all of you."

"I know, sweetie. We all miss you, too. It's been so long since we've seen you." Melanie tried to lighten his mood. "Did you get my letter? I mentioned the reporters are no longer camped out on our doorstep. They haven't been for ages. Naturally, Jetta is disappointed. She won't be able to sell them refreshments anymore."

Devon grinned with pride. "That's my little entrepreneur."

"She took it to heart. She knows their absence means you'll come visit soon. When are you coming home, anyway?"

"Soon, Mel. I promise. Enough about me. How's Carl doing?"

Melanie sighed. "As fine as ever."

"Stop drooling."

"I can't help it. I love my wonderful, talented, sensitive, and incredibly sexy husband."

"So much so, you had to open up a dental practice with him? If you ask me, you just did it to keep all the cute assistants away from him."

She laughed. "I keep my husband on his toes, and he keeps mine curled. It's quite an arrangement."

Her brother groaned. "Seriously, spare me the intimate details."

After he hung up, Devon's spirits lifted. His sister had always had a calming effect on him. Still, he was in no mood to deal with the opposition. He needed some time to compose himself before he crossed paths with Jayde Seaton again.

Outside the gallery, Devon took a few deep breaths. Five minutes later, he was still taking deep breaths. It gave him time to observe the hustle and bustle of Seventh Street. The controlled chaos calmed him, just like his grandmother had always done.

The nation's capital was in his family's blood. Though most of his mother's side of the family had moved, his grandmother had been adamant that she wasn't moving. She was born at Georgetown University

Hospital, and she'd vowed she'd die there. For over twenty years, her gallery had stood regal and proud, while businesses around it had come and gone. The latest boom in the Chinatown corridor over the last few years was astounding. Observing the abundance of life thriving steadily around him caused him to smile.

The Verizon Center a block away was a state-of-the-art arena that housed the men's and women's professional basketball teams and the men's hockey team. Entertainers performed there, and cultural events were held there. Down the street, the Shakespeare Theatre Company, the Smithsonian American Art Museum, and the National Portrait Gallery drew connoisseurs of the arts to the area. All walks of life and ethnicities came together and blended cohesively for work and leisure.

Devon glanced up at the Wells Gallery. He took in every inch of it. Most of the buildings in the area were an architectural blend of past and present. Some buildings had brick fronts; some glass and steel; others smooth concrete. Cecilia Wells had chosen a concrete facade of deep burgundy for the exterior of the gallery. It stood apart from its cohabitants without clashing.

Once you stepped inside, there was no doubt you were in an art gallery. The floor-to-ceiling brick-walled great room welcomed visitors. Nearby, several smaller, intimate rooms held paintings and sculptures. In the middle were comfortable black leather benches on which to sit and admire the works.

The second level had a large, white-walled viewing area, which was also used for receptions. The lower level was comprised of storage rooms for the paintings and other works of art. There were additional rooms for framing, preservation, and supplies. The top level was strictly for employees. Offices, a conference room, bathroom facilities, and an employee break room took up the entire floor.

Devon placed his hand on the side of the building and closed his eyes. "There's no way I'll ever let anything happen to you," he vowed. With a heavy heart, he pulled the glass door open and walked back into the gallery.

CHAPTER 5

Avalon Wells Mitchell leaned back while her butler poured piping hot tea into her Wedgwood teacup. "Thank you, Selby."

"My pleasure, Mrs. Mitchell," the tall, impeccably dressed man acknowledged.

His dark brown skin was wrinkle free despite his mature years. The only thing that gave Jonah Selby's age away was the stark white hair atop his head.

Sipping Earl Grey, Avalon scanned her morning appointments.

"What do you mean you won't be home soon?"

Devon's mother looked up from her date book. Her husband always had a way of disturbing her morning calm. Sighing, she lowered her pen. "Sterling, who are you talking to, dear?"

"Devon," he mouthed.

At hearing the one-sided conversation, her anticipation grew. She missed her son terribly. His self-imposed seclusion had been difficult for them all, especially her daughter, Melanie, Devon's fraternal twin. Her children had always been extremely close.

Perched sideways in her chair, she held out her jewel-laden hand. "Darling, hand me the phone."

Grudgingly, her husband relinquished the cordless phone.

"Hi, honey. It's Mom. What's this I hear about you not coming home?"

Devon's father sat in the elegant Biedermeier chair across from his wife. He disliked tea and pondered getting coffee. Out of nowhere, Selby appeared holding a cup and saucer. Sterling wasn't surprised. His butler had a unique way of ascertaining his employer's needs.

Taking the proffered brew, Sterling nodded his thanks. His attention returned to the conversation, and then he started one of his own with nobody in particular.

"What I can't understand is why he isn't ready to come back? We haven't had a reporter loitering at the front gate for months," he complained, loud enough for his son to hear. "If he doesn't want to stay at his own house, he can stay with us. For goodness' sakes, he's practically got his own wing here."

With a hand over the mouthpiece, Avalon shushed her husband. "Darling, I can't talk to both of you at once."

"Well, put him on speaker," Sterling groused.

A few minutes later, the Mitchells bade their son good-bye.

Coffee cup in hand, Sterling sipped and paced around the room. "This makes no sense." His gray eyes flashed angrily. "I don't see why he's lollygagging around Henry's ramshackle farm. If he needed seclusion, he could've stayed here. We have a fourteen-thousand-square-foot mansion. He has his own wing. It's not like he has to see us, unless he really wants to."

"Sterling, it was his choice."

"The crisis is over, Avalon. He should be here with

his parents, not slogging through manure, listening to my brother sing off-key to that decrepit old cow."

His wife smiled. Sterling Mitchell was a force with which to be reckoned in the business world. He was widely respected by his employees, within the community, and in their social circle. Too bad he was putty in his family's hands. He was as soft as a melted marshmallow when it came to them.

"Now, dear—"

"Honestly, I don't know which is older," he continued, "the house or the damned cow."

"I'm not thrilled by our son's news, either, but he's been through such an ordeal." She reached for his hand. His fingers closed over hers. "We've waited this long for him to return. If he feels he needs more time to get his head straight, I say we give it to him. In the grand scheme of things, a few more weeks won't matter. Besides, he's good company for Henry. I never liked the idea of him being alone on that big farm. I can hear it in his voice. He enjoys having his nephew around."

"Ava," Sterling said, using his nickname for her, "I'll wait a few more weeks, and that's it. We've got a business to run. Devon is second in command, and I'm not getting any younger. I'd like to retire soon, while I . . . while we can still enjoy it."

Avalon heard this speech at least once a week. Each time, her response was the same. "Nonsense. You're in excellent health, dear."

"You mark my words, Avalon, if my son isn't back in Chicago soon, I'm going to go get him myself!"

Jayde placed her key in the door lock and heard the familiar thump of her dog, Boomer's tail hitting the foyer floor. Though distraught, Jayde refused to alter their daily ritual. After she set down her briefcase, purse, and keys, she gave her golden retriever the signal that he was free to pounce. He jumped up on his hind legs and wrapped his front ones around her middle.

"Okay, boy, let's go get changed and take you for a walk." After going upstairs, she discarded her suit for a pair of sweats. Jayde was tying her shoelaces when the telephone rang.

"Hello?"

"Is that my sweetie?"

Jayde grinned. "Hi, Mom."

"Hello, darling. How are you?"

"Fine," Jayde replied in what she hoped was a cheerful voice.

A few seconds lapsed before Harriette Seaton replied, "No, you're not. I can hear it in your voice. Something is wrong."

Staring at the phone, Jayde wondered how on earth her mother knew.

Her mother replied as though her daughter had spoken. "I'm your mother, dear. It's my job to know."

Dumbfounded, Jayde threw up her free hand. "I give up."

"That's wise. Now tell me what happened."

"Mom, I've got to take Boomer out for his walk before he explodes. I'll call you when I get back, I promise."

"Honestly, why anyone would want to have a horse in a condo is beyond me."

Jayde couldn't help but laugh. "He isn't a horse, Mom. He's a golden retriever."

"The way that dog eats, he might as well be a horse."

"I'm going now, Mom."

"Okay, but if I don't hear from you soon, I'm calling back."

Against her parents' suggestions, Jayde had purchased a condo on the waterfront in Southwest D.C. instead of in the upper Northwest neighborhood where she'd grown up. The Metrorail was nearby, allowing her to catch the subway to work. An added bonus was being minutes from Ronald Reagan Washington National Airport and walking distance to the wharf. Jayde loved being by the water. That selling point alone overrode all objections from her family.

"What do ya say, boy? Should we get some shrimp for dinner?"

An hour later, Jayde was sitting at her dining room table, enjoying steamed, spiced shrimp and an iced glass of Dos Equis, her problems momentarily put aside. Boomer lounged happily on his doggie bed, munching on a rawhide. Sighing, Jayde couldn't help quoting an antiquated beer commercial. "It don't get much better than this."

The phone rang, interrupting her shrimp fest. Her hands were buried in spices and discarded shrimp shells, so Jayde decided to let the answering machine pick up. After three additional rings, her machine kicked in. Sipping her beer, she listened to her greeting. The beep followed.

"Hey, Tree. It's Christy. Get your tall booty off the couch, and answer this phone." Seconds passed. "Okay, hit me back on my cell when you get in, and don't take all night," she yelled loudly before laughter kicked in and she hung up.

Jayde smiled and continued eating her dinner. After she cleaned up and put away the leftover shrimp, she flopped on the couch before picking up her cordless phone. She dialed her girlfriend's number and waited.

"Who are you calling a tree, Battle Cat?"

Best friends since elementary school, Jayde and Christy Denton had developed nicknames for each other. To an outsider, they sounded unflattering, but they were actually terms of endearment.

"Hey, girl. Where were you? I know you weren't out on a date." Christy laughed into the phone.

"No, smarty, I was eating spiced shrimp, and you know I wasn't about to interrupt that for you."

"Uh-huh. Well, what happened? Are you the new director of that bourgeois art gallery, or what?"

Bitterness crept into Jayde's voice. "Or what."

"You're lying!"

"Afraid not. One of the bigwigs came down to introduce me to Devon Mitchell, my new boss."

"Run that by me again."

"Heck, run that by *me* again. It seems the powers that be didn't think I was capable of being director on a permanent basis."

"Did you quit?"

Jayde put her feet up on the couch. "No, I didn't. Truthfully, Chris, I'm still in shock. I don't know what I'm going to do. I guess I'll take the weekend to consider my options."

"Girl, if you want me to stage a protest, just let me know. I've got friends at Channel Nine. We can get a write-up in the *Post*, and . . ."

"Girl, it's not that serious."

"It most certainly is. You can't let them bulldoze over you like that. If you start now, they'll be doing it at every turn. You have to fight this, Jayde."

Jayde heard a beep. "Hold on. I've got another call."

Clicking over, Jayde said hello. When she heard her mother's voice, she groaned.

"I heard that," her mother replied. "I told you I was going to call you back. So, did you get the job?"

Jayde sighed. "I'm afraid it's a long story, Mom."

"It is? Then hang on, honey. I'll go get my microwave popcorn."

Devon had arrived at the gallery without a thorough game plan, which was unlike him. Even with the emotionally draining day he'd had, he should have remained cool and unflappable. He felt as cool as a skewer of bread dipped in his mother's infamous cheese fondue. "I should've had this worked out from start to finish," Devon admonished himself, disrupting the silence within his car. "All the time off's got you rusty, man."

Maneuvering the powerful Mercedes in and out of traffic, he recalled his father's words. *A person should be prepared for any circumstance, however remote. A contingency plan should be developed at the beginning in case things go awry.* Devon tightened his grip on the steering wheel. "Clearly, I don't have a plan, contingency or otherwise."

His sole objective had been to get his foot in the door. Now that his goal had been accomplished, he'd have to tread carefully. He didn't think anyone would discover he owned the gallery, but his instincts told him to watch his back.

Forty minutes later, Devon stepped over the threshold of his family's home off Sixteenth Street in Northwest D.C. A large home, it was on a tree-lined street in a prestigious neighborhood at the tip of the D.C./Maryland border, near Rock Creek Park. Disarming the alarm, he threw his keys on a table, dropped his suitcases, and went straight for the family-room couch. Devon plopped down with the ceremonious *oomph* of a body hitting leather. When a massive dust cloud failed to disperse into the air, Devon made a mental note to thank Maxwell for getting the house livable. While massaging his temples, he allowed an audible sigh to escape his lips.

His first day back on the job had been a disaster to the fifteenth degree. To accentuate the point, he had a pounding headache, rivaled only by his bad mood. His thoughts turned to Jayde—again. Her anger had been as genuine as her surprise at being replaced. Could that have been an act? Had she been in a bad mood because her plans of sabotage had been thwarted? *More questions with no definitive answers.* The events of the last few days were catching up to him. Devon rose from the couch. He'd had enough thinking for one day. Wearily, he climbed the massive staircase that led to his bedroom and another restless night.

CHAPTER 6

A week later, Devon had gone over every employee's dossier and the gallery's inventory. He'd been impressed. All his employees were well educated and experienced in their field. There was still the matter of delayed or incorrect shipments, small mishaps, and equipment malfunctions. All had been dismissed as accidents. Considering the gallery had never had numerous incidents like this before, he pondered the timing. Then there was the elusive Miss Seaton. Jayde hadn't returned to the office since their initial meeting. She was starting to bug him.

Maxwell defended her actions when Devon questioned her absence. "She called in and asked to take personal leave. This isn't like her, I assure you. It's completely out of character. I've read Paolo's review reports and promotion recommendations on her. Jayde's conscientious, and she always gives more than one hundred percent on the job. I know she was upset at not being promoted, but not showing up for work—I can't fathom why."

Devon could. "Her absence is because of me. I hope

she comes to terms with the new arrangement over the weekend. If she's the best at what she does, I need her here, not pouting around her house because I took away her favorite toy."

"There's more to it than that, Devon. She was expecting to be promoted. You can't blame her for being disappointed. What if she's looking for another job?"

Devon leaned back in his chair and rubbed his hand over his jaw. "Highly unlikely. She doesn't seem the type to give up something she wants so badly," he said, recalling their previous run-ins. "Not without a fight, at any rate."

Maxwell couldn't help but grin. "I'd say your assessment is accurate."

Sitting upright, Devon picked up the telephone receiver. "Call her. See when she's planning on gracing us with her presence. I'll catch up with you later. I've got a few calls to return."

Jayde showed up for work Monday and finished the week without incident or argument. Her low-key attitude had Devon on high alert. He had an overall knowledge of the gallery but hadn't expended much energy on learning the day-to-day responsibilities of a director. By Wednesday, his lack of suitability was more than apparent to him and certainly didn't get past Jayde.

Each time he asked a question, she'd give him the same serene look and then provide him with the answer. It wasn't long before Devon started hating those looks.

Seeing him rub his temples one afternoon, Jayde couldn't help but ask, "There's a great deal more to this than you expected, isn't there?"

He stopped mid-rub. "For once, we're in agreement."

"And it's back to my favorite theory."

"Excuse me?"

"You know, someone owed you a favor, so here you are. Nice cushy job, benefits . . ."

His eyes darkened to a color Jayde could only describe as storm-cloud gray. Deciding she'd prodded the bear enough, she switched gears. "So, let's recap. What is the director's function?"

Devon put his feet on his desk and pondered his sanity. Hiring a detective to get to the bottom of things was looking more appealing by the minute. Dueling with Jayde was taking up more time than he'd ever anticipated. Their constant repartee was draining his reserve of patience and snappy comebacks.

"The director's function?" she repeated.

"Maintains the premises, or in my case, hires someone else to do it." Devon couldn't help the laugh that escaped his lips.

Jayde rolled her eyes. "And?"

"The director works with the artists to put together shows and exhibits." He paused, checking his notes. "He also handles all PR for the gallery, national and international. Invitations fall under his realm, too. Along with sales, marketing, distribution, legal contracts, etcetera."

Jayde put up a hand to stop him. "The etcetera part would be planning and projections. Creating all exhibit programs also falls under your umbrella, mighty overlord. As do community outreach, direct contact and fostering relationships with the artists, securing loaned items, funding and—"

"Okay, I get it," he interrupted. Devon got up, walked around his desk, and patted Jayde soundly on the back. "You've been promoted."

"Pardon me?"

"You're now the exhibition director. You report directly to me and are responsible for all the stuff you just mentioned, plus a few other things not previously mentioned."

"You—you can't do that." Her eyes grew wide. "Can you?"

"I can and just did. You handle all creative aspects. I'll do what I do best."

"Take up space?"

He pinned her with a glacial stare. "It's time we come to an agreement about that acerbic tongue of yours."

"There is no end to your audacity or ego."

"Jayde," Devon warned.

"Fine," she conceded, "but I want a bigger office and a salary increase."

"Done. Now, I know you're busy, so I won't keep you."

Jayde's curiosity increased tenfold. Unable to resist, she stepped closer. "So tell me, Devon, where did you work before coming to the gallery?"

He didn't miss a beat. "I held an executive management position for a company based in Chicago."

"What did you do there?"

"Executive management."

Devon thought the look of annoyance that crept across her face was priceless.

"If you don't want to talk about it, just say so."

"I just did."

Exasperated, she grabbed her briefcase. "Good night, Mr. Mitchell. Don't forget I'll be in late tomorrow. I've got a meeting."

"I haven't forgotten. Have a good evening, Jayde."

"Oh," she said, turning. "I want your entire proposal in writing."

He grinned shamelessly. "Would've surprised me if you didn't."

The moment Jayde got back into her office, she pulled a card from her Rolodex. After dialing the number, she tapped her finger impatiently on her desk while waiting for the line to connect.

She got voice mail. "Mr. Shaw, this is Jayde. I'm calling to confirm our appointment for tomorrow morning. Please call me back at your earliest convenience." Hanging up, Jayde grabbed her purse and hurried out.

"You thought you could elude me?" the man staring out the window asked aloud. He waited, as if expecting an answer. Turning, he paced the thickly carpeted floor of his study while talking to himself. Nobody could just drop off the face of the earth. If something had happened to him, wouldn't there've been some news? *No. You're alive, Devon. You have to be.*

The calls he'd made pretending to be a reporter hadn't produced the desired effect. The Mitchells remained tight lipped about their son's whereabouts. He moved his hand over his firm, stubble-laden face to stroke his jaw. "They can't protect you all the time. Eventually, I'll find you, Devon."

Unexpectedly, a woman's figure appeared in the doorway. She was scantily dressed in a dark blue laced teddy that stopped mid-thigh. Her shoulder-length black hair hung in voluminous waves. Red lips curved into a seductive smile that illuminated her face.

"Sweetheart, I'm bored. When are you coming to bed?" she called.

Instantly, his demeanor altered. When he saw her standing there, the smile that crossed his face was genuine. His eyes twinkled in appreciation of her curvaceous body—a body that would please him repeatedly before the night was through.

"What are you doing up? I told you I'd be there shortly."

Her hips swayed as she walked toward him. The buxom woman slid her arms around his middle. The rigid muscles flexed under his chocolate silk shirt. She purred like a contented kitten. Running her smooth cheek over his textured one made her shudder with delight. "I know you did, baby," she said, pouting. "But you were taking too long."

Molding her body to his, he lowered his head and swept her lips up in a powerful, sensuous kiss that left them both breathless. She wasn't his beloved, but she'd do. In seconds he'd be buried within her honeyed walls, delirious with passion.

His cell phone vibrated in his pocket. Carnal intentions were put on hold. Easing a hand into his slacks, he retrieved the phone. Flipping it open, he answered it. When he heard the voice on the other end, he lowered the phone, turning his attention back to his latest distraction. "Sorry, baby, but this is business. You go ahead up. I'll be there in a sec."

She unraveled herself from his embrace, but not before sliding a manicured finger over his lips. "You'd better hurry, lover. I don't want to idle too long."

Slowly, the curvaceous beauty walked out. In fact, she took her sweet time, accentuating the task with each deliberate sway of her hips.

She had his undivided attention, until she left. The moment she did, his smile faded. "Go ahead." After a few seconds, he nodded. "Yes, I got it. I just haven't opened it yet."

Walking over to his polished cherrywood desk, he sunk into the leather chair behind it. Opening his right desk drawer, he retrieved a large white envelope. Turning it over, he ripped it open, then pulled out several papers.

As he scanned the documents quickly, his face mirrored his growing delight. Leaning back in his chair, he tossed the papers he'd been holding onto his desk. *Perfect.* "This is the news I've been waiting for. I'll call you back the moment I've finalized my plans." Ending the call, he slid the phone back into his pocket. For the first time in months, he felt pure, indescribable pleasure.

"Finally, everything's falling into place." His eyes grew bright with purpose. "Don't worry, Candace, my love. It's payback time for your ex. I knew you'd have to resurface sooner or later, Devon. Now that it's happened, I'll make my move."

Though the hour was late, sleep evaded him. Sighing, Devon groped in midair. Eventually, his fingers connected with the lamp beside his bed. Switching on the light, he grabbed a book off the nightstand and headed to the connecting sitting room.

With a bottled water from the wet bar in hand, he settled on the plush Italian leather love seat. Devon flipped to his bookmarked page. Fifteen minutes later, he slammed the book shut. Angrily, he threw it on the coffee table.

"Why am I still dreaming of her? It was an accident. I've done the therapist thing. You have to come to terms with your loss," he mimicked.

He got up. Angrily, Devon paced.

"I am past it. She's dead. There's nothing I can do to

change what happened." Flopping across the love seat, Devon rested his arm across his forehead and stared into nothingness. "I can't bring her back—neither one of them."

Eventually, his thoughts came back to the present. He needed to concentrate on the matter at hand. Maxwell had mentioned an increase in incidents at the gallery over the last month, but there'd been no mysterious accidents or delays since his arrival. The timing was too perfect to be coincidence. So far, everyone had been friendly, helpful, and civil. All his employees had accepted his being there without question. That is, everyone except Jayde Seaton.

I don't get it. Why is she still being difficult? So I took her job. Big deal. That's hardly a criminal offense or out of the ordinary. "It's just business," he muttered. "Besides, I just promoted her. You think she'd be happy." *Unless she's behind the mishaps.*

He thought about the animosity she radiated when he entered a room. It was tangible. If they were in court, she'd be dubbed a hostile witness. "I've got to kick this investigation into overdrive. The sooner I find the culprit, get things back on track, and get out of here, the better."

To help him achieve his objective Devon had hired a detective to check out Paolo's whereabouts and current business dealings. He was certain it was just a matter of time before the guilty party was identified and he was heading back to Chicago. Putting his hands behind his head, he imagined Jayde as the saboteur. In his mind's eye, he saw her being led out of the gallery, handcuffed, kicking and screaming. A sadistic smile crept across his face. He turned out the light. Whistling a happy tune, Devon headed back to bed.

CHAPTER 7

Maxwell Shaw motioned for Jayde to be seated. "Can I have my assistant get you anything? Coffee? Tea?"

"No, thank you, Mr. Shaw."

"Jayde, you can call me Maxwell or Max. I insist."

"Fine, Max. I'll get straight to the point. This isn't working. The man's been here a few weeks, and it's painfully obvious he hasn't got a clue what working at a gallery entails. What possessed the company to hire him, anyway?"

"Jayde, we've been through this before. It was our intention to promote you to director, but for reasons I'm not at liberty to discuss, we had to bring Devon on board. None of us can disregard a direct order from the top. Besides, I was under the impression he'd just promoted you."

Her cheeks colored slightly. "He did. Personally, I think he did it to keep me from needling him every chance I get." Jayde willed the headache forming behind her eyes to dissipate. Now wasn't the time. She had to stay focused. "The truth is, I'm still wondering *why* he needs to be here." Puzzled, she folded her arms across her middle. "This whole thing doesn't make sense."

The older man leaned back in his chair. "Jayde, may I offer you some advice?"

Jayde threw up her hands. She knew where this was going. "Sure. Why not?"

"You've just been given a well-earned raise and a promotion. You're doing a job you love, despite a boss you have issues with. In today's arena, this arrangement is hardly uncommon. I suggest you make the best of it— that is, if you want to continue working here."

When Jayde returned to the gallery, it was with purposeful strides that she headed to Devon's office. She didn't bother knocking before going in and shutting the door behind her.

Looking up from his desk, Devon frowned. "Knock much?"

Sitting across from him, Jayde began as if they were already in the middle of a conversation. "Some things just don't add up."

Here we go again. He lowered his pen. "Such as?"

"Like why a man who's obviously not qualified is in charge. What are you doing? Community service or something?"

He decided to have some fun at her expense. "I wouldn't exactly call me unqualified. Besides, I happen to like art."

"My mother likes art, too, but she's not working in a gallery, doing a job she's not qualified for."

Devon traced circles on his left temple, something he'd done more frequently since meeting her. The woman was relentless. She reminded him of a pit bull with a bone—she just wouldn't let go. "Didn't we go through this last week? I thought you'd accepted my position here. Not to mention your new promotion," he added. "I suggest you get past this animosity, Jayde. It isn't conducive, and quite frankly, it's wasting my time, which translates into company time—and money."

Absentmindedly, she put her fingernail in her mouth and bit down. "I don't like it when things don't make sense. It annoys me."

Throwing up his hands, Devon leaned back in his chair. When he spoke, he didn't bother hiding the sarcasm. "What doesn't?"

Standing, she paced around the office. "There's more to this picture than you've painted. No pun intended. Are you hiding from the mob? Did you sleep with some rich guy's wife, and now you have to lay low?"

She'd gone too far. Bolting out of his chair, Devon was around his desk and in her face in seconds. His close proximity caused her to back up. "No, Jayde, I'm not hiding from the mob or anyone else, and I don't discuss my love life with my *employees*," he stressed. "I'm here because I choose to be. That's all you need to know."

She shook her head. "That evasive answer just won't cut it, Devon. I know you're hiding something— I intend to find out what it is."

He'd had enough of her insubordination. It was time to put her in her place. "Need I remind you that I'm in charge?"

"No." Jayde turned and walked out of his office.

It took less than five seconds for him to go after her. Spotting Jayde descending in the glass elevator, Devon took the stairs down three flights to the lower level. He saw her heading into a storage room. She spun around when she heard the door closing behind her.

"No, wait," she yelled, running for the door. "Don't let it—"

The metal door shut with a thud.

"Close," she said.

He didn't give the door another thought. "We weren't done."

"You just let the door close," she accused.

"So what?"

"So, it doesn't work right, genius. It won't open from the inside, which you'd have known if you'd been here long enough."

He looked at the door before glaring back at her. "Don't try blaming me for this. Someone should've mentioned that the darn thing didn't work before now. Besides, you were the acting director. If it wasn't working, why didn't you just get the thing fixed? How much sense does accepting a broken door make?"

"Now isn't the time for this. In case you hadn't noticed, we're trapped in here."

"Well, hey, don't let me stop you." He swept his hand toward the door. "You're the one who knows everything. You get us out of here."

Shaking with rage, Jayde walked a wide berth around him and banged on the door. She tugged on the doorknob. It wouldn't budge. "Why did you even come in here?"

He looked at her like she'd lost her mind. "We need to finish our conversation—right now."

"I'm not about to have a talk with you when we're locked in a room," Jayde argued. "Now isn't the time for an in-depth discussion."

"Why not?" He waved his hand through the air again. "We're stuck in here, and it doesn't appear we're getting out any time soon." Devon found the closest crate and took a seat, crossing his legs in front of him.

Jayde stared openmouthed. "What are you doing?"

Is the woman blind? "Uh, sitting."

Jayde expelled the air in her lungs through her mouth in a deafening whoosh. "I can't believe you."

"What's to believe? It's time we hashed this out, if we're going to work together professionally," Devon reasoned. "Don't you agree we have to try being civil to each other?"

Her anger flared. "That's just it. We aren't supposed to be working together. You know squat about this position or what it entails."

"Correction. Thanks to you, I know a lot now."

"Yeah, well, having to show you how to do your own job has me more than a little pissed."

Devon shrugged. "Then I suggest you get over it or get a new job, because I'm not going anywhere."

His nonchalant attitude sent her ire through the roof. "Do you have to be so cryptic all the time? Just admit why you're really here, because I know you don't give a fig about art."

"Are you this hostile to everyone you meet, or am I special? You've been giving me attitude since I walked through the door, and I don't believe for a second that it's all because I took 'your' job or ruined your precious suit. I think there's another reason you're so annoyed with me."

"Really? Well, great and powerful Oz, don't keep me in suspense. Enlighten me as to what it is."

"Gladly." Devon leaned in a few inches. "Despite the pretense, Jayde, you like me—and that bothers the hell out of you."

She recoiled. "What? Have you gone berserk?"

"Just admit it, Jayde."

"No! If you think there's more to this than my barely tolerating your presence, the cheese fell off your cracker two picnics back."

The smug look in his eyes spoke volumes.

"I'm outta here. I'm not going to spend one more minute with a crazy person." Jayde strode to the door, then twisted and yanked the knob hard. It wouldn't co-operate. Turning, she glowered at Devon, as if he'd intentionally caused their predicament.

"Don't glare at me," he said, laughing for the first time all day. "It's not my fault."

"This isn't funny, and it is your fault. Admit it. You planned this."

He let out a snort. "Please. Like I'd lock myself in here on purpose with a raving lunatic."

"Me? You're the lunatic," she countered. "If you hadn't followed me in here and closed the door behind you, we wouldn't be locked in."

"If *you* had stayed and finished our conversation, in-stead of running away like a spoiled child, we wouldn't be locked in here."

"Will you stop arguing and help me get us out?"

He shook his head in disbelief. "Are you always this annoying?" Devon went over and tried the knob. He tried turning it in opposing directions, but no luck. Glancing down at her, he shrugged.

"This can't be happening," Jayde said in dismay. She pushed past him to pound on the door. "Help," she yelled loudly. "Can anybody hear us? We're locked in!"

"As I previously stated, we're stuck—at least for the moment," Devon conceded. It was quite some time before he spoke again. When he did, a wicked grin wasn't far behind. "Any thoughts as to how we can pass the time?"

CHAPTER 8

Perched on a shipping crate, Jayde ran a shaky hand through her hair. The last thing she needed was being locked in a storage room with *him*. She didn't know how long they'd been in there, but whatever it was, it was too long. *Why isn't someone coming to rescue us? Don't they hear the banging?*

With each passing second, she was more aware of him. The heady scent he wore was well known. XS by Paco Rabanne was one of her favorite men's colognes. It assaulted her senses, making her tingle. Jayde refused to give Devon any credit. That scent on a dead man would affect her. *Any thoughts as to how we can pass the time?* His words echoed in her head.

How dare he suggest she liked him? She barely stomached being in the same room with him. *Get a grip,* she scolded herself. *Why are you even thinking about the minutiae when there are more pressing matters? Like being trapped.*

Every breath brought her closer to becoming unglued. "Where could everyone be?" She voiced her concern. "Why haven't they heard us?" Her tone grew shrill. "For the love of Pete, this place isn't soundproof, you know."

* * *

Devon watched the cacophony of emotions cross her face. It was obvious a crescendo was imminent. He just didn't know why. Putting joking aside, Devon tried to calm her. "Take it easy, Jayde. We've only been in here a few minutes. I'm sure we'll be out of here soon."

"Take it easy? How can I take it easy when I'm stuck in a storage room with you." Her look was venomous. "I don't understand how can you be so calm. Aren't you the least bit interested in getting out of here?"

"I'm calm because there isn't much we can do. We have to be patient. Eventually, someone will notice we're missing and start to get suspicious. Either that or they'll hear you banging and shrieking in here."

She wrapped her arms around herself. "This is all one big joke to you, isn't it?" Jayde backed up toward the wall. "I can't stand being cooped up in here. I can't take it anymore. I've got to get out," she cried, wringing her hands. "Too small . . . It's too small."

Running to the door, Jayde banged on its solid frame again. Aching hands didn't slow her determination. She couldn't recall how long she was yelling at the top of her lungs when suddenly she was forcibly turned and pulled into a strong embrace.

Holding her tightly, Devon tried to allay her fears. "Hey, it's okay."

Jayde was oblivious. Shaking her didn't get her attention, either. Her flushed skin, glazed expression, and hyperventilating were clear indications she was having an anxiety attack.

"Jayde," Devon shouted over her rambling, "listen to me. This isn't helping you. You've got to calm down. You have to breathe slowly."

Words of encouragement were futile. She needed something to snap her out of it. He had to find something else on which she could focus. Slapping her was the least appealing option. At a loss for what else to do, Devon cushioned Jayde's thrashing head between his hands, leaned down, and kissed her.

Considering their brief history, he didn't know what type of response he'd get—a slap or a well-placed kick to the groin wouldn't have surprised him. Since none was forthcoming, he continued to increase the pressure on her lips until Jayde ceased fighting.

Eventually, she became a willing participant. By the time her arms wound around his neck, Devon was lost, too. A few moments later, he reluctantly broke their kiss. Devon noted that Jayde's face was still flushed, but the frenzied look was gone.

Dismayed, Jayde couldn't believe what had happened. He'd kissed her. The trouser snake had actually *kissed* her, and without a thought, she'd responded to it. Her stomach churned. Beads of perspiration on the back of her neck and her fluttering stomach were clear signs she wasn't repulsed by the exchange. *Good grief. Am I that hard up?* Her eyes shut to block out his face. She struggled to breathe. The ramifications of their actions weighed on her mind, as did her body responding wholeheartedly to the encounter. *Office flings don't last, especially when you dislike the other person. Right?* What was she thinking? It was a kiss. Why in the world was she acting like it wasn't a random, crazy act that would never, ever happen again?

"Jayde, are you all right?" Devon questioned.

"Yes," she croaked. Embarrassed at her outburst, Jayde

looked away. Her throat felt raw. When she swallowed, she grimaced with pain. "I'm sorry I lost . . . control."

"Don't apologize." Though they were alone, he lowered his voice. "Jayde, you're claustrophobic?"

Jayde blushed, looking everywhere but his face. "I don't like admitting it. It seems silly to mention it when most of the time it's not a problem. It only happens . . . sometimes."

He nodded, running a finger down her tearstained cheek. "Like when you're locked in confined spaces with people you hate?"

Gazing into eyes the color of polished steel, Jayde felt that crazy thing her heart did when she was . . . intrigued. "I don't hate you, Devon." *God help me. I am crazy!*

A slow smile crossed his face, causing her to stare like she'd never seen the expression before.

"Saints preserve us," he said loudly. "You finally admitted it."

She went to hit him, but he deftly captured her hand in his. Before either one could overthink their actions, they were locked in another embrace.

She felt as rigid as a brick wall. "Relax," he whispered against her mouth. Keeping the pressure firm and consistent, Devon eventually felt her soften. Only then did he release her. When a contented sigh escaped her lips, she pulled away.

"I retract my earlier statement—I hate you," she said.

Devon grinned. His thumb traced a line over her swollen lips. Her cheeks glowed. He was happy to see that familiar fire dancing in her eyes. She was back to normal. "That's a shame, because this has been the only time since I've met you that you haven't annoyed me." Suddenly his smile faded, and his expression grew serious. A look of wonder crossed his face before he spoke again. "You know, for once I'd love to hear my name on your lips, spoken in something other than anger."

Thoughts flittered through Jayde's mind, but she was too dumbfounded to manage a reply. How could she respond to a statement like that? Not too long ago she'd been ranting at him, and now the only thing she wanted was for him to kiss her again. How did that happen? she asked herself. Jayde's mind contradicted her body. The skirmish left her dazed and way too confused.

Devon tilted his head. "I take it you weren't expecting blatant honesty. I suppose I could apologize for it, but I'm not going to. I haven't enjoyed this war between us, Jayde. Truthfully, I've been trying to think of ways to end the conflict without having to send you packing. I think we just came up with a viable solution, don't you?"

She pushed him in the chest. "What . . . oh," she sputtered. "You are so arrogant. I was barely coherent when you kissed me. It was just a fluke."

Devon nodded in agreement. "It could have been. I doubt it. It happened twice, you know." The dimple in his chin deepened. "Of course, we could try it a third time, just to be sure."

Jayde didn't utter a word. Instead, she backed away and put herself on the opposite side of the room. She sat in perfect silence while Devon tried in vain to engage her in conversation.

Salvation arrived shortly after by way of the gallery's receptionist. The tall, impeccably dressed man jumped ten feet when he opened the door to find Jayde and Devon casually sitting there.

"Girl," the receptionist said, grabbing his heart, "you both gave me a scare. I was walking by and saw the door closed, and since it's never closed, I thought it was an accident."

Jayde looked pointedly at Devon. "It was." She ignored Devon's mocking expression. "Where the devil was everybody? We've been here a long time."

Devon's gaze traveled to his watch. He decided not to tell Jayde it had only been fifteen minutes.

The receptionist chuckled. "Hel-lo, it's Thursday, remember? We planned to try out that new sushi place. The whole office went"—he surveyed them both and chuckled—"except you two."

As they headed toward the elevator, Jayde recounted what had happened, purposely leaving out bits of information. Each time she did, the smug look on Devon's face grew. Her face grew hot, and she told the inquisitive receptionist that she'd finish the rest of the story later.

Devon's rich, booming voice stopped her. "So, was there anything else we needed to . . . discuss?"

She turned to face him. The saccharine smile on her face spoke volumes. "No, I think we covered everything."

Devon's reply was immediate. "Trust me, we're not even close."

Two weeks later . . .

Maxwell slid the report across his desk. "Your man is very thorough. I don't think there's a stone he isn't overturning."

Devon took the report. "It's his job. Besides, I wanted to make sure I don't leave anything out. Thus far none of the staff investigations have turned up anything unusual."

"That's good news, isn't it?"

"We still don't have a suspect, Max."

"So where's your detective now?"

"Italy. Paolo Gambrini's next. If he's guilty, I want undeniable proof. Gambrini left two days after he resigned. We have to find out what he's been up to."

"Good thing you hired the PI."

"Purely practical. I can't keep an eye on Gambrini *and* what's going on here."

"Speaking of which, how's it going? You and Jayde make nice yet?"

Devon's expression was unreadable. "Something like that."

The sigh of relief escaping Maxwell's lungs was audible. "Great. I'm glad you two are on the same page, because we'd hate to lose her. She's a valuable asset."

Devon scoffed. "I said we were getting along, Max, not thinking alike."

Maxwell regarded the younger man. "It's been two weeks since she's been to see me or called. You don't call that progress?"

Devon recalled their storage-room encounter. The left side of his mouth rose slightly. "I'll call you later."

Jayde stared at the notes sprawled across her desk. She was coordinating an upcoming exhibit showcasing a local artist. It would be a glitzy event with plenty of media coverage, and she loved every minute of it. She enjoyed being part of the planning process. Since the budget for each event was flexible, it ensured everything was personalized and done on a grand scale.

"How are things going?" Devon poked his head into her office later that day. "Everything on track?"

"Of course. This is the first gallery event since you

became the new overlord. Wouldn't want you to crash and burn, would we?"

Devon wasn't the least bit intimidated. "Easy, Jayde. Your claws are showing."

She purred loudly before bursting into laughter. Her lightheartedness was infectious.

Soon, Devon was chuckling, too.

When the laughter died down between them, Devon stared at her. Unable to help himself, he pondered the stark difference between Candace and Jayde. The latter's feelings were never hidden. He could look into Jayde's eyes and see exactly what was on her mind, even if she was angry. No pretense, no games—just honest emotion. As he gazed at her with an open frankness, his voice relayed the awe he felt. "I like when you do that."

She looked up in confusion. "What?"

"When you laughed just now, it was with such abandon. Whatever the reason, you weren't cautious or wary, just open. It was . . . refreshing."

Taken off guard, she didn't have a snappy comeback.

Devon decided not to point it out. Instead, he changed the subject. "So, what do you do on the weekends?"

She smiled. "Just the typical stuff. I hang out with my friends, take my dog, Boomer, for walks at Hains Point."

"What kind of dog?"

"He's a golden retriever."

"Okay, what else?"

"I get seafood from the wharf at least twice a week and spend time with family."

"Really? I would've pegged you as a party girl."

Jayde smirked. "Me? Nah. Don't get me wrong. I like to go out and party, just not till the wee hours of the morning. Did that when I was young, dumb, and stupid." A laugh bubbled up. "Now I'm grown, wise, and selective."

You forgot beautiful. His gaze was contemplative. "My instincts tell me you were never dumb—or stupid."

For the first time since their encounter in the storage room, he became aware of her appearance. Devon subtly scanned her six-foot frame. What a body it was. Jayde was a work of art in her own right—shapely, well proportioned, with an unusual beauty. Her hair was dark brown, with curls that rested on her shoulders.

Within her oval face were slightly slanted, warm brown eyes, which complemented her hair color. Her nose and lips were equally proportioned, and she had a lone mole on her right cheek. Her complexion was almost the same as his—a warm, sun-soaked brown. Her style of dress was classy and ultrafeminine. It was appealing.

Devon wasn't surprised at the direction in which his thoughts had strayed. He'd been doing it off and on since their intimate run-in. Aware of the heavy silence, he stopped assessing her and tried lightening the tense air around them.

"Whoa. Are we having a conversation?" he asked.

Jayde placed her hands on her hips. "Yeah. What of it? It's not like we haven't talked before."

"True. Just not about anything personal."

"Well, don't get too excited."

There was no way he was letting that skate by. "Why shouldn't I get excited?"

She ignored his suggestive tone. "Because it's only temporary. One of us will do something to mess it up. Probably you," she teased.

Walking around her desk, Devon sat on the top so that he was next to her. "Tell me why it has to be a temporary cease-fire. We're on the same team, aren't we? I'd wager both of us want what's best for the gallery. I know you don't think that's me, but it is. You have to trust me on that. I wouldn't do anything to ruin its reputation. I thought very highly of Cecilia Grayson Wells." His expression became unreadable. "She was an unforgettable woman."

"Come on. How did you know Mrs. Wells?" Her expression turned wary. "There's something you're not telling me. I can feel it, Devon. You want me to trust you? Well, that works both ways. Trust is earned, and so far you're coming up short."

Devon grasped her hands. Feeling her about to pull away, he tightened his hold. "Jayde, I promise you that soon, everything will be explained. I just need a little time. Don't you think a battle-free work zone is worth some patience?"

There was something in his expression that drew her in. He actually looked sincere when he spoke. His eyes implored her to understand. He was extending an olive branch. Now Jayde had to decide whether to accept it or hand it back to him, snapped in two. Time ticked by, and still she pondered. Finally, decision made, she nodded. It was almost imperceptible, but it was enough. Devon caught it.

She retrieved her hands from his grasp to poke him in the chest with her finger. "You'd better not make me regret this."

The smile on his face made his dimple more pronounced. "I wouldn't dream of it."

CHAPTER 9

True to his word, Devon had the documents drawn up to make Jayde's promotion official. She was now the exhibition director. The job was identical to what she had been doing before, except it included more interaction with artists for exhibits. In addition, her responsibilities extended to searches for new talent, outreach programs, and all public relations. She was in her element.

Jayde added an after-school art series for children and teenagers. The weekday courses fostered youngsters showing natural aptitude in painting and sculpting. Once a month local art teachers selected students for special recognition. Their works were displayed in a special wing at the gallery. Invitations to the unveiling were mailed out to fellow students, parents, and teachers. An after-party followed, with a catered buffet of kid-friendly hors d'oeuvres. On occasion, the media covered the event. The programs were great PR for the gallery, boosting foot traffic and community awareness.

Devon couldn't have been prouder of Jayde's hard work and dedication. It was obvious how enamored she was with all things artistic and creative. She wasn't the only one who appreciated the difference Wells made. Working at the gallery had allowed him to glimpse the true importance of his grandmother's life's work. Her gift to the world became clear. It filled him with more pride and insight into Cecilia Wells's passion.

However, he never forgot his original reason for being there. He'd received another communiqué from his detective in Italy. Gambrini had recently opened the Galleria d'arte di Gambrini in Lazio. Though small by Italian standards, the gallery had substantial collections of paintings and fine art. Based on the report Gambrini's gallery was flourishing.

Devon was flipping through some of the information on Paolo Gambrini one day when Jayde walked in.

"Hey, what are you up to? It's rather late for you, isn't it?" she asked.

Closing the folder, he slid it to the side. Devon glanced at his watch. "It's only six," he replied. "Hardly considered burning the midnight oil. Did you need me?"

"As a matter of fact, I do. I've just hung a painting, and I want to get your feedback on its location. We've got a small reception tomorrow, so get off your duff, Mr. Mitchell, and come help."

Standing, Devon met her in the middle of his office. He placed a hand at Jayde's back, then ushered her out. "You know, Miss Seaton, someone should've told you that insubordination is not the way to professional advancement."

Arching an eyebrow, Jayde gave Devon a quizzical look. "Really, that's odd. It seems to work just fine for me."

Jayde wore special gloves to keep the oils on her hands from damaging the painting. Perched on a ladder, she was all business. Behind her, Devon looked critically at the display.

"So? How's it looking from down there?" she called.

"A little to the left." Smiling, Devon tried to sound disinterested. In truth, he was far from it. Seeing her six feet in the air and practically straddling a ladder was making him sweat.

"Now?"

"Nope, a tad bit to the right."

Jayde let out an exasperated sigh. "Devon, would you hurry this up?"

"You've almost got it, Jayde," he said encouragingly. "Trust me, just a little more to the right."

After moving the painting, she turned her head to look at him. It was too quick. She caught the mask of concentration his face had become. The problem was his gaze was riveted to her backside and not to the painting.

Carefully, she climbed down the ladder. Once her feet touched the ground, she glared at him. "You are so busted."

"What?"

"I saw you staring, and it wasn't at the painting. Fess up, Mr. Mitchell. You had me up there, pushing that painting to and fro, and it didn't even need adjusting." She punched him on the shoulder for good measure.

"Ow." Devon grabbed his arm. "Don't even feign innocence, Miss Seaton. You knew that painting was fine before you came to get me. Personally, I think you wanted me to check out *your* work of art."

Indignant, Jayde scoffed, "Ha. I did no such thing. I simply needed a second opinion."

Playful eyes captured her gaze, refusing to relinquish it. "And you got it. Come on. Let's get out of here."

"Excuse me?"

"You heard me." Devon placed his hand in hers and

pulled her along behind him. "I've been putting off taking you shopping for that replacement suit long enough."

"That isn't necessary—"

"Oh, yes, it is. We're getting along much better these days. It's the perfect time to add a stone to that wall of a truce we've erected," he reasoned.

They headed to Neiman Marcus. Devon accompanied her as far as the entrance to the women's clothing department. When Jayde turned to ask him a question, he wasn't there. Puzzled, she peeked over her shoulder. She spotted him, with his hands in his suit pockets, holding up a nearby wall.

"That's as far as you're coming?" she called.

"You've got it. This is where I draw the line. When you're ready, just come get me."

"Coward," Jayde taunted.

"I've got a mother, a sister, and a niece. I've paid my dues. I refuse to be used as a dressing-room clothes rack."

She was astonished at the bit of personal information he'd supplied. Unable to help herself, Jayde walked over to him. "You know, you said more about your personal life in that one sentence than you have the entire time I've known you."

"Jayde."

Hearing the warning in his tone, she smiled brightly. "Yes, Devon?"

"Go shopping."

Twenty minutes later, Jayde narrowed it down to three suits. She called over to Devon to let him know she was going to try them on. The only indication he'd heard was an almost nonexistent grunt. Several minutes later, the decision was made. Jayde had chosen an Albert Nipon three-piece suit. It was champagne-colored silk, with a textured jacket, matching camisole, and pencil skirt. The size-twelve ensemble fit her like a second skin. Eyeing the price tag, Jayde couldn't help smiling in anticipation of Devon's reaction. *This will give him a coronary.* The expression he'd have when seeing the cost would be priceless.

Eagerly, Jayde went in search of Devon. He was exactly where she'd left him.

"Ready?" he asked.

Jayde noted his hopeful expression. Holding up her outfit, she couldn't refrain from asking his opinion. "What do you think?"

"It looks great."

"You said that awfully quick."

"I'm not crazy. I told you I've done this before."

They took Jayde's purchase to the counter. The sales associate smiled pleasantly at Jayde as she took the suit. That smile went into overdrive when she spotted Devon. The woman practically fell over herself. Rolling her eyes, Jayde made a barely audible comment about the woman drooling on the keypad of her register. Hearing it, Devon chuckled.

When the sales associate announced the total, Jayde waited for an outburst from him. It never came. Instead, he deftly pulled a credit card out of his wallet and handed it over. Jayde deflated quicker than a punctured balloon. Not even a blink. If anything, he looked bored. *So much for hitting him in his wallet,* she griped to herself, taking the proffered shopping bag.

As they walked past the shoe department, a pair caught Jayde's eye. Entranced, she went straight to the display and held one shoe up for closer inspection. The

Manolo Blahnik ankle-strap, cream-colored sandals went perfectly with her new suit.

While she pondered her purchase, Devon's voice drifted around her. "You should get them."

"I don't know."

Coming around, he had stood in front of her. "Sure you do. They'd go well with your suit, and you like them. I can tell by the way your eyes glazed over just now. I thought I saw drool, too."

She shoved him playfully. "You did not," Jayde protested, but she didn't put the shoe down. Instead, she found a salesman and asked for her size. Once seated, she waited for the man to return.

Lowering himself into a chair next to her, Devon stretched his legs out in front of him.

"Do you have to look so bored?" Jayde asked.

He looked up in question. "This is the standard look men wear when they shop."

She snorted. "Unless it's for themselves."

"Don't be fooled. I don't like to shop for myself, either."

Their exchange was cut short when the salesman arrived, waving a box. Trying on the shoes, Jayde turned repeatedly in front of the mirror. "They fit and look amazing. I'll take them."

While the salesman rung up her shoes, Jayde retrieved her wallet from her purse. Devon's hand stayed her motion.

"I've got it."

"Oh no, you don't. We agreed on the suit, not on the Manolos to go along with it."

"Jayde, it's an outfit. I agreed to buy you an outfit. Now stop arguing and let me pay for them."

"Absolutely not." Her determination brooked no arguments. "I will not have you paying over a thousand dollars for my clothes, Devon."

He turned. "You didn't mind a moment ago. In fact, you looked quite pleased with yourself."

Was I that transparent? she wondered. "You got me. I was looking forward to hitting you in the wallet."

"Then what's the issue?"

"Devon, it's obvious you can afford this excursion, but we agreed you'd replace my suit, nothing more."

Between point and counterpoint, the salesman chimed in. "How will you be paying for this?"

"Charge," they said in unison.

She turned toward Devon. "I'll pay for my shoes, and that's final."

Devon threw his hands up in surrender. "Fine, Jayde. You win. If I don't agree, we'll be standing here till next Thursday, arguing about it."

"I'm glad you see it my way." Handing her card over to the salesman, Jayde reveled in her undisputed victory.

Exasperated, Devon strode off to reclaim his spot at the front.

When she walked by, Devon fell into step beside her. "So, are we squared away?" he asked.

"Yes. I'd say you more than compensated me for your clumsiness."

"That was, by far, the most expensive coffee I've ever had," he said dryly.

Jayde couldn't help laughing at that.

He looked down at her. "So, can I assume you're done playing the suit card?"

The smile on Jayde's face was dazzling. "Yes, I believe I am." Suddenly she stopped him. "Thank you for the suit, Devon. I love it."

Her sincerity got to him. "It was my pleasure. Now, how about having dinner with me?"

Jayde's mouth dropped open. "Are you serious?"

"Of course, I'm serious. Why wouldn't I be? Neither one of us has eaten, so why don't we grab a bite together?"

Frowning, she shifted her weight. "I don't know . . . I don't think it's a good idea for us to—"

"For us to what?" Crossing his arms across his chest, Devon pinned her with an amused look. "Jayde, we're going to dinner. I haven't asked you to fill out a bridal registry, and don't give me the no-mixing-business-with-pleasure speech. You go out with coworkers all the time. Just last week a group of you went to Andale."

Jayde was shocked. "How'd you—"

"Besides," he interrupted, "we're way past that."

"Way past what? Just what is that supposed to mean?"

His eyes took on a lascivious glint. "Do I really need to mention the storage room?"

Her breath stuck in her throat. She blushed furiously. "I can't believe you brought that up."

"Trust me, if it's to my advantage, I'll use it, but it's not just that. If you recall, I just bought you a suit, and last time I checked, a man buying a woman clothing was unmistakably personal."

Jayde fiddled with the shopping bag in her arms. "It's not like I let you pick it out or anything."

"True, but I was there," he teased. "And my credit card was, too."

Frantically, Jayde tried to think of the ramifications of dinner with Devon. *Say yes. It's just dinner, no more, no less,* her conscience reasoned. *You're getting along. Don't blow it.*

"Jayde? Uh, hello?" Devon said, snapping his fingers. "Now who's daydreaming?"

Jayde came out of her reverie. "Sorry about that."

"Well, what's it going to be? You . . . me . . . dinner?"

"I was just . . . oh, never mind. I'd love to go to dinner with you. Where to?"

Devon was thoughtful for a moment. A flash of light crossed his face, and suddenly his eyes brightened. He retrieved his cell phone from his suit jacket. "I've got just the place."

One phone call and thirty minutes later . . .

They were being escorted to their table at the Sequoia at Washington Harbour. Located on K Street in Northwest D.C., it was the place to see and be seen. Jet-setters, young professionals, waning socialites, and local diners all flocked there to enjoy the food and ambience. The menu, though exemplary, was surpassed by the beautiful decor and extraordinary views of the Potomac River.

The evening was clear and the temperature warm enough for them to eat at one of the intimate tables outside. Multiple levels afforded diners a tranquil look at breeze-blown trees adorned with soft lights. Occasionally, boaters sailed lazily by, with music drifting and glasses clinking in the air.

Jayde was awestruck. "You know, I've lived here all my life, and I've never been here before. This is exceedingly beautiful, Devon. I'm stunned I almost missed out on this experience."

Her honesty moved him. "An oversight I'm happy to correct."

She smiled at him.

After ordering a drink and appetizers, Jayde lost herself in her surroundings. Studying her profile, Devon found himself as entranced by her as she was with the harbor.

"You have an undeniable passion for the water," he said.

"Yeah, I do. My love for it consumes me like nothing I've ever felt before. It's like a calming buoy amid the turbulence of life."

Devon's smile widened. "She's a poet, too."

"Hardly. I just know what I like."

His gaze became fixed. "So do I."

CHAPTER 10

Unable to help herself, she returned his frank stare. A connection formed between them where words were spoken without the need for sound.

Desperate to ease the tension fluttering around them, Jayde asked Devon about topics that were less personal in nature.

They conversed easily over dinner. Jayde was amazed how similar their tastes were in music, television, and sports, except Devon wasn't an art aficionado. Over dessert, Jayde discovered that Devon was also well traveled and fluent in French, Spanish, and conversational Japanese.

"Wow, growing up, you must've had your pick of the ladies," Jayde noted. "I'll bet they thought you were to die for."

Devon's fork clattered against his plate. Jayde looked up in alarm. The absolute pain etched on his face made her gasp.

"Devon?"

He couldn't hear her. Traveling back in time, Devon was oblivious to his surroundings. His apartment materialized before his eyes. It was just before he'd left on his business trip before the accident. He saw Candace sitting on the couch, smiling like she had just moved a piece on a chessboard and was about to form her lips to say "Checkmate." Those perfectly shaped lips, which used to keep him busy for hours, were painted a dark, shiny crimson. Her immaculate silk dress and the body underneath would never drive him to distraction again.

"Why can't we talk about this?"

"There's no need," Devon replied curtly. "It's over, Candace. We've known this for quite some time. I'll be in Japan for the next three weeks on business. That should give you time to make other living arrangements. You've been out of my bed for some time. Now I want you out of my life."

Standing, Candace closed the distance between them with sexy, purposeful strides. Flinging her arms around his neck, she pouted up at him. "Devon, I love you. We just had a tiff. What couple doesn't? Besides, we always have such fun making up."

He untangled her hands from around his neck. "This isn't working for me, Candace. You and I have run our course. Besides, we both know love isn't in it—for either of us."

Candace's eyes narrowed. "Did your father put you up to this? Your parents would just love for you to break up with me. I'm sure they are beside themselves with joy."

"Let's not do this. Look, I've already called my assistant to make arrangements. You have your choice of apartments throughout Chicago, or anywhere you'd like. I'll cover six months' rent and all moving expenses."

She jerked out of his arms. "Forget it," she yelled. "I'm not going to let you cast me aside like last year's fashion. I've got you, and I'm not letting go. Do you hear me, Devon? I'll be a Mitchell if it kills me!"

* * *

"It did kill her," he said.

"What? Devon, can you hear me? What killed who?" Shaking his forearm harder, Jayde grimaced when he still didn't respond. "Devon," she whispered loudly, "snap out of it."

He blinked rapidly, and the haze eventually cleared. Devon cleared his throat. "Jayde?"

"Yes, it's me."

He took in his surroundings. He ran a hand over his face. "That was closer to hell than I've been in a while."

Placing her hand on his, she gave it a firm squeeze. "Are you all right? You were far away and so angry just now. You should've seen your face."

"I'm fine. It was nothing."

Her eyes widened. "Devon, a blind man could've seen that it was something."

He ran his fingers over her hand. "It's nothing," he assured her. "I'm not letting the past ruin our evening. So, where were we?"

After dinner, Devon drove her home. Jayde put her window down to enjoy the feel of cool air on her face. The soulful melodies, her food-laden stomach, and the plush seats of his Range Rover were nirvana.

"You don't strike me as the SUV type," she said.

Devon didn't let his eyes leave the road. "Is that so? And just how would you know what my type is?"

"A car is a representation of its owner. I think that there is a perfect car for everyone."

"Uh-huh. Well, you drive a Jeep, so what does that say about you?"

"That I'm a risk taker. I'm not trying to prove anything to anyone. I'm my own boss, and I can tackle any obstacles that come my way."

"Interesting analogy, Miss Seaton."

"So, back to the question. Whose truck?"

At the next red light, he looked over. "Why the sudden interest in what I drive?"

"No reason. Just making small talk. And don't think I don't realize that you didn't answer my question."

What he drove, what he bought for her, and with whom they socialized had been the cornerstones of Candace's universe. He'd been naive enough to fall for the honeyed words that had dripped from her lips and the sweet nectar she'd dished out in bed. Toward the end, it had been a bitter pill to swallow. *You were a fool.*

"Does it really matter what I drive?" He tried, but Devon couldn't keep the edge out of his voice.

Minutes passed before she spoke again. "It only matters that you won't tell me."

Jayde heard the heavy sigh. A clear indication he wouldn't divulge the source of his torment—at least not tonight. Jayde dropped the subject. It was another piece of the puzzle that was Devon Mitchell to be filed away for future reference.

Silence descended in the vehicle's cabin. By the time they pulled up to Jayde's condo, the damage was irrevocable. Devon's disturbing walk down memory lane was a cloud that had descended over their impromptu outing, snuffing out the lighthearted fun between them.

Jayde turned sideways in her seat. "Thanks for the suit, dinner, and the ride."

With purse in hand, Jayde bounded out of the car. Leaning into the backseat, she grabbed her packages and headed for her door.

Devon caught up with her by the time her foot hit the building's third step. He placed a hand at the small of her back. "It was my pleasure, though we could've gone back to the office and picked up your car."

"No need. I'll take the subway in tomorrow. Good night, Mr. Executive Director."

Devon frowned at her reference. "Good night, Jayde. See you in the morning."

She let herself into the inner sanctum of her building. Waving, she opened the security door and disappeared down the hall. Eventually, Devon turned and strode angrily to the big behemoth idling at the curb. Once he'd secured his seat belt and slid the truck into drive, he punched the accelerator. The engine sprang to life, propelling him faster down the street than necessary.

Great going, Mitchell. He chided himself for upsetting her. His inner musings on Candace had put a damper on the wonderful time they'd been having. It was obvious his inability to open up affected Jayde. Her reserved behavior after his last comment was proof enough. Once again, she'd retreated into her zone of wariness. This time it was his fault.

"One step forward, two steps backward," he muttered.

Devon punched a button on his cell phone, activating the speed dial.

"Hi, Mom. It's me."

"Hello, me. I was wondering when you'd touch base. Your father has been beside himself. You know, he is actually contemplating visiting Henry if you don't come home soon. They enjoy rubbing each other the wrong way, so you can imagine how that would go."

Despite his somber mood, Devon couldn't help the laugh that escaped. "Scary."

His mother didn't respond right away. "What's

the matter, darling? You sound like something's troubling you."

Devon brought the car to a stop and closed his eyes. "You mean other than the usual stuff?"

"It's bothering you only because you let it. It's been so long, honey. When are you going to stop this self-imposed exile and resume your life?"

A horn honk caused him to snap his eyes open. He resumed driving. "I already have, Mom. I'm at the gallery."

"What? Sweetheart, why?"

"I'm not ready to come back to work, Mom—not yet. Besides, some issues cropped up here that I need to take care of, so I figured a detour was in order."

He could hear the frown in his mother's voice. "Your father isn't going to like this one bit. Just how long will this detour last?"

"I can't say, but don't worry. I'll keep in touch. Maybe I'll take a long weekend and drop in soon. It'll have to be in a few weeks, though. We've got a new exhibit opening next weekend that's taking up most of my time."

There was a pause before his mother spoke. "This is a first. You've never involved yourself directly in gallery business before."

"Maybe it's time I did. Tell Dad I'll call him later."

"I'll tell him when he gets home. He's working late, tying up some loose ends. Something about a merger he's working on."

"Merger?" Devon said, surprised. "I don't recall anything in the mail from the office regarding a merger. Why didn't Dad mention it the last time we spoke?"

"I don't know, dear. Don't worry about it. I'm sure he didn't want to burden you with business. There'll be time for that later."

"I guess you're right." Emotion constricted his throat, making his voice sound gruff. "Love you, Mom."

"I love you, too, honey. I can't wait to see you. None of us can."

"I know."

Smoothing back the covers, Jayde slid into the welcoming warmth of her bed and stared at the ceiling. Beethoven's Piano Sonata no. 8 drifted through the CD player on her nightstand. Boomer settled himself on his doggie bed a few feet away. Sighing loudly, he shifted until he found a comfortable position. It was their bedtime ritual.

She closed her eyes and willed herself to drift into blissful slumber. Seconds later her eyes popped open. "Devon Mitchell, you're the most infuriating man I've ever met. Why the sudden mood swings?" she wondered aloud.

Dinner had started out amicably enough, but then it had taken a swan dive toward disaster. For once, they'd been getting along without the need for white flags or dueling pistols; now it felt like they'd just taken a huge step backward.

Just then Jayde's phone rang. Picking up the receiver, she heard her friend's voice before she'd spoken a word.

"I know you're on the phone. Save the hello."

"Hi to you, too, Chris. What's going on?"

"You know I didn't call to tell you about *me*. You left me some cryptic message on my machine about a suit and dinner tonight with gallery man. A date! What in the world is this about? I was on pins and needles waiting for your tall butt to get home. Tell me all, and don't

even think about leaving anything out. I'm dying to hear
about all the sexy, heart-stopping, stomach-fluttering,
toe-curling action," Christy said and laughed. "I mean it.
Don't you dare scrimp on the details."

Despite her earlier pensive mood, it was hard not to
get caught up in her friend's enthusiasm. For now,
Jayde set the misgivings aside. "Okay, okay," she said,
giggling. "Let me get settled."

"When last we left our virile superhero," Christy said
in her best television announcer voice, "he was throwing a well-placed monkey wrench into your artistic program. Seconds later, he's expertly overloading your
senses while necking in the coat closet." She laughed.
"Girl, I can't keep up! This is way better than a soap
opera."

Jayde's laughter echoed around her bedroom. Her
best friend was incorrigible. "For your information, it
wasn't a coat closet. It was a storage room."

"Yeah, whatever. Get back to the story. What's up
with Dr. Jekyll and Mr. Fine?"

Lowering herself under the covers, Jayde got comfortable. "Settle in, girlfriend. I got a tale for you."

CHAPTER 11

Henry was spreading an over-the-counter analgesic on his latest war wound courtesy of Abigail when his telephone rang. Stretching, he attempted to answer it without getting up. He failed. The phone receiver slid onto the floor. "Hold on," he yelled, setting his liniment on the nightstand. He wiped his hand on his jeans, then picked up the receiver, holding the earpiece close.

"Hello?" Hearing the voice on the other end caused an immediate frown. "What do you want?"

"Is that any way to speak to your older brother?"

"Yes. Besides, you're my *only* brother," Henry shot back. "Why do you insist on calling yourself older? It's a fact we're both aware of. Makes no sense, if you ask me."

"I didn't."

Ignoring that comment, Henry went to the window. He spotted Abigail. He could've sworn the obstinate bovine was looking right at him. *One day she is going to push me too far.* Sighing, Henry turned his attention back to his sibling. "What d'ya want, Sterling?"

"For starters, I'd like to know where my son is."

Henry loved riling his brother. Next to Abigail, it was

his favorite pastime. "If he wanted you to know, he would've told you."

"Don't play games, Henry. My patience has run thin. Devon has responsibilities—to himself, our employees, and me. It's time he took them up again."

"Oh, give it a break, will you? His first priority is to get his head straight. That's what he's been doing. I suggest you give him the time he needs, and I'm not telling you squat, so quit your whining."

Before his brother could retort, Henry hung up on him. "Told him," he said and smiled at the phone. Not even his bruised backside was going to spoil the moment.

It was ten in the morning and still no Devon. Where could he be? Jayde wondered. She was stirring creamer into her tea when he entered the break room. The tea sloshed over the side of her cup. Annoyed, she grabbed a napkin and sopped up the mess. *Why?* she asked herself. *Why in the world does he affect me the way he does?* Dealing with Devon meant dealing with extremes. One minute she wanted to riddle him with paintball capsules, and the next . . .

She'd see him walk by, and her gaze would follow him until he was out of sight. Looking at him coming through the door now, Jayde couldn't deny the obvious. He looked good in his dark blue suit. *No, not good,* she corrected. He looked spectacular. Hanging perfectly on his muscular frame, the tailored garments were the perfect backdrop for his powerful presence.

Wait a minute. Jayde shook her head to clear the unwanted thoughts. *You're supposed to be ignoring him,* she chided herself. *Drooling all over yourself at his good looks isn't the plan. Cool indifference. Yeah, that's what you want to use.*

Boldly, Jayde made eye contact. It was a mistake. His gaze was disturbing. It spoke volumes, telling her he knew exactly what she was thinking. She hated clairvoyants. They were too nosy for her peace of mind.

"Morning," she said, with exaggerated indifference.

Silence filled the room.

Devon glowered. She could act stiff and aloof with what's his name at the front desk, but not with him. Walking over, he poured a cup of coffee. "We need to talk."

She took a loud sip. "We are talking."

"While the tone you're using could sweeten my coffee, it's not what I had in mind." He headed for the exit. "My office in five."

"Go to the devil" was poised on her lips, but his next words halted the acerbic comeback.

"I wouldn't advise it, Jayde. Five minutes. Not a moment more."

Devon noted the time on his watch. He was about to go looking for Jayde when she entered. Shutting the door, she walked over and calmly took the seat across from him. She stared at him defiantly.

He relaxed in his chair.

Jayde crossed her legs. "I'm here, mighty overlord. What did you need to say?"

"First off, sarcasm this early in the morning doesn't suit you, so stop calling me that. Second . . . I'm sorry."

"For what?"

"My behavior last night. I don't want you to think my reticence was because of you. It wasn't."

She shrugged away his apology. "I didn't think that at all—actually, quite the opposite. I figured out something was bothering you when you went missing during dinner."

Confusion etched his features. "Missing? What are you talking about? I didn't leave the table."

"Your body was there, but your mind was in a galaxy far, far away."

"A sci-fi fan to boot," he quipped. "I've got a lot on my mind right now, nothing more."

"Care to share it?"

Devon rolled his Montblanc pen between his thumb and index finger. He grappled with his conscience. Were things ever simple? "The reason I was so—"

"Annoying? Cranky? Preoccupied?"

"All of the above," he conceded, with a grin. "I can't go into details about it, not now or here, but soon. How about a rain check? I ruined our evening, and I'd like a chance to make it up to you."

She looked skeptical. "Another man with drama," Jayde mumbled. "I swear I don't have the stomach for another trip on that crazy-go-round."

"What did you say?"

Uncrossing her legs, she stood. "Tempting as it may be, I don't think that's a smart idea."

He got up and came over to lean on his desk, next to her. "What isn't?"

She shrugged.

"Jayde, look at me."

Picking a spot on his suit jacket, Jayde gave it her undivided attention.

He tilted her face up until their eyes were parallel. "Tell me."

"You and I doing the dinner thing again. It seems like a . . . bad idea."

He dropped his hand. "So you're telling me you never need to eat? Or that you do, just not with me?"

His tone startled her. He actually sounded hurt. She could've sworn his outer hull was titanium. "It's just that things ended rather awkwardly. Add the whole zone-out thing you did at the restaurant and you've got a certified bad evening."

"I already explained it was my fault and that I'd fill you in later. What else is there to know?"

Is he kidding? "How about why you need to fill me in later? While you're at it, you can admit why you're really here. What's with the cloak-and-dagger routine?"

He stared at her incredulously. "We're back to that again? I thought you'd accepted I'm here to do a job. That's all."

"My gut is telling me there's more to the story. I just want the truth. It's not like I'm demanding your life story, only a few explanations, which I've earned the right to hear."

Exasperation gave his voice an edgy tone. "Why can't you leave well enough alone—at least for now?"

"Because I'm the only one in the room who doesn't know the punch line." She took a breath to calm down. It didn't work. "Everybody has something in the closet, Devon. I just don't want the dress walking up and asking me to step outside."

He couldn't help chuckling.

"This isn't funny," Jayde snapped.

He moved a piece of her hair behind her ear. "Are you referring to a complication of the feminine nature? Trust me, it's nothing like that."

She stilled his hand. "That remains to be seen."

Abrupt silence enveloped the room. Their attraction was palpable.

"Devon, can't you see it's a mistake to start blurring white and black lines? We're just getting to a point where we're not squaring off at fifty paces with staple guns every other day. I don't think we should tempt fate by delving into shades of gray."

"You call us getting to know each other better shades of gray?"

Jayde looked away. "If that were all it was, I wouldn't have a problem, but there's more, isn't there?"

"You're asking if we're drifting past the confines of a business relationship?"

"A bit wordy, but yes."

"I'd say that's a choice we both have to make."

"I think the choice is clear, Devon. The answer's no. I can't allow myself to get caught up with personal feelings. Not when there is so much about you I don't know. We're business associates. It should stay that way."

Devon thought about the complexities of his life of late. Truthfully, the last thing he needed was a complicated relationship. There wasn't a thing about Jayde Seaton that seemed simple or casual. Opting for strictly business between them would be wise. Besides, the steel resolve in her voice and posture were enough for him. He'd drop the subject—for the moment.

"If . . ." The ringing telephone interrupted his reply. He cursed the interruption. Picking up the phone, Devon barked out a quick "Mitchell here." After a second, his expression grew glacial. Holding his hand over the receiver, he looked at her. "I'm sorry. I have to take this."

She turned to leave. "That's fine. I've got work to do. Besides, I think we've covered everything."

Devon pressed the hold button on the phone and slammed the receiver into the cradle. He was across the room, with Jayde in his arms, before she even knew what he was about. Backing her up against the closest wall, Devon proceeded to kiss Jayde senseless. Unable to help herself, Jayde wrapped her arms around his neck. Eventually, her fingers snaked through the curls in his hair. He explored her mouth with calculated voracity. Then, without warning, he ended their heated embrace. Jayde slid a few inches down the wall. Devon reached out to steady her. Dumbfounded, she gaped at him.

"I got news for you, sweetheart. We're way past shades of gray," he said.

CHAPTER 12

After leaving Devon's office, Jayde didn't know how, but eventually she made it to hers. Anxious, she circled the room. Shaking her arms at her sides, Jayde willed the simmering need coursing through her body to go away. It didn't listen. *If he had kissed you any harder, your clothes would've fallen off,* she thought to herself. Her hand moved to her throat. The pulse she felt there was rapidly beating against her fingers. The thought that she was getting in too deep galvanized her into action. She had to find out more about him.

Suddenly she looked at her computer. Within seconds an idea came to mind. "Of course," she said aloud. Sitting down, she typed her password on the keyboard and waited. Using her mouse, Jayde clicked on her Web browser icon. After going to her favorite search engine, Jayde paused. Her face crinkled in concentration. "Let's see." Jayde typed, "Devon Mitchell" and "art community," then hit ENTER.

There were a few hits. Jayde double clicked on each one. A few minutes later, she sat back in frustration. She'd turned up nothing useful. There were numerous

Devon Mitchells, but none of them were *her* Devon. *My Devon.* Jayde bit her lower lip. When did he become mine? *When he claimed your lips like you owed him money. Stop thinking like that,* she scolded herself. *He isn't yours and never will be.*

Next, she did a search of just his name. The results were enormous. Scanning the list, she tried narrowing it to any Devons in the local area who met her criteria. "Wait. Where did he say he worked before coming here?" Jayde said aloud. Racking her brain, she tried to remember what he'd told her. "Got it." She grinned. "He said he worked in executive management at a company out of Chicago." She was entering those keywords when her telephone rang. "Great," she muttered, reaching for the receiver. "This is Jayde."

"*Buon giorno,* Jayde. *Come sta?*"

Jayde smiled. "*Bene, grazie,* Paolo. *E lei?*"

"*Bene. Bene, amica mia.*"

Since Jayde's Italian was sorely lacking, she switched to English. "It's good to hear your voice, Paolo."

"Yours, too. How are things?"

Sighing, Jayde leaned back in her chair. "How much time you got?"

Over the next twenty minutes, Jayde filled Paolo in on what was going on at the gallery. He was so upset by the news, he was almost speaking straight Italian. He was surprised and outraged they'd replaced her as director.

"I promise you I'll get to the bottom of this."

"That isn't necessary. I'm over it. Well, mostly over it." She sighed. "Please, Paolo," she begged, "don't stir the pot."

"If you insist. You must come visit me soon, yes?"

A coworker poked his head in her door. "Got a minute?"

Jayde nodded and stood up. "I'd love to Paolo. I just don't know when I'd be able to."

"Make it soon, *bella*."

"Paolo, I have to run, but I will visit soon," she promised before hanging up.

For the next three days, gallery business monopolized Jayde's time. All thoughts of digging deeper into Devon's past were put on hold. Everyone geared up to present a new gallery artist, Samuel DeVoe.

The gala event would be held the following Friday. Invitations had gone out to the media, to local art critics, and to art enthusiasts, in addition to their loyal patrons, family, and friends. Secretly, Jayde prayed there would be a large turnout, because the artist's work was exceptional. After finishing the promos for the event, Jayde went to find Devon to get his feedback. He was in a meeting with someone, so he told her he'd stop by her office shortly.

Looking at a painting entitled *Sadness,* Jayde was lost amid the abstract strokes of the artist's brush. The well-chosen splashes of color beckoned her to explore the painting's textured depths. She welcomed the distraction. Anything was a welcome diversion to thinking about her personal life. Since the day in Devon's office when he'd kissed her silly she'd avoided him as much as possible. Aside from addressing work-related issues that couldn't be ignored, Jayde had kept to herself. The cacophony of emotions brought about by reminiscing about that encounter would have to wait. Right then, she wanted to lose herself in the simplistic beauty of the painting.

"Jayde?"

Jumping, she turned around to find Devon inches behind her.

"Oh, sorry," she said, backing up. "Did you want something?"

"Yes. I told you I'd meet up with you in your office, remember?" Devon noticed she was distracted. "What are you doing?"

"Hmm? Oh, just . . ." She stared at the easel consuming her attention. "This painting . . ." Her brow creased as she struggled for the right words. "I get lost in it."

Devon's gaze traveled over the abstract painting. Normally, he disliked abstract art. Returning his attention to her, he was baffled by her absorption in the canvas. Her eyes were riveted to the assortment of colors, while her blouse rose and fell faster with each breath. Her reaction reminded him of the passionate melee in his office. Suddenly something dormant surfaced. A primal force invaded his logical mind, making him want to experiment with ways he could elicit from her body that same reaction. Squelching the dangerous urge, he focused on his initial reason for seeking her out. It almost killed him.

He cleared his throat. "What did you want to see me about?"

"Hmm? Oh." Reluctantly, she turned toward him. "I stopped by to go over the press releases with you."

"Sorry about that. I was meeting with a colleague of mine. I'm thinking of creating a 'Meet the NSO Musicians' contest. We're hammering out the details."

"As in the National Symphony Orchestra?"

Devon nodded. "They have an event series starting in a month. It's a 'Meet the Artists' event, followed by dinner and then a concert. I'm thinking of having a raffle for the kids in our art programs. Six winners and their parents will enjoy a special evening at the Kennedy Center compliments of the gallery. Complete with a limo ride, of course."

Jayde's mouth hung open. "Are you serious?"

"Quite." When Jayde remained quiet, Devon scowled. "What's the matter? You don't think it's a good idea?"

"A g-good idea?" Jayde stammered. "I think it's a wonderful idea. I just can't believe you came up with it."

He arched an eyebrow. "You know, occasionally, I do have a few."

They shared a laugh. She gazed at him with newfound appreciation. "You never cease to amaze me."

"Then I'd say we're even."

The silver glint in his eyes captivated her. She wasn't sure how long they stared at each other, but one thing was clear. She couldn't look away.

Devon decided to break the spell before they changed the status quo. "I was thinking. Since everyone has worked so hard to make the upcoming event memorable, I'd like to have the staff over to my house for a dinner party, as a way of saying thank you."

Blinking, Jayde needed a moment to switch gears. "That isn't necessary. Everyone here loves what they do."

Not everyone. While the businessman in him appreciated his grandmother's ability to turn her passion into a lucrative reality, initially, he hadn't shared her vision. Devon had been all about business. He'd never had time to indulge his artistic side, not that there was much there to use, anyway. Before arriving at the Wells Gallery, Devon had been more comfortable managing the company's stock portfolios and various holdings than running a gallery. But thanks to Jayde, it was growing on him. If he was honest with himself, he'd acknowledge that everything about *her* was growing on him.

He turned his attention back to their conversation. "I'm sure they do, but all work and no play isn't productive in the long run. It's bad for morale, which affects the bottom line."

Taking the hint, Jayde agreed. "Fine, a party it is." Heading out, she called over her shoulder. "Let me know if there's anything I can do to help."

Devon pounced on her offer before the resonance of her voice vanished from the air.

"Actually, there is. I need help in the planning and implementing department."

She eyed him skeptically. "Oh, come on. Like you've never had a dinner party."

"Actually, I have them all the time, but usually I am a spectator," he admitted. "My mother frequently handles those details for me."

Her interest piqued, Jayde leaned against the wall and crossed her arms. "Your mother? I would've thought you had some Martha Stewart–type girlfriend just sitting around waiting to whip out the floral centerpiece and doilies."

"Hardly. My ex-girlfriend wasn't the home-and-hearth type. The only thing she made was reservations. If she couldn't order it, she didn't eat it."

"Oh, one of those types? I figured as much."

He snorted. "You did no such thing. Anyway, I need someone with your talent for event planning to help me pull this off." Moving closer, Devon slid his hand up and down her shoulder before whipping out the smile that got him anything. "Come on, Jayde. Help a man out."

Mesmerized, she tried to focus on what they'd been discussing. "When you go through the trouble of bringing out the heavy artillery, how can I say no?"

"Come on, Jayde," she mimicked. "Help a man out."

After she retrieved a sheet of bacon-wrapped scallops from the oven, Jayde checked the time. The staff would be there in less than an hour. Setting the baking sheet on the black and gold speckled granite countertop to cool, Jayde wiped a hand across her forehead. "Why did I say yes?" she moaned. *Because he touched you, then smiled at you till your toes curled*, her conscience reminded her. "Focus, Jayde," she admonished herself. "Oh, there's no way I'm going to be ready in time."

"Come now. Everything looks fantastic," Devon said from the doorway.

His appreciative glance made her face warm.

Her short-sleeved purple dress rested off her shoulders before continuing down her body to stop just below her knees. It wasn't one he'd seen before—he'd have remembered. Her hair was swept up into a decorative clip. Even in the chef's apron, she looked ravishing.

Devon sauntered toward her. "Especially you."

Flushing, Jayde glanced up from her task. "Thank you. I just hope the crew likes dinner."

"You really need to work on your obsessive tendencies. Everything doesn't have to be perfect."

"Don't just stand there. Point me in the direction of the food processor."

He gallantly motioned behind her. Her eyes followed his hand to an overhead cabinet. On tiptoes, Jayde opened the cabinet door. Her fingers fanned out in the black recesses of the cabinet in an effort to locate her quarry. It was futile.

She jumped when Devon's voice teased her ear. "Here, let me help."

When Jayde turned around, she was brought up short by his massive body.

Leaning closer, he pressed his body against hers in an effort to retrieve the appliance.

There was nowhere Jayde could move. He had her trapped between the counter and the cabinet. She had no alternative but to wait until he released her. It was a few moments before Devon retracted his arm from the cabinet—the longest moments in her life.

"Got it," he said triumphantly, offering her the appliance.

She shot him a murderous look. "Took long enough."

"Yes." He beamed, not the least contrite. "It did."

Jayde tried her best to look unaffected by their closeness. She maneuvered past him. "Would you mind handing me the cream cheese from the fridge? I've got to finish the hot crab dip."

Smugly, he went off to do her bidding. When he returned, he was also carrying two glasses and a wine bottle. He handed her the carton of cream cheese and then eased the wine bottle onto the counter. The glasses followed. "Would you care for some?"

Intent on her task, she shook her head. "Thanks, but not yet. Maybe after the gang arrives."

Devon propped himself against the counter and watched her work. "You know, when I asked you to help with this, I didn't think you'd try to do everything yourself."

She looked up. Jayde recalled her reaction to seeing the large house he called home. The decor hinted at professional designers or someone with an eye for decorating. Warm butter-colored walls anchored the color scheme of the entire first floor. Variations of cranberry, navy blue, and olive added to the palette. The decor made Jayde feel warm and relaxed, but Devon had disturbed the mood when he'd answered the door in his bathrobe, obviously just out of the shower.

He'd told her to hire caterers, but she knew that would be an expensive endeavor. Seeing the chateau on a hill outside Rock Creek Park made her realize he could've afforded to hire a whole team for the evening and would not have blinked twice. Another line item to add to the long list of mysteries about Devon Mitchell.

"Is there anything else I can do to help?" he asked.

Yes, stop staring at me with those penetrating eyes. "Not right now. I love entertaining and always work myself into a state preparing for things, so this is nothing new. I enjoy doing this."

"Yeah, right. You enjoy simulating a nervous breakdown?"

I'll have a nervous breakdown only if he keeps encroaching on my three feet of personal space, Jayde thought to herself. Tonight he looked way too hot. She noted that his eyes appeared darker and more mysterious when highlighted by his black slacks and a short-sleeved gray silk shirt with black piping. His hair was still damp from his shower. The visual on that made her palms moist. A few other body parts would be, too, if she didn't get herself together. She banished the dangerous thoughts from her mind. Playfully, she scrunched her nose and stuck out her tongue. "Shut up and hand me a large serving bowl."

CHAPTER 13

The man staring out the window sighed loudly. He switched the receiver to his other ear. His patience was evaporating with his associate on the other end of the line.

"I went to the farm, but he'd already gone. I know he didn't go to his place in town, because I have someone keeping tabs on it. There's been no contact with his parents or his sister. It's like he's taunting us to find him."

"I suggest you think outside the box. People hide best in plain sight. If I were you, I'd enlarge the search area. Try looking someplace outside of Chicago, but still in the continental United States."

"I really don't think—"

Gritting his teeth, he barked into the phone, "D.C., you moron. He's in Washington, D.C., at his grandmother's gallery."

"What's he doing there?"

"We sent him there."

"We did?"

"Have you been paying attention? The accidents sent him there! You know, someone that charges as much as you do shouldn't be so unbelievably stupid! As long as we continue creating havoc, he won't be going anywhere. Now, I suggest you hop on a plane and take care of the things we discussed."

Unable to help himself, he slammed down the receiver. The motion soothed his frazzled nerves. "I don't get paid enough to deal with this, but I will soon. Everything is going according to plan, but there can't be any foul-ups. Devon has to stay put until I get old man Mitchell where I want him. I'm just about done being your whipping boy and taking orders," he said in a menacing voice.

Yanking his desk drawer open, he took out a legal document. Scanning the contents, he imagined Sterling's face when he signed his company over to him. "You'd do anything for that son of yours, wouldn't you, Sterling?" Fingering the document, he couldn't help the smile that wrapped itself around his lips. "Soon enough, this company will be mine, and the Mitchells will finally get what they deserve."

So far so good, Jayde mused. All the gallery staff had turned out for the party at Devon's house. Circulating through the crowd, Jayde finally allowed herself to heave a sigh of relief. A feeling of being watched washed over her. She spotted Devon leaning against the kitchen counter. Their eyes locked. He winked before displaying a boyish grin. Returning his smile, Jayde swallowed hard. A prickly sensation drifted over her body. Her hand traveled to her throat. The pulse at her neck was erratic, a clear indication he was affecting her on a seriously sexual level. Suddenly self-conscious, Jayde headed in the opposite direction.

The company receptionist yanked her into the nearest corner when she walked by. "Girl, this place is a resort. I told you the man was loaded."

"No, you didn't," Jayde corrected.

He put a finger to his lips. "I didn't? Well, I meant to. From the looks of this place, the only reason our commander in chief needs to work is to fill idle time. Of course, I could—"

"Spare me," Jayde said quickly.

"Oh, all right, but tell me you aren't wondering why he's at the gallery. I tell you, there's more to our gorgeous young director than meets the eye."

"Amen to that," a female coworker chimed in from behind them.

"Funny," Jayde said, wearing a perplexed look, "this doesn't look like a water cooler."

"Things are never what they seem," her female colleague replied.

Jayde started to mingle. The weather allowed the crowd to spill out onto the patio.

"You didn't think you could hide from me all night, did you?"

Devon came to her side.

"It's a lovely party," Jayde replied.

Devon elbowed her arm. "Thanks to you, everything's going fantastic."

There were some coworkers eyeing them. Jayde ignored their raised-glass salute.

Devon tilted his head toward the group. "What's that about?"

"Beats me. Um, wouldn't you like to make your speech now?" Jayde prompted while gently pushing him toward the throng of people.

"I was planning to, yes. And, Jayde?" he called over his shoulder.

"Hmm?"

"I know a diversion when I see one."

Devon walked to the center of the patio. Clearing his throat, he greeted the crowd and then asked for everyone's attention. "When I first started at the Wells Gallery, I wasn't sure what to expect. I realize my coming on board was an unexpected surprise to all of you. I also realize that my transition wouldn't have gone smoothly if it hadn't been for each of you." Scanning the crowd, his gaze found its target. "Especially Jayde Seaton."

Startled, Jayde stood rooted to her spot.

Devon went on. "Having me here hasn't been easy for her, and I'm sure there are times when she'd prefer it otherwise. But, trust me when I tell you," he said, glancing directly at her, "I have only the gallery's best interest at heart." He focused on the crowd. "It's imperative to me to preserve everything that our founder, Cecilia Grayson Wells, held dear. Mishaps have plagued our day-to-day operations as well as our gallery events. It's my job to get to the bottom of these incidents, and it's not one I take lightly. I promise you all that if there are culprits responsible, I'll find them. I'm counting on everyone here to support me in my endeavor to ensure this gallery continues to thrive and be a positive monument in our community."

Applause echoed into the night, as did cheers from the small motivated crowd. After his big speech, Devon mingled.

Jayde decided to take a sweep around the tables to see if anything needed replenishing. A few of the dishes needed more food, so she headed to the kitchen. She unwrapped a fruit platter she retrieved from the fridge and headed back outside.

Devon knew the moment Jayde returned. It was hard to explain, but the air just felt different whenever she was around, almost like an electric current surging through him. His eyes followed her around the party of their own accord. Several times he saw her conversing with coworkers. From the looks on her face, some of those conversations were personal in nature. He wondered what they were about.

"You're deep in thought."

Devon looked down into Jayde's observant eyes. "Not that deep."

"Deep enough."

"Actually, I have been getting to know quite a few of my employees. It's been nice to converse with them outside the office. They're quite loyal to you, you know. Several people tried to pump me for information regarding my intentions for the gallery. I'm hoping my speech put their worries to rest."

"I hope you don't think I put them up to that," Jayde told him.

"No, of course not."

"Good. For a minute I thought you were going to try and pump me."

For a moment he was too stunned to reply.

Jayde's hands flew to her mouth, and her eyes registered her embarrassment. "I . . . Oh gosh, that didn't come out right. What I meant was . . ."

Devon placed his right hand on the dip between her waist and hip. Guiding her to him, he whispered in a voice only for her, "Believe me, I can't wait to get you alone and pump you."

Pump me? her brain queried. "For what?" she said in a voice that wasn't close to being her own.

He backed her up until she was in a quiet alcove surrounded by trees and heady-scented lavender. "Why, information, of course. What else would I pump you for, Jayde?" he said, trying his best to sound innocent.

He was having too much fun at her expense. She decided to get back at him. "Oh, I dunno," she shot back. "You could use your imagination."

He whispered into her ear, "I assure you, my imagination is quite . . . expansive."

"That remains to be seen."

Jayde could feel her cheeks grow hot. She didn't doubt they were flaming red by now. This little game between them had gone way too far. What was she thinking, flirting with him? Clearing her throat, she stalled for time, which was something she desperately needed to gather her wits about her. When had she lost control of the conversation? Heck, did she ever have control of it?

They both stood there, transfixed; neither had the strength or the good sense to turn away. A kiss was inevitable. Slowly, their heads moved toward each other, but before their lips connected, a partygoer poked her head around a lavender bush.

When she spotted the couple, a fiendish smile crossed her face. "Ah, here you two are."

Devon reacted first. "Yes, sorry to disappear like that. I was helping Jayde go over the speech she's giving at our next event," he explained, stepping back slightly but keeping his hand at her waist.

The woman observed the still-silent Jayde for confirmation.

Devon gave Jayde a nudge.

"Good one," Jayde said, nodding vigorously. "Um, the speech, that is."

"That's great," the woman said and smiled. "Actually, Jayde, I think it's high time you had your speech . . . edited. Don't let me interrupt. I just came to tell you I think everyone's calling it a night. People are heading for the Saran Wrap. Mr. Mitchell, you don't mind if we take a few doggie bags?"

"Not at all, please help yourselves," replied Devon.

"Thanks. If you two will excuse me, I'm off to fix a plate." The woman winked, then retreated.

"I've got to speak with her before she leaves," Jayde whispered.

Devon arched an eyebrow. "Why? You practically talked her ear off a minute ago."

"This isn't funny," she chided. "She thinks we . . . that we . . ."

"What?"

"Don't give me the big eyes and the innocent 'what.' You know what. We were about to kiss."

Turning, Devon headed out of the alcove, pulling her with him. "Easy, Jayde. Don't get all wigged out on me."

Yanking her hand away, she dug in her feet. "What's that supposed to mean? I'm not . . . wigged out. I just can't believe I was stupid enough to play cat and mouse with you at a company function. Now everyone thinks we've got something going on."

"All I wanna know is which one of us is the cat?"

"Devon," Jayde practically hissed, "this isn't funny. She thinks we were fooling around in the rosebushes. The gallery historian thinking we're having a fling is the last thing we need. Oh, I can't believe this. She's like the town crier!"

He simply couldn't resist the fire in her eyes, which appeared every time he baited her. Just seeing the expressions play across her face was worth the risk of a third-degree burn. Without cracking a smile, he replied, "They are lavender."

"You're impossible," she said, with annoyance, before sidestepping him and heading back to the party.

Stroking Boomer's head, Jayde laid her head back against the couch. She contemplated the evening. The party had been a success, no doubt about that. The dilemma was how to handle being drawn to a man she disliked with a passion that rivaled her attraction.

Picking up the cordless phone with her free hand, Jayde hit the second speed-dial number.

"What's up?"

"Hey, Chris. It's me."

"Girl, I do have caller ID, you know. How was the party?"

"It went a little *too* well. That's why I'm calling," Jayde said, frowning into the receiver.

"Uh-oh, hang on. I've gotta get comfortable."

After Christy settled in, Jayde gave her the rundown of the evening's events.

"So what you're saying is you think director man's got it going on."

"I don't know what I'm saying," replied Jayde. "I'm confused about it all. Every time he kisses me—"

"What! Wait a minute! He's kissed you more than once, and you're just now telling me about it?"

"I thought I told you about it."

"Uh, no, you didn't. I'm so mad at you, but never mind. What was it like?"

Jayde was thoughtful. She ran a hand over her lips. "So good, I almost forgot my name."

Christy let out a whistle. "That's definitely worth pursuing, Tree."

"I don't deny there's something there. The question is whether I should pursue it. We didn't exactly start out on the best of terms. Even now the truce is a bit shaky. How do I know it'll last?"

"If I recall, the last time we had this conversation, you had the hots for Marcus Moore. You liked him so much, you drank yourself silly and threw up all over the floor at his feet."

"I can't believe you're bringing that up now. I was nineteen when that happened," Jayde groaned.

"Come to think of it, he helped you into bed and put a trash can by the side of it. He was such a gentleman."

"No, he just wanted to appear to care so I'd sleep with him," Jayde replied.

Christy snickered. "True. Hey, remember the other guy? Steve, I think it was—"

"As much as I enjoy the reminder of my momentary lapses in good judgment," Jayde interrupted, "can we get back to the present, please?"

A long silence ensued. When no response came forth, Jayde looked at the phone. "Christy?"

"Jayde, you've always had the same problem. You think things to death. You always have to know what comes next."

"So, what's wrong with that? There's no crime in being cautious."

"No, cautious is what everyone else is. You're flat-out paranoid. You want to know the end of the story before you've written the beginning. There's never a guarantee things will work out or that you won't get hurt."

"I know that."

Christy let out an exasperated sound. "Then act like it. Give the man a chance, and if it works out—great. If it doesn't, chalk it up to experience and move on."

"I don't know if I could be that cavalier with my heart again," Jayde confessed.

"Girl, I suggest you blow the dust off the thing and find out. That is, before life passes your tall butt by."

Despite feeling apprehensive, Jayde couldn't help but laugh. "Battle Cat, you'd better be right."

"When have I ever been wrong? At least when it comes to you?"

Adamant about clearing up the last remnants of the party himself, Devon had sent Jayde home. At least that was the excuse he'd given her. Every inch of him had wanted her to stay longer, but he knew that course of action wouldn't be wise.

Placing the dishes in the dishwasher, Devon closed the door and set the timer before turning out the lights in the kitchen. He was walking into the family room when the telephone rang. As he reached for the phone, Devon wondered if it was Jayde.

"Mitchell."

"Start talking."

"Dad?"

"Of course, it's me," Sterling snapped. "What I want to know is why my son is at our house in Washington, D.C., and not in Illinois, where he belongs."

This wasn't a conversation Devon wanted to have right now. Sighing, he sat down on the couch. "I had to come here. There was a problem at the gallery that demanded my attention."

"Devon, you have a whole company that runs that gallery. Why can't they handle it? What was so important that you had to lie to your parents?"

"I didn't lie. I just didn't volunteer any information."

"Devon, I'm not amused. You know full well what I'm getting at. You led us to believe you were at Henry's farm. I called that no good brother of mine, looking for you, and do you know he didn't once mention you'd left?"

"I know, Dad. I asked him not to. I wanted to tell you myself."

"Well, when were you planning to get around to it? I had to find out from your mother that you decided not to come home and that you are in D.C. Since when am I the last person to hear about what you're doing? Have you forgotten we have a company to run and that you are second in command at that company? Are you purposely trying to cause me to have a heart attack?"

"No, sir."

"Then I suggest you start talking, because so far you aren't making a bit of sense—"

"I've got trouble, Dad."

Instantly, Sterling stopped his ranting. "What kind of trouble?"

After filling his father in on the mishaps at the gallery, Devon was surprised that he felt considerably better. He hated keeping things from his father, but he wasn't sure how his father would react to the news that he wasn't coming back to the Mitchell Group any time soon. Surprisingly, his father was more understanding than he'd anticipated.

"Son, it disturbs me that you felt you couldn't be straight with me about this whole thing."

"I apologize, Dad. I know you want me back at Mitchell, but I couldn't get back to work with things unsolved here. I just can't let anything happen to this place. I can't."

"I know, Dev. So, what have you come up with so far?"

"I have a detective investigating the previous director, Paolo Gambrini. He's moved to Italy. So far he's the only lead I have."

"There are a few friends of mine that could help you out. Two of them are on the police force. I could make a few calls and—"

"I'll keep that in mind. I'm sorry I didn't tell you about this sooner. I just . . . I wasn't ready to pick up where I left off. Everything has changed."

"I can't say that I completely understand, son, but it's your decision. We really miss you here, and I'm not just talking about work. Your family misses you."

Devon closed his eyes. He could hear the disappointment in his father's voice. It tore at him. "I miss you all, too. I really do."

When he spoke, his father's voice was gruff. "Call if you need anything—and even if you don't."

"Yes, sir. I promise."

By the time Devon hung up the phone, he was exhausted. When the phone rang minutes later, he wondered what his father could've possibly forgotten to mention.

"Did you forget something?"

"Mr. Mitchell?"

Hearing his detective's voice, Devon sat back down. "Sorry about that. What do you have?"

Sometime later, Devon was still in the family room, processing the information he'd received. Phone records indicated that Paolo had telephoned the gallery regularly over the past few weeks, confirming his suspicions of an accomplice. The problem was that all calls to the gallery had come in over trunk lines before being routed to the employee's individual extension.

There was no way of knowing whom Paolo was calling, but Devon's gut told him something was there, right under his nose. Excluding the storage-room incident, Devon found it odd that nothing unusual had happened since he'd assumed command at the gallery.

The timing was too much of a coincidence. Obviously, the saboteur was waiting for something, but what? His detective would continue shadowing Paolo. Something would turn up soon. He could feel it.

Of their own accord, his thoughts returned to Jayde. There was the possibility that she was involved, but his gut told him that she wasn't an accomplice. There were no facts to prove that yet, but he was certain he wasn't going to find out that she was embroiled in the mishaps. Her being embroiled in his psyche was another matter altogether. Jayde was deeply rooted in his thoughts, and he couldn't get her out of them. Her presence at his house for most of the day had been soothing. They'd joked and engaged in witty banter while she'd prepared the food for the party.

He'd seized every opportunity he could to be near her or touch her. His intuition had told him that she was just as affected as he was by their close proximity. The longer he was around her, the more his body ached to possess her. He wanted Jayde with a singleness of mind that he couldn't begin to explain. The question was, what was he going to do about it?

CHAPTER 14

Devon heard the sound of tires screeching and smelled the acrid scent of smoke. Ignoring the pain, he staggered around to Candace's door. He jerked on the handle, attempting to free her from the mangled wreckage. "Candace," he shouted. "No." His anguished cry was harsh against the eerie calm of night. Suddenly he felt a warm hand on his shoulder. Turning, he saw Jayde standing behind him. She was dressed in all white. Her hair flowed around her shoulders. Her smiling face held acceptance and understanding.

"Devon," Jayde said softly, "it's all right. You've done all you can."

"I didn't," he cried out. "I have to get her out. I've got to help her."

With Herculean strength, Devon wrenched the door open. The sounds made by the crumpled metal and shattered glass were sickening.

Crouching in front of her still form, Devon gently shook Candace. "Please, you've got to wake up. I'm sorry, so sorry, I let this happen."

"It's not your fault," Jayde said above him. "It was an accident, Devon. You tried to help her. It was her time."

"Time?" he said angrily. *"What about our baby? Was it the baby's time, too? He never had a chance. I took it from him."*

Slipping her hand in his, Jayde guided him away from the mutilated car. Stopping next to a nearby rock, she sat him down. "You have to forgive yourself. You can't move past this moment until you do. Your soul won't rest until you make peace with her death."

Devon shook his head. "I don't think I can do that."

Jayde raised her hand to stroke his cheek. When she stood, her hand fell to her side. "When you're ready to try, I'll be there."

"Wait," he called out as she walked away. *"Jayde, don't leave me. I need you. Jayde!"*

Devon bolted upright, Jayde's name still ringing in his ears. His breathing was unsteady; his body soaked from perspiration. Seeing Jayde in his dream rattled him. It was the first time his subconscious had placed someone else at the scene of the accident. Quickly, he recounted the dream before it faded. Jayde was trying to bring him peace, to make him realize he wasn't to blame. If only that were true, he thought. His gaze traveled from the clock to the telephone. He wanted to call her, but it was two o'clock in the morning. There was no way he'd disturb her at this hour. Besides, what would he say to her? "Oh, by the way, I had a dream about my dead girlfriend, and you were in it?"

Devon headed downstairs. One thing he knew for certain: sleep wasn't coming back to him that night—in any form.

A few hours later Devon arrived at work. He unlocked the front door and immediately went to the alarm pad to deactivate the system. His hands were poised over the keypad to disarm it when he noticed that the system had already been turned off. Startled, Devon squinted. The lights in the main gallery were out, as were the lights in the hallway leading to other areas of the building. He sat his briefcase down and headed cautiously toward the stairwell door. Devon headed down the stairs. As he walked toward the storage rooms, a loud thump reverberated off the walls in the darkened hallway. The hair on his neck rose. Something was wrong.

With heightened senses, he crept stealthily toward the noise. Upon entering one of the low-lit storage rooms, he looked around for something to use as a weapon. He found a crowbar next to an opened crate and picked it up. Another thump, followed by a whispered expletive farther into the space, made Devon tighten his grip on the crowbar.

When he came upon the dark figure, he sighed in relief. Luck was on his side. The man had his back to him and wasn't aware he had company. Devon poked the crowbar in his back. His voice was a hushed, icy tone. "Just what the hell do you think you're doing?"

The man dropped the crate top he'd been holding and raised shaky hands in the air. "Don't shoot, man. I'm not armed. I work here. I'm just an employee. If you let me go, I'll make it worth your while."

"Wrong answer," Devon said, shoving the man forcibly against the opened crate.

The man crashed into the crate and slid down the side. Terrified, he held his hands over his face, not bothering to turn around. "Please," he yelled, "I'm begging you. Don't hurt me. I'll give you anything you want."

"What I want is information," Devon ground out. "What are you doing here? Who put you up to this?"

He yanked the man off the floor and none too gently ushered him to the door. He flipped the rest of the lights on, then pushed the man away from him to get a better look. A dark scowl deepened his features upon seeing the culprit.

It was one of their college interns. Devon looked down at the nervous young man with contempt.

"Mr. Mitchell," he said, with relief. "I didn't know it was you. This is all a big misunderstanding."

"Save it." Devon flipped his cell phone open. "I asked you a question. You've got twenty seconds to answer before I call the police and have you arrested for burglary."

"I wasn't doing anything wrong. I was just opening a shipment, and I—"

"Don't insult my intelligence. You're on someone's payroll—other than mine. Fifteen seconds left."

The young man stood, wiping the back of his pants. "I'm telling you the truth."

"Don't tell me," Devon said, dialing 911 on his phone. "Tell the police."

"Wait!"

Devon lowered the phone.

"Okay, okay. A man approached me."

"What man? What's his name?"

"I don't know his name."

Devon started dialing.

"I'm not lying! I swear to you, I don't know his name. He said he'd pay me five thousand dollars if I rigged a couple of accidents for him. He said it was nothing major, just a few botched deliveries and some near misses around the gallery. He promised me nobody was going to get hurt, said it was just some prank-type stuff between the two of you."

"Pranks. And you believed him?"

The young man shrugged. "Why not? He told me he was an old friend of yours and that the two of you take turns messing with each other and that it was his turn."

"How long has this been going on?"

"Just a few months, I swear to you."

"How did he contact you?"

"A lady caught up to me outside of the Metro. She said she'd noticed I worked at the gallery and asked me if I could help them out. Seemed harmless enough."

"Then you're an idiot," Devon snapped and dialed the police.

"What are you doing? You promised you wouldn't call the police."

"I never said that," Devon replied just before his fist connected with the young man's jaw.

Devon watched him hit the floor. "By the way, you're fired," he said above the cowering intern.

After the police arrived, Devon gave them his statement and the information that his ex-intern had volunteered. He also voiced his suspicions about the gallery mishaps and the possibility of another accomplice. Devon turned over all the information his detective had gathered on Gambrini to the Metropolitan Police Department. Later that day he filled Jayde in on the incident. She was devastated to learn the news of the intern's part in the sabotage.

"This doesn't make any sense. Why would a friend of yours hire someone to wreak havoc at the gallery? You just started here. What kind of friend would play such a sick joke?"

"It wasn't a friend of mine, Jayde. The man was obviously lying, and the intern was too stupid to realize he was being set up."

"I still don't understand why this all happened. Who would want to harm the gallery? We have been here forever and have never had any type of incident."

"Maybe someone has an ax to grind or a previous employee is holding a grudge," said Devon.

Jayde shook her head. "We've had the same employees here for years. The only recent changes are the addition of the interns and Paolo resigning."

When Devon remained quiet, Jayde glanced across the desk at him. His firm gaze locked with hers.

"You . . . My God, you think Paolo had something to do with this?"

"You said it yourself, Jayde. The only changes have been the addition of two people and Paolo leaving. It seems like fair speculation."

Jayde bolted out of her seat. "What? You're seriously trying to pin this on Paolo Gambrini?"

"I'm saying we should look at every possibility."

"You're crazy. Paolo is the most admirable man I know. Not to mention one of my dearest friends. There is no way he has anything to do with this, Devon. You have no proof to substantiate such a baseless accusation," she argued.

"Jayde, there's no way that nitwit I caught red-handed is the mastermind behind all this. He had help—smart help."

"I agree, but it wasn't Paolo."

"How can you be so sure?"

"Because I know him, Devon. He loved this place like it was his own. He and Mrs. Wells were the best of friends. He wouldn't betray her—or her gallery."

"I hope you're right, Jayde. But I would be remiss in

my duties as the director if I didn't at least consider the possibility."

"I didn't for one minute entertain the idea when I was acting director. So you're saying I was remiss in my responsibilities to the gallery?"

"I'm saying no such thing. I'm merely trying to keep this place open and thriving. To do that, I need to be sure we locate the person, or people, responsible for these ongoing problems and ensure they're stopped. If that means delving into Paolo's background to rule him out as a suspect, so be it."

"You'd be wasting your time."

"I hope you're right."

Jayde turned and left Devon's office.

Leaning back in his chair, Devon closed his eyes. He knew he'd just lost some footing with Jayde by accusing Paolo of possible wrongdoing, but the former director was his best lead. He'd personally interviewed every employee that worked at the gallery. Every one of them had expressed trepidation about the incidents and a deep admiration for Paolo Gambrini. Besides, he'd had investigations done on each of them. Nothing out of the ordinary had come to light.

"Am I grasping at straws?" he said aloud.

Just then the phone rang. Picking up the receiver, Devon leaned back in his chair. "Mitchell."

"How are things on the front lines?"

"Same as usual, Max," Devon replied. "Except I caught an intern sabotaging us this morning."

At Maxwell's loud exclamation, Devon filled his second in command in on the details. He also admitted that he'd told Jayde about his investigation of Paolo.

"Was that wise, Devon?"

"Probably not, but I wanted to clear the air between us. We've been making some headway lately."

"I'm sure you voicing your suspicions about Paolo set you back considerably," Maxwell noted.

"You could say that."

"I'm sorry, Devon, but I'm going to have to agree with Jayde on this one. Paolo wouldn't do anything to harm the gallery. It means as much to him as it does to me. We both called your grandmother our dearest friend. There isn't one thing either of us wouldn't have done for her."

"Then, by your reasoning, my investigation should turn up nothing, right?"

"That's right, Devon."

"Then you and Jayde should have nothing to worry about, Max."

Eventually everyone had to put the sordid incident aside. Last-minute details for the upcoming gala were monopolizing everyone's time. Everyone's except Devon's.

Thoughts of Jayde filled most of his waking hours. Ever since the dream he'd had the week before, she hadn't strayed far from his mind. That being said, the stubborn woman was throwing a monkey wrench into his program. She did her best to keep him at arm's length. When they weren't discussing gallery business, she was nowhere to be found. Devon wondered if her disappearing acts were to keep them from getting too personal or if she was still upset with him for admitting he was investigating Paolo.

It had taken a while, but Devon had finally admitted to himself that the reason she drove him to distraction was that he cared about her—deeply. Despite his reason for being there, he was glad he'd met her. His life had been too lonely for far too long. It was time to move the past to the back burner and concentrate on the future.

He still mourned Candace's death, but the nightmares haunted him less these days. While Jayde's presence in his life diminished the inner demons, time was running out. He had to return to Chicago and his life. Every time he spoke with his parents, his father would ask when he was returning. He couldn't hold off indefinitely. He also couldn't ignore the fact that the longer he was at the gallery, the more he wanted to make Jayde a permanent part of his life.

Fresh out of the shower, Jayde tied a robe snugly about her damp body. Looking at her crumpled bed, she decided five o'clock on a Friday morning was a perfect time to change the bed sheets. Besides, she couldn't sleep another minute. Her thoughts were tormenting her. Retrieving fresh linens from the closet, she stripped the bed. As a crisp sheet billowed out in front of her, Jayde's mind wandered. Soft jazz from her stereo filled the room.

Appealing thoughts of Devon came to mind. It was about as impossible to stop herself from thinking about him as it was trying to stop Boomer from chasing after the neighbor's cat. Suddenly, she gazed toward the door. Going over to turn the volume down on her stereo, Jayde tilted her head to the side, listening intently. *Nothing.* Twisting the volume dial back to its original setting, she returned to changing her sheets.

Devon Mitchell. Those two words were becoming synonymous with sweaty palms and an upset stomach. She'd done her best to avoid him for the last week. Despite being angry at him for accusing Paolo of wrongdoing, she was having a hard time not thinking about him. There wasn't a moment that went by when Jayde wasn't aware of his presence. It was like she'd developed a second sight where he was concerned. The awareness was so strong, she could predict his location and then divert her course so they wouldn't run into each other.

Smug looks from several coworkers weren't enough to dissuade her from her mission. She might be attracted to Devon, but she wouldn't pursue it. They were colleagues. Wanting him to make love to her so bad that her eyes crossed was irrelevant. Besides, if it didn't work out between them, there'd be the awkward moments and pitying looks from everyone at the gallery. She refused to put herself in that predicament, no matter how much she ached to get her teeth rattled.

With her task accomplished, Jayde sat at the foot of her bed, staring off into space. Pent-up desire had made her edgy. She closed her eyes. For the moment, she'd make good use of her imagination. She would create, in painstaking detail, all the things she'd love to do to and with Devon. At night, her dreams were so vivid, she had to wake up to keep from going insane. As if summoned to do so, her mind conjured him up in all his glory. Jayde drew an intake of breath at the realness of him—right in front of her—during the day no less. *Wow,* she thought, her skin growing sensitive. They weren't authentic, but images frolicked brazenly in her imagination. They were accurate enough to make her mouth water. She was on a roll.

Now she prayed her brain would be able to get the voice right. If she had a picture and sound, she'd die a happy woman. Concentrating, she put her creativity to good use. "Say something," she commanded aloud.

"You're beautiful," he replied, smiling.

The mind is a wondrous thing. A feline smile was plastered on her face. *So far so good.* "Say something else."

Dream Devon took a step forward. His gray eyes darkened, just like the real thing. "I want you."

Good answer. In her dream, she swayed slightly, and he reached out to steady her. In reality she laid back on her bed. This was *her* fantasy. She could do whatever she wanted.

"You don't know how long I've waited for this," he said, dipping his head to kiss the pulse at her neck. He was one step closer to claiming her lips. To eventually claiming her.

A loud, rapid pounding, combined with Boomer barking, caused Jayde to snap her eyes open. She almost rolled off the bed and onto the floor.

"What the . . . ?" Jayde said, disoriented. Standing on shaky legs, she walked awkwardly into the hallway and cautiously down the steps. Since the knocking was at her front door, Jayde figured it was one of her neighbors. *Don't they know what time it is?* Jayde wrenched the door open with more force than necessary. She gasped, seeing the object of her fantasy staring at her.

It was Devon, leaning against her doorjamb, and at five thirty in the morning. She stood there openmouthed, speechless, and as red as a ripe strawberry. Seconds passed. She was unable to form a coherent thought. The air drifting in from the hallway felt cool on her half-damp skin. As casually as she could, she drew the sash of her robe tighter.

"A little late for modesty, don't you think?" Devon inquired.

She stepped aside to let him enter. "Uh, what are you doing here?" she finally managed. "How'd you get in without buzzing me?"

"I did, several times. Your neighbor saw me frantically pushing your buzzer on his way out. He let me in."

"So much for security," she quipped.

He walked farther into the foyer, until Boomer stopped him. Extending his hand, he knelt, giving the canine time to sniff.

Eventually, the retriever determined that he was a friend, not a foe. No longer interested, Boomer trotted off to another part of the house.

Jayde shook her head. "My attack dog, Boomer." She motioned for Devon to go into the living room.

"I phoned you but didn't get an answer. It's pretty early, so I took a chance you'd be here."

"I was . . . just getting dressed."

His gaze roamed her entire body in a not-so-discreet way. His jaw clenched. "So I see."

They stood staring at each other until Devon remembered why he was there. "We've had a problem at the gallery."

His frank scrutiny was causing Jayde's heart to flutter. "Oh?" she said breathlessly.

"It appears someone relieved us of a few paintings featured in the gala on Friday."

That got her attention. Jayde's hand rose to her throat. "What? How is that possible? The intern's still in police custody, and though it's crazy, Paolo's under investigation, too, so we know it's not him."

"Yet here we are. How fast can you be ready?"

"Give me ten minutes."

CHAPTER 15

From the moment they stepped through the doors at the gallery, Jayde was a whirlwind of activity. After assessing the situation, she began giving orders to the disorganized staff mulling around.

"Okay, people, listen up. I know this isn't how we'd like to start our workday, but there's no help for it. Only four paintings are missing from our exhibit, so there's no need to postpone the gala event. We'll replace what's been stolen and change the theme to compensate. Devon's already spoken with the authorities, and a detective will be arriving shortly to interview everyone, so please make yourselves available."

Someone handed her a cup of tea. Taking a sip, she paused for a moment before turning to her assistant. She fired off a list of items. "I need the artist's phone number. Call our insurance company, and give them the police report number when you have it. Devon and I will look over our inventory and choose replacements. Call the printer and see if they can edit and reprint the programs and deliver them this evening, or no later than three o'clock tomorrow afternoon."

Jayde's assistant, who had been rapidly writing, stopped mid-sentence. "Trying to get a rush job reprint of the programs at this late date will cost a fortune."

"Tell the manager I asked him to work with us on this. We do enough business with him to put his kids through college. I'm sure he'll waive the rush fee if we ask him to," Jayde replied.

"What about the press? What happens if they get wind of the robbery?" one of her team members asked. "They'll be all over this like people driving by Krispy Kreme Doughnuts when the HOT sign comes on."

Jayde nodded. "If anyone calls from the press, route the call to me. If they stop by, inform them that they'll need an appointment with me and that that's not likely to happen until tomorrow evening." She turned to the receptionist. "Under no circumstances are they to get past your desk to interview anyone."

"Got it," the receptionist replied.

"Any questions?" Jayde asked the group.

Silence confirmed that everyone understood. "Good. The gala is in one week. We've got plenty of time to pull this off. Now let's get to work."

Heading to her office, she sat down at her desk. Taking a cleansing breath, she pinched the bridge of her nose.

"I'm in awe."

Jayde looked up and quirked an eyebrow. "You mean there's nothing the great Devon Mitchell would've done differently?"

"I'm sure there is, but it doesn't matter. You handled the situation admirably. I'm sure things won't turn out the way our thief intended."

"By thief, you mean Paolo, don't you?"

"Honestly? It doesn't seem likely. My man's been

tailing Paolo for some time. I just spoke to him, and both he and Paolo are in Italy. It couldn't be him."

"I told you he wasn't involved in this."

"Maybe not this time, but it's a week before a big show. A random robbery at this point is unlikely. That intern could barely get a crate open without help. There's a mastermind behind this, and I'm going to flush him out. It's possible Paolo had an accomplice."

"It's not him, Devon. You don't know the man. I do. He's dedicated his life to art. He loves what he does."

"You're right. I don't know him. Until I'm convinced otherwise, he's my primary suspect. Nobody messes with what's mine. If he's guilty, he'll answer to me."

"Why? What has he cost you? We have insurance. The artist will be compensated for his works if they're not recovered. The way you're acting, you'd think this was a personal attack against you. It's not like you own the place." Jayde laughed.

Devon cursed his slip of the tongue. He didn't want to make Jayde suspicious. Striding to her desk, he hauled her up against him.

"You're wrong, Miss Seaton. He's cost me plenty. For starters, a call from the D.C. police department that totally destroyed my morning calm, plus missing the opportunity to revel in my good fortune at finding you half naked—and wet. I won't mention that you blushed *before* you realized your robe was open." Devon raised a finger to his lips. "I wonder why? My instinct tells me you were thinking about me."

"That isn't instinct. That's male ego."

"Same thing. Are you telling me I'm wrong?"

"Please. You're so full of yourself."

"Won't say, huh? Okay. You leave me no choice but to

prove my theory." Without warning, he kissed her. He was pleased when she responded without protest.

After a few moments, Jayde ended the kiss by playfully shoving him away. "Enticing as it may be, I have to take a rain check on your seduction scene, Mr. Mitchell. We're at work, and you know my policy on office romances."

"Everyone here knows your policy on the subject," he said dryly. "Have dinner at my place tonight. It won't be a late evening, I promise."

"I don't think . . ."

Raising a finger to her lips, he silenced her. "Don't think, Jayde. Feel."

She didn't have time to go round for round with him. She guided Devon toward the door. "Fine, but on one condition."

"Name it."

"You go away. There's a ton of work to be done if we're going to cover our butts for this event."

Devon stopped in his tracks. His expression was unmistakably carnal. "Now, there's an entertaining idea." Devon left Jayde's office before she could retort.

While walking to his office, Devon was thoughtful. He was surprised that Jayde hadn't ribbed him for being able to handle the situation better than he could have. Without hesitation, she'd stepped in, taken charge, and gotten them back on track. Jayde knew her job. She was sure of herself and her abilities. He hadn't exaggerated when he'd told her he was impressed.

Aside from his personal feelings toward her, Devon now had proof that Jayde wasn't involved in the scheme to derail the gallery. The police had indicated that the woman that had approached the intern was a Caucasian woman in her late forties, with short blond hair. That ruled Jayde out.

Sitting at his desk, he leaned back and stared out the window. Now more than ever, Devon wanted to confess to Jayde why he was there. The only problem was how she'd react to the news. He couldn't risk that unknown right now. They had to get through the upcoming gala event, and he needed her in top form. He'd been to events like this before, but never in a working capacity. Before this, he'd been ignorant of how much was done behind the scenes to make one of these exhibits successful.

Now he knew, and it humbled him. He wanted the best for his legacy, and that appeared to be Jayde Seaton at the helm. When their big event was over, he would nail Gambrini's butt to the proverbial wall for jeopardizing the gallery, and then he'd tell Jayde the truth and make her director, like she deserved.

Hearing the bedroom door open, Avalon Mitchell lowered her book. Her husband walked in, looking like he'd gone through a root canal with no anesthetic.

"Rough day, dear?"

When he saw her, his demeanor softened. "That would be an understatement, darling." Placing a kiss on his wife's lips, Sterling sauntered to the wet bar in the sitting room to fix a drink. Then, lowering himself on the plush love seat across from her, he sipped the brandy while swishing the ice around in his glass.

"Do you really think it wise to drink so close to bedtime? You know how it makes you toss and turn."

Sterling pulled the knot at his neck. After loosening

his tie, he unbuttoned his shirt. "I'm sorry, dearest, but if I don't have this to help me unwind, I'll be pacing instead of tossing and turning."

"Heavens, lucky me."

He looked at her thoughtfully. Her sarcasm hadn't been missed. "Maybe I should sleep in one of the guest rooms tonight. Just because I'm out of sorts doesn't mean you should suffer, too."

"Don't be silly."

Sterling walked into the wardrobe room to change his clothes.

"The question is," she called after him, "why are you out of sorts?"

"I don't want to talk about it. It's water under the bridge."

"More like brandy under the bridge," she countered. "You'll feel better if you get it off your chest."

He peeked from around the corner. "Says who?"

"For starters, your doctor. He's always telling you that de-stressing is the key to longevity."

Sterling walked back into the bedroom, fastening the last button on his silk pajamas. "Ha," he barked loudly. "That man will say anything to keep me coming every two to three months." Throwing back the covers, Sterling eased into bed, then arranged the covers over most of his head. "I swear, he'll be the death of me."

Turning out the light, Avalon joined her husband. He'd already turned away from her. "Forget something?" Jabbing him gently in the side, she waited for him to kiss her good night.

"Sorry, darling." Turning over, Sterling gave his wife a sound kiss. "Good night."

For a few minutes, there was complete silence. Eventually, Sterling ended the stillness.

"There isn't anything I wouldn't do for my family, Ava."

"I know, sweetheart. We all do."

"I want us to be provided for well into the future. Everything I do is for the continued growth and financial stability of the Mitchells. I wish our son could see that."

Upon hearing their son mentioned, Avalon sat up on her elbow. "What does Devon have to do with this mood you're in? He's seven hundred miles away."

Sterling sat up and cut the light on. "I'm in the middle of a business deal, and I could use Devon's help on this one. I just wish he were here. Don't get me wrong. I understand his need to get away from this place for a while and the whole thing about the gallery, but I just can't understand why he feels he has to stay away. We're his family, Avalon. We should be helping him through the tough patch he's in. He just up and left and hasn't been back for months. That's not how I raised him to handle problems. You have to face them—head-on."

"He's doing just that. He has a problem at the gallery, and he's tackling it. He'll be back when it's cleared up. You have to have patience, dear."

"It's not just the gallery, Ava. The whole accident has him messed up, too."

Avalon sat up and faced her husband. "Sterling, Candace died in his car. He lost a child that night, too. Granted, they weren't on the best of terms, but that doesn't matter. She's dead, and nothing can change that. Darling, we haven't had to come face-to-face with someone dying like that. Our son has. Sure we can tell him we understand what he's going through, but truthfully, we'll never know that kind of pain unless we've been through it."

"I just want to help him. For him to know we're here for him and he doesn't need to shut us out."

Avalon placed a hand on Sterling's shoulder. "He does, sweetheart. I know he does. No matter how much we want him to come home, we can't put a time frame on his pain or dictate how he should deal with it. He has to heal on his own. Nobody can help him with that."

Sterling picked up her hand and pressed it to his lips. "You continue to amaze me, Ava. You always know what to say to make someone feel better. That's a wonderful gift you have."

"It comes very easily with the people closest to my heart," she replied, kissing him.

He hugged her to him. "I love you, Mrs. Mitchell."

She smiled at her husband. "And I love you, Mr. Mitchell."

CHAPTER 16

Jayde leaned back in her chair, heaved an enormous sigh, and rubbed her stomach.

"I stand corrected. That meal was a delight to the senses and, as Emeril Lagasse would say, bam," she said loudly, imitating the famous chef.

Devon's rich laugh boomed around the patio. Jayde felt his warmth reach out and caress her. His smile that followed made her tingle all over.

"I'm glad you enjoyed the dinner. It was truly my pleasure. I'd forgotten how much I enjoy cooking for someone other than myself." He was thoughtful. "It's been a long time."

There was a question forming on Jayde's lips, but she pushed it aside. If he'd wanted to elaborate, he would have. Jayde looked around, taking in her surroundings. The house was different from the last time she'd seen it. Of course, she'd been the hostess of an office party then. She'd barely had time to breathe, much less scrutinize every nook and cranny of his chateau on a hill.

Tonight the patio was perfect for a secluded, romantic evening. There was no doubt it was turning out to be just that. There were miniature white lights laced throughout the trees. Somehow Jayde had missed those the last time. Several tall candle stands held burning pillar candles. Closing her eyes, Jayde listened to the sensual song flowing from Devon's outdoor sound system. The soulful melody swept her along. She couldn't resist its pull. Her head and upper body moved languidly in time to the music.

"That's entrancing. I've never heard it before. Who is it?" she said.

"Robin Berry. She's a harpist."

Jayde closed her eyes again. "She's amazing. What's the name of this?"

"The song is called 'Night Sky.' It's one of my favorites. Every time I see her, I beg her to play it for me."

"You know her?" Jayde said incredulously. "Wow! How did that come about?"

"I met Robin in Chicago a few years ago. She has a sister there that's a friend of the family."

Devon watched her for a few moments. Unable to resist the unspoken invitation, he got up. Walking around the small table, he smiled, then drew her smoothly up against him. "It would be my pleasure, Miss Seaton."

"What would? I don't remember asking anything."

"You asked me to dance, and I accept," he said, steering her away from the table to give them more room.

"Wait a minute. I didn't ask you to dance."

"Well, your body did."

There was no arguing with logic like that. Jayde didn't bother trying. Giving in, she swayed around with him in time to the music. Jayde inhaled and immediately recognized the masculine scent of Devon's cologne. Issey Miyake was driving her insane. Was he reading her mind? Next to the Paco Rabanne from the storage-room fiasco, it was her second favorite scent.

Devon rubbed his hand methodically against her back. Jayde leaned closer. The meal, the music, the mood lighting, the cologne, and the man had all conspired against her defenses. She was slipping fast. If she didn't stop soon, she'd be lost.

Sensing a quiet victory, Devon didn't hesitate to claim his reward. Lowering his head, he captured her mouth for a slow, deliberate kiss. Jayde's body responded like it had been starved of a precious nutrient. She molded herself against him. Her arms encircled his neck. Relenting to the magic transpiring between them, neither one of them had the strength or ability to end their embrace.

Devon literally swept Jayde off her feet. She sighed against his lips and tightened her hold. In what seemed like seconds, Devon maneuvered them back inside the house and to the family room. He released her and set her in front of him. He traced a finger over her mouth.

"You don't know how often those lips have driven me to distraction since the storage room," he whispered.

"Couldn't be as often as I've imagined it," Jayde confessed.

Her admission made him grin. Devon claimed her mouth again in a heart-stopping kiss. Time slowed as they gave themselves up to the current of passion dragging them under.

"I can't think straight when I'm around you anymore." Devon buried his face in her neck while his hands roamed her body.

"Me either."

"I'm serious. Since the moment we kissed, you've tormented my dreams, and frankly, I didn't think there was any more room."

"Why?"

"Long story. I'll tell you later. Jayde, I really think I'm losing my mind. That's how much I want you."

"I want you, too. I can't deny it—or you—anymore."

Before he could respond, the doorbell chimed loudly. Devon stifled a curse. "I won't answer it."

Jayde ran her hands along his back as the doorbell rang a second time. "You think they'll just go away?"

Devon buried his head in her hair. "I can't imagine who it is in the first place. Don't move," he commanded, walking around her. "We haven't finished . . . conversing."

"Perhaps I should go."

Loud knocking replaced the ringing of the doorbell. "Whoever it is, I'll get rid of them. Don't even think about leaving." Devon strode to the front door and wrenched it open.

A woman barreled into the foyer like a steam engine. A man followed, wearing a mischievous grin.

"Lucinda, Xavier, what in the world—"

"Surprise, darling," Lucinda said, throwing herself in Devon's arms. "I hope you don't mind us dropping in unannounced like this, but Xavier said you'd probably be climbing the walls with boredom by now."

"What are you two doing here? How did you find me? What didn't you just call?" Devon asked.

"Don't be mad, darling," Lucinda replied. "Your mother mentioned she'd spoken to you. She was just so elated, it slipped out when I was on the phone with her last week. I promised her I wouldn't tell anybody."

Devon looked at Xavier pointedly.

"Well, I had to tell, X. We're your best friends, Dev,

and we've missed you terribly." Lucinda wrapped her arms around his neck and kissed him.

"We have missed you, buddy," Xavier chimed in. "Work isn't the same without you. Your father is driving everyone crazy. If you don't come back to Mitchell soon, we're all going to demand a mental health day."

"Guys, don't get me wrong. I am glad to see you both. I've missed you, too," said Devon.

"Really? Is that why you look like we've just interrupted the last play in the Super Bowl?" Xavier replied.

"Trust me, I'm thrilled to see you both, but now isn't the best time for a reunion. Why don't the two of you come back tomorrow?" Devon said, ushering them out the way they'd come.

"Nonsense, darling," Lucinda purred, planting her feet. "X and I aren't going anywhere. Not after coming all the way from Chicago to see you. It's been three months, Dev, with no communication whatsoever. It seems like ages since we've seen you. Now that we've found you, horses can't drag us away."

Devon nodded. "Luce, I'm elated you've come all the way here to see me. How about you and Xavier get settled in your hotel, and I'll drop by tomorrow, and I'll fill you both in on what's been going on, and we'll do breakfast?"

"The Ritz Carlton was booked, and you know that's my favorite hotel, so you're stuck with us," Lucinda explained. She leaned up and planted a firm kiss on Devon's lips while wrapping her arms around his neck again. "I'm just happy you're back in the land of the living."

Devon extricated himself from her embrace as Jayde walked into the foyer. Xavier saw her first and cleared his throat to get Devon's attention. Devon turned, registering Jayde's hesitation. He knew that look. His overbearing friends and their untimely entrance would take some explaining.

Jayde watched Lucinda peruse her with slow deliberation. Jayde stiffened under the direct scrutiny. Devon's friend looked like a runway model from head to toe. She was dressed to the nines, and saying she was gorgeous would be an understatement.

"Shame on you," Lucinda said, pouting. "You didn't tell us you had company, darling. Who's this? Your secretary?"

"No," Devon said in a warning tone. "She's not."

"Well, don't be rude. Introduce us to your . . . friend here," Lucinda ordered.

"Lucinda Davenport, Xavier Taggert, this is Jayde Seaton. Jayde, this is Lucinda and Xavier, friends of mine from Chicago, who would appear to be here for a visit."

Xavier quickly moved to Jayde's side. He raised her hand to his mouth and kissed it. "Hello, Miss. Seaton. It's wonderful to meet you, but I can tell by Devon's scowl, we interrupted something . . . important," he said, grinning.

"No, you didn't," said Jayde.

Devon looked at Jayde, but he was talking to his friends. "Yes, you did."

"Dev, you're being quite testy over nothing," Lucinda chimed in. "I'm sure Miss Seaton doesn't mind our being here. Now, why don't you help Xavier bring in our bags while we ladies get acquainted?"

Devon glanced at Jayde. The muscle in his jaw ticked

rhythmically. "I'll be right back." Opening the front door, he nudged Xavier out into the night.

Lucinda eyed Jayde briefly before walking into the family room. "I always thought this house was charming but way too small. Then again, I don't think Devon plans on being here long, so I guess it's adequate. So tell me, dear, how long have you known Dev?"

One of Jayde's pet peeves was a woman her age calling her "dear." Her mental bourgeois meter rocketed off the scale. "A few months." She smiled sweetly. "How long have you known each other?"

"Devon and I grew up together. We didn't meet Xavier until college. Where did you and Dev meet?"

"Dev," she said, mimicking Lucinda's pronunciation, "and I work together at an art gallery downtown."

"He works in a what?" Lucinda snorted. Her mascaraed eyes widened. "You can't be serious. Why would a man of Devon's means be working in an art gallery?"

Lucinda's question gave Jayde pause. She'd had enough of the prima donna in the five-inch heels. It was time to exit. *Like right now.* "I suppose you'll have to ask Devon. Now, if you'll excuse me, it's late, and I'd better be going."

"Well, I hope you aren't rushing off on our account, Miss, uh . . ."

For a dime, Jayde would've loved taking all her frustration out on Miss High and Mighty in front of her. "It's Seaton, and no, I'm not." She smiled, making sure to show all her teeth. "It's been a pleasure meeting you, Miss, uh . . ."

Lucinda's eyes narrowed. "Davenport, of the Boston Davenports. I suppose you haven't heard of them. Somehow I doubt you travel in the same circles as we do."

"Thank God for that," Jayde quipped under her

breath. Grabbing her purse from the coffee table, she glided past Lucinda. At the front door, she almost collided with Devon and Xavier.

"Where are you going?" Devon demanded.

"Home. It's late, and I've got to be up early." Jayde stepped around them. "It was nice meeting you, Mr. Taggert."

"Please, call me Xavier, or X will do."

Jayde's not-so-subtle running away irritated Devon. "Did you enjoy dinner?" he said bitingly.

"Yes, thank you, I did," Jayde told him.

Xavier's eyebrows rose a few inches at the exchange. "I think I'll go see what Lucinda's up to," he said quickly.

Devon turned to Jayde. "Wait. I'll walk you to your car."

"That isn't necessary. You should see to your guests. Good night." Jayde left, closing the door firmly behind her. She felt stupid. How could a man have friends like the catty Lucinda and still be someone to whom she wanted to get close? It defied reason.

The comment the horrible woman had made about Devon and his means had stuck in Jayde's head. What was that all about? Once again, Jayde had too many questions, not enough answers. Walking slowly to her car, she second-guessed herself. It was clear there were hurdles that would have to be overcome to be in a relationship with him. Were there too many?

There's only one solution, she concluded. Their fledgling romance, which hadn't really started, would have to end. "Makes sense to me," Jayde said out loud, with false conviction. "Devon and I are over."

Suddenly, her disorderly emotions overwhelmed her. Unlocking her car door, she slid into her seat. *Car door shut? Check. Seat belt secure? Check. Keys in the ignition?*

Check. Now it's safe, her inner voice soothed. Jayde leaned her head against the steering wheel and let the tears of doubt slide down her cheeks of their own volition.

   Parting the curtain, Devon looked at the car still parked at the curb. He could see Jayde slumped over the steering wheel, her shoulders shaking rhythmically. He ground his teeth in frustration. What went wrong? He couldn't figure out Jayde's abrupt mood change. Granted his friends dropping in and Lucinda's over-the-top behavior had dampened their evening, but he hadn't misread the signals. Jayde wanted him as much as he wanted her. They'd both been willing to let things proceed naturally between them. If they hadn't been interrupted, he'd be deep inside her, consumed by erotic bliss, consummating their not-so-business-like relationship. With a frustrated sigh, he let the curtain fall back into place.

CHAPTER 17

Jayde reached back until her hand encountered the box of Kleenex. Grabbing the last tissue, she quickly brought it to her nose. The blow was deafening.

Startled, Boomer stared at her.

"You're an idiot, Ralph de Bricassart. How could you let Meggie marry a creep like Luke O'Neill when you love her?" Jayde asked the television screen for the third time in two hours.

After leaving Devon's house, Jayde had driven straight home, taken a shower, and put on her most comfortable lie-around-the-house pajamas. Her mood had practically mandated watching one of her favorite miniseries, *The Thorn Birds*.

She dropped the tablespoon into the container on her lap. She heard the dull thud of the utensil hitting the container's bottom. She looked down in dismay at the empty pint of Chocolate Peanut Butter Häagen-Dazs ice cream. When had she eaten the whole thing?

The intercom buzzer stunned Jayde. She lowered the TV volume and dragged herself off the couch. Scuffling to the wall, she pressed TALK on her intercom pad. "Who is it?" she asked in a voice laden with tears.

"It's me, Jayde. Open up." There was a three-second delay before he spoke again. "Are you crying?"

Devon. She groaned inwardly before slumping against the wall. She stole a glance in the nearest mirror. What she saw made her cringe. Her appearance was a science experiment gone wrong. The curls on the back of her head were smashed from rubbing against the couch cushions. Her bloodshot eyes, complete with bags under them, and her ripe-tomato nose were the finishing touches. She tried running a hand through her hair and drying her tears on her pajama top, but it was useless. She was a big wreck.

She pressed TALK on her intercom again. "Now's not a good time."

"Jayde, it's easier to curse me out in person than on an intercom, so may I come in?"

Shrugging over her disheveled appearance, Jayde pressed the enter button. She opened the door and waited. "I wasn't cursing you out," she clarified when he walked up. "What are you doing here?"

"Why do you sound surprised? You knew I'd come." Once inside he looked around.

"I did? Well, I guess I should've let myself know, because I didn't have a clue."

Silence permeated the room. Jayde remained still, staring at him. Finally, he voiced the question that had plagued him during his drive over.

"Jayde, why did you leave?" He held up his hand before she replied. "And don't try that nonsense about having to get to work early. We both know it was an excuse."

She glanced past him, wondering how she could lie

her way out of this. "It was a long, emotion-packed day, Devon. I'm wiped out."

He snorted. "That isn't the reason, either."

Jayde shrugged. "I felt it would be better if I left."

His expression blazed skeptically. "Better or easier? Was it Xavier and Lucinda who caused you to leave?" He caressed the hair out of her face. "Or what was about to transpire between us?"

Jayde backed away. "I-it wasn't anything like that. Shouldn't you be home, entertaining your friends?"

"My friends are entertaining themselves quite nicely at the Marriott downtown. Luce will never forgive them for not having a suite available at the Ritz or the Four Seasons, but who cares?"

"Oh," Jayde murmured, eyeing her socks.

He tilted her face up to meet his eyes. "Sweetheart, talk to me. It's obvious you're upset about them barging in, and rightly so. I just didn't expect you to leave— at least until morning."

Jayde gasped, jumping as if she'd been burned. Though she hadn't, her face was red enough to simulate a first-degree burn. The distance she put between them was immediate and obvious. "Upset? I'm not upset. Why would you think that?"

"Well, I'm no expert," Devon said, following her, "but with the women in my family, I've seen enough chick flicks to know you've been sitting here in your pity pajamas, eating ice cream and crying your eyes out." He glanced at the television. Devon did a double take. "The *Thorn Birds?*" he said incredulously. "Okay, now I know you're insane. That movie is over twenty years old. I think my mother has it on videotape."

Protectively, Jayde marched over to the remote and pointed it at her television. Ralph and Meggie faded into the darkness. Before she could protest his assessment of the situation, Devon pointed to the tissue box and the empty ice cream container littering her couch. He grinned knowingly.

Jayde wished she didn't have on her Mickey Mouse pajamas and white sweat socks. Defiance flashed in her eyes. "For your information, I always cry when I watch *The Thorn Birds*."

Devon visibly shivered. "I'd cry, too, if I watched a movie that old."

Leaning over a chair, Jayde picked up a pillow, intent on whacking him with it. Catching her hands in his, Devon flung the pillow away, then kissed her knuckles. "I'm sorry Xavier and Lucinda interrupted us. X is cool, but Luce can be a bit much to handle if you're not used to her."

"She acted as if you and she—"

He silenced her with a well-placed finger on her lips. "The only thing that's ever been between Luce and me is air, and lots of it. She and I have been friends since childhood—platonic friends. If she gave you any indication otherwise, she was just being—"

"Bitchy and possessive?" Jayde interrupted.

Laughing, he drew her into his arms. Jayde relaxed against him, inhaling his scent. Devon lowered his head and kissed her.

There was such passion behind the exchange, Jayde's knees almost buckled. She wasn't prepared for the tension growing in the pit of her stomach. It was unnerving.

Feeling her respond with a want that matched his own humbled Devon. Taking her hand, he guided them both to the couch. When she was seated, he spoke. "I watched you leave tonight. When I realized you were crying, it tore at me." He traced a path along her palm. "I didn't know what I'd done to bring you to tears."

"It's the uncertainty of it all, Devon. Being around Lucinda tonight brought that point flying home."

"Baby, I already told you nothing's going on between us. We're just really old friends."

"I know that now, but that doesn't allay the doubts I have about me . . . you . . . us."

"About our attraction to each other?"

Jayde nodded. "Among other things. Your friend wondered why a man of your means would be working in a gallery. Why would she say that?"

Devon took her hands in his. "Jayde, I told you I held an executive position in Chicago. What can I say? It was lucrative. I can't look into the future, at least not too far into it, but I do know that the here and now is my priority. My life for the last year has been hectic, stressful and, quite frankly, without joy. Then, quick as spilled coffee, my life was turned upside down. I met you, and it's been fireworks every since."

"Fireworks?" Jayde said disbelievingly.

"Absolutely. Of course, some of those have been pointed at me and not the sky."

They shared a mutual laugh.

"Has it been that bad?" asked Jayde.

"Hell, yes." Devon chuckled. "I never expected to find a woman I was interested in exploring a relationship with and choking at the same time."

Jayde snorted. "You haven't been a walk in the park, either, you know. There've been more puzzle pieces trying to figure you out than I've ever dealt with before." She grew somber. "It scares me sometimes, Devon."

"I know." He rubbed her shoulder. "Yet, here we are."

She took a shuddering breath. "Here we are."

Devon leaned back on the couch and ran a hand across his eyes. Jayde remained silent. Finally, Devon opened his eyes and focused on Jayde's face. "I realize I haven't been forthcoming in a lot of ways. I've kept my own counsel for quite some time now, but I assure you, I will tell you everything. Soon."

"Why can't you just tell me everything now? Are you worried my feelings might change?" A thought passed through Jayde's mind, causing her to bolt off the couch. "You aren't married, are you?"

Devon looked indignant. "Would we be here if I were?"

She stared at him incredulously. "You're kidding, right?"

"No, Jayde," Devon said, standing. "I'm not married. There are no kids in my life, except my niece and nephew."

"You have siblings?"

"Sibling. I have a twin sister, Melanie."

"You see? That's what I'm talking about. I don't know anything about you, and I—"

Devon silenced her with a kiss. He probed and explored her mouth until, on a languorous sigh, her lips parted.

Ultimately, a heavy, tense quiet drifted around them. Devon ran his finger along her jaw. "Jayde, you and I can't keep running circles around each other. There's a strong connection between us. If you don't feel it, tell me now, and I will walk out that door and won't bother you again."

Just hearing him say he'd leave caused her body to protest. Her breath caught in her throat. "I do feel it, Devon, and it scares the hell out of me," she said haltingly.

"I want you, Jayde. It's that plain and that simple. My

desire for you has never wavered, and honestly, I don't have the energy to deny my feelings anymore."

Jayde bit her lower lip. "I don't, either."

"Music to my ears." Picking her up, Devon enveloped her in his strong embrace. Her legs dangled over his arms. She kissed him with a heat she couldn't conceal. While he climbed the stairs, Jayde babbled from pent-up desire and nervousness.

"I can't remember if my room is clean," she told him.

"I'm not making love to your room."

"What about, um . . . birth control? I don't . . . I mean it's been awhile, and I . . ."

"I came prepared," Devon confessed. "You weren't getting away from me twice in one night."

Thank goodness, she thought. It was too late to play coy. Jayde almost laughed aloud as Christy's words rang in her head. She wanted to get her teeth rattled, and she wanted Devon to do it!

She closed her eyes tight. "I can't believe this is happening."

"Why?"

"Well, for one, I wanted to be wearing sexy lingerie, not Walt Disney pajamas."

"What's the other reason?"

"We work together."

"I'd say it's time to get over that one. Where's your bedroom?"

She pointed her foot straighter than a pointer's tail. Devon walked toward the door farthest from them. Once inside he set her down. Running his hands up and down her arms in a calming gesture, he whispered, "Sweetheart, the themed pj's don't matter to me. In a few seconds, they'll be the same place the sexy lingerie would have been—on the floor."

She couldn't help but laugh. After a few seconds, Devon joined in. After the mirth subsided, they walked hand in hand to the bed. Jayde sighed in relief. *At least the bed's made.*

Devon looked her over from head to toe. A slow smile traveled up to his eyes. They were as bright as polished silver. "You're so damn beautiful. You're a tall, deliciously sexy, smart, and amazingly talented woman, Jayde Seaton. I just wanted you to know that."

Jayde beamed like the village idiot at his compliment. It warmed her heart with a heat that was steadily traveling south. *Devon Mitchell.* Still a name she'd never forget.

Slowly, Jayde eased back onto her mattress. After kicking off his shoes, Devon joined her. His gaze traveled from her eyes to Mickey Mouse's ears, and lower still. After his blatant appraisal of her body, he stared at her face. His expression smoldered with increasing heat. "You're incredible. All of you."

A nervous giggle escaped her lips. "Aren't you supposed to save that observation for afterward?"

Devon ran his hand down her side. On the way back up, he stopped and slid his thumb over her left breast. He delighted in hearing her sharp intake of breath and watching her pupils dilate. "No."

"Do me a favor," Jayde said softly.

"Anything."

"Tell me you want me."

His smile was lascivious. "I'd rather show you."

"Please. I need you to say it."

"I want you, Jayde."

Closing her eyes, she reveled in the fact that the real Devon was as painstakingly thorough at melting her insides as the dream Devon. "You don't know how much I've longed to hear that."

"A fantasy of yours, huh?"

She didn't bother denying it. "Uh-huh."

Returning his hand to her breast, Devon drew circles around it, concentrating on the sensitive areas that made her squirm. "So, what else have you fantasized about?"

Jayde's breathing turned shallow. Her insides clenched, and her body tingled. "Now that you're here in the flesh, I'm too embarrassed to say."

There was no way Devon was letting her off the hook. He moved closer and whispered into her ear, "Then show me."

His words had the opposite effect on Jayde. Instead of feeling discomfited by his challenge, she felt emboldened. Heady with desire, Jayde allowed her hands to roam over his chest and sides. Her lips sought out his neck. Placing kisses everywhere, her tongue snaked out to tickle his ear.

Devon's hand tightened on her rear end. "That's going to get you in trouble."

"I certainly hope so."

Before Jayde could blink, Devon had turned her over and had her under him. He pressed his middle firmly against hers, leaving no doubt about the extent of his arousal. She drew him closer. Slipping his leg between hers, Devon inflicted a friction so intense, they both moaned aloud. Before Jayde could recover, Devon sat up.

"Where are you going?" she asked.

"Time to unwrap the canvas and look at my masterpiece."

With slow deliberation, Devon eased her pajama top over her head. The satin and lace bra he discovered was a definite contrast to the theatrical sleepwear. When he moved to her pajama bottoms, she raised her hips off the bed to help out. Devon ceremoniously lobbed both garments across the room.

"Told you that's where they were headed," he replied to her questioning glance.

Taking a moment, Devon allowed his gaze to travel over her body.

Slightly self-conscious, Jayde asked nervously, "Is the picture worth a thousand words?"

Thoughtful, Devon ran his hand down her bent leg. "Not yet."

In seconds, he removed her bra and panties. They, too, went sailing through the air. He looked at her solemnly before shaking his head in awe. "I don't think a thousand words could describe what I'm feeling at the moment." His voice shook. "Jayde, you truly are a work of art."

Raising herself off the bed, Jayde kneeled in front of him. "No man has ever told me that before," she admitted while helping him out of his shirt.

"That's their lack of foresight. Not every man can see what's right in front of him. At the moment, your raw beauty is the least of my problems."

She sought out his belt buckle with her fingers. Sliding the belt out of the loops, Jayde made quick work of unbuttoning his pants and unzipping them. "Care to elaborate?"

Before she could finish the job, Devon edged off the bed. Gravity took care of the rest. His pants dropped to the floor, exposing black boxer briefs. The dark fabric was a stark contrast to his skin.

When she joined him to stand at the foot of the bed, she stared. Her eyes drank in his rock-hard, well-defined body. "The sight of you leaves me breathless."

Hearing her words, Devon closed his eyes, and he took a deep breath. His jaw flexed rhythmically.

"You look like you're going into battle," she noted.

Devon splayed his fingers over her abdomen before traveling lower. "It's been a while, sweetheart. I don't want this over before it begins."

His fingers began to work their magic on Jayde's hypersensitive skin. She swayed slightly before she reached out and locked on to his muscular shoulders. His fingers increased their sensuous torture of her body.

Jayde sucked in her breath. "Devon?"

"Relax, baby. I'm right here."

Devon continued the onslaught of her body with one hand, while he supported her with the other. His face was a mask of concentration. The goal was to bring Jayde to pleasure, and he wasn't about to let her down.

Jayde's teeth clamped on her lower lip. She squeezed her eyes tightly shut. Her body was overwhelmed by Devon's ministrations. Soon, very soon, she'd shatter before him like ice dropped on a frozen pond.

"Devon," she repeated.

Leaning her back against his arm, Devon lowered his head and rained kisses over her chest and the sensitive area on her neck. It was Jayde's undoing. Her body shuddered in ecstasy as waves of undiluted pleasure crashed over her.

Suddenly, her body slowed, and she slumped against him. Effortlessly, he picked her up and carried her back to the bed. He wiped her hair away from her glistening face.

The smile Jayde wore was radiant. Her hand caressed his face. "Now I'm at a loss for words."

"Jayde Seaton at a loss for words? Wow, I must be fantastic."

"Shut up," she said, shoving him slightly before a yawn escaped her lips.

"Uh-uh, I'm not done with you yet," he promised. "Not even close."

"I certainly hope not." She stretched languidly. "I think I'm getting my second wind."

Rolling over, Devon pinned her to the bed. "That's good to know, because you're going to need it."

CHAPTER 18

After a few minutes of exploration, both of them became impatient for more. After donning protection, Devon concentrated on the task at hand. When they finally came together, the first moments of awkwardness dissipated, and their syncopated rhythm left them both speechless. Jayde lost herself in the unhurried intensity of their lovemaking as indescribable pleasure pummeled her.

When Devon's body spoke, hers answered. When his body demanded, she gave. Even with her eyes closed, she could see their desire as if it were tangible. The energy they generated took on a form all its own. Hues of color twirled in intricate patterns across her mind's eye. Each time their bodies connected, the colors intensified. When their movements ceased, Jayde eagerly anticipated their return.

Melding in perfect harmony, they explored each other with fearless abandon. Jayde's hands repeatedly roamed over Devon's sweat-slicked body. When her fingers connected with the dampened curls on his head, her hand sought to keep him close. Shortening the distance between them sent tingles catapulting through Jayde's body.

The sensations caused her to expel a startled gasp.

Devon immediately stopped. "Jayde, are you okay?"

Nodding vigorously, Jayde pulled him closer. "If you stop—I'll kill you." Too worked up to remain passive, Jayde gave as good as she got. She pushed at his shoulders until he got the hint and flipped them both over. "My turn," she said eagerly.

Her legs settled on either side of his hips. Now in the driver's seat, Jayde grinned.

Content to let her set the pace for a while, Devon gave himself over to her delicious ministrations. "Whatever my lady wants," he replied.

Time had no meaning for her. It could've stopped, for all she cared. The only thing that mattered was the two of them and the pleasure they were giving each other. When the yearning overwhelmed her, Jayde found it hard to catch her breath. Tears pooled in her eyes as she struggled to stay adrift amid the bittersweet tidal waves.

Devon rubbed her cheek, his voice considerably gentle when he asked, "Hey, what's wrong?"

"It's too much," she said, sobbing. "I can't . . . Please end this."

Turning Jayde over, Devon whispered into her ear, "Hold on to me." With quick, forceful strokes, it wasn't long before he coaxed Jayde's body into a pleasure-filled abyss.

Hearing the tenderness in Devon's voice, urging her to let go, was her undoing. Hearing Jayde call his name like a litany was his.

It took some time, but eventually, they mastered again the art of breathing and lucid speech.

Tracing circles on her arm, he smiled wickedly. "So, was that better than Häagen-Dazs?"

Opening her eyes, she scrunched her nose at him. "If I had the energy right now, I'd hit you."

"If I had the energy right now, you'd be too busy to hit me."

Settling into a peaceful state, Jayde started drifting off to sleep.

Devon broke the silence. "Jayde?"

"Hmm?"

"Are you okay?"

"I am a little sore," Jayde admitted, yawning, "but that's to be expected. I mean, it has been a while and—"

"For me as well, but that wasn't what I meant. I was wondering if you're worried about this . . . about us? Because after what we just shared, there's definitely an us, Jayde."

Opening her eyes, Jayde raised herself slightly off the pillows. The sheet wrapped around her slid precariously low. Devon's eyes glimmered like liquid silver at the view. The renewed heat sparking between them caused her mouth to go dry. Covering herself, she concentrated on his question.

"A little," she admitted. "This has the ability to become . . . so complicated. We work together. There's still so much about each other we don't know—"

Devon put a finger up to her lips. "I know I want to make love to you every time I see you. I have since you flounced out of my office in all your glory."

"Which time?"

"Every time."

"Devon." She poked him. "Be serious."

"When aren't I?" He chuckled, then grew somber. "I meant what I said earlier. There are things I want to tell you. I should have before we ended up here. In retrospect, I probably did things ass backward. For that I apologize. I guess I let my need for you cloud my judgment."

Giving him a pure feminine smile, Jayde cuddled closer. "Me too." Wrapping one leg around his middle, she took pleasure in hearing his sharp breath.

"You'd better stop," he warned, "before you end up at a very unusual angle."

"I'm not scared of you," she taunted, moving her leg lower.

In an instant, he had her securely under him. Jayde shrieked at the sudden action.

"You should be," Devon countered, then made good on his claim.

Sunlight streamed into Jayde's bedroom through the pleated shades. Blinking several times, Devon opened his eyes. It took a few tries, but eventually they focused. The first thing that came into view was Jayde's dog, Boomer. His head was resting on Devon's elbow, his big brown eyes surveying him with interest.

Smiling at the retriever, he returned the canine's stare. "What? Is this your side?"

Boomer thumped his tail on the carpeted floor. Devon reached out and rubbed the dog's head with his free hand.

Great would describe how he felt. It was the deep down, soul-cleansing great that had been missing in his life for some time. He looked at the woman sleeping next to him. It put an immediate smile on his face. Jayde was the difference. This time when he'd been awakened in the middle of the night, it was because of Jayde's pleasurable kisses, and not a violent nightmare. The knock-down, drag-out fights they had; the times he wanted her so much, it consumed him; her sharp, witty intellect and caring heart—all of it made a difference to him. To his life. He'd been given a second chance at happiness. It humbled him.

With a languid stretch, Jayde opened her eyes and rolled over. She'd caught the tail end of the exchange between her dog and her man. It had made her smile. *Did I just call him my man? Yeah, I guess I did,* she told herself. She was amazed that the thought didn't make her want to bolt out of her bed and run screaming into the hallway. Yes. There had been definite progress between them. They'd come a long way from the mocha chiller and the ruined suit.

"Morning," Jayde said shyly.

Leaning over without lifting his hand from the dog's head, he kissed her. "Good morning yourself. How'd you sleep?"

She snorted loudly. "What sleep? You kept me up most of the night."

Devon placed his arm under Jayde's shoulders and hauled her up against him. "I kept *you* up? If memory serves, it was the other way around."

"Nope. I remember it clearly. It was you and—"

"My what?" he countered. "Snoring?"

"Hmm. I heard you make a lot of noises last night. Early this morning, too, yet I don't recall a snore being on the list. Groans, moans, sighs, a few grunts, but no snoring," she teased. Jayde yawned loudly. "I don't know how we're going to get through the day."

His face almost split from happiness. "Who cares? It

was worth every sleepless, heated, erotic, sweaty, earth-shattering minute."

Blushing, Jayde looked at the clock. She was determined to relish every minute before they had to get up. "That was quite a list, Mr. Mitchell."

His gray eyes darkened. "It was quite a night, Miss Seaton."

"We're supposed to be at work in an hour."

"Not today we're not. Besides, I've got to go home to get showered and changed." He kissed the tip of her nose. "Come with me?"

Jayde sat up, hoisting the bedcover up her body. "Devon, how is us coming in together going to look?"

"Like I gave you a ride, because we were at your house, making love all night long?"

"Good-bye, Mr. Mitchell. Go home and get changed. I'm going to hop in the shower and get ready for work."

She scooted off the bed, taking the bedcover with her. It trailed in her wake as she hobbled into the bathroom.

Her modesty made Devon chuckle. "Want company?"

"If I say yes, we'll never get to work," she called out.

Jayde screeched when two arms snaked around her waist.

Devon made quite a show of lobbing the bedcover into the bedroom. He pulled Jayde firmly against his front. His need to pick up where they'd left off was more than evident. Dipping his head, he kissed the pulse on her neck. "That's the whole idea."

CHAPTER 19

Devon decided to tell Jayde the truth before the gala. So far he'd done a spectacular job of staying away from the media, but there would be too many reporters present for one of them not to recognize him or to mention his past or ask where he'd been for the last several months. To think otherwise would be naive. He couldn't allow her to get blindsided. An early-morning phone conversation with his sister, Melanie, helped him realize the dangers of going into the evening unprepared. He cursed his stupidity for not coming to the conclusion on his own.

He had to admit, making love to Jayde the last five nights in a row had addled his brain, but he didn't mention the matter to his sister. During their talk, Devon brought her up to speed on what was going on at the gallery and told her that his involvement with Jayde was turning serious.

After ending the call, Devon phoned Jayde to ask her to dinner at Papa Razzi in Georgetown. He suggested they go to his house afterward. That would afford them the privacy he needed to confess everything. True to form, Jayde refused. Since consummating their relationship, they'd been inseparable both at work and at home. However, almost like clockwork, Jayde had been trying to put barriers back up, in fear of how the gallery staff might view their recent attachment. Devon had to contain his mirth at her suggestion that they take things slow.

"Maybe we're moving too fast, Devon. We've been with each other around the clock since—"

"We slept together?"

"Yeah. I don't want to give anyone the impression—"

"That we're sleeping together?"

After a moment of silence, Jayde started laughing. Even she couldn't deny the ridiculousness of her argument. "Fine. Give me an hour."

He laughed at the resignation in her voice. He hoped that meant she'd given up trying to hide behind office protocol. "I'll see you soon, sweetheart."

Once he hung up, he started pacing the floor. Now that he'd decided to tell her, he wanted to get it done. Part of him dreaded the outcome. Would she understand why he'd come there incognito? Would she trust that their coming together was by chance? That it was just mutual attraction? Or would she think it was part of a bigger plan?

The more he mulled the questions over in his head, the more it made him nervous. He prayed Jayde wouldn't judge him before he had a chance to explain. There was too much at stake for this evening to turn out badly. Her opinion of him mattered more than he'd ever envisioned.

Despite their rocky start, he was drawn to Jayde in a foreign way. Since they'd slept together, he simply couldn't get enough of her. How she felt from the inside, as well as out, drove him to distraction. How passionate and giving she was of her body and mind enthralled him, but it wasn't just the sexual aspect of their relationship that thrilled him. Though she got on his nerves, drove him crazy, and made him want to throttle her, there was nothing he'd rather do than spend time with her, getting to know every nuance that was the foundation of who she was.

What made her laugh and cry? Besides him stealing her job. What did she do when she was nervous or scared? Besides hyperventilating and yelling at him. How did her family interact? What were her dreams for the future? With each passing day, Devon desperately wanted to know more about her, because he'd finally admitted the truth to himself: he'd fallen in love with Jayde Seaton—broom and all.

When dinner was over, Devon drove them to his place. The moment they made it through the garage and into the house, Jayde threw herself into his arms. Without hesitation, he enveloped her within his embrace. Finding the nearest wall, he reached down and picked her up. His hands rested on her rear end. She wrapped her legs around his waist, and he leaned against the wall.

"What about those reservations you had about our relationship?" Devon asked between kisses.

Jayde ran her fingers through his hair. "Lost them on the ride over."

"I just can't seem to get you close enough." Moving to the couch, Devon sat, with Jayde straddling his hips. She took advantage of the position to start unbuttoning his shirt. Nipping his neck, she moved down his chest, kissing everywhere she could reach. Sliding his shirt open wider, she marveled at the chiseled muscles of his stomach.

"I want you, Devon."

"I want you, too, Jayde. So bad that all I can think of is burying myself inside you."

"I know. I don't know how we lasted through dinner."

Devon began easing her skirt up her thighs, but then he stopped. Suddenly his subconscious reminded him why she was really there. Leaning back, he expelled a harsh breath. It took a moment for the lust-driven haze to dissipate. With slow, painful movements, Devon slid Jayde off his lap. His body protested, but he ignored the need pulsating through his veins and his lower extremities. "Sweetheart, I'm sorry. I . . . We can't do this." He smoothed her skirt down her thighs.

"You're worried how this may look at work, aren't you? I know I was the one who said no mixing business with pleasure, but—"

"The hell with that," he said roughly. "I don't care what people think about our relationship. That's not why I stopped, Jayde. We need to talk. Actually, I need to talk, and you need to listen. We don't have much time. I want you prepared."

Confusion crossed her face. "Prepared? For what?"

"There's a slim chance some additional things about me might surface tomorrow. I want you to know the facts."

Devon noted her uneasy expression, and he hadn't even started the conversation. Turning sideways on the couch, she took a deep breath. "Okay, I'm ready."

No, you're not. With a deep breath, Devon plunged in. "At the gala tomorrow, there's bound to be a lot of media."

"I know," she replied, with a laugh. "That's what we wanted."

"It's possible someone there could recognize my name."

"Oh. Look, if you're concerned that questions may come up about the gallery to which you don't know the answer, just give me a sign. I'll jump in and answer them. No problem."

He shook his head. "No, that's not what I meant. It's time—past time—I told you the truth about why I'm really here."

Jayde frowned. "The truth?"

Devon braced himself. "Jayde, the truth is . . . it's mine."

"I don't understand. What's yours?"

"The gallery. I own it. It was bequeathed to me by my maternal grandmother."

"Wait. Cecilia Grayson Wells is—"

"My grandmother," he finished.

"You own it? As in 'Look, Ma. I've got a butt-load of money' own it?"

"Jayde—"

She jumped off the couch. "Answer me."

He stood. His expression was grim. "Yes, as in I have money."

"How much?" she said hoarsely.

"It isn't relevant."

"The hell it isn't." She stalked around the room. "Don't hold back now, Devon. You're telling me the truth. You might as well tell me all of it."

"I'm trying."

"You aren't trying fast enough," she cried. "Just how far down does the rabbit hole go?"

With a pained expression, Devon put his hands in his pocket. "I'm vice president of the Mitchell Group, based out of Chicago. We specialize in finance, technical and business consulting. It's a family-owned business. Always has been."

She staggered backward; a trembling hand went to her chest. "Why are you here?"

"It appeared someone was sabotaging my gallery. I figured the best way to find the culprit was to hire myself as the director."

Tears dotted her blouse. Angrily, she wiped at them, but more trickled down her face. "I don't understand. How could you have been here this long without someone figuring out who you really are?"

"I stayed away from anyone in town that might recognize me. Only a few of the older employees actually remember me. I asked them not to say anything. Everyone else here had never met me. As you know, Wells Inc. owns the gallery. I never involved myself until recently in the day-to-day operations of the gallery. That made it relatively easy to be here incognito."

She shook her head in disbelief. "You upset my life, took my job, and lied to me just so you could save your precious money?"

"Jayde, there's more to it than that. I wanted to protect my grandmother's legacy. There isn't anything I wouldn't do to ensure the gallery continues to thrive, to grow in the community."

"And make a profit."

Devon bristled. "That's not fair."

"Fair? You have the gall to tell me what's fair?" She crossed the room in seconds, her face inches from his. "You turned my world upside down, Devon Mitchell—in more ways than one. Now I find out you were lying the whole time."

"Not the whole time. At least not about everything," he said meaningfully.

She recoiled. "Spare me. Like I could trust your feelings were genuine, or your motives pure."

Devon's eyes turned glacial. "Motives? What the hell does that mean?"

"Tell me, was I part of the plan? To gain my cooperation, you thought it imperative to sleep with me?"

His temper flared in earnest. "Of course not."

"Ha!"

Devon grasped her by the shoulders. "I care about you, Jayde. My involvement with you wasn't an act. My feelings for you are real, not contrived."

"You lied to me. *To me,*" she accused. "After everything we've been through, how can I ever be sure I wasn't just some fringe benefit? Just someone to do while you were wasting time at your dead grandma's gallery?"

He shook her. "Stop being pigheaded, and calm down. There's more to this story. I need you rational enough to hear it."

"Rational?" she scoffed, wrenching her shoulders free. "The only rational thought I have right now is how much I'd like to stuff your head into a bowling-ball bag. Better yet, tie you down, naked, to a fire-ant hill." Jayde swiped her purse off the glass table. She ran to the front door.

Devon was there before she opened the door. He pressed a hand against it. "Where are you going?"

"Away from you."

"If that's what you want to do, then let me take you home."

"No. I can manage on my own. I'll walk down to Sixteenth Street and catch a cab."

"No, you won't. If you want to go home, I'll take you."

"I'm not going anywhere with you!"

Devon sighed. "I know you're upset, but don't leave. Not like this. I'm begging you, Jayde. Hear me out."

"No," she cried. "I don't want to hear anything else you've got to say. How could you?" She struck his chest with her fists. "You shattered my world, Devon Mitchell. You invaded my heart, my body. I trusted you, and you betrayed me."

His clenched his jaw with each hit, but he didn't stop her.

Finally spent, Jayde pulled away. Her chest heaved with exertion. She stared at him. Her hands throbbed, and her eyes burned from too many tears. A cold, desolate feeling engulfed her. Her throat was raw and dry from ranting.

Devon was at a loss for words. Jayde was plain lost.

Then he felt it, the moment she erected a wall between them. It was almost an audible noise echoing through the room, announcing her heart was now off-limits. Untouchable. Forever. His heart caved in on itself.

"I'm leaving," she whispered hoarsely into the deafening silence.

"Jayde . . ." He stopped abruptly. Defeat shone in his eyes. Finally, Devon cleared his throat before speaking. "I'll call a cab for you. It will take only a few minutes to get here."

She remained in her spot.

Grabbing the cordless phone off the table, Devon called information and asked for a local cab company. When the line connected, he gave the dispatcher his address, then Jayde's, and asked him to hurry. He hung up and placed the phone on the nearby table before leaning against the couch.

He could tell by Jayde's body language that further

conversation between them would be futile. Painful minutes ticked by. When a horn finally sounded outside, Devon was almost relieved. Jayde was opening the door when he reached out to push it shut.

She refused to look at him. "Let me go."

He closed his eyes momentarily, shaking his head. "I can't, Jayde. Leave this house if you must, but I can't let you go." His voice faltered. "Don't ask me to."

Jayde remained silent.

Lowering his hand, Devon opened the front door and stepped aside.

She left without saying good-bye. This time, she didn't make it to the car before losing her composure. Crying uncontrollably, she climbed into the cab. *Damn him.* She'd been right all along. Devon the Destroyer had cut her swiftly—and it wasn't painless.

The water gave her solace. It was that simple. She leaned over the metal railing to peer into the murky depths of the Potomac River. The waterfront was quiet, a stark contrast to the deafening beat of her heart. *Why? Why aren't things ever simple?* Her relationship with Devon had been fraught with emotion and turmoil from day one. *He owns the gallery.* Jayde could barely think it, much less say it aloud.

After the cab had dropped her off, Jayde had gone inside long enough to grab her dog and his leash before heading back outside. She'd lost track of how long she'd walked along the water's edge before stopping to gaze at the water. "How big a fool can I be?" she cried into the night. "I mean, really, I ask you, how long before I stop getting emotionally involved with men that use my heart as a doormat?"

"I'd say that would depend on you."

Startled, Jayde whipped her head to the left. She flinched when a pain shot through her neck. "What?"

"I said that would depend on you," the man replied.

"I know what you said. I'm wondering why you answered."

"You asked me a question. I answered it," he said matter-of-factly.

Jayde rubbed her sore neck. "I'm sorry. I was talking to myself. I didn't really expect to get an answer."

Drawing his worn coat closer, the stranger shrugged. "Just because you didn't expect an answer doesn't mean it's not valid."

Jayde moved a little to the right. She chided herself for even talking to someone she didn't know on the street at night when no other people were around. "Who are you? The waterfront psychologist?"

The old man chuckled. "Hardly. Just a man with some time on his hands and a good ear."

"Thanks, but I don't need your ear right now, so if you'll excuse me, I'd like to be alone."

"Your dog's sitting there. I'd say that means you're not alone."

"You know what I mean," Jayde snapped.

"Your prerogative," he replied before walking off. The stranger got a few feet away before adding, "Don't forget, you have the kind of love life you choose."

Jayde let out a very unladylike snort. "You think I choose to have men lie to me, or that I chose to have my ex-boyfriend cheat on me under the guise of needing his space?" she called after him, not caring who overheard.

"Yeah, I do."

"That's insane. I'm not a masochist. I want a normal,

trusting relationship, just like every other woman on the planet."

"Well, I guess I'll let you get to it, then." Without another word, the old man went on his way, strolling nonchalantly down the walkway like he didn't have a care.

Jayde threw imaginary daggers at his retreating form. "Kind of love life I choose. Yeah, right!" she yelled after him. "Shows how much you know. I am so over Devon Mitchell. He means nothing to me anymore. You hear that, Mr. Coat Guy?" She swept her hand through the air. "Nothing. He's just a careless memory gone in the blink of an eye."

Jayde strode angrily back to her condo, Boomer easily keeping up with her fervent pace. With every stride, the heels of her shoes tapped her frustrations out on the concrete sidewalk.

CHAPTER 20

Swirling the teaspoon around in her novelty mug, Jayde glanced at the clock on her desk—again. Devon was always in by eight o'clock. In moments he'd be standing in her doorway, wanting to talk about what happened. Jayde didn't know if she was ready to face him after the fiasco of the previous night.

She rocked back and forth in her chair. The gentle swaying motion was comforting. It allowed her to focus on the bombshell that had been dropped on her. Devon Mitchell owned the gallery. It was strange enough to think it, much less say it aloud. She mentally recited her list of grievances about him, while her heart defended him.

He'd derailed her chances at becoming director. He'd made love to her. He'd lied to her and the entire staff since day one. He'd brought her body indescribable pleasure. He had more money than a small European country. He'd got past her defenses, causing her to feel again, to believe in someone again. He had a stuck-up friend whom she wanted to punch. It was all more drama than she could've imagined—or could bear.

Worst of all, heaven help her, Jayde still liked him. *Don't lie,* her mind scolded. *You love him.* "Nothing good can come of it," she whispered. "Not now."

As usual, her heart didn't agree. It ached to recapture the moments before he'd made that blasted confession. Outside she could hear the early morning downtown traffic. She tried to focus on the horn honks and tire screeches. With her soul in such turmoil, the chaos outside was soothing.

"Jayde?"

Yes? her heart answered. Wow. It was amazing how real his voice sounded, its rich timbre easing the upheaval inside her despite having caused it.

"Are you going to open your eyes?"

She shook her head. "Why bother?" she said aloud. "The real world is outside, with problems and confusion, things I'd rather not deal with right now."

"Well, you're going to have to, because one of those problems is standing two feet in front of you."

That sounded too close for comfort. Probably because he was too close. Reluctantly, Jayde opened her eyes. What she saw confirmed it. She endured another embarrassing moment, one that claimed the title of Worst Nightmare Imaginable. Devon was standing in front of her desk, looking at her like she was a mental patient. *More like daymare,* her inner voice replied.

"Do you talk to yourself often?"

She bristled at his tone. "Don't you dare tease me. You've lost the right to tease me."

"I'm sorry. You looked so troubled."

"Gee, I wonder why. Could it be from the bombshell you dropped last night? Which, by the way, was one hundred times worse than introducing me to your snotty friend, the uppity little . . ."

He arched a brow before she could get out a well-chosen expletive.

"Besides," she continued, "she's so thin, she looks like she'd kill someone for a sandwich. Honestly, I got hungry just looking at her."

Devon looked at her skeptically. "I doubt the reason you didn't answer any of my calls last night, or the bereft look on your face just now, has anything to do with Lucinda."

"It could be," she said haughtily.

"It doesn't."

"It was a long day yesterday." She scrutinized him. "An even longer night."

"For me as well."

Angrily, she leaned forward. "Here's a news flash for you, Mr. Mitchell. This isn't about you. It's because of you."

"I realize that."

"Good. Then do me a favor. Stop acting like the victim. I'm the one who got my world turned upside down."

"My world's been turned upside down for the past year. Trust me, you're getting off light."

She threw up her hands. "What does that mean? Do you expect me to be able to follow you? I only came on board this party boat last night. Remember?"

He took a few steps forward. "I've apologized for that. I would've finished telling you everything, but you didn't look like you could handle it."

"Can you blame me?"

He strode around her desk to sit on the edge of it. She backed her chair up in the opposite direction.

"Jayde, we've got to clear the air between us. We can't leave things like this."

"Like what? Fouled up beyond all recognition? Surprise, Devon—it's too late. This isn't something you can explain away in the course of an hour." Tears slid down her cheeks. "It's too late, anyway. I don't know if I can ever trust what you'd be telling me is the truth."

"What you mean is you believe my making love to you was part of my plan."

She nodded.

"Jayde, I care about you. All of you. Your contributions to the gallery aren't why you are special to me."

Her complexion turned mottled. "Don't you dare say you care about me," she choked out. "You haven't earned the right to say those words to me."

He let out an exasperated sigh. "Woman, why would I lie?"

"You mean more than you have already?"

"Touché. Look, Jayde, all I'm asking is that you listen to what I have to say before the reporters arrive."

"Why? What difference does it make if they're here or not?" She put her hand up. "You know what? Never mind. I know all I need to. When you first got here, I knew something was fishy. Deep down I had nagging suspicions, but I ignored them. I knew things weren't all they seemed. I let myself get sidetracked from trying to find out the truth, and I just accepted your presence without further opposition." When she thought of the closeness they'd shared, her heart ached. "That was my fault, and it's cost me." Bracing herself, she got up to sidle past him. "Besides, it's irrelevant now. As my employer, your past doesn't concern me."

Devon's outstretched arm delayed her departure. "You don't mean that."

Her laugh was hollow. "Think I don't? It was a mistake trying to make this personal. I've been saying that from day one." She blinked back tears. "I just didn't think my words would come back to haunt me so soon."

Closing the distance between them, he tilted her face to meet his. "Jayde, don't do this. Don't erect the wall again. Not now, not after how good things have been between us."

Angrily, she removed his hand from her cheek. "I don't have to, Devon. You did it for me."

He watched her storm away. His stomach tightened. Instinctively, he knew the worst was yet to come.

"Remind me again why we have to go to this shindig."

Lucinda pursed her lips, smiling into the mirror. "Because Devon's our best friend, and he needs our support."

Xavier rolled his eyes while readjusting his tie. "He's not having major surgery, Luce. He's holding a party at his gallery."

"This is the first time we've seen Devon in a formal setting since . . ." Noting Xavier's grieved expression, Lucinda stopped.

"Go ahead. Say it. Since Candace's funeral."

She stared at his reflection in the mirror. "Does he know?"

Xavier shrugged. "Know what?"

Lucinda whirled around. "That you're still in love with Candace?"

He forced a laugh. "Past tense, Luce. I was in love with her, and then she died. End of story."

"I think you should tell him everything."

"Why? What good does dredging up the past do?"

"It can heal the future. My therapist Tina says—"

Xavier clasped his hands. "Dear Lord, please spare me Lucinda's regurgitation of her last therapy session."

"Fine. Forget I said anything, but it's true. There are latent issues between the two of you. Trust me, X, if you don't resolve them, eventually they'll come to the surface."

"Amen. Thank you, Dr. Davenport." He smiled, pulling her up from her chair, then pushing her toward the door. "Now, if you're done with the psychoanalyzing, we've got to go."

Since Lucinda was in front of him, she missed seeing his playful smile turn into a dark scowl.

"Is he coming?"

The sigh that followed could've blown out a candle. "You're killing me. For the last time, yes, he'll be here. It's his freaking gallery. Of course, he'll be here," Jayde snapped, trying in vain to suppress her anger.

"Put a cap on it, girl. When you're pissed, that little vein in the middle of your forehead sticks out. That's not sexy."

"Does not."

"You want a mirror?"

"Hi, ladies," the gallery receptionist said, prying himself between the two friends. "So, who are we waiting for?"

"Nobody," said Jayde.

"Devon," Christy whispered.

"Got it," the receptionist said.

Jayde raised a brow at him suspiciously. "Got what?"

"Oh, nothing. Only the perfect thing to wear to the next soiree. Let me just say, it's exquisite. I got it from

one of those cute shops in Georgetown. Girl, it fits me
like a second skin."

"Everything fits you like a second skin." Christy
giggled.

"Don't hate," he warned, leaving them to mingle.

"He's here," Jayde said emotionlessly.

"He is?" Christy scanned the room excitedly. "Where?"

"Ten o'clock. Why are you excited?"

Christy did the mental calculations, turning her gaze
accordingly. What she saw standing there made her
gasp. "Oooh. I'm not ready. That's him?"

Jayde followed her stare. "Yep. In all his glory."

"He is glorious, tall, and so handsome, he makes me
wanna get a massage. Gray eyes to boot? Mercy." Christy
glanced at him again, then at Jayde. "He's the guy that
rattled your teeth?"

"Christy," Jayde hissed.

"Blew the dust off your—"

Jayde pinched her friend's arm.

"Okay," Christy said, laughing. "All jokes aside. Tree,
you're in a mess."

"No." Jayde spoke with slow deliberation. "I'm not.
There's nothing between us." Her lip quivered. "Not anymore."

"Correction. I'd say there're twenty people between
you, and since he's headed this way, the number's getting smaller. Now it's more like fifteen . . . ten . . . four."

Jayde turned just in time to see Devon heading
straight toward them. She heard Christy's not-so-quiet
laugh. She elbowed her friend. "This isn't funny."

Christy took a sip of her drink. "Yeah, it is. Three . . .
two . . . one."

"Good evening, ladies."

Only Christy responded. "So far it is."

When Jayde didn't make the introductions, Devon extended his hand. "Hi, I'm Devon Mitchell."

Christy clasped his hand. "I'm Christy Denton. Jayde's best friend."

"Oh?" Devon flashed her a smile. "Welcome. It's a pleasure meeting you, Christy." Devon blinked at the still-silent Jayde.

Jayde's skin glowed in a silver sequined gown. The high neck called to him. His fingers itched to run over the front of her bodice. The low back made him want to kiss the expanse of her flawless skin. Her strappy silver sandals made her loom over every woman there. Not that they could eclipse her if they tried. Jayde simply took his breath away with such a force, he never wanted it back.

Just visualizing their intimate encounters made Devon's body constrict painfully with need. Even when Jayde glared, like she was doing at the moment, and looked ready to kill him, he wanted her. He could tell her hostility was barely in check, and yet all he could think of was burying himself deep inside her. *Get a grip, man*, his inner voice cautioned. He balled his fists at his sides to reduce the urge to touch her.

Unable to help himself, he lowered his voice. "We need to talk."

Jayde looked past him. "I'm sure if you thought about it all night, there'd still be nothing you could say that I'd want to hear."

"Stop being stubborn. Meet me in your office in five minutes," said Devon. "There's someone here I need to speak with first, but I won't be late."

Jayde pondered his request.

Her deliberation made his jaw clench. "Jayde?"

It was more a warning than a question.

"Fine," Jayde whispered loudly. "Five minutes—not a minute longer."

"Fair enough." Backing away, he turned his attention to her best friend. "It was nice meeting you, Christy. I'm sure we'll meet again soon."

"One can only hope." Christy beamed. Her smile stayed fixed until Devon left. The moment he was out of view, she turned toward her friend. "Girl, you've lost your mind."

Jayde arched a waxed eyebrow. "Excuse me?"

"You heard me. Your ever-loving mind. I may have gotten a C in college chemistry, but I know enough to see it's there between you and Mr. Mitchell."

"What is?"

"Jayde, focus. Chemistry. Chemistry's there between you."

"Chris, please."

"Uh-uh. Don't 'Chris, please,' me. You two have angst written all over you. It's amazing watching you. It's like I set my TiVo for *The Young and the Restless*."

Jayde glared at her. "Stop making fun of me."

"Then stop sabotaging yourself. Good grief, Tree. Be happy for once. You deserve it."

"I was quite happy the last time."

"Sorry, dear, but two weeks in a relationship doesn't count. It's been years since you were involved—really involved—with anyone."

"Don't remind me."

"Apparently, someone needs to. Give the man a chance. Sure, he has drama. What man doesn't these days?"

"Drama would be a child with his ex-girlfriend,

bad credit, living with his parents. That kind of thing I can handle."

"Since when?"

"The point is," Jayde continued, ignoring her friend, "I can't deal with him lying to me about whose gallery I'm working in, being wealthy, or sleeping with me under false pretenses."

"Get serious, Jayde. He admitted to you the attraction was mutual and not part of the subterfuge. The way his eyes burned the sequins off your dress when he saw you just now, I'd say he cares for you—a lot. You're going to fault the man for being loaded? Now that's just wrong. Since when is having money a liability?"

"Since yesterday," Jayde snapped.

"Don't bite my head off. My last name isn't Mitchell."

"I'm sure that's another problem. I'll bet there are generations of Mitchells who have left an indelible and quite lucrative legacy behind. Somewhere on a college campus, there's a wing named after his family or a library or something just as grandiose."

"Personally, I think you're blowing this whole thing out of proportion."

"Really?"

"Of course. I mean, do you know how much money you'd have to donate before they'd put your name on a building?"

Jayde laughed in spite of herself. "Go mingle, Chris, and stop worrying about my love life. I'll be fine."

Jayde surveyed the room. Their featured artist's debut was a major success. Everyone loved his work. As promised, the media was on hand covering the event. Jayde's eyes lit up when she saw her mother from across the room. She sought her out.

"Mom, what are you doing here?"

Her mother's eyes sparkled. "Hello, darling. I've missed you. I wanted to make sure you were okay. You do realize you haven't called in a week? A week, Jayde. That's unlike you, so I wanted to come down here myself to see what's going on."

Jayde hugged her mother. The moment they touched, she was overwhelmed at the rush of calm suffusing her soul. In that second, Jayde realized how much she missed their closeness. She longed for her mom to listen to her problems, then tell her everything would eventually work out.

"There's nothing going on, Mom. I've just been tied up with work. I'm glad you made it. I've missed you, too."

"You know, you wouldn't have to miss me if you called more often," Harriette admonished. "Now, where's that new boss of yours? I'd like to give him a piece of my mind for stealing my baby's job."

"Mom, now is not the time for a showdown."

"Nonsense. Any time is the right time. Now, darling, you can either point me to that job-stealing man, or I'll get on the loudspeaker and find him that way. It's your choice, sweetie."

Jayde's stomach churned at her mother's barely veiled threat. Silently, she pointed.

CHAPTER 21

"You sure everything's in order?"

"Of course. We're on schedule. Now we just need the guest of honor, and we're a go."

He closed the cell phone. He ran a hand over his stubbled jaw. His plan was actually coming to fruition. He needed to cause one more nice, neat little accident at the gallery, then move on to the next Mitchell. Sterling would be beside himself if something happened to his precious son. Getting him to hand over the company to keep his son safe from harm would be a piece of cake. After all, if the golden boy's life was threatened, the elder Mitchell would move heaven and earth to keep him safe. That was where he'd come in.

He'd force Sterling to name him his successor. It would finally become his. *As it should.*

Then there was the lovely Jayde. He ran his tongue over his bottom lip. She was an added bonus. Once he got rid of the competition, he'd assume command before making his move. He'd offer her a job heading up her own gallery. She'd be so thrilled, there wouldn't be anything she wouldn't do to show her gratitude.

Yeah, it was almost showtime. Checking his watch, he smirked. The time was near. His henchmen had better not let him down.

The gala was in full swing when Devon's friends arrived. Always one to make a grand entrance, Lucinda swept in, heading straight for the cameras. Xavier took a few minutes to scan the crowd. When he found his target, he zeroed in.

Devon stared down at Jayde's mother. He'd spotted her talking to Jayde. The familial resemblance was undeniable. When their eyes had connected across the room, a look of determination had crossed her face. With purposeful strides, Harriette Seaton had swept across the crowded room, never breaking eye contact. Once at his side, Jayde's mother had introduced herself.

Now, skipping the pleasantries, she went straight for his jugular. "So, I finally meet the man responsible for turning my daughter's professional life upside down. I'd love to hear your side of it. I'm sure it's a doozy. Tell me, how do you sleep at night?"

"It's a complicated story, Mrs. Seaton, one I'm sure would bore you."

"On the contrary, Mr. Mitchell. I find the whole scenario of how you inveigled my daughter into a web of subterfuge far from dull."

Devon cleared his throat, praying for an interruption. When he saw his friend heading toward them, he wanted to run up and hug him. "Ah, there you are, X. I've been wondering when you'd arrive. Mrs. Seaton, I'd like to introduce you to a close friend of mine, Xavier Taggert. Xavier, this is Jayde's mother, Harriette."

"It's a pleasure to meet you, Mrs. Seaton," said Xavier.

"Not if you're anything like this joker." She smiled pleasantly.

Xavier made a choking sound, then cleared his throat several times.

"If you two will excuse me, I've business to attend to, but rest assured, Mrs. Seaton," Devon said to the woman impaling him with her eyes, "we will finish our conversation."

"We'd better," she warned, noting the amused and slightly startled look on the newcomer's face. She returned her attention to Devon, with steely determination in her eyes. "I'm not fooled, Mr. Mitchell. I know a diversion when I see it. We're far from done. I plan on telling you exactly what I think about your ill treatment of my daughter. Make no mistake about that."

"I wouldn't dream of it, ma'am," Devon replied. He practically threw Xavier in his place before bolting in the opposite direction. Devon prayed Jayde was in her office, waiting for him. He glanced at his watch. He was late. Swearing under his breath, he scanned the crowd until he found Jayde. She was talking to someone. Across the room, their eyes connected. He wasn't prepared for the shock and utter desolation in her gaze.

His step faltered; then he came to a halt. There was so much turmoil in her eyes, he felt overwhelmed. She turned away, which set his feet in motion. Devon reached her side, instantly recognizing the man talking to her. A real estate developer, Robert Loomis had never gotten along with Devon's grandmother and, subsequently, Devon's family. He'd been trying for years to purchase several properties along their corridor, but none of the owners would give him the time of day.

"Ah, Devon, there you are. I was just speaking with the

lovely Miss Seaton. Imagine my surprise when a colleague of mine told me about the gala."

"Mr. Loomis, while this isn't a nice surprise, it's a surprise nonetheless. Why are you here?" asked Devon.

"You're a hard one to catch up to, Devon."

"Mr. Mitchell," Devon corrected.

"Right. Mr. Mitchell it is. I haven't seen you since Cecilia's funeral years ago. So, how've you been?"

"Loomis, you don't give a damn how my family and I are doing, so why are you here?" Devon queried.

"I wanted to see how the gallery was faring. I sent several letters and never received a response."

"That was your response, Loomis."

"I see." Robert Loomis looked around. "Seems things are going well for you. I'm sure your grandmother would be pleased to know her baby is still going strong. I was shocked to hear that she left it to you, though. You never struck me as the art enthusiast."

Devon shrugged. "I have a myriad of interests you know nothing about."

"Evidently, but I'm still interested in buying it when you're ready to sell."

"The answer hasn't changed since you were hounding my grandmother. This gallery will never be for sale, Loomis."

"Never say never. Invariably things do change. I was just chatting with your employee here. I was asking Jayde—"

"Miss Seaton," Jayde corrected.

"I was just asking Miss Seaton how you were doing since your car accident. I was sorry to hear about it. Losing your fiancée and unborn child had to be devastating. Yes, indeed, a terrible, tragic accident." Loomis stressed the last word.

Devon inched forward. "It *was* an accident, you bastard."

"Then why haven't you told anyone here about it?"

"I don't discuss personal matters with my staff, Loomis, and considering that she doesn't live in the area, it's not unusual that Miss Seaton wouldn't have heard about a car accident in Chicago."

"I did," Loomis related.

"You have a vested interest, don't you? You've been waiting in the wings to gather any dirt you can on my family to aid your cause. It won't work. You don't deserve to step foot in this gallery, and I promise you hell will freeze over before you own it." Devon placed himself between the man and Jayde, and his voice came out in a deadly whisper. "I won't allow you to harass Miss Seaton any longer. This is a private party, Mr. Loomis. Unless you want to be thrown out on your ass for trespassing, I suggest you leave. Now."

Loomis's face turned a mottled red. His nostrils flared. "I'm with an invited guest. I've every right to be here."

Grabbing his arm, Devon discreetly pulled the portly man toward an approaching plainclothes security guard. "Escort Mr. Loomis out of the building. See that he doesn't return. If he so much as raises his voice a decibel on his way out, have him arrested for trespassing."

The guard obliged, grasping Loomis's arm. "Yes, Mr. Mitchell."

Surprisingly, Jayde was in the same spot he'd left her. Her face was ashen; her breathing stilted. Devon frowned. The damage had already been done.

"Jayde, I'm taking you someplace private where we can talk."

She shook her head, putting her hand up to her head. "No, I'm not going anywhere with you."

"You're in shock. That's obvious. But it wasn't how Loomis insinuated."

She backed up. "So, it's true?"

Devon sighed deeply. "Yes."

Her face contorted with pain. "No."

He ran a hand through his hair. "My ex-girlfriend was killed when the car I was driving crashed, but it was an accident. I didn't harm her, nor would I ever have. Now, can we please leave so we can talk about this?"

"I'm not going anywhere with you," Jayde repeated, rushing away.

"Jayde," Devon whispered loudly. "Wait."

Walking swiftly behind her, he'd barely caught up when a loud crash splintered the air behind them. Screams and shouts echoed around the room. Diving for the floor, Devon shielded Jayde under his body. After catching his breath, he glanced over his shoulder. Seeing the turmoil behind them made his blood run cold. One of the track-lighting fixtures lay in a crumpled heap right where they'd been standing.

Steel and glass were scattered across the hardwood floor. If they hadn't moved, they'd have been seriously injured—or killed. Squirming under him, Jayde peeped around his massive body. Shakily, she followed his line of sight. When she saw where they'd been standing, she gasped.

The gravity of the situation made Devon's chest tighten. They could've been killed. "Jayde, are you all right?" Rolling her over, he searched for injuries.

After recovering from the initial shock, Jayde realized she was still under Devon, with dozens of people looming over her. A few reporters were actually taking pictures of the couple sprawled on the floor.

"Yes, I'm fine," Jayde responded, with a forced smile. "Would you help me up?"

Devon rose to his feet. Immediately, he helped Jayde stand, then gave her a hand smoothing her disheveled dress. Instinctively, she wanted to bat his hands away, but she couldn't. People still stood wide-eyed and open-mouthed around them. She heard her name screamed from across the hushed room. In a matter of seconds, her mother cleared the crowd, with Christy in tow, shouting for Devon to remove his hands from her daughter's person. At this point, creating a scene was the last thing Jayde wanted to do.

"Mother, I'm fine. I just got the wind knocked out of me," Jayde said hastily.

"No, you're not fine. It's obvious you're upset," Harriette declared.

Of course, she was upset. Devon still had his hands on her, making it difficult to get a coherent thought out of her emotionally tattered brain.

"I think you should go to the hospital," Harriette added.

"Mom, I don't need a doctor. What I need is . . ." Jayde halted before she could admit that Devon was the source of her consternation.

Sensing her best friend's dismay, Christy stepped in. "Actually, Mrs. Seaton, with all the commotion down here, I think it would be best if Devon took Jayde upstairs to help her get herself together."

Devon shot Christy a look of gratitude.

"Well, okay, but if you need me—," Jayde's mother began, but Devon interrupted.

"I'll come get you, Mrs. Seaton," he assured her.

Harriette pointed her finger at him. "You'd better."

Jayde allowed Devon to usher her out of the room.

The second she was out of view of the swarm of people, she wrenched her elbow from him. "Get your hands off me."

Devon released her immediately. Without another word, Jayde bolted for the back door.

"Where are you going?" he called.

"Anywhere that's away from you."

The whole sordid nightmare was too much for her to process. She couldn't take another strain on her senses. Devon called her name, but that didn't slow her down. Once her feet started moving, they didn't stop. She'd catch up to her mother and Christy later. Right now she had to get out of there.

Jayde ignored Devon's second request to wait. Once outside she hesitated. *Damn,* she hadn't brought her car. She'd ridden with Christy. The Archives–Navy Memorial Metro stop was down the street, but she'd never make it before Devon came out of the gallery. Raising her hand overhead, Jayde frantically hailed a cab. The motion caused her to flinch. She grabbed her side. Apparently, Devon saving her life wasn't without side effects. The pain would have to wait. She had to be gone by the time he came outside. She had to.

Her prayer was answered when she saw an Elite cab cross two lanes of traffic and careen to a screeching halt at the curb. Opening the door, she gathered her dress and eased herself in. Before giving the driver her address, she shut and locked the door and then collapsed against the seat.

Devon yelled her name from outside the cab. He tried the door, but it was locked. Through the closed window, his eyes sought hers. "Jayde, open the door."

"Go away," she shrieked through the glass. "I don't want to hear anything you have to say. Just leave me alone." She tapped the Plexiglass separating her from the driver. "Go. Go!"

The cab peeled away from the curb. The tires screamed in protest at the accelerated speed.

Jayde didn't have to look out the window. She knew Devon was still standing there, staring. She didn't care. *Let him stare till his eyes fall out.* She never wanted to listen to another one of his lies or explanations again. The farther she got away from Devon Mitchell, the better.

Numb. That was how Devon felt. As he watched Jayde's cab roar down the street, his first impulse was to go after her. He was about to run to get his car from the parking garage when a hand on his left shoulder stayed him.

"Let her go."

Startled, Devon looked around to see Lucinda. "Why?"

"You can't go after her now. Give her time. She's had to digest a lot, Dev. She needs to sort through it all before you pile more onto her head."

"You overheard?"

Lucinda nodded. "Enough to figure out what happened."

"She doesn't know the whole story, Luce. She thinks that I killed Candace and that it was premeditated murder. You didn't see her expression after hearing that snake Loomis insinuate that it was no accident. I did."

"You think going after her now is a smart choice? What are you going to do? Stand on her steps and yell at a closed window?"

Devon turned around. "There's more to this than just misunderstandings, hurt feelings, and deception. The track lighting that crashed to the floor was no accident."

"What?" Lucinda looked incredulous. "How do you know that?"

"That's why I've been here," he admitted. He pinched the bridge of his nose. "There've been unexplainable accidents occurring at the gallery for some time, so I went undercover to get to the bottom of it. One of my employees ended up being embroiled in this craziness. I don't buy for one second that he was the ringleader. That's why I want to keep an eye on Jayde. If we hadn't been arguing, if she hadn't walked away at that precise moment . . ." Devon struggled to maintain his composure. "I want to make sure these idiots don't harm her trying to get to me."

"You're sounding awfully paranoid."

"I don't care how it sounds," he said harshly. "I'll do any and everything to keep her safe."

Lucinda covered her mouth with her hand. "Oh my," she said in awe. "Why didn't I see it sooner?"

He glanced down. "What?"

"You love her."

His nod confirmed it. "Yeah, I do, but I'm scared, Luce. I just hope I don't end up loving her to death."

Standing in the shadows, Xavier had heard enough. He waited until his friends left before he moved away from the wall. Stealthily, he walked back undetected the way he'd come. At first he'd assumed Devon's fascination with Jayde was a fleeting attraction, but this was much better. He was in love with her. All the ammunition he needed to bring Devon down had just pulled off in a cab. Jayde was the catalyst to his revenge coming to fruition, and he wouldn't hesitate to use her to even the score.

CHAPTER 22

"Miss?" A chipper blond woman bent down. "Can I get you anything else?"

Jayde glanced up. "No, thank you. I'm fine."

"Then, if you'd like to put your seat back in its upright position, we'll be preparing for landing."

Jayde thanked the woman before adjusting her seat. Sighing, she returned to reading her magazine.

"Tree, if you're going to sulk the whole darn trip, I'm leaving as soon as we get there."

"You'll do no such thing. You've never been to Italy, either. Besides, you'll be spending the whole time wondering if you missed something."

"True, true."

The captain came over the loudspeaker. "Ladies and gentlemen, we are on the final approach and will be landing in twenty minutes. . . ."

As the pilot continued speaking, Christy couldn't help but ask, "Still thinking about him?"

Jayde bit her bottom lip. "Not as much as when we started this long flight."

Christy checked her watch. "Since I don't even know

what darn time it is, I'd say that was good. Seriously, Jayde, I understand getting away from your man by going across town or a few blocks away. But across the ocean?" Jayde didn't answer so she kept talking. "I guess I can understand the need for distance. First off, he's enough to make a crazy woman sane. Then he knocks the bottom outta that thang and—"

"Do we need to go over this again?" Jayde interrupted.

"Secondly," her friend continued, "you never even told me how good it was. I mean, was it good? Or was it scrumdillyumptious? And to make matters worse, you think he planned the accident that killed his ex-girlfriend and their unborn child? I swear, this sounds like a made-for-TV movie."

Jayde turned toward her best friend. "You know, Chris, you missed a spot. How about twisting the dagger a little harder so you can get my whole heart in one shot?" she replied tearfully.

"I'm sorry, girl. Truly. I just have a hard time believing someone who makes you feel like he did could harm his girlfriend—to death. It doesn't fit. Don't you think you owe it to him to hear his side of the story?"

"Owe him?" Jayde snapped. "I don't owe him anything. My life has been ripped apart by that man. From this moment on, I'm not expending any more energy on Devon Mitchell."

"Fine. Forget about owing him, but seriously, Jayde, don't you think you owe it to yourself to hear it all?"

Silence ensued.

Christy patted Jayde on the shoulder before turning her attention to the window.

It had been three days since she'd ridden off, leaving Devon on the sidewalk outside the gallery. She had ignored his calls and hadn't bothered answering her door. The only people she'd contacted were her mother, to let her know she was going on vacation, and Christy, to invite her along. If Harriette Seaton was skeptical of her daughter's motivation, she didn't let on.

Calling Devon's work number at two o'clock in the morning had ensured she'd get his voice mail. While struggling for composure, Jayde had told his recorder that she needed time away to clear her head. Then she'd said she'd be gone about ten days. As an afterthought, she'd added that she wouldn't be reachable or checking messages until she got back. Once she'd hung up, Jayde had sat cross-legged on her bed, eyeing the phone. Her heart had hurt. The thought of facing him again had sent spasms through her chest. If it hadn't been for Paolo's request to visit, she'd have nowhere to go. She'd e-mailed him to make sure his invitation was still good. A day later, an elated Paolo had phoned her with detailed travel plans.

"Of course, you'll be staying with me," he had informed her. "I'll pick you up at the airport, so don't worry about anything."

"I won't." Jayde had almost broken down in tears. "Thank you, Paolo."

"*Arrivederci, cara mia.*"

"Ciao," she'd whispered. "Oh, Paolo?"

"*Si?*"

"Do you . . . Would you mind if I brought a friend along?"

"*Si, bella. Porta una amica,*" he'd gushed. "Bring a friend."

"Grazie." Jayde thanked him before hanging up.

She took a few deep breaths and tried to relax. *Forget him,* she told herself. It was hard to do when her whole body trembled just thinking about him. She'd get over him. No matter how painful the process was. Before long she'd be walking the streets of Rome, Italy. She knew the city was famous for romance, but she also hoped it was the perfect place to repair a broken heart.

After disembarking from the plane, Jayde and Christy retrieved their luggage. When they cleared customs, Jayde took out the itinérary Paolo had sent her. After rereading the documents, she elbowed Christy. "We're going that way. Paolo and his driver should be waiting for us."

"He has a driver?" Christy looked impressed. "Now we're riding in style."

"You're too much." Jayde gathered her suitcases and wheeled them along behind her. Not wanting to get left behind, Christy was right on her heels.

Jayde heard her name yelled over the airport din. "Jayde, over here."

She scanned the throng of people. When her eyes fixed on a short, impeccably dressed older man, she waved and headed toward him.

"Ooh," Christy gushed. "He's so cute. Short, but cute."

Bags momentarily forgotten, Jayde went straight into his arms. Being enveloped in a big bear hug was just what she needed. She was crushed against him while being shaken to and fro. She loved every minute. "Paolo, it's so good to see you."

"Welcome to Rome. Let me look at you," he said, setting her away from him. "Ah, you're still as beautiful as ever. Simply *meravigliosa*." He kissed her cheek. Turning in Christy's direction, Paolo turned on the charm. "Who's this gorgeous creature with you?"

"See? I knew I liked you." Christy leaned in to hug Jayde's friend.

After the introductions, Paolo signaled for his driver to take the bags to the car while he strolled arm in arm with his guests. "You two are lovely. Beyond compare. I'm the envy of every man in this *aeroporto*."

Jayde and Christy exchanged looks behind Paolo. Oh yes, Jayde definitely needed this vacation.

"My house is in Lazio, about two hours from here. My gallery isn't too far from home but you'll see that soon enough. For now, you'll soak up the scenery while we sit back and enjoy ourselves with some of the finest Umbrian vino. I have a friend in Umbria. His family owns a vineyard. Excellent vintage, I assure you."

Once she'd reclined against the leather seat of Paolo's limousine, Christy looked to Jayde and winked. "Now this is how we roll."

Devon paced his home office. He'd just retrieved Jayde's message from the gallery voice-mail system. Where could she be? He realized she was upset, but to up and leave, without so much as a word, was unlike her. Then again . . .

He recalled his first few days at the Wells Gallery. This was Jayde's modus operandi. When she got upset, she bolted as fast as her Prada pumps could carry her. Inspiration struck. Devon grabbed the cordless phone off the desk. Dialing Maxwell's number, he waited impatiently. After two rings, the older man answered.

"What took so long?" Devon complained. "Max, I need an alternate number for Jayde. I've already tried her home number. Check her personnel file, and then get back to me." He disconnected before Maxwell could get two words out.

Minutes later, Devon slammed the receiver down in disgust. Maxwell had given him several numbers that he'd received from the receptionist. The man had informed Maxwell that Jayde's grandparents had left her their beach house. Remembering her love of the water, Devon tried that number first. If she was there, she wasn't answering. Her mother was listed as a contact, as well as Christy Denton. Taking the path of least resistance, Devon phoned her girlfriend. When Christy's voice mail picked up, he left a brief message. Seeing her mother's number gave him pause. He was desperate to get a hold of Jayde, but he wasn't ready to take that bullet.

Two days later . . .

"You're delusional if you think I'm telling you where to find my daughter," Harriette said bitingly.

"Mrs. Seaton, please tell me where I can locate Jayde. I'm concerned about her. She hasn't been to work in a few days."

"Mr. Mitchell, I don't know what's going on between you and my daughter, but I'm no fool. I know there's more to this than the obvious employer-employee relationship. I'm not blind, and I was young once. I'd wager whatever sent my daughter flying outta here on the first thing smoking was your doing. Am I right?"

Devon clenched his teeth. Nothing was worth this headache. "Yes, ma'am," he replied. "I'd say that was a fair assessment."

"Uh-huh. Well, since that's the case, I'm not at liberty

to tell you where she went—or with whom," she added happily.

The chair in which he was sitting snapped upright with a loud clunk.

"With whom? What do you mean with whom? She's gone out of town with someone? Mrs. Seaton, I need to know where she is. It's . . . imperative."

Jayde's mother had the temerity to chuckle. It grated on his nerves.

"No, Mr. Mitchell. You *want* to know where my daughter is. There's a difference."

"I can't believe we're arguing over semantics. I'm still her employer," he groused.

"That being said, I suppose you should treat your employees better. Good day, Mr. Mitchell."

Devon heard a dial tone. "Thanks, Mrs. Seaton. No surprise now where Jayde gets her attitude from," he said loudly into the receiver. "Like two argumentative peas in a pod. The next gift you get your daughter should be track shoes, because every time she gets in a situation she doesn't like she turns tail and runs."

Tossing the phone down, Devon leaned back in his chair. Angry didn't begin to describe how he felt. Was *frustratingly angry* a term? If so, Devon was two degrees past that. Granted he was mad, but he wasn't an imbecile. Jayde was avoiding him. That much was obvious, but the question was why, and more importantly, for how long? He knew that the secret he'd harbored finally coming to light had pushed Jayde to flee to parts unknown, and that it was his fault. *You should never have allowed her to leave before you got the whole story out,* his inner voice chided. "Easy for you to say," he muttered aloud. "You try stopping her next time and see how far you get."

Devon leaned forward and placed his head in his hands. She had to believe he'd never kill Candace. How could she think otherwise? She didn't, he told himself. Jayde would calm down eventually, and when she did, she'd realize he cared about her and would never purposefully harm anyone. Not feeling any better, Devon stared absentmindedly at the ceiling. His thoughts returned again to the woman he loved. "Jayde." Her name escaped his lips in a tortured whisper. "Where are you?"

"Please, I can't take any more." Jayde groaned, holding her stomach. Pushing her plate away, she slumped back in her chair. "Signora Capelli, you're killing me," she wailed.

The older woman dropped the dish she was carrying. She turned frantic eyes toward Paolo.

Paolo explained the English vernacular to his housekeeper. "What a way to go, hey?" He laughed while his newly enlightened housekeeper cleared away the broken dish.

"Personally, I can think of another way I'd like to go," Christy said, moaning.

"Christmas," Jayde hissed. She always used that nickname when Christy shocked her.

Her friend looked indignant. "Uh, hello? I was referring to death by chocolate. Get your head outta the gutter."

"I knew that." Jayde blushed, then stared into her wineglass.

"Lazio fare is rich in pastoral tradition. Lamb is our staple," Paolo explained. "Here we use simple ingredients from local shepherds and farmers to create dishes that tantalize the palate."

"What do you call the roast lamb we had?" Christy asked.

"Ah, that was *abbacchio al forno*. The pasta dish was *gnocchi alla Romana*," said Paolo.

"I even liked the zucchini dish," Jayde interjected between labored breaths, "which is amazing, considering I don't usually like zucchini."

Christy turned to Paolo. "And that other one, with the stuffed olives. I was all over that one." She stood and stretched languidly. "I think I'll go submerge myself in a scented bubble bath. It's a good thing you float in water. As full as I am, I'd probably sink to the bottom."

Paolo spoke to his housekeeper. She nodded before turning to Christy. "Would you like me to run for you, signorina?" she asked haltingly.

"*Grazie*, Signora Capelli." Elated, Christy followed the older woman up the stairs in an undignified waddle. "If I'm not back in an hour, send in reinforcements. Preferably male and single."

Alone, Jayde looked at her host. "Your home is beautiful, Paolo."

Jayde had taken a tour of the farmhouse earlier. Nestled among the greenery and lush countryside, the three-bedroom home was tranquil and welcoming. The ground floor had a spacious, wood-beamed great room with a well-used fireplace. The kitchen was big enough to dine in. The old wooden kitchen table looked like it had accommodated diners throughout the centuries. Upstairs were the bedrooms and a large bath with an extra-wide tub. She and Christy shared a bedroom, which left Paolo the master suite and his housekeeper her private sanctuary. Cradled in the bosom of the rustic home, Jayde's frazzled nerves receded.

"Come," Paolo beckoned. "Let me show you my pride and joy."

Jayde walked arm in arm with her old friend. The house was surrounded by gardens and a quiet, lush meadow. Somewhere nearby music was softly playing.

To constant chatter, Paolo led Jayde through a maze of paths until they ended up in a secluded area. A vine-covered wooden pergola sheltered a well-worn patio.

On it was a café table, two chairs, and a lounger. A wood-burning stove occupied part of the space, while potted plants and flowers dueled playfully with wild ones.

It moved Jayde to tears. "There are no words."

"I felt that way when I first saw this place. Amazingly, I still do."

Directing her to sit, he followed suit, folding his short arms across his chest. "Okay, Jayde. I let you recover from your travels yesterday. It's time you tell me what brought you here. I have a feeling it wasn't just my *invito* to tour the European countryside, no?"

Not trusting her voice, she shook her head.

"I didn't think so. Could this have something to do with Signor Mitchell?"

Her eyes widened. "How did you know?"

Paolo winked. "I have my ways."

Uncrossing her arms, Jayde rubbed her temples. "I don't think you have time to hear the whole sordid story."

Snorting, Paolo waved his arm around. "My dear, this is Italy. We have nothing but time."

In less than a week, the entire gallery staff developed an amazing ability to walk on eggshells. The longer Jayde was gone, the grouchier Devon became. Lucinda and Xavier had departed a few days after the gala. Though he hadn't had that much time to spend with his friends, Devon missed them. They always made him feel better.

"Honestly, Dev," Lucinda complained their last night in D.C., "I don't know why you're moping around at the gallery on our last night here. We could be out on the town, painting it chartreuse."

"You gotta be kidding me." Xavier scrunched his nose. "You can't think up a better color than that? I mean try the standard red, or fuchsia, periwinkle . . . something."

"Honey, haven't you figured out by now that I love standing out?" she quipped.

Raising his head from his laptop, Devon arched an eyebrow. "Periwinkle?"

"Shut up," Xavier warned.

"Kinda girly is all I'm saying," Devon joked.

"You get the gist," said Xavier.

Devon snickered before returning his attention to his project. "Just give me another thirty minutes. I've been asked to be a keynote speaker at a luncheon focusing on community-sponsored programs for kids. Since Jayde is missing in action, the task falls to me."

"Some vacation." Lucinda pouted.

"I'm not the one who asked you guys to come here, you know. It's not good timing, which I would've told you had you called first," Devon retorted.

Lucinda took her feet off the front of his desk. She stood stiffly. "Well, excuse us for being your friends, for being concerned about your sorry butt. You go away without warning or a phone call. We haven't seen you in months, and when we do visit you, the first thing you try to do is get rid of us. Well, I, for one, don't need the aggravation. I'm leaving. My apologies for disturbing your perfect little life."

Devon sighed. "Wait, Luce." Standing, he walked around his desk and placed a hand on her shoulder. "I'm sorry. I should've called you both sooner, but I needed the time away to get my head straight. I realize now that keeping the truth from my friends was a mistake. Please forgive me for taking my frustration out on you, too. I'm glad you're here, and I've missed you both. Seriously."

"Fine," she sniffed, hugging him tightly, "but we're still leaving."

"Speak for yourself," Xavier replied. "I've a mind to take some time off from work. Might as well spend it in the nation's capital, driving Dev crazy."

"Please," Devon said, groaning. "I've had enough of that lately. Aren't you due back at Mitchell? Doesn't Dad have you working on some project?"

"I've got my laptop with me," Xavier replied, leaning back in his chair, grinning. "I'm all set."

"Suit yourself," Lucinda told Xavier. "I'm heading to New York. If I came this far and didn't go shopping, I'd never forgive myself."

"Let's get out of here. We'll do dinner. My treat," Devon offered.

Lucinda kissed him on his cheek. "Great. I'm starved. Darling, for what it's worth, I like your little secretary."

Somewhat startled, Devon walked with his friends to the door. "She's not my secretary, but I'll tell Jayde you asked about her when she returns. I'm sure she'll be thrilled at this new development."

"No, she won't." Lucinda smiled mischievously.

"No, she won't," Devon agreed.

"You two meet me out front. I'm running to the ladies' room," Lucinda said.

Once outside, Devon turned to Xavier, who was standing next to him. "Aren't you going to ask what that's about?"

Xavier shook his head. "I already know. You and Jayde are an item. I knew that the moment we walked through your front door. It doesn't take a PhD to figure out something that obvious."

Devon shook his head. "I don't know what I'm going to do about her, X. One minute I want to love her till she's catatonic, and the next I want to shake her till she passes out."

"Sounds vaguely familiar," Xavier said dryly.

"Oh no," Devon said quickly. "There's no comparison. I never loved Candace the way I do Jayde. Honestly, since I know the difference now, I can truthfully say I was never in love with the woman."

Surprise etched Xavier's features. "Surely, you don't mean that. You told me once you couldn't do without her."

"That was stupidity and hormones talking. Toward the end, any feelings I had for that conniving . . . woman were gone. She didn't love me . . . just the brand name."

"That's funny."

"What's funny about it?" Devon replied. "Consider yourself lucky. You escaped the wrath of Candace and all the ministrations that went along with it. Trust me, X, you got off light. If I hadn't come along after you two broke up, just think how much misery you'd be in now. I took a bullet for you."

Xavier's jaw clenched. "Don't worry, Dev. Someday soon I hope to repay you in kind."

"You don't have that much money," Devon joked.

Xavier was silent for a while. When he finally spoke, his voice was cold. "So what? After Candace died, you decided to go off and get a change of scenery? How long did you mourn her, Devon?" Xavier said sarcastically. "A day or two, or was it a whole month?"

Devon's jaw clenched. "That was out of line."

"I must admit I'm at a loss as to why you ended up here. This is an art gallery, Devon. Creativity isn't exactly your forte. You're the heir to one of the most lucrative technical services companies out there right now. You have it all, and yet you're here, collecting dust. Do you know how many men would kill to be in your position? To have the opportunities you take for granted? Do you even care what this is doing to your father?"

"My father is aware of my intentions, and the last time I checked, he's the only person I report to."

"Can't you see that he needs you now? No, I guess you can't. You aren't there every day. I am. Your absence affects him, Devon. Taking time off to mourn a woman you never gave a damn about is one thing. Being gone as long as you have is flat-out selfish. Though your father would never say it to your face, it's the truth."

"My decisions are my own, X. I don't need to clear them with you."

"You know, the night we arrived at your house, it took two seconds for me to guess why you're spending so much time here."

"What the devil is that supposed to mean?"

Xavier's smile was brittle. "The works of art are—breathtaking."

Devon grabbed Xavier by his shirt. His tone was barely controlled. "You seem to have forgotten one important fact, so let me remind you. You work for me,

Xavier, not the other way around. We may be friends, but I don't need you telling me how to handle my affairs—business or personal. If you want to continue collecting that six-figure salary, I suggest you keep your insubordinate opinions to yourself. That also includes derogatory comments about my staff." He shoved Xavier backward. "Do I make myself clear?"

Xavier eyed him pointedly. "Crystal."

"What's going on out here?"

Turning his attention to Lucinda, Devon missed the expression of hatred on Xavier's face.

Though she pressed both men for answers, they remained silent. Xavier bowed out of their dinner plans. Devon agreed to take Lucinda back to their hotel. Xavier took the time alone to drive around the city. He couldn't stop thinking of the woman he'd lost—or his child. The taste of bile was so strong, he almost choked on it. It probably wasn't a good idea for him to prod Devon like he had, but he couldn't help himself. His need for retribution was insatiable. To avenge the woman he'd loved was tantamount.

Xavier had squelched his craving to lunge at his best friend when he'd confessed he didn't love Candace. He *had* to wait. It wasn't time to reveal his hidden agenda. Soon, everyone would know who he really was: a Mitchell and the rightful heir to the family dynasty.

Once you're out of the way, I'll make our father sign over the company to me. A tragic accident seems fitting, his conscience reasoned. *One that'll leave the old man so grief stricken that he won't think twice about handing me the reins. All of it will be mine. Only then will my grievances against all of you be made right.* "That's the time, Devon. The time you'll pay for destroying the family I could've had, the one I always wanted," he said aloud. "You'll pay in the worst way imaginable, my friend. I promise you that. You'll pay with your precious Jayde, and I promise you, I'll make her suffer—just like you did Candace."

Satisfied, Xavier returned his attention to the road. When his car glided to a halt at the red light, he looked to his right. A beautiful woman in a spotless red sports car winked at him. Smiling, Xavier winked back. Why shouldn't he? Everything was going his way. Blowing her a kiss, Xavier slammed his foot down on the gas pedal. His rented Mustang roared to life under him. He liked the feel of power emanating from it. The screeching tires spun in circles as the car jetted off the white line. In his rearview mirror, he glimpsed the woman and her car fading behind him. A distant memory—just like Devon would be.

CHAPTER 23

On the walk back to the house, Jayde found it easy to confide the whole story to her old friend. With her eyes planted firmly on the ground, Jayde recounted almost every moment since she'd met Devon. Paolo remained silent until Jayde was finished. When she finally came up for air, Paolo took a sip from the wineglass he was still carrying, cleared his throat, then went into a monologue in Italian that was so vehement and so loud, it brought Signora Capelli running from the house.

"*Scusa,*" he told the startled woman, who was gasping for air and waving a broom around like it was a bayonet.

Contrite at terrifying the older woman, Paolo apologized again to his housekeeper in subdued, comforting tones. Signora Capelli gave Paulo a rapid response of her own before waving her broom at him and stomping off toward the house.

Unable to contain his mirth, Paolo turned his attention back to Jayde. "Forgive me. I got carried away." He wrapped Jayde's hand in his. "My wonderful housekeeper told me that the next time I use words like that and there isn't an intruder, she'll use her broom on me.

I'm sorry, but I couldn't help my outburst. It makes my blood boil hearing the things that man has been up to. *Ridiculo.* Now he accuses me of sabotage. That's the straw on the cake."

"The straw that broke the camel's back," Jayde corrected.

"What?"

"It's the straw that broke the camel's back or the icing on the cake. You've got them mixed up."

"Oh. Well, whatever." Paulo threw his hands up in disgust. "If the beloved Cecilia were alive today, she'd be disgraced. To believe her grandson could dishonor her memory with this foolish behavior."

"You knew he was her grandson?" Jayde sputtered. "All this time?"

"Of course, *bella.* Cecilia was very proud of her *famiglia.* If you had mentioned him before now, I would've told you." Paolo threw up his hands again and fired off another round of angry, rapid words. "I swear to you, I'm so angry right now, I could—"

"Please, Paolo," Jayde pleaded. "If you're going to be angry, do it in English. I can't follow you in Italian."

Paolo took her hands in his and sighed. "Jayde, I swear to you on my mother's grave, I had nothing to do with these sabotages. I cared deeply for Signora Wells. I had the utmost respect. I would never besmirch her good name or the gallery. Art is my life, my passion—*mi amore.*"

Jayde squeezed his hands. "I know, Paolo. I never thought for a minute you were behind any of it. You're a good man and an even greater friend. Devon Mitchell could learn a great deal from you."

Paolo raised her hand to his lips. "Ah, *bella.* I don't know why you fell in love with such a donkey's hind end."

Her throat constricted painfully at the truth she

could no longer deny. With a heavy heart, Jayde looked out over the lush countryside. "Why indeed?"

In bed that night, Jayde mulled over Paolo's words. The conversation she'd had with Devon and Mr. Loomis invaded her mind. Was Devon capable of what Loomis had hinted at, or had it been just an accident? She'd told Devon she didn't want to hear anything else he had to say, but not knowing was causing more problems than knowing. If she did love Devon, how could she love someone capable of such a heinous crime? What if what Devon had started to say was true? If it was just a horrible accident, didn't she owe it to him to hear the whole story?

She turned over, yanking the covers over her head. She pleaded with her mind to cease the questions and with her body to quit burning with need. The latter was more of a challenge. In bed at night her body betrayed her the most. Desperately, Jayde wanted her subconscious to forget the way Devon had made her feel, to forget the passionate embraces, the intense loving, the way his body molded perfectly to hers—and the heat. The slow, unrelenting burning was so deep, it suffused her soul.

Devon. She slammed her eyes shut, and sweat trickled between her breasts. She prayed the wanting would ebb long enough for her to drift into a frustrated sleep. There was no way she'd come up with a solution that night. Her problem was just too big.

Morning came way too soon. Paolo sent Signora Capelli to rouse his houseguests, with instructions for them to get dressed, wear comfortable shoes, pack an overnight bag, and hurry. After a light breakfast, Paolo herded the ladies into his Mercedes to go exploring.

"Our first stop is Casperia," he said as they set off. "It's an amazing hilltop village in the Sabina Mountains. The village is accessible only by foot—no cars allowed. We'll visit St. Francis of Assisi's hermitages. We'll see medieval culture at its best. We'll visit the abbeys and soak up plenty of history. Wait till you see the mountain views. Ah, they're *fantastico*," Paolo said proudly. "When you're hungry, we'll stop at one of my favorites, Café La Fontana, for lunch. Afterward, it's off to my gallery for a tour."

Jayde and Christy both looked overwhelmed. "From there it's home, right?" Christy asked.

Paolo laughed loudly. "Oh, no. We're going to sample the nightlife in the Eternal City. In the morning, we'll tour the Vatican before visiting the Fontana di Trevi, the Pantheon, and loads of other architectural treasures, with culinary delights unsurpassed. This is your vacation, yes? You can sleep anytime. Come, my beauties. Rome awaits!"

After their whirlwind tour of Casperia, they visited Paolo's gallery and then headed to Rome. Jayde was impressed. The old stone building had a massive door with a black, circular iron knocker. It reminded Jayde of a small palace. The building held a maze of rooms containing paintings, statues, and tapestries. Each section had a different theme. There were areas with rich red walls, plush carpets, and gilded frames. One room had a white decor, dark casings, and wood floors.

Jayde's favorite was a small space with marble statues.

Every inch of the space was the color of warm cream, even the window treatments. Jayde could've sat there for hours. Walking along the corridors, with a practiced eye, she identified each painting's artist, then the year it was made.

Paolo nodded approvingly. "I see my protégé hasn't lost her touch. *Bene.*"

"How could I? Paolo, everything is wonderful. I'm in awe of your collection," Jayde replied.

"I thought it essential to combine the old with the new. Most of our patrons have tastes running from eccentric to downright passionate. We try to accommodate the variety," Paolo told them.

Examining a nude statue of lovers, Christy arched an eyebrow. "I wish I were that limber," she whispered.

Stifling a giggle, Jayde pushed her friend along behind their host.

Paolo's assistant interrupted to bring him a message.

"I'm sorry, ladies, but I have a phone call I must take. You two explore the gallery. I'll catch up to you as soon as I'm done," Paolo said, hurrying away.

After fifteen minutes of watching the back of Jayde's head, Christy yawned. "Okay, I've hit my art quota for today. If I stare at another painting, my nose is going to bleed. I'm off to find the ladies' room. You coming?"

Jayde eased onto a bench. "No," she answered distractedly. "I'll wait here."

Taking keys out of his jacket pocket, Devon flipped through until he found the right one. Sliding the key into the lock, he was about to turn it when the heavy wood door eased open, and the family butler, Jonah

Selby, greeted him with a warm smile. "It would appear the prodigal son has returned."

Devon couldn't contain his smile. "Morning, Selby. Never could beat you to the punch, could I?"

"Afraid not. It's good to see you, sir. Were your parents expecting you?"

"No," Devon answered on the way in. "I didn't want all the pomp and circumstance. And, Selby, we've known each other for thirty-five years. Would you please call me Devon?"

"As you wish." Selby went to retrieve Devon's luggage. "Will you be sleeping in your old room, or should I put these in the guesthouse?"

"Don't bother. I've got them." Devon hauled his garment bag over his shoulder and headed up the stairs. "I'm staying in my old room. What time's dinner?"

"Six o'clock."

"Mode?"

"Casual this evening, sir."

"Perfect." Devon smiled. He hated his parents' habit of dressing up for dinner. He thought it archaic.

Taking the stairs swiftly, Devon was on the second floor in no time. Heading down the long hallway, he turned and went in the second door. Striding to the leather couch, he laid his garment bag across it. Once he'd shrugged out of his suit jacket, he threw it across an adjacent chair. Devon unfastened three buttons on his dress shirt and walked to the windows at the back of his room. He scanned the well-manicured grounds of his boyhood home.

Usually, he loved the view, but today he was preoccupied. He didn't see the large pool, the spa, or the brick-paved patio leading to the poolside guesthouse. He wasn't looking at the acres of grass leading to an enclosed gazebo, either. Instead, he was focused on the reason he'd hopped the first flight out of D.C. on a brisk Friday afternoon, why he'd finally decided he needed the solace of his family, a welcome distraction to the chaos his life had become. He'd pondered Jayde's defection and Xavier's unprovoked attack until he was cross-eyed. Both disturbed him, but he'd acknowledged that the one constant in his thoughts over the last week was Jayde. She'd been under his skin, in his gut, traipsing through his mind every day since she'd pulled off in that damned cab.

Nighttime was worse. His cursed memory was too acute when it came to remembering the curve of her skin, the scent that was unmistakably Jayde. The way her body responded when he touched her or was engulfed by her. Every nuance of her was branded in his mind—and his heart. Loving her consumed him with an intensity he'd never experienced before. It was simultaneously a pleasure and a curse.

When she'd left, the agonizing emptiness he'd felt had driven him to flee the city, to escape it. In D.C. there were no diversions. It was *her* city. Everywhere he went, he was reminded of her, but in Illinois, he had family that loved him, things that could occupy his time, and a family business. He had roots. Yes, this was a much-needed break from all things Jayde and from his bizarre run-in with Xavier.

Backing away from the windows, Devon felt renewed hope that this trip home was exactly what he needed to restore his soul and his sanity.

Things would settle down. His old life would assuredly take hold, pushing all the tumultuous emotions aside. He'd be calm again.

With anticipation, Devon put his clothes away. He was

eager to resume a few of his old habits. Right now his heart felt like it was being ripped asunder. The sooner he controlled the bleeding, the better off he'd be.

His task complete, Devon changed into a pair of jeans and a T-shirt. With confident strides, he headed down the back stairs that led to the kitchen. He'd get a bite to eat and search out the matriarch of the family before she got wind that he was there and ripped him a new one.

If his mother was going to read him the riot act, it would be best to have it happen on a full stomach. Avalon Mitchell was a force with which to be reckoned without the hassle of hunger pangs.

Devon headed straight for the refrigerator. He grabbed deli meat, lettuce, tomatoes, mayonnaise, and mustard. He was in the process of getting pickles when a loud crash and woman's scream sounded behind him.

A pained expression crossed his face in anticipation of the trouble he was in. Devon slowly turned around. Spying his shocked mother behind him, he gave her his widest smile. "Hi, Mom."

CHAPTER 24

Paolo turned out to be the consummate host. He showed Jayde and Christy all the hot tourist spots in Rome so they could take pictures and revel in Italian history. They toured the Coliseum, marveled at the inexpressible colors on Michaelangelo's tribute in the Sistine Chapel, and visited the Piazza Navona to look at the fountains. The Eternal City was bursting with traffic. Pedestrians, automobiles, and Vespa scooters jockeyed for position on the crowded streets.

Jayde cringed as the cars whizzed in and out of traffic. Anyone brave enough to drive in Rome deserved a medal. After Jayde and Christy drank their fill of antiquities, they were shown Italy as only a true native could. They toured the small, quaint shops off the beaten path. Paolo insisted they stop for a glass of wine, so they walked down a narrow alley to one of his favorite trattorias. Later, the threesome visited with friends of Paolo's for cocktails before a fashionably late dinner. Not one to go anywhere without sampling the nightlife, Christy insisted they check out the club scene.

Paolo politely declined. "Clubs are not for me. I need

my sleep, but not to worry. I asked a friend to accompany you. I've made all the arrangements."

Their guide was a bona fide, living, breathing Adonis. Six feet, four inches, with black hair, brown eyes, and a physique that bordered on criminal. Christy took one look at him and almost swooned. She whispered to Jayde, "I'd follow this fine man anywhere. *Anywhere.*"

"You young people have a good time." Paolo waved. "I will be here when you return tomorrow."

"Tomorrow?" Jayde's eyes widened. "Somehow I don't think we know what we're in for."

They had the time of their lives. Their guide took them to a few clubs, where Jayde danced until her eyelids hurt. First, he took them to Big Mama, Rome's home of the blues in Trastevere, one of the city's most romantic areas. Afterward, they went for a scenic drive, then headed to Gilda, another famous hot spot.

"All the VIPs hang here," their guide informed them. As they entered the club, the man at the door welcomed them to the "greatest city on Earth." When Paolo had said he'd see them the next day, he hadn't been kidding. They didn't make it back to his friend's villa until 7:00 a.m., where an exhausted Jayde and Christy said both good morning and good night to everyone. Paolo gleefully waved the women off to bed.

Much later, their host, accompanied by his crisp-looking friend, took them shopping.

"You get less than four hours of sleep, and you look that good in the morning?" Christy gaped at Paolo's friend as he held the door open for her. "I must be doing something wrong," she grumbled, putting on dark sunglasses to hide her bloodshot eyes.

"It takes years to perfect." The man winked.

Out shopping, Jayde was looking at a purse when Paolo sought her out. "You remain so sad."

Startled, she dropped the purse. "Sad? I'm in one of the most beautiful cities in the world. What's there to be sad about?"

"Your eyes are mirrors into your soul, Jayde. They speak to me. They tell me your heart is still heavy," Paolo explained.

It wasn't a question.

Stunned, she could only stare at him.

"Tell me, *bella,* do you think he's in as much pain as you?"

A pair of gray eyes and a well-placed dimple invaded her thoughts. Jayde grinned sardonically. "I certainly hope so."

Avalon Mitchell was given a proper shock as she entered her kitchen. There was her only son, standing matter-of-factly in front of the refrigerator. Screaming first from shock, then elation, she ran around the kitchen island. By the time she reached him, Devon had already set the food on the counter and was waiting to pull his mother into his arms.

"Oh dear Lord, what a wonderful surprise! I prayed you'd come home, and here you are, my darling boy." Holding him tightly, Avalon cried with sheer joy. "I've missed you, sweetheart."

Racked with emotion, Devon's throat was so tight, he was barely able to croak out a response. "I've missed you, too, Mom. You'll never know how much."

They held each other in silence for some time before Avalon spoke. "Dear, it's not that I'm not thrilled to see you, but why are you here?"

Devon chuckled and set his mother away from him. Except for a few additional wrinkles around her eyes, she looked exactly the same. "I've come to visit—not long, though, so don't get too excited."

"Are you kidding?" Avalon ran a hand down his cheek. "You being here for any amount of time is excitement enough."

He took her small hand in his and kissed it.

"I think I'd better sit down before I fall down," his mother murmured.

Devon ushered her to the table. Avalon reached behind her for a chair. Before she could grab one, Selby was there, helping position it under her. Avalon smiled in gratitude. "Thank you, Selby."

"Quite welcome, Mrs. Mitchell."

"My goodness, Dev," she said, appalled. "What have you done?"

"Done?" Devon looked confused. He sat down across from her. "What are you talking about, Mom?"

"You look like something the cat dragged in on a cold, rainy day."

"Gee, thanks."

"Don't sidestep, Devon Andreas Mitchell. I know when something's wrong, so don't try faking stupidity with me. It's obvious you haven't slept properly in days, and you've lost weight. There is definitely something wrong."

"I'm fine."

"Don't lie to me," she chided. "I spoke with Henry a few weeks ago, and he assured me you were fit and healthy when you left. I can see now that wasn't the case."

"Mother, relax. Uncle Henry wasn't lying. I was just fine there. I've got issues I'm dealing with right now, that's all."

His mother looked skeptical. "So these issues you're dealing with wouldn't have anything to do with Jayde Seaton, would they?"

Devon's head snapped up. "What? How . . . Mother, how'd you know about Jayde?"

"Oh, please! You really thought your sister wasn't going to mention this young woman? You know Melanie better than that. She knows she'd have to answer to me if she withheld any news about you. Dev, I know you're hurting. I can see it. A mother can read her own children, so you'd better tell me what's going on."

Devon opened his mouth, but she interrupted. "And don't leave anything out."

The next twenty minutes were spent bringing his mother up to speed on his tumultuous life. She remained silent the entire time Devon spoke. When he was done, his face was strained, his expression grim. "There you have it." He sat back. "So, is this where you tell me everything will be okay and to have faith?"

Avalon studied her son. "No, darling, this is where I tell you you're being a jackass and I hit you upside your head."

"What?"

Making good on her claim, Avalon popped him. "Don't 'what' me," she snapped. "I can't believe someone as intelligent as you claim to be could do something so incredibly stupid. How'd you expect her to react? Did you think she'd stand there quietly after the bombshell you dropped? Honestly!" his mother ranted. "It's clear you've inherited your father's inability to think things through to their logical conclusion."

"This isn't exactly the welcome I'd envisioned," Devon complained.

"Well, honey, if you wanted someone to blow sunshine

up your heinie, you should've visited my sister. You know you're her favorite nephew. She wouldn't dream of telling you you've done something asinine."

Avalon pushed her chair back and got up. Despite her annoyance at her offspring, she kissed his cheek. Before she got to the door to open it, Selby was there.

"Selby."

"Yes, Mrs. Mitchell?"

"Make sure you tell the cook we're expecting four more for dinner in addition to Devon. I've a feeling Melanie and her brood will be arriving shortly."

"Certainly," Selby replied, stepping aside to let Devon's mother exit.

Selby glanced into the room. Quietly, he closed the door to give the bewildered-looking Devon time to recover.

"So, did it help?" Christy asked her friend.

Jayde looked at the mountain of bags on either side of her legs. "I don't know what you mean."

"Come on, Tree. We've been friends since you set my hair on fire in elementary school. I know you. When you're upset, you spend money. My question is, did it help? Is Devon off your mind?"

Jayde calculated her purchases and couldn't help but grin. It felt good to have someone who knew her inside and out. "No. It didn't. I can't help—"

"What?"

"I dunno. Sometimes I feel like I should've given him the benefit of the doubt. Maybe I should've stayed to hear his side of it. What if I'm wrong about him, Chris? What if I turned my back on him when he needed my understanding most? I'm just confused about everything. It wasn't that long ago when I threw mental daggers at him every time he walked by."

"Now you mentally undress him every time he walks by."

"Christy."

"What? I'm just saying . . . he worked you over. Now he's working you over."

"Huh? What does that mean?"

"He used to drive you crazy outta bed. Now he's driving you crazy in bed."

"I don't know why I bother confiding in you."

"'Cause you love me." Christy poked her friend in the ribs. "Now, let's see where Paolo and that hunk of a friend went."

Jayde and Christy went in search of their hosts. They found them by the car. Paolo's friend relieved them of their numerous bags, carrying them back to the car. Christy took the opportunity to ogle his physique from behind.

"Was there anything else, signorinas?" the Adonis said over his shoulder.

A strangled gasp left Christy's mouth, and a splotch of red emerged from her cheeks to her hairline. Jayde's burst of laughter only made Christy blush more.

He'd caught Christy's line of sight before she'd had time to look away.

"Yes," Jayde began.

"No," Christy quickly added.

Jayde thought a little payback was in order. "Actually, sir, Christy was just admiring the . . . view."

Even Paolo had to chuckle.

At that revelation, the man stopped walking. Placing the bags down, he sauntered back toward them. He gave Jayde's friend his full attention. The look with which he pinned her was hot enough to melt an Italian ice. "*Ti piace quello che vedi*, Christy?"

Christy bit her lower lip. "*Non . . . non parlo Italiano.*"

He moved closer. Bending down, he whispered in Christy's ear. "I asked if you like what you see."

Moving closer, Christy dipped her head to whisper back, "*Assolutamente.*"

They laughed and conversed together in hushed tones.

Seconds later, Jayde interrupted their tête-à-tête. "Uh, hello?" she teased. "Standing right here."

CHAPTER 25

"Uncle Devon, Uncle Devon," Mitchell and Jetta chorused while running through the house.

"In here," Devon called from the library.

"Mom, we found him," Jetta called.

Once over the threshold of the large, book-lined room, Devon's niece and nephew headed straight for him. The force of impact knocked the three of them over and onto the carpet. Devon went down with a loud umph, followed by the giggling children.

"How are my favorite niece and nephew?" Devon beamed.

"We're your *only* niece and nephew, silly," Jetta reminded him.

He swung them both into a big bear hug. "Good thing. I don't think I'd have the strength to keep up with more than two of you."

"We missed you," Jetta cried. "A whole lot."

"Yeah," Mitchell said, pouting. "You missed all my soccer games."

"I know, sprout. I'm sorry I couldn't be there, but

GiGi and Granddaddy went, didn't they?" said Devon. Mitchell and Jetta called their grandmother GiGi.

Mitchell nodded but frowned nonetheless. "Yeah, but they don't cheer as loud as you do. Granddaddy doesn't do a good enough job."

"I see. Well, I promise you I'll be at the next one. When is it?" asked Devon.

His nephew chewed his bottom lip, deep in thought. "Jet, when is it?"

"Mitch, you know when it is," his sister sighed. "Every Saturday."

"Every Saturday," Mitchell replied.

"You're in luck, my man. I'll be here all weekend. I'll come tomorrow, and I'll make sure I'm the loudest one there. Deal?" said Devon.

His nephew gave him a high five. "Deal."

"Devon," Melanie said breathlessly from the doorway.

Standing, Devon set Melanie's children aside and headed for his twin sister.

Meeting him halfway, Melanie was crying before he'd finished wrapping his arms around her.

"Oh, Dev," she said, sobbing. "It's really you."

"It's really me," he said gruffly. "I've missed you, Mel."

Closing his eyes, Devon felt the tension drain from his body. His twin revitalized him down to his soul. "Just this instant, I realize how much I've missed you. All of you." Devon's voice was gruff with the strain of holding himself together.

"Move over, little girl," Sterling called from the door. "It's my turn."

Devon's sister turned to see her parents in the doorway. Sterling walked over to them. He usually shook Devon's hand, but not this time. He gathered his son in his strong embrace. "It's been so long, my boy. That's too long for family to be apart."

Devon patted his father on the back and winked at his mother. Her eyes aglow with unshed tears, she gave him a look that he knew well. Unconditional love.

Devon looked around. "Mel? Where's that husband of yours?"

"Root canal. He said he'd see you before you left, though."

"Can we eat now?" Mitchell interrupted the tender moment.

Melanie laughed, scooping her son up into her arms. "We sure can, baby. You get to sit next to Uncle Dev."

"Yeah," Mitchell yelled, making a beeline for the dinner table.

As was tradition, after dinner everyone adjourned to the family room to talk and commune with each other. After Devon brought everyone up to speed on the gallery, Sterling spoke.

"So, are you back to stay?"

"No, sir. I'm only here for the weekend. I plan to fly out Monday," said Devon.

Sterling nodded. "I see."

Devon heard the disappointment in his father's voice. He was sorry, too. He missed his work at Mitchell, but the gallery needed him. He'd come back to work with his father after the Wells Gallery was turned over to Jayde to run—if she didn't leave him first.

That thought didn't sit well with him. In fact, it was his frown that drew his niece's attention.

"Uncle Devon, are you okay?"

Devon nodded automatically.

"Uncle Devon's got a girlfriend's troubles," Mitchell announced, with authority.

Devon glared at his sister. "Melanie."

"It's girlfriend troubles, Mitch," Melanie corrected sweetly.

"Melanie," Devon repeated.

Ignoring Devon's hostile tone, Melanie turned to their mother. "Mom?"

Avalon looked at her grandson. "Mitchell, we don't gossip about things we overhear, sweetie. Either in private or over the phone. Understood?"

"Yes, GiGi." Mitchell lowered his head repentantly, and then, quick as a flash, he raised it. "But, Mommy was talking to you, so does that make it okay?"

"Mom," Devon muttered.

"Devon," said Avalon, mimicking his appalled tone.

"Is *anything* off-limits in this house?" Devon asked.

"Dear, don't be so dramatic," Avalon chided. "Besides, we had to hear about it sooner or later."

"I would've preferred the latter," Devon returned.

"What's all this about?" Sterling chimed in.

"It's a long story, Dad," Devon replied tiredly.

Interest sparked in Sterling's gray eyes. "Good thing we've got all weekend."

Since Devon's time at home was limited, his sister and her family spent the night. It was after nine o'clock when the kids were sent off to bed, protesting all the way. Once Devon tucked them in and read them stories, they drifted off into a peaceful slumber. Mitchell's soccer game was first thing the next morning, so Devon and Melanie's parents bid them good night. Devon and Melanie stayed up till the wee hours, talking and getting reacquainted. When they both started to yawn, they turned in.

Up in his room, Devon used his cell phone to check his messages at his D.C. home and at the gallery. He had a few business calls, but none from Jayde. Halfway between worried and annoyed, Devon hit the power button to turn off his phone. He tossed it on the nightstand. Lying back on his bed, he closed his eyes. His homecoming had been long overdue. It was a joyous time spent with his family, one he would've liked to share with Jayde. It was useless thinking about it. She wasn't there, nor would she ever be if he didn't find a way to make amends for deceiving her.

Agitated, Devon got up and headed downstairs to his father's study. He wasn't surprised to see the light still on. Knocking, he waited until his father bade him to enter. Devon shut the door behind him and took a seat across from his father's desk.

"About time you made it down here," said Sterling.

Devon stared at him. "You were expecting me?"

"I've known you all your life, son. No matter how many smiles you paste on that mug of yours, I always know when you've got troubles."

"You sound like Mom," Devon replied, stretching his legs out in front of him. He was thoughtful for a while. "It's the gallery, Dad."

"More mishaps?"

Devon nodded.

"This nonsense has gone on long enough, son. I know you wanted to handle this yourself, but it sounds like you're no closer to finding the SOB responsible for these incidents than you were weeks ago."

"I know," Devon admitted. "And this latest accident could've proved fatal. Jayde and I had barely cleared a set of track lights before they crashed to the floor."

"What?" Sterling bellowed. "Devon, I think it's time you filled me in—on everything."

Thirty minutes later, Sterling was barely controlling his anger. He snatched a piece of notepaper from his desk drawer, wrote a few lines, and handed the paper to his son. "There are several numbers here. You're to call all of them. The first is my buddy at the police department. I want you to tell him what's been going on and see what he suggests. The second number is for a private investigator friend of mine. He can use his contacts to help you get a surveillance system installed at the gallery. You need to ensure the front and rear entrances are monitored as well. You have an alarm system, don't you?"

"Yes."

"Do you arm it?"

"Of course, it's armed."

"Then how is anyone able to get in and set up these mishaps?" asked Sterling.

"Dad, if I knew that, I'd have solved this mystery a long time ago."

"Someone at the gallery is an accomplice."

"I know. The question is, who?"

They went over several theories before Devon decided to call it a night. "Thanks for the phone numbers."

"You're welcome. I want you to call them, Dev. We need to turn up the heat on this before someone gets hurt."

"I agree," Devon said tiredly.

"Sorry about your girlfriend. I hope it works out for you, son. You deserve to be happy. That's all your mother and I want for you."

"I know. She makes me happy, Dad. That is, when she's talking to me."

After Devon left, Sterling ran a hand over his eyes. His son was embroiled in quite a mess. Picking up the phone, Sterling dialed a telephone number. When the line connected, he leaned back in his chair. "I'd like to speak with Detective Calvert please."

When Devon got back to his room, he went straight to the bathroom. Turning the shower knob all the way to the left, he stripped while waiting for the water temperature to rise just short of boiling. The searing heat felt soothing to his overwrought nerves. He breathed deeply, clearing his mind of everything except the moment. He would find a way to get things back on track—with Jayde and the gallery. He had to.

Jayde and Christy spent their last night in Italy at Paolo's villa. They enjoyed a wonderful meal of lamb cooked with roasted potatoes, vegetables, and freshly baked focaccia prepared by Paolo. Glass of wine in hand, Jayde toured his land one last time. Words couldn't describe the natural, unaltered beauty of Lazio. She closed her eyes and inhaled the air around her, committing the land, the house, and all she'd seen to memory.

"You seem to have enjoyed your stay."

Jayde smiled but didn't turn around. "It was just what I needed. I'm glad I came."

"As am I, *bella*. Are you ready to go home?" asked Paolo.

Jayde was thoughtful for a moment. She turned to face him. "As ready as I can be. I don't know how it'll be when

I get home, when I see Devon again . . . after all that's transpired between us, but I'm sure I'll be fine."

"Of that I have no doubt. You're a survivor, Jayde. Never question your ability to brave life and love, under any circumstances."

She hugged her friend, took a final look at the countryside, and then, with determined steps, strode back to the house.

CHAPTER 26

"Make way for the greatest soccer champ of all time," Devon shouted, entering the house from the breezeway connecting the garage. "Mitchell Thomas scored the final shot that won the game."

"Congratulations, Master Mitchell," Selby remarked. "I'd say this calls for celebratory sundaes."

"All right!" Mitchell and Jetta chorused.

Devon set his nephew down. No sooner had Mitchell's feet hit the ground than he and his sister were running at breakneck speed to the kitchen.

"Slow down," Melanie called after her children.

"You and Devon were the same way," Avalon reminded her. "You two would always bolt through the door after a game, requesting Selby's special sundaes."

"Whether you'd won or lost," Sterling added.

"Race you to the kitchen?" Devon asked his sister.

"You're on," Melanie challenged.

The two took off running, each determined to win. They almost collided as they rounded a corner. Before they even reached the kitchen, Selby, hearing the approaching commotion, was holding a white paper towel up to signal the winner.

"I won," Melanie screamed. "Did you guys see me? I beat your uncle Devon."

Her kids cheered her victory, scooting over on the banquette so their mother could squeeze in.

Selby handed Melanie and Devon a bigger version of his signature treat.

"No fair," Devon bellowed, pushing in next to Melanie. "You elbowed me in the ribs."

Melanie took a spoonful of her sundae. "All's fair in love and ice cream."

She maneuvered her spoon toward her brother's dessert. Devon used his utensil to block her. "Don't even think about it."

"I forgot to mention there was a large envelope delivered for you, sir. It's in the foyer," Selby said.

Wiping his mouth on a napkin, Devon stood. "Thanks, Selby." He took his bowl with him.

"Don't you dare get ice cream anywhere," his mother called after him.

"Uh-huh," Devon mumbled through a mouthful of sundae. Walking to the foyer table, he picked up the manila envelope and scanned the return address. It wasn't one he recognized. He shoved the envelope under his arm. "I'm going upstairs for a minute. I'll be back," he called out.

"Devon," his mother called back.

"I know, I know. Don't spill anything. Did you forget I'm a grown man?" he said, grousing.

"Did you forget I'm still your mother, and if you ruin my carpet, you'll answer to me?" Avalon called.

He couldn't help the laugh that escaped him at her stern warning. He walked up the stairs and into his

room and headed for the couch. He sat the sundae
down on the table and ripped the envelope open. He
retrieved the letter inside it. His expression went from
jovial to serious in a matter of seconds. He read the
letter again before tossing it on the table and dumping
the rest of the envelope's contents out. His face contorted with rage. Devon pushed the correspondence
aside and collapsed against the couch.

"It can't be."

Jayde arrived home on Saturday after many heartfelt
good-byes to Paolo and promises to return. She spent
the whole day Sunday in bed, jet lagged. When she woke
up, she grabbed some food, used the bathroom, and
begged her mother to keep Boomer another day before
going back to sleep. Eight hours later, Jayde awoke, ravenous. She headed to the kitchen to forage for food.
The selection was scant. She opted for a peanut butter
and strawberry preserves sandwich. She eyed the cur-
dled milk in her fridge with distaste, pushed the plastic
gallon jug aside, and retrieved a bottled water.

She sat at her dining-room table and thought about
going into the gallery the next day. Her thoughts drifted
back to her plane ride home. Jayde had convinced herself it was time to hear the rest of Devon's story. She
owed him the benefit of the doubt. Thankfully, a
partied-out, sleep-deprived, and hungover Christy had
been in no shape on the way home to bend her ear with
advice. After making her decision, Jayde had slept peacefully the rest of the flight.

Monday morning dawned. Jayde chose a pale green
Tahari bouclé suit jacket with a slim black bouclé skirt.
She stepped into black pumps. Jayde chose the silver

earrings and matching necklace she'd purchased in Italy to complete her ensemble. Her hair tumbled in riotous curls around her shoulders. Ready, she grabbed her keys and purse and headed confidently out the door.

The walk to the gallery from the parking lot gave Jayde the time she needed to gather her thoughts. *You can do this,* she told herself. *Go in there and listen to what he has to say. Hear his side of things, keep an open mind, and let him explain about his dead ex-girlfriend, or was it his fiancée and their unborn child? You love him, right? He is worthy of that love and won't do anything to screw it up.*

Once inside the gallery, Jayde took a deep breath. *The elevator is straight ahead. Come on, girl. You can do this.* Two conversations with herself later, the elevator swooshed shut.

Devon's door was closed, so she knocked. After a long pause, she heard his brusque reply to come in.

This is it. Cut him some slack, be open to his confession, then apologize for running out on him. Good plan, Jayde told herself.

Opening the door, she strode into the office. Devon was at his desk. Even though his face was down, she knew something was wrong. He wasn't wearing a suit. Devon always wore a suit. Instead, he had on a black silk shirt. She couldn't see his pants but wagered they were black.

When he raised his head, their gazes connected. He appeared ready to battle with Satan himself. His eyes were hard. Against his somber clothes, they glowed like molten steel. Devon's mouth was set in a thin, rigid line, and the shadows under his eyes made her wonder if he'd slept since the night of the gala.

"You look like crap," she told him.

"Thank you." Devon's eyes raked over her. His blatant scrutiny made Jayde blush. "Welcome back."

What's going on? Jayde thought. She wasn't stupid. She could see Devon was livid. She'd have to be in a coma not to notice his mood. Sitting, Jayde crossed her legs. "Thank you."

Devon leaned back in his chair. "How was your trip?"

"It was fine." She stopped. "How'd you know I'd gone out of town?"

"Your mother. She took great pleasure in not telling me where you'd gone. Just that you'd gone."

She shifted in her chair. "Oh."

"I tried calling you several times. You didn't return my calls."

"I mentioned in my voice mail that I wouldn't check my messages until returning."

Devon snapped his fingers. "Ah, yes. The infamous voice-mail message you left me at two o'clock in the morning, at work no less."

"I didn't want to talk to you."

His jaw ticked. "That was obvious. At the time I thought it was warranted, but that was before."

Jayde looked confused. "Before? Before what?"

"You haven't said yet where you went. Any particular reason why?"

"I needed to get away—from you. What would've been the point in telling you where I went? I needed time alone. To digest what I'd learned."

"You mean what you'd assumed. And were you alone while you were doing all that digesting?"

Jayde bristled. "Devon, where's this going? Why the inquisition?"

"You don't think I have a right to know where you went? You ran out of here like the hounds of hell were nipping at your heels. You wouldn't let me talk to you, try to explain my position. No, you just ran away in typical

Jayde fashion. Honestly, I should've seen it coming. Running seems to be your thing."

"That's not fair. I'd just been given the second shock of my life. Both times were because of you, I might add. I needed time to digest it all."

"That's bull. You played the judge and jury, finding me guilty before I even had a chance to defend myself."

"Could you blame me? I'd just had my whole world turned upside down in less than forty-eight hours. Everything I'd believed about you was a lie."

"I didn't lie to you about everything—and you know it," he snarled.

"How, Devon? How was I supposed to know? By blindly trusting you?" She sniggered. "Look where that got me last time."

Bolting to his feet, Devon leaned over the desk. "I can't believe you've got the gall to come in here talking about trust. You've been gone almost two weeks, without so much as a telephone call to let me know you were all right. I thought we meant more to each other than that. That we . . . I was the fool. But I see the big picture now."

She jumped up and bent over his desk, too. "You do? Great. Fill me in, because I don't have a clue what you're getting at."

Devon wrenched the manila envelope out of his top desk drawer. He threw it across the desktop.

Jayde yanked the envelope off the desk. When she tugged the contents out, her mouth dropped. With a shaky hand, Jayde leafed through a stack of photos. Almost her entire trip was documented in front of her—from Paolo's villa to their trip to Rome. Christy, Paolo, his friend, even Signora Capelli.

"You won't tell me where you went? Fine. I'll tell you.

Italy," he roared. "Party enough with your partner in crime, Gambrini?" Devon snatched a photo from her and shoved it under her nose. "Tell me, Jayde. Who's the slick dude in the photo with you? Is he another one of your cohorts sabotaging my gallery or your attempt to get back at me?"

Stunned by his accusations, Jayde could feel her eyes widen. "You . . . you had me followed?"

"No. I didn't have *you* followed," he stressed. "I had Gambrini followed, but lo and behold, an unexpected twist. Here you were, nice and cozy with the man I'm investigating. I'd say that was too convenient, wouldn't you?"

"He didn't do it. I've told you that from day one. Apparently, you were too paranoid to hear me."

"You're right," Devon shot back. "He didn't do it alone. He had help. Inside help—from you."

She quivered with indignation. "I had nothing to do with the mishaps here. Besides, you fingered the saboteur."

"The intern? Give me a break. Admit it. That idiot was just a scapegoat. You two were the real geniuses at work here."

"You're accusing me of plotting to bankrupt the place where I work? How stupid is that?"

Her tone was his undoing. He stomped around the desk and gripped her by the shoulders. "About as stupid as my trusting you'd accepted my being here. I believed you were finally working with me. I was a fool. I thought you cared about me and about what we shared. All along you were lying to my face."

Jayde wrenched herself out of his hold. She walked across the room. When she turned around, the battle line was drawn. "You fake. You talk to me about lying?

You've got the benchmark on it. I came here to give you a chance to explain how your ex-girlfriend or fiancée, or whatever she was, and your baby ended up dead."

His pained expression made her want to push the knife deeper. "You're right. I didn't give you the benefit of the doubt. I believed what that real estate developer guy told me was the truth. I did run to get away from you, because I was confused and scared. I dunno. Maybe I was wrong to condemn you before listening to everything. But now . . . now I know I was a fool to believe in you—in us. I was out of my mind to think our initial reaction to each other should be ignored. I didn't trust you from day one, but I let my physical attraction to you blind me to the facts."

Getting in his face, Jayde pointed a finger at him. "You, Devon Mitchell, are the liar. I'm just glad you didn't get rid of me and make it look like an accident. I was insane to sleep with you or ever think I—"

"That's enough," he said menacingly.

Luckily, he'd stopped her before she'd confessed to loving him. She'd submit to invasive brain surgery before declaring her love for him.

"It'll never be enough," she fired back. "To top it all off, you're the biggest hypocrite I've ever met. I had to find out damaging information about you from some guy on the street with a grudge. Not from you, the man I'm involved with, but from a stranger."

"I was going to tell you. If you'll recall, I tried telling you, but as usual you ran. You couldn't take more enlightenment. You begged me to stop. Remember?"

"And you begged me to consider your side, to hear the truth. Now you have pictures you think say a thousand words."

"Don't they?"

"As usual, you're dead wrong. You spew accusations out of your rear end that are way off base, but do you give me a chance to explain or give you the truth? No. You draw your own caveman conclusions, and they're ridiculous. Now who's trying to be judge and jury?"

"Then, by all means, set me straight. Tell me, Jayde. What's the real reason you were in Italy?"

"I told you. To clear my head."

"So you say."

"I think you're . . ." At a loss for words, Jayde threw her hands up. "Forget it."

"There's something you're not telling me. I can feel it."

Arms crossed, Jayde remained silent.

Devon's eyes glinted. "It appears we're at an impasse."

She shrugged. "I don't have anything else to say."

"Maybe you don't, but I do. I need loyal people by my side, not ones who hide behind lies and subterfuge."

Jayde snorted. "Look who's talking."

"I've had enough deception to last me a lifetime. I won't have anyone working for me or in my life that I can't trust. You're fired."

Jayde did a double take. "Did you say fired?"

"Fired."

"Don't bother. I quit."

"You can't quit. I just fired you."

"Watch me." Livid and needing to hit something, Jayde was about to leave when he grabbed her arm.

"If you promise to end the attempts to close my gallery, I won't press charges."

The slap she delivered to his face echoed through the entire room, then back again. She took sardonic pleasure in seeing her handprint emblazoned on his reddening skin.

"You pompous, possibly murdering, devious, hypo-critical, lying jackass!" she screamed. "Stay away from me, or so help me, I'll get a restraining order."

Leaving, Jayde tried her best to slam the door so hard, it would break the glass. God must've been on her side of their heated argument, because she hadn't gotten two feet when she heard the telltale crack, then the shattering of the glass in his door.

Later that afternoon, Devon sat eyeing the brown paper covering his glassless office door. Leaning back in his chair, he stared at the ceiling. For the second time in a year, his world had spiraled out of control. Devon lowered his head on the desk. Skin connected with glossy paper. He opened his eyes, focusing on what he'd laid his head on. The offensive photos again sent him over the edge. With a string of curses, he snatched them off his desk and flicked his wrist, sending the photos sailing across the room.

Images of Jayde laughing and smiling with Paolo Gambrini went fluttering to the floor. His stomach tightened viciously. The need to take his aggressions out on something was overwhelming. He scanned the contents of his room and spotted an empty trash can. Devon moved in for the kill. Grasping either side of the can, Devon brought his hands together until the metal collapsed. He threw the misshapen receptacle across the room. It gave him no pleasure. An acrid taste filled his mouth. He'd been duped—again.

CHAPTER 27

Xavier looked down at the piece of paper. "This is it." He found a parking space reserved for guests on the side of the building. He climbed out of his rented car, then used one of its windows to check his appearance. Satisfied, Xavier walked down the sidewalk to the front of the building. He pulled the outer door open and walked into the foyer. He perused the last names on the metal mailboxes, found the one he was looking for, and pressed the button.

After a second, a woman's voice answered, "Who is it?"

"It's me. Xavier."

"Xavier Taggert?"

"One and the same."

There was a long pause before she spoke again. "What are you doing here?"

"I . . . uh . . . came to talk to you."

"I can't imagine what for."

"Jayde, while I love the repartee over the speaker, I can't help but wonder if you're going to let me in, or do we converse through this box on the wall for the next fifteen minutes?"

After another long pause, the buzzer sounded. Xavier hauled the heavy door open and stepped into the large foyer. He walked down the hall to Jayde's door. It was opened before he had a chance to knock on it. "Hi."

"Hello again," she replied.

When she stood back, Xavier breezed through the door. Shutting it firmly behind him, he looked around. "Nice place."

"Thanks. Can I get you anything?" Jayde asked out of habit.

"No, I'm cool."

Jayde offered him a seat. "I'm a bit surprised to find you on my doorstep. I didn't even know you were in town, much less that you knew where I lived."

Xavier shrugged and sat down. "I'm resourceful. I take it I'm the last person you expected to see."

"Actually, it's more like second to the last." She sat on the couch almost a person's length away from him. "No offense, but what are you doing here?"

"None taken. I came to check on you. To see how you were."

This time Jayde shrugged. "You mean since Devon and I had the big blowup two days ago, where he fired me and I quit?"

"You don't say. That I didn't know."

"It's no big deal. I'm fine. Never better. I've put it behind me. I'm moving on with my life."

A laugh escaped his lips. "It's been two days."

"So? Where's it written how long it's customary to wait before moving on?"

"Uh, nowhere."

The silence was awkward.

"I thought you left town," she said.

"I did, but recent developments prompted me to return."

"Recent developments? Like what?"

Something like you and Devon parting ways."

"I'm not anyone's opportunity."

"Boy, you don't mince words, do you?" Xavier replied, taking her hand and bringing it to his warm lips. "I like that in a woman."

Jayde removed her hand from his grasp. "You're a charmer, Mr. Taggert."

"I'd hoped you'd think so."

Jayde went into the kitchen to make herself a cup of tea. "I don't believe you'd come all this way to inquire about my state of mind."

Jayde grabbed the sugar from off the counter. Measuring a spoonful, she dumped it into her ceramic cup. She was just about to get the cream out of the fridge when Xavier appeared in the doorway.

"Not exactly. I thought you'd be interested in joining me for dinner tonight."

His stealthy arrival had startled her, but not as much as his dinner invitation. "Why would you think that?"

"Why not? I'm charming, the perfect gentleman." He winked. "Not bad on the eyes."

Ignoring his not-so-subtle observation, Jayde poured steaming water into her cup. "Not modest, I see."

"You're right, I'm not. Tell me what else you see."

Jayde blew on her tea. She observed him with a practiced eye. "Honestly?"

Leaning against the doorjamb, Xavier folded his arms across his chest. "Critique away."

"You're a suave, good-looking man who has an air about him, like you're used to getting your own way. The way you carry yourself, it's obvious you're used to being noticed, too. You're intelligent and witty. You're as tall as Devon and just as good-looking. Actually, there are similarities between you two. You both have dark hair, a bronzed complexion, and dimples. Unlike Devon, your eyes are the color of warm sherry, and you're not afraid to use them."

"To get what I want?" he asked.

"Your words, not mine."

Moving away from the doorjamb, Xavier crowded her. "What about to get *who* I want?"

"I'm not on the market, Mr. Taggert."

"You never answered my question," he continued. "Have dinner with me."

She backed up a few inches. "You're asking me on a date, and you don't see why I'd refuse? I'm involved with the man that's supposed to be your best friend. You've known each other since college. Doesn't that mean anything to you?"

"Correction. *Were* involved. By your own admission, that was two whole days ago, surely enough time for you to be completely over him. Besides, Dev and I are the best of friends. We share everything." He ran his finger down her cheek, then to her shoulder. "You should ask him about our college days. There wasn't much we didn't share back then."

His laugh echoed around the small kitchen. It wasn't an endearing sound. Jayde flicked his finger off her shoulder. "This isn't college, Mr. Taggert. I'm not a besotted groupie who can't see past your profile, and I don't play both sides against the middle—ever. So you can take your suaveness and charm and go drape them over some other woman's shoulders, because I'm not interested."

"Fascinating. Are you really that attracted to Devon.

or did you finally find out how many zeros come after his name?"

Recoiling, she took a step back. Her face mirrored her disgust. "You really are a piece of work. I find it inconceivable that Devon could actually consider you a friend. I'll wager he'll think twice when I inform him of our *stimulating* conversation."

Faster than she could blink, Xavier hauled her up against his chest. His embrace was as unyielding as granite. Backing her against the refrigerator, Xavier moved suggestively against her with his body. "I wouldn't suggest doing that. I'd hate to harm this beautiful body, but I would if I had to. No, I don't think it would be wise to tell Devon about our little tête-à-tête. It could prove harmful—for all concerned. My best friend owes me something, and I intend to collect my payment in full. So if I were you, I'd keep that pretty little mouth shut. It would be a shame if anything unforeseen happened, wouldn't it?"

In an instant, she was released. Jayde watched in disbelief as he blew her a kiss before letting himself out. She felt cold, then burning hot. She couldn't help the shiver that climbed up her spine. What just happened?

Her gaze traveled to where her dog was usually lying. Christy had taken Boomer for a walk while Jayde searched the Internet for a new job. "I wish you were here, boy. You could've bitten the arrogant SOB in his overinflated behind." Eyeing the phone, Jayde felt an overwhelming urge to call Devon.

"What would I say? 'Hi, Devon. I hate you, you're a creep, and guess what? So is your friend'?" she said aloud. "How about 'Hi, Trouser Snake. I know I'm not supposed to be talking to you, but I thought you'd like to know your supposed best friend just made a pass at me and threatened my life—and yours.'" *Great! That sounds unbelievable, too,* she told herself.

The whole encounter had freaked her out. When Christy opened the front door, Jayde screamed at the top of her lungs. Boomer lunged into the room, barking, with his teeth bared. He pulled Christy behind him. By the time they reached Jayde, she'd whipped out her pepper spray.

"What! What's the matter?" cried Christy.

"Sorry," Jayde said sheepishly. "You scared me."

Christy put her hand up to her heart. "I scared *you?* Girl, you scared *me.* You knew I was out with the dog. Who else has a key to your condo?"

"Nobody. It wasn't that. I just thought you were somebody else, that's all." Jayde removed Boomer's leash and petted him reassuringly. She reached down and picked up his water dish and filled it with water.

Christy scrutinized Jayde. "Something's wrong. You're all pasty, not to mention the wild look in your eyes. What happened while I was gone?"

"Nothing. Well, not exactly nothing. Devon's friend Xavier showed up."

"Come again?"

"He said he'd heard what happened, so he stopped by to see how I was doing."

Christy waited for Jayde to elaborate. When that didn't happen, she spoke. "I can tell that isn't the whole story."

"No, it isn't." Jayde walked over to the window and stared at the trees outside her patio. Her voice was barely audible. "He made a pass at me and then threatened to harm me if I told Devon about it."

"You're lying!" Christy stepped back. "That nasty creep."

"Tell me about it. I didn't know what to do. Especially since when I rejected his offer, he got—"

"He got what?"

"He turned a bit mean."

"Did he hurt you? I'm calling the police." Christy stormed to the phone.

Running over, Jayde put herself between her friend and the telephone. "Don't. There's no reason to call the cops."

"Like hell, there isn't. That pervert made a pass at you and then threatened you. I think that's one reason too many why we should have his sorry butt arrested for harassment."

"Let's just forget it happened. I've been through enough this week. I don't want to add filing a police report to the laundry list of disasters in my life."

"Okay, we'll do it your way for now, but if the millionaire's wingman gets out of hand again, I'm going straight to the authorities, no matter how much you protest," said Christy. "Trust me, I know from experience never to discount crazy people, no matter how good they look."

Jayde was pensive.

"I've got an idea. How about I spend the night and we have a good old-fashioned girls' night? I'll make margaritas, we'll fondue something, or better still, we'll make nachos," Christy offered. "Then we'll do our nails, wear pajamas with the feet in them, and watch *The Original Kings of Comedy*. Now if that doesn't cheer you up, I don't know what will."

"Sounds great, but I don't want you feeling obligated to baby-sit me. I'm a grown woman. I can take care of myself."

Christy stood her ground. "You'd better take me up

on this offer, girl. I don't make my signature margaritas for just anyone. Whoever I make them for, we gotta go way back. I mean way, way, way back."

"Okay, I get it," Jayde said, giggling. "Yes, we'll have girls' night. If you don't mind, just not tonight."

"Suit yourself," Christy remarked, hugging her. "If you need anything, call me, okay?"

Jayde saw her friend out and then double-locked the door behind her. Going back into the living room, she flopped on the couch. Boomer immediately sidled up next to the couch to lean on her leg. Petting his coat made her feel better. Jayde recalled Xavier's threat. He'd meant what he said, of that much she was sure. He wouldn't hesitate to do her bodily harm. Worse still, Jayde knew if she involved Devon, it could have ramifications. She might be mad at Devon, and he might not be worthy of her love, but she wouldn't do anything to cause him harm. If Xavier got out of line again, she'd find a way to deal with him—on her own.

Thinking about Devon, she wondered what he owed Xavier. More importantly, how long would it be before Xavier decided to collect that debt?

With no word from Devon, Jayde went about her business as usual, except for one fact: she didn't have a job. It wasn't from a lack of offers. Over the last week, she'd gone on several interviews at local galleries. Walking around the state-of-the-art spaces, Jayde hadn't felt the connection she'd felt at the Wells Gallery. There, she'd felt an almost tangible energy flowing throughout the old building. It had beckoned her, inspired her, giving her a sense of well-being and purpose. Her bond with the Wells Gallery had been established long before Devon arrived. It hadn't been a job. It had been equivalent to a vacation. She'd enjoyed making a difference in people's lives and affecting the community in a positive way.

Setting their individual differences aside, Jayde and Devon had concentrated on the gallery, not their animosity. Eventually, neither could deny they made a good team.

Thoughts of Devon were driving her crazy. She was still angry with him, but she'd be flat-out lying if she didn't admit to missing him. Firing her notwithstanding, Jayde couldn't keep erotic images of Devon out of her mind. Though the sexual aspect of their relationship had been brief, it had been explosive. He'd awakened a long-dormant passion in her. Now that it had resurfaced, the craving refused to be denied. Longing kept her up at night, making her restless.

Tired of pining for him, Jayde decided to get out of the house. She changed into a gray and pink running suit and hooked the leash to Boomer's collar. "I know you just went out, sweetie, but this can't wait." She slipped into a pair of white cross-trainers. Her purse and dog in tow, Jayde took the elevator down to the parking garage. Jayde decided a trip to her parents' house was in order. She took the scenic route through Rock Creek Park to get there.

Purposely ignoring Sixteenth Street, she exited at Military Road. *Don't need to get too close to his house,* she thought. There was no need to tempt her self-control that much.

Elated to see her, her mother hugged her fiercely while pulling her into the house. "What a nice surprise. I was beginning to wonder if you'd forgotten you had parents."

Jayde followed her mom to the kitchen. She reached

for a banana and then sat at the table. "As if I could. Sooner or later you'd call to remind me of my transgression."

"Fair enough." Her mother laughed. "I see you brought the horse. You should've seen the trouble I had keeping this house free of dog hair. I almost burned out the engine on my vacuum."

"Trust me, I appreciate you watching Boomer while I was in Italy, Mom. I really didn't want to leave him at a kennel for that long."

"I wish you'd let me fix you something more filling than that banana."

"No thanks," Jayde replied between bites. "Where's Dad?"

"Golfing," her mother called over her shoulder.

Retrieving a plastic container from the refrigerator, Harriette spread butter on leftover biscuits before warming them in the oven.

"Mom, I'm not that hungry," Jayde protested.

When the timer went off, Harriette pulled the biscuits out of the oven, put them on a plate, and set it in front of her daughter. Then she retrieved strawberry preserves and milk from the fridge. "I know, dear."

The aroma of homemade biscuits wafted through the air. Targeting Jayde's nose, the tantalizing smell overrode her protests. Her stomach growled.

"What were you saying, dear?"

"Nothing." Jayde smiled, shaking her head at her mother's foresight. Sliding the plate closer, Jayde picked up the nearest biscuit, then slathered preserves on it. As she bit off a section of the circular piece of ecstasy, she rolled her eyes heavenward.

Two biscuits later, they adjourned to the family room. Once settled on the couch, they brought each other up to speed on recent events. Harriette was in awe hearing about her daughter's Roman holiday. By having her digital pictures converted to printed photos, Jayde made it easier for her mother to envisage the places she and Christy had visited.

"I'm so glad you got away for a while. After the gallery fiasco, you were right to put some distance between you and Casanova."

"Mom," Jayde protested.

"Don't even think about defending that man," her mother warned.

"I'm not defending him."

"I can't believe the arrogance—the temerity—that man has. You know, he actually called here, expecting me to just tell him where you went. Oh, I told him all right. I told him he should learn to treat his employees with respect. I swear, it felt incredible when I hung up on his—"

"Mother," Jayde interrupted, "you actually hung up on him?"

"He's lucky that's all I did. I really wish you'd find another job and just be done with him. "

Jayde looked at her mother. "Funny you should mention that."

Jayde filled her mother in on the latest development at the Wells Gallery. Harriette was so incensed about Jayde's firing/quitting, she bounded out of her chair. It took three minutes before Jayde could get a word out.

"I can't believe what I'm hearing. When did this happen?" Harriette asked.

"Over a week ago."

"You've known about this for a week, and you're just now telling me?"

"Mom," Jayde said, groaning, "it's not a big deal. I can handle it."

Finally, her mother sat, but she was still pensive. "I can't believe that man had the audacity to fire you."

"It wasn't actually a firing. It was more like I quit."

"I don't give a flying fudge what it was. If he thinks we're going to take this lying down, he's crazy! I'm going to talk with our family lawyer. Surely we can sue him for a hostile work environment, unlawfully terminating employment, sexual harassment—"

"Whoa, Mom," said Jayde, finally interrupting her mother's tangent. "First of all, I'm not suing him. Secondly, anything sexual that occurred wasn't harassment, trust me." Her eyes glazed over. "If anything it was—"

"Jayde Elizabeth Seaton, I do not need vivid details of your in flagrante delicto," Harriette said, admonishing her daughter. "It didn't take long to figure out there was more going on between you two than paintings. I don't need a visual."

Blushing, Jayde quickly changed the subject.

A few hours later her father returned home. Jayde decided to stay for dinner and spend more time with her family. Harriette insisted that she take the leftovers home. As she was leaving, Jayde assured her mother she'd be fine.

Jayde parked in the underground garage. Balancing her purse and the doggie bag, and leading Boomer, she walked slowly through the basement security door to the elevator. After hitting the button for her floor with her elbow, she stood back. Once they were in the elevator, Boomer started growling and circling her in the confined space. The closer they got to their floor, the louder his growling became.

Jayde looked at him in surprise. "Easy, Boomer. It's okay, boy," she soothed.

She struggled to hold his leash while keeping everything else in her arms, which turned out to be a juggling act. When the elevator door opened, Boomer bolted into the hallway. The things in Jayde's arms went crashing to the hall floor. "Boomer, come!" Jayde commanded. She gathered up her things and trailed after her dog. All the people standing around brought Jayde up short.

What's going on? she wondered. Upon further inspection she realized they were standing in front of her door.

She recognized a few of her neighbors. One neighbor looked scared, another angry, while a third looked sorry. She hurried past them to get to her door. The first thing that hit her was that it was ajar. "Boomer," she cried out, frantically following. She was brought up short by a man in uniform.

"Just a minute, miss. Is this your condo?"

"Yes, it is. I need to get my dog."

"Your name?"

"Jayde. Jayde Seaton."

"May I see your identification?"

She pulled her driver's license out and handed it to him. "Now can you let me in?" she replied, trying to get around him.

"Sorry, ma'am, but I had to check. I'm Officer Harris. It appears you've had a break-in. Your neighbor called nine-one-one after hearing a loud disturbance outside her door. Whoever did this was long gone by the time we arrived. I'm sorry, Miss Seaton, but they did a thorough job on the place. Eventually, we'll need you to tell us if there's anything missing for the police report. We'll, uh, give you some time."

She entered her home and skidded to a halt, gasping. The whole first floor of her home has been turned upside down. Nothing had been left undisturbed or in its original place. "Boomer," she choked out. Jayde saw his head poke out; then her dog crawled out from under the table. Her heart tightened as she watched him cautiously maneuver around the devastation to come to her side.

Sinking to her knees, Jayde wrapped her arms around the nervous dog. He whined and licked her face. "Oh, sweetie, it's okay," she cooed into his ear. Boomer placed his head in the crook of her neck and went still. Jayde gave him a reassuring squeeze. "It's going to be fine."

Several officers came down the stairs from the second floor. When they saw her, they discreetly filed out the front door.

On wobbly legs, Jayde climbed the stairs. She entered her guest room first. Seeing the destruction there made her stomach cramp. The first thing that came to mind was that what she'd told her dog was wrong. It wasn't fine. It would never be fine again. The timeworn cuckoo clock her grandfather had given her was lying on its side, cracked in half. Books were scattered all over the floor and the bed. Her Lladró figurines, given to her by her paternal grandmother, had either been shattered or had had their heads snapped off at the neck.

Everywhere Jayde looked, there was deliberate, concise obliteration. She eyed the wall separating the guest room from the master bedroom. Dread swirled around her like a harsh winter wind. Instinctively, she knew her personal haven would be much, much worse.

"I can't go in there," Jayde whispered aloud.

Sensing her distress, Boomer came up to her side

and placed his head under the palm of her hand. He lifted his head up so that she pet him.

"I know, boy. We have to go in there."

Jayde walked with slow steps toward the master bedroom. The door was partially closed. She took a deep breath. Her palm sweaty, Jayde gave the door a firm push.

A cry of anguish started slowly, building momentum as it traveled upward to her throat before eventually releasing itself from her lips. She collapsed just inside the door. Her back collided with the wall as she sank down to the carpet.

She eased her cell phone from her pocket. Numbly, she dialed her best friend. It seemed like an eternity before the phone was answered. With each passing second, Jayde's fragile hold on reality slid farther away.

"Ch-Chris?" she choked out.

"Jayde? Girl, you won't believe my day," Christy began, then stopped short. Dead silence traveled across the line. "Jayde? What's wrong?"

Try as she might, Jayde couldn't get a sound out of her mouth. She struggled to release a noise, a croak, anything, but nothing happened.

"You're scaring me, Jayde. What's wrong?"

"House."

"Huh? What about it? Honey, I don't understand."

"My house. Someone broke in. . . ." Jayde stopped. She couldn't get any more out.

"Are the police there?"

Jayde nodded. When her friend asked again and louder, she realized she hadn't answered. "Yes."

"Jayde, listen to me. Stay put. Don't leave, no matter how bad it is. Wait for me to get there, okay?"

"I can't. . . ."

"Jayde, don't move. I promise you I'm on my way."

CHAPTER 28

They'd saved the best for last. The master bedroom had been given extra attention. The burglars had spared no expense when invading her privacy. If they'd wanted to humiliate her, they'd succeeded. Clothes ripped from the closet had been tossed everywhere. Lingerie from every drawer had been cut into pieces. The mattress and box spring were across the room, with as much care given to destroying them as the bed linens. In the bathroom, toiletries had been dumped in the bathtub. Shattered glass was everywhere. Not a square inch of the room was devoid of debris. Unable to process the destruction in its entirety, she slogged through the chaos to the window.

Jayde simply stood there. Outside it looked so peaceful, the breeze calmly swaying the trees. The moonlight cast a glimmer onto the Potomac River. It was serene. Hearing the distinctive horn of the *Odyssey* in the background, she wondered if the ship was coming in or going out on its dinner cruise.

"Jayde?"

She heard her name being called but didn't turn

around. If she did, she'd see the devastation that was once her home.

It was almost as if a hurricane had blown through, destroying everything in its path. Was this how people felt when it happened—when their world was crushed by natural disaster? *Raw. Vulnerable.*

"Jayde."

There it was again. This time the voice was urgent. It implored her. She glanced over her shoulder toward the door. Devon filled the doorway, his expression one she'd never seen before. Their eyes locked.

"It's gone," she whispered. "Everything . . . is gone."

"I know."

She continued to stare at him. "Why are you here?"

"Christy called me."

Christy. Her steadfast friend. "Where is she?"

"Downstairs. We arrived about the same time. The police said it was okay for us to come in. They've already dusted for fingerprints. She's downstairs tidying up," he said, rambling. He didn't care how he sounded. She needed time to process the carnage. He did, too.

When she remained silent, he spoke again. "Jayde, you can't stay here."

Gazing around, she smiled remorsefully. "I know."

"Have you called your parents?"

She shook her head. "I'm not ready for that yet. Later."

Devon moved toward her and stopped. He didn't touch her. "Jayde, please come home with me. You shouldn't be alone. Not now."

Rubbing her shoulders, she realized how cold she was. "I can go to Christy's house."

"I realize that, but . . ." Devon's voice faltered. "I'm to blame."

"That's not true."

"I don't think this was a random act. Someone is sending a message. It's clear this was about the gallery."

Slowly, her wits were returning. Jayde couldn't fathom that her house being trashed was about the gallery. Suddenly, Xavier's threat came to mind. Could he have done this? She hadn't said anything to Devon about Xavier, to protect him. Maybe Xavier didn't believe she'd keep quiet and was trying to scare her into silence.

Before Jayde could think on it more, Christy poked her head in. Seeing Jayde's room brought tears to her eyes. Approaching her friend, Christy embraced her. "Hey, girl."

Jayde's eyelids drifted closed. She shuddered. "Thanks for coming."

"Like I wouldn't," said Christy.

"Oh, Chris, it's a mess," Jayde moaned.

"Yeah, it is, but don't worry. We'll fix it," Christy said, staring at Devon. "All of it."

Devon returned Christy's gaze. Her frank stare was meant to remind him of the animosity between Jayde and him. He got it. "I've asked Jayde to come home with me. I realize she could stay with you, but this mess is my fault. I'd feel better if I could keep an eye on her."

Christy studied her friend's face. "Whatever you decide is what we'll do."

"Could you give me a minute?" asked Jayde.

Both agreed and reluctantly left her alone.

She knocked the debris off a nearby chair and sat down. Placing her head in her hands, Jayde thought about her options. She knew it'd be less of a strain if she stayed at Christy's house, but part of her wanted to go with Devon. She felt a tangible pull in his direction. When she considered the blowup they'd had, she realized her response was baffling. But his concern was genuine. She could tell it wasn't a contrivance. His eyes had told her he meant every word. Devon wanted her to come home with him. Deep down Jayde wanted to go.

With her decision made, she searched in the closet for luggage. Thankfully, all its contents hadn't been destroyed. Finding her overnight bag, Jayde grabbed it, then stopped. There wasn't anything that hadn't been touched by some maniac. With tears in her eyes, she dropped the small bag and went downstairs.

The moment her foot hit the landing, Boomer rushed to her side.

She lowered herself to his level and wrapped her arms around his neck. She stayed like that for some time before standing to look at her friends. "I'll go with Devon."

Christy came to her side. "That's fine." She squeezed her hand. "Would you like me to take Boomer with me?"

Jayde shook her head. "I think he needs to stay with me. We'll both feel better." She turned to Devon. "Is that all right?"

He smiled reassuringly. "Of course." Seeing no bags, Devon asked, "Is there anything you'd like to take with you?"

Jayde's lip quivered. "No. There isn't anything that hasn't been—"

"Don't worry," he interrupted. "I've got everything you need. I'll go get Boomer's stuff." Devon started to walk away, then stopped. "Where is Boomer's stuff?"

The consternation on his face made Jayde smile. "His doggy bed was by the patio door," she said, pointing. "It could be anywhere now. His toys and food were in the cabinet to the left of the fridge."

Devon nodded. "I'll check it out."

When they were alone, Christy turned to Jayde. "Sweetie, are you sure about the arrangements?"

"Yes. Boomer and I will be fine."

Removing her purse from around the bathroom doorknob, Christy gave her a final hug. "Call me if you need me. No matter what time it is."

"I will."

Soon after Christy left, Devon returned with a plastic bag holding the only items of Boomer's that were undamaged. "There's not much left. We've got some food and two toys. The bed isn't salvageable."

"Thank you."

Finding Boomer's leash, he called the dog. Surprisingly, Boomer left Jayde and carefully made his way through the debris to Devon's side. Praising him, Devon attached his leash securely. He extended his left hand to Jayde. "Ready?"

Slipping her hand in his, she nodded. "Yes."

Thankfully, there wasn't anyone left in the hallway. Her neighbors had returned to their homes. All was quiet outside. Devon helped Jayde settle in the front seat of his father's Range Rover before escorting Boomer and his accoutrements to the back. "Officer Harris left a card with his contact information. We'll need to give the police a list of anything that's been stolen."

Her gaze traveled to her building. Her thoughts centered on her disarrayed apartment. Tears trickled down her face.

Devon slipped into the driver's seat of the Range Rover. Oblivious to her surroundings, Jayde was unaware he'd gotten into the truck. She jumped when he touched her shoulder. At Jayde's panicked expression, Devon immediately apologized.

"I'm sorry I scared you. We'll get through this," Devon assured her. "I promise."

Jayde didn't trust her voice, so she simply nodded. Guiding the truck away from the curb, Devon headed home.

When they were close, he glanced at the clock on the dashboard. "CVS is still open. Would you like to stop to pick up some toiletries?"

Not up to a crowd, she declined. "I'll use whatever you have."

"Fair enough. I'm sure between my mom and Melanie, we have whatever you need for tonight. We can go shopping in the morning if you feel like it."

The rest of the drive was done in silence, each caught up in personal thoughts. By the time Devon opened the garage door, Jayde was asleep.

"We're here," he said quietly.

Opening her eyes, Jayde stretched. "When did I fall asleep?"

"Somewhere in Rock Creek Park. You can go in. The alarm isn't armed. I kinda left in a hurry. I'll take Boomer out back. I'm sure he has to go by now."

She entered the house. She walked straight through the kitchen to the family room. She sat on the couch and turned on the lamp on the side table next to the couch. She put her feet under her. The room was warm and inviting. Taking a few deep breaths, she attempted to relax.

Boomer bounded into the room, heading straight to his owner. She ran her fingers over his head. Within seconds he left her side to roam around, sniffing everything in sight.

"Getting acclimated, I suppose?" said Devon as he entered the family room.

"Uh-huh. I can see he feels at home already."

"I hope so." His gaze included Jayde. "I hope his mommy feels at home, too."

Jayde patted the seat next to her. "I do."

Devon sat down, then turned sideways on the couch. Hesitantly, he ran a finger under the dark lines circling her eyes.

"How can I thank you for coming to my rescue? You and Christy are wonderful," said Jayde.

"Don't even try. I don't need your thanks. Making sure you're safe and sound is my priority."

Awkward silence wafted through the room. Unable to take it, Jayde was the first to speak. "So, are we going to mention the big gray elephant in the room, or are we going to act like it's not here?"

Devon was thoughtful. "I acknowledge that it's here, but I don't think either of us is in any shape to discuss it. Not tonight. I suggest we get some sleep. It's been an emotional evening—for both of us. How about we talk tomorrow, after we've rested?"

The word *sleep* made her yawn. "Sounds like a plan."

Standing, Devon held out his hand.

Biting her lip, she placed her hand in his. *What am I getting myself into?* she asked herself. Realizing they hadn't even broached the subject of sleeping arrangements, Jayde worried about the hasty decision to spend the night.

After Devon checked the doors, he turned off the lights and then set the alarm. He pulled her behind him up the long staircase. Boomer happily followed.

Jayde's face registered her surprise when Devon stopped in front of a door she knew wasn't his.

Perceptively, he rubbed her arm. "Under the circumstances, I thought the guest room would be best."

She looked at her shoes. "I wasn't sure . . . I mean, I didn't want you to—"

Devon tilted her chin until their eyes connected. "Jayde, I didn't ask you here to take advantage of the situation. I wanted you to stay because I think this is the safest place for you. We can talk about where we stand later. Deal?"

"I didn't think you'd take advantage of me," she added quickly. "I just didn't . . . The last time we saw each other, we didn't part on the best of terms. It's a little awkward."

A troubled expression crossed his face. "Jayde, you do know I'd never hurt you, don't you?"

"Of course."

He expelled the breath he'd been holding. "I'm glad. Besides, we've been through too much for there to be any discomfort between us." He winked.

Jayde smiled. *Chivalry is not dead.*

Devon opened the door, then stood aside while she entered. He flipped the wall switch, bathing the room in soft light. "This is my sister, Melanie's room when she's in town. I know she leaves stuff here, so let's see if we can find you something to put on."

Despite her anxiety, his smile made her stomach flutter.

Walking to the closet, Devon studied its contents, while Jayde looked around.

Melanie's room was a soft yellow. Her furniture was white, with a queen-size wrought-iron bed dominating the room. Spacious, the room had a desk and love seat in the corner, plus a three-drawer dresser, an armoire, and two nightstands. The bed linens were a green, yellow, and purple floral pattern. They complemented the muted green chenille love seat, with purple and yellow throw pillows.

"There's a television in the armoire, in case you want it. A stereo system pipes music through the house. The console is on the wall near the door. I think I've got it on a jazz station. If you want to listen to something else, just let me know and I'll change it."

"I'm sure I won't be awake for long, but thanks."

"I found a few choices for you." He grinned. Devon held up a lavender cotton nightgown, some blue striped cotton pants with a white cotton camisole, and a red silk nightshirt that buttoned down the front.

"I think I'll go with the pants and top."

Handing her the pajamas, Devon returned the others to the closet. He showed her to the bathroom and opened the medicine cabinet. Finding an unopened toothbrush, he handed it to her. "I'll go get toothpaste."

When he returned, he was holding an unwrapped basket from Bath & Body Works, containing shower gel, body cream, and body spray. "Look what I found in my parents' linen closet." Devon removed the plastic surrounding the basket. He scrunched his nose while reading the label. "Cotton Blossom?"

"Don't laugh. It smells really good."

"Right," he drawled.

Devon scanned the drawers under his sister's sink. He found some feminine toiletries and sprays. Dropping them immediately, he told Jayde she could explore those at her convenience—without him. Jayde realized all men were the same when it came to feminine hygiene products. They wanted no part of them. Refraining from comment, she followed him out of the bathroom.

"Is there anything you'd like from the kitchen before bed? I've got milk, orange juice, tea, soda, and bottled water, unless you're hungry."

"No, thanks. I'm fine."

"In that case, I'll bid you good night."

Scratching Boomer's head a few times, he smiled at Jayde before leaving. Once he was gone, she picked up the pajamas she'd chosen and headed to the bathroom for a much-needed shower.

While the water warmed up, Jayde undressed. She filled the sink with hot water before adding her bra and panties. She washed them with the liquid soap, wrung them out, and hung them on the towel rack to dry. Jayde found towels and washcloths in a small linen closet. She selected two fluffy yellow towels and one washcloth. Jayde wrapped her hair in one of the towels before easing into the shower. Once the water connected with her body, a moan escaped her lips. She squeezed the shower gel onto a bath sponge. Running it over her body, Jayde inhaled the feminine scent.

She took her time drying off, then lathered on body cream. Almost finished, she heard a knock. With the towel securely around her middle, Jayde went to answer the door.

They stared at each other.

Devon wore gray lounging pajamas with a matching robe; Jayde a towel. It took a few seconds for either of them to speak.

"Uh, I forgot to give you some toothpaste," he said shakily.

"Thanks," she replied, accepting the proffered tube.

She had trouble focusing on additional dialogue. He looked incredible and smelled even better. Rivulets of water occasionally slid down his face. Jayde fought the urge to follow the trails with her finger or to run her hands through his damp hair. Suddenly, it became way too hot for her towel. She'd been put through an emotional wringer that evening. She wasn't capable of sifting through the mess her life had become, yet her baser instincts were alert and fully functional. Her body was causing her a great deal of trouble.

Realizing she still hadn't said more, Jayde focused on a reply. "Thanks," she said again. She saw his eyes rake over her.

Devon swallowed. Hard. "You're welcome."

The awkward silence was back.

Finally, Devon moved away from the door. "Good night, Jayde."

"Good night, Devon. Sleep well."

When she closed the door, he spoke. "You're wrong, Jayde. It won't be a *good* night. It'll be a *long* night."

Sleep didn't come quickly, but eventually it did come. Then, in the middle of a vivid dream about Jayde, something woke Devon. Bolting upright in his bed, he was immediately alert. The first thing he realized was it was raining. He craned his ears. He scanned the dark room, his eyes adjusting to the lack of light. There wasn't anything out of place. That didn't matter. He sensed something wasn't right. *Jayde.*

He shoved the covers aside and slid out of bed. He hurried out of the room. Down the hall, he stood outside of her room, in the darkness. He leaned his ear against the entryway. He heard Boomer whining.

He opened the door as quietly as he could and eased into the room. Despite the darkness, Devon moved effortlessly toward her bed. He didn't know what he expected, but Jayde crying wasn't it. He was torn between giving her comfort or privacy. He turned to leave. Her choked plea stopped him.

"Don't go."

Devon was beside her bed in seconds. He sat on the edge of the bed. Gently, he eased her into his arms. It wasn't until she came willingly that he released the breath he'd been holding.

Jayde fought to hold herself in check. When she felt his hand slowly moving up and down her back, she lost the battle. His tenderness was her undoing. Unable to stem the flow of her tears, she gave in to them. Her body, racked by the force of her crying, shook violently against him.

He began rocking her. "It's all right, Jayde. I'm here."

Jayde wrapped her arms around his neck. "I'm sorry," she said, hiccuping. "I just . . . I lost everything."

"Not everything," Devon corrected. "The most important thing is you. Material things can be replaced. You're safe. That's all that matters." He held her tight until her body was spent. Devon picked Jayde up and walked toward the door. "Come on, Boomer," he called behind him. Jayde's dog followed suit. Once he got her to his room, Devon laid her down on his bed. He hoped the familiarity would calm her fears. He climbed in behind her and engulfed her with his arms. "You're safe, Jayde." Devon buried his face against the back of her neck. "I swear we'll find out who did this."

Jayde felt the imminent pull of sleep. She yawned and snuggled deeper into Devon. "I think I already know," she barely got out before drifting off.

His eyes popped open at her semiconscious admission. Staring into the darkness, Devon held her close. In the morning he and Jayde were going to have a long, long, much-needed talk.

CHAPTER 29

Devon awoke with a start. A loud, constant noise sounded in the distance. *Is that the alarm?* Sunlight streamed through his window. It was morning. He remembered his companion. He rolled over. He saw the indentation of Jayde's body, but no Jayde. No Boomer either. "Jayde?" he called out groggily. He got out of bed and staggered to the door and opened it. At the foot of the stairs was the keypad. He entered his code, and the shrill tone ceased. Jayde must've accidentally opened a window or door. Devon headed to Melanie's bedroom. He knocked softly before he turned the knob. He poked his head into the room. Empty.

He called her repeatedly but didn't get an answer. In the kitchen, Devon found a note on the granite countertop. He scanned it. Swearing, he balled it up and tossed it across the room before taking the stairs two at a time.

Ten minutes later . . .

Devon backed his father's Mercedes coupe out of the driveway. Shifting the gears, he revved the engine before popping the clutch. The tires squealed as the car accelerated, catapulting him down the street. Since Jayde had activated the alarm by opening the front door, he figured she wasn't that far ahead of him. All the cars were in the garage, so he figured she'd called a cab.

At this hour, Sunday morning traffic headed out of town was minimal. According to the note Jayde had left, she planned to stop by her condo before going to her beach house. For that reason alone, he would throttle her. She shouldn't face that devastation again without someone with her. *Without him.* Devon navigated his way down Sixteenth Street toward the southwest waterfront. She didn't have that much of a head start. Hopefully, he'd intercept her before too long.

Fifteen minutes later Devon turned down her street. Making a U-turn, he screeched to a halt outside her building. Jumping out, Devon ran around the car and up the stairs. Once inside, he pressed the button to buzz her condo. About the fifth time, he decided to give up. He was turning to leave when he heard the door open. He spun around to see an elderly woman.

"You looking for Jayde?" the woman asked.

Devon nodded.

"I've seen you a couple times. You her boyfriend?"

He didn't hesitate. "Yes."

"She's gone. Left a while ago like a bat out of . . . well, you know."

Despite being in a hurry, Devon smiled. "Thanks, Mrs. . . . ?"

"Just call me Ms. Patty."

"Thanks, Ms. Patty," he said, hurrying back to his car.

After dialing a number on his cell phone, Devon switched it to speaker. When a woman answered, he silently thanked God.

"Hello?"

"Christy, it's Devon."

"Is Jayde all right?"

"No. She left me a note this morning. She's headed to her beach house. I need to catch up to her."

"She called earlier," Christy informed him. "She said she'd be on the bay a few days to clear her head. She wouldn't give me details. Devon, what's going on?"

Annoyance crept across his face. "Your friend runs a lot. She spent the night at my house. She woke up crying early this morning. I thought I had calmed her down. I'd planned for us to talk things out this morning."

"What things?"

"Everything. I was hoping to get all our problems out on the table—Jayde, me, the accident, where we go from here."

"So why'd she leave? What did you do?"

"I didn't do anything," he snapped. "To paraphrase her note, she's absconding to her beach house. She doesn't want to deal with our relationship right now. She doesn't want to deal with her home being ransacked, either. I swear, the woman must be part ostrich. I guess she's looking for sand to bury her head in."

"So what can I do to help? If she's not ready to talk, I can't coerce her."

"I don't need you to convince her. I need the address."

Devon got the information. "Thanks, Christy."

"Don't make me regret it, Devon."

"I'll get to the bottom of this, I promise you."

He hung up from Christy and pulled away from the curb and back into traffic. Shifting, he accelerated. "Where are you?" he said aloud. He scanned the cars on the road as he sped past. Devon tried to remain calm. He'd talk to her rationally—without yelling. He'd reason with her, allay her fears about the future. Together, they'd come up with a game plan. Happy with his solution, Devon concentrated on the road. Several minutes later, he exited onto New York Avenue heading towards Route 50.

Jayde guided her car onto Route 50 toward Annapolis. She took another tissue from her purse. After blowing her nose loudly into the cottony fluff, she tossed the tissue onto the passenger seat. It landed in a noiseless heap next to ten others. Images of Devon's reaction after he read her note came to mind. He'd be livid at finding her gone, but it was for the best. Her life was spiraling out of control. Nothing made sense anymore. The only way she could get a handle on the chaos was to go off by herself to sort things out.

Jayde got into the fast lane and set her cruise control.

She passed Freeway Airport on her right. Her exit, Davidsonville Road, was up ahead. Suddenly, her cell phone rang. Her hand roamed through the tissues on the seat. She checked her rearview mirror. Once she depressed the brake pedal, cruise control disengaged. She got in the slow lane. Letting a car go past, Jayde guided her vehicle onto the shoulder of the road.

Rifling around, she finally found her phone in her purse. She pressed the talk button. "Hello?"

Hearing nothing, Jayde spoke a second time. Deciding she'd missed the call, she dropped the cell phone back into her purse. She had just maneuvered back into traffic when it rang again.

"Hello?"

"Thank God, I got you. What are you doing?"

She bit her lip. It was Devon. By the time he'd woken up, she'd expected to be halfway there. "Driving."

"Yes, I know you're driving. That's my point. You should be at my house, in my bed. Not running away."

"I'm not running away."

"Fine. What do you call it?"

"A change of scenery."

The expletive he let out caused her to frown. "If you're going to use that kind of language, I'm getting off the phone."

"Jayde, don't you dare hang up. We're going to talk about this. Right now."

"No we're not. I—"

"I don't understand you," he said, cutting her off. "Why do you feel the need to hightail it every time something occurs in your life that you don't like? Were you the only kid in elementary school escaping to her beach house when you didn't get picked for the school play?"

"Stop being dramatic. Besides, I think better when I'm by myself."

"Fine," was Devon's terse reply. "You could've asked me to leave the room if you wanted to be by yourself. Hell, I could've left the house to give you time alone. Why'd you feel it necessary to take a cab back to your trashed condo without me? That could've been dangerous, Jayde. What if whoever wrecked your home came back for a repeat performance?"

"They didn't."

"Well, they could have," he reasoned. "You shouldn't take unnecessary risks."

Devon continued railing for a few more minutes before he realized there was silence.

"Jayde?"

When she didn't answer, he raised his voice.

"Jayde! Can you hear me talking to you? Jayde, did you hang up?"

"Just a minute," she snapped.

"Don't get snotty. You were ignoring me, remember?"

"I wasn't . . . Okay, I was ignoring you, but I think someone is following me," she said.

Devon's eyebrows arched. "How do you know? Have you tried changing lanes?"

"Of course, I've tried changing lanes. I do watch television, you know. I've looked out my rearview mirror a few times, too. A black sedan with heavily tinted windows has been shadowing me since you started your monologue. They're definitely following me."

He ignored her biting remark. "Where are you?"

"I really don't think—"

"Where!"

"I'm on Route Fifty, heading east. I'm almost to the Davidsonville exit. Good grief, I wish the car would go around."

"Just slow down. Eventually, they'll pass you."

The next thing Devon heard was a loud bang, followed by Jayde's startled gasp and Boomer's barking.

"Jayde," Devon yelled into the phone. "What the hell was that?"

"He rear-ended me," she said, shocked. "I slowed down, and he . . ."

A piercing crash was followed by Jayde's scream. From the loud thud and her distant voice, Devon realized she'd dropped her cell phone. "Jayde," he shouted as loud as he could, "I'm on my way." Switching his cell phone to speaker, Devon tossed it next to him and jammed his gas pedal to the floor.

In less than seven seconds, he'd exceeded one hundred

miles per hour. Devon concentrated on his objective. He heard another crash. Jayde cried out his name.

Helpless, Devon picked up the phone, barking into the speaker, "Hang on."

Up ahead, he saw two cars weaving between the two lanes. He recognized Jayde's swerving Jeep. If he didn't get there soon, she'd roll it over. He hated to do it, but Devon disconnected their call. Dialing 911, Devon gave the dispatcher his location and described what was going on ahead of him. The woman asked him to stay on the line until help arrived.

He flashed his lights to get a car in front of him out of his path. Before he could reach Jayde, the black sedan slammed into the left side of her Wrangler. The driver persisted until Jayde's mangled 4x4 was forced off the road.

"No," Devon roared in anguish as he watched Jayde's Jeep slide onto the graveled shoulder. It rolled onto its side before disappearing into a ditch. The black sedan slowed to a halt. "God, no," Devon pleaded as he saw a car door open. He was almost there when a police car raced in front of him.

The door of the black sedan suddenly closed. Seconds later it sped off.

Stomping on the brakes, Devon reined in the Mercedes and pulled onto the side of the road. Parking, he bolted out of the car and slid down into the ditch as fast as he could. By the time he reached Jayde, the police officer was trying to wrench open the driver's side door. His heart stopped. There was no movement inside the Jeep.

CHAPTER 30

Removing the keys from Jayde's trembling hand, Devon opened the front door to her beach house. He guided her slowly to the nearest couch, flinching when she grimaced in pain.

"The pain medication hasn't kicked in?"

"No, not yet," Jayde replied between clenched teeth.

"Where's the kitchen?"

Jayde pointed past him.

"I'll be right back."

Walking into the next room, Devon turned on the lights and scanned the cabinets. He poked his head through the door after he located some tea.

"Earl Grey with cream and sugar, right?"

"You remembered," Jayde replied weakly. "Sounds delicious."

Once his head was back in the kitchen, Devon's smile faded. He leaned against the counter. With shaky hands, he gripped the edge for support. His emotions had been in turmoil since the moment he'd seen her vehicle pushed off the road.

"Are you finding everything okay?"

Jayde's voice interrupted his descent into self-condemnation.

"Of course, be out in a minute," he called.

Sipping the hot, aromatic tea, Jayde closed her eyes, sighing audibly. When she opened them again, she saw the look of unguarded pain etched in Devon's features. "Devon, what's wrong? I don't look that bad, do I? I mean, a sprained wrist and a few cuts and bruises aren't worth the look you were wearing just now. Boomer and I are a bit banged up, but we're going to be okay. Aren't we, Boomer?"

Her dog's tail thumped loudly on the carpeted floor.

Sitting down next to her, Devon ran his hand over the arm that wasn't in a sling. He shook his head. "I'm so sorry, sweetheart. I didn't mean for this to happen."

"Don't be silly. It wasn't your fault. I'm to blame."

"No, you aren't. If I hadn't insisted you stay with me, you wouldn't have felt the need to run off. Dammit, Jayde, you could've been killed. It would've been my fault . . . again," he whispered hoarsely. "I seem to have a strange way of protecting the women in my life."

Jayde's attempt to sit up failed when a stabbing pain in her back halted her actions. Instead, she held out her hand. Eventually, he took it.

They looked at each other in silence. Devon scanned her face. Seeing the large lump on her forehead made him frown with worry. "You need to rest."

"I'd rather talk with you. There are some things need to say. You have to listen."

"Later," he promised. Standing, Devon picked he up as gently as he could. "You should get some sleep.

He took her into the bedroom and got her settled i

bed. He removed her shoes and asked if she needed help disrobing.

"Maybe with these jeans," she said, yawning.

"Sure."

He unbuttoned her jeans. When he eased them down, he spotted a bruise on her thigh. He was careful not to rub the heavy material against it. Devon pulled the covers up and knelt beside the bed. "If you need anything, I'll be right outside the door, so just call."

"I will."

He left the door slightly ajar. Out in the living room, he sank onto the couch. At a loss, Devon placed his head in his hand. Moisture formed in his eyes, visual proof of the emotions warring inside him. Eventually, Devon drifted into a tortured slumber.

Devon was in his car. Jayde was in the passenger seat; her stunning smile illuminated her face. His hand caressed her stomach. It was a flat surface, but he joked that pretty soon it would be burgeoning with their child. Jayde captured his hand and brought it to her lips for a kiss.

Devon's knuckles glided over her soft cheek. "I love you," he said solemnly.

Her smile was radiant. She looked so beautiful, his breath almost stopped in his chest.

"I love you, too, daddy-to-be."

Returning his hand to the steering wheel, Devon focused on the road. Without warning, they heard a loud noise. Before either of them could react, the car lunged to one side. He gripped the steering wheel and fought to get the car under control.

"Devon?"

He knew what she was thinking. "We'll be okay, I promise."

The car jolted again before spinning out of control. Jayde's scream echoed through the cabin. Plunging down a steep embankment, the car careened through bushes and dense brush before smashing into a large tree.

Coming to, Devon looked over at his wife. She wasn't conscious. "Jayde?"

She didn't answer.

"Jayde," he yelled. "Wake up." Devon felt the side of her neck. He didn't get a pulse. "No! Jayde, no. Don't leave me. Don't you dare." His hand shook violently as it traveled to her stomach. Grief racked him. Bile churned in his stomach. Kissing her lips, he tried breathing air into her lifeless body. "Jayde," he repeated over and over.

"Devon, wake up. Devon! You're dreaming." Jayde shook him with her good hand.

He bolted upright. The quick movement sent Jayde falling to the floor. She let out a pained cry.

Disoriented, it took him a second to figure out where he was. Seeing her prostrate on the floor caused him to remember. "Jayde!" He rushed to help her onto the couch. "I'm so sorry! Did I hurt you?"

"It's fine. No harm done. You were having a nightmare. Actually, I guess it was a daymare."

Devon looked tortured. "I—I thought it was real. I was driving, and you were in the passenger seat. Something happened to our car. We hit a tree." His voice was hoarse, and he grimaced. "I tried . . . I couldn't save you or the baby."

Anguish crossed his face. His look of desolation made her heart ache.

Jayde eased her uninjured arm around him. His head rested on her shoulder. She caressed his face. "You were dreaming, Devon. I'm fine. I'm not dead, and by the way, I'm not pregnant, either."

He's reliving the accident he had with Candace, substituting me instead, Jayde thought, grasping his hand. Hold ing it against her face, she kissed his palm. "Devon, please tell me what happened. I want to know. Don't keep it bottled up inside anymore."

His tortured expression was heartbreaking. He switched spots with her. He helped her lie back on the couch so that she was comfortable, and then he seated himself on the floor beside the couch. He reclaimed her hand. He wasn't looking at her, but out the window. Oddly, the dark water lapping roughly against the shore was calming.

Jayde watched him, imploring him with her eyes to open up, to finally release what had tortured him for so long.

Devon told her how he'd met Candace and how she had been dating Xavier before him.

"Xavier didn't tell me what happened, but their relationship ended. He and I worked together at Mitchell, so I wanted to make sure he was okay with me dating Candace. He said he was okay with it, but occasionally I'd glance over at him, and he'd have this look on his face. Anyway, a year later, things began to fall apart. There were changes in her that put a strain on our relationship."

Devon recounted the party they'd gone to and the heated argument they'd had after she'd announced to the crowd that she was pregnant and they were engaged.

"What!"

Devon laughed harshly. "I'd underestimated her determination to get what she wanted. I couldn't believe she'd do something like that. I was livid. I'd never proposed to her, and I knew nothing about her being pregnant."

"Oh, Devon," Jayde said tearfully. "I'm so sorry."

"I felt like such a damned fool. Needless to say, I was geared up for a fight. We argued in the car. It got pretty heated. That's when I knew it was all about the money. It had always been about the money. She didn't love me, and I realized I had never loved her."

When he stopped talking, Jayde leaned in. "What happened?"

"Somehow I lost control of the car. The accelerator got stuck. We went skidding off the road, and a tire blew. The car flipped over a couple times. I guess I blacked out. When I came to, I tried to help her, but it was too late. Candace was already dead."

"I'm so sorry."

"The media had a field day at my expense. They made all sorts of nasty innuendos, saying I'd purposely crashed my car to get rid of her and my unwanted child. I couldn't go anywhere without stepping over a reporter. The phone calls were fierce—at work, at home, my cell. When my father stepped in, that only made matters worse. Rumors spread that my family was trying to use their wealth to cover up everything. None of it was true. Two weeks after the accident, the police ruled that the crash was due to mechanical failure. I was free to resume my life, but the damage had already been done."

He told her about staying at his Uncle's farm to clear his head and mourn the loss of his child.

Getting up, Devon went to the window and stared out.

"I've relived that night in my head and dreams repeatedly, Jayde. I have always wondered if I could've done something differently—anything to keep from crashing my car. I'd never harm Candace. I admit I was plenty angry with her and I wanted her out of my life but I didn't want her dead," Devon said emotionally "Never dead."

Tears pooled in Jayde's eyes. She heard the pain. The

complete devastation in his voice gripped her soul. Slowly, she made her way to where he was standing. She turned his face toward her. "Listen to me. You aren't to blame—for any of it. It was an accident. It wasn't your fault Candace died. You can't keep condemning yourself. You've got to let it go, or your guilt will eat away at you until nothing's left."

He looked down. Bitterness tinged his voice. "Knowing that doesn't make me feel any better. There was more I could've done, that I should've done. Seeing you run off the road brought it all back."

"I can see how it would, but, Devon, I'm all right."

"Yes, but I was helpless to save you." He encircled her shoulders with his hands. "Like I was Candace."

Though Devon's grip was firm, his fingers trembled. His expression ripped her apart.

"You can't imagine how frantic I was reaching your truck. I wasn't sure if you were alive or dead. It felt like my heart was being ripped out of my chest. If anything had happened to you, my . . ." His voice faltered. "My life would be over."

He buried his face in her hair. Devon held her like his life depended on their embrace.

Jayde relished the closeness. "I felt the same way when I rolled down that embankment. At that moment, everything became clear—how foolish I'd been, how fragile life is. Suddenly, everything seemed so trivial— our arguments at the gallery, me walking out."

"Which time?"

"Every time." She blushed. "Then I was livid at your deception, so I ran. I wanted so badly to shut you out of my heart," Jayde admitted. "It didn't work, though."

Devon's gaze was penetrating. "You sure about that?"

Jayde returned his stare with equal frankness. "As sure as I know how to breathe."

He tweaked the bridge of her nose. "I'm familiar with the feeling."

The air left her lungs in a gush. "All the drama we've been going through seemed inconsequential when I thought I'd never see you again. That we'd never get another chance." Her voice was barely audible. "To make it right."

Squeezing Jayde's hand in his, Devon kissed it, then her lips. Shaking his head, he grinned boyishly. "I love you, Jayde. I guess it's time I told you that."

"And I'm ridiculously in love with you." Her voice held similar awe.

Devon's features relaxed. "How in the world did that happen?"

Jayde shrugged. "I guess it's been there for some time. I was always too mad at you to see it."

"Me, too, but then you came to me in a dream. It was the first time anyone had invaded my mind, changed how the accident played out. I was baffled by its meaning. When I woke up, it just hit me. I'd rather argue with you than have sex with someone else." He held her chin with his finger as he lowered his head. Kissing her tenderly, he leaned back. He wiped the tears from her eyelids with his thumb. He grinned. "I'm sorry I fired you."

She laughed. "I'm sorry I quit."

He snorted. "What about all those names you called me?"

"Oh, I meant all of those," she teased. "At least at the time."

Devon went back to the couch, taking her with him. Once settled, he kissed her again.

For a long time, the couple quietly observed the moonlight shimmering across the water.

"Jayde?"

Cuddled against him, she was comfortable yet exhausted from their declarations. Her voice was heavy with sleep. "Mmm?"

"At my house, after your condo was ransacked, you were drifting off to sleep when you whispered you knew who did it. Now you get run off the road. Jayde, what is it you aren't telling me?"

CHAPTER 31

The cease-fire between Devon and Jayde was a joyous and tender moment. They'd finally admitted their fears, concerns, and true feelings for each other. They were in love, and they were together. That joyous and tender moment lasted about ten minutes.

The more Jayde tried to divert the conversation from the subject at hand, the more wary Devon became.

Feeling the tension seeping into the room, Jayde finally confessed her suspicions. "I think Xavier had something to do with this."

If she weren't ensconced in his arms, Devon would've bolted off the couch. "Xavier?" he said incredulously. "What does my best friend have to do with this?"

"He stopped by my condo the other day, before it was ransacked," Jayde replied.

Devon disentangled himself and stood up. "Come again?" His expression was severe.

"Xavier came to visit me after we had our big blowup.'

"I didn't even know he was in town. How did he ever know where you lived?" Devon asked.

"I don't know. He's resourceful, I guess."

friend's involved in all this, I'll deal with him. The gallery is my responsibility."

"I'm not."

His eyes darkened. Moving back slightly, he tilted her face up to look at him. "This isn't a joke. When I'm done yelling at you, we're going to call the police. Now, about Xavier . . ."

By the time Devon got through lecturing her about personal safety, Jayde was exhausted. The pain medication had begun to wear off. Her eyes were clouded with pain. It took some time, but Devon noticed her condition. Scowling, he walked over to where she was leaning against the wall.

"In pain?"

Unable to lie, she nodded.

Devon walked into the kitchen. He returned with a glass of water and her medication. He handed her the pill, then the glass.

Popping the painkiller into her mouth, Jayde took a sip of water before handing the glass back. "Thanks."

Devon took the glass back, to the kitchen. When he got back, his eyes roamed over her. "I'm sorry. You're exhausted. We both are. It's time we called it a night."

Jayde looked hopeful. "No more yelling?"

"No more yelling." Hoisting her in his arms, he carried her into the bathroom, watching while she brushed her teeth and washed her face. When she tried to do more, he walked over and gently took the washcloth.

"Wait. I feel cruddy. I really want to get the grime off," she told him.

"I wasn't protesting. I was merely trying to help." He

flipped the shower on. "My lady wants the grime off. Her wish is my command."

"Since when?" She snorted.

He kissed her lips. "Since right now." Devon adjusted the water. As gingerly as he could manage, he removed the sling on her arm. While the room filled with steam, he helped her out of her clothes. Sitting her on the commode, Devon removed his own clothing.

"I'm perfectly capable of washing myself," she protested.

"I know you are, but this is for me," he whispered. He assisted her into the warm water. "I need to feel you against me, to convince myself you're here, safe and sound."

In the shower Jayde watched the play of emotions cross his face. She wrapped her good arm around his neck and leaned her wet body into his. Devon's hands came to her waist, holding her steady.

"I love you, Jayde. All I could think earlier was, God, please let me get another chance to tell her how much I love her, how much she means to me."

Jayde ran her fingers over his face. Next, she slid them across his lips. "I'd rather you show me."

He swallowed hard. "Jayde, I don't want to hurt you."

"You won't."

A low moan escaped his lips. Unable to help himself, Devon lowered his head and kissed her thoroughly. Possessively.

Later . . .

Devon carried Jayde back to the bed. He helped her into her pajamas before easing her under the covers

More than anything, he wanted to sleep next to her, to revel in the incredible moment they'd just shared, but he didn't want to jostle her during the night. Watching her thoughtfully, Devon snaked his fingers through her hair. "Do you want me to stay with you for a little while?"

The pain medication was kicking in, making her drowsy. Forcing her eyes open, Jayde looked dreamily at him. "A little while would be nice. Say, eight hours?" she said, plastering a silly grin on her face.

"Far be it for me to argue." Devon slipped under the covers. He eased Jayde into his arms. "I don't know if this is wise. I don't want to accidentally jostle you while we're sleeping."

"If you try sleeping somewhere else," she threatened between yawns, "I'll hurt *you* while we're sleeping."

After kissing Jayde, Devon was quiet for some time. She'd almost drifted off to sleep when he spoke again. "Jayde, don't think I didn't notice we never got around to calling the police. We'll phone in the morning about our suspicions regarding the accident—that it could've been Xavier. You're not safe here. Whoever ran you off the road could try here, too. Tomorrow I'll call for my company's private jet. We're out of here."

Jayde opened her eyes an inch. "Gee, that was a laundry list. Where are we going?"

He stroked her stomach. "We're going to my family's place in Illinois—Bellehaven. I need you somewhere safe, away from harm. Under the circumstances, that's the best place I can think of."

"Mmm." Jayde closed her eyes. "Have you told them about me?"

"Yes."

"That's too bad."

Devon chuckled. His smile was unseen in the darkness.

"Will they like me?" she asked.

He kissed the top of her head. "In spite of how you treat me, yes. They'll like you." Devon waited. He expected her to protest going to visit his family, but she didn't. *Those drugs are stronger than I thought.* "Jayde?"

"Huh?"

"Do you trust me?"

"Now I do."

Devon shook his head. She was great on a man's ego.

As if she'd just thought about something, Jayde sat up partially, turning to him. "What about Xavier? Do you think he's still in town?"

At hearing his name, Devon glowered. "I'm counting on it."

The next morning, while Jayde was at Christy's, dropping off Boomer, Devon paid Xavier a visit. Going to his hotel room, he knocked on the door. When it opened, he found a half-naked woman looking at him speculatively.

"I hope I can help you," she said, licking her lips.

"Afraid not," Devon said, walking around her. He spotted Xavier on the bed. "We need to talk, in front of her or not. It doesn't matter to me."

Standing, Xavier looked Devon in the eye. "I suppose Lucinda told you where I was?"

Devon didn't bother responding.

Xavier's eyes raked over the tall, dark, and gorgeous woman against him. "I'm sorry, darling. Would you mind waiting in the other room? This won't take long."

The woman looked at both men appreciatively before she flounced into the bathroom, shutting the door behind her.

The moment she was gone, Xavier turned his attention to Devon. The moment he did, Devon punched him in the jaw. Xavier staggered back against the bed.

"Good to see you, too, Dev. What brings you by—and unannounced?"

"Save it. You're not surprised to see me. Not after what you did."

Xavier retrieved his pants and his shirt from a nearby chair. He sauntered to the small bar and grabbed a bottled water. Twisting the cap off, he gingerly took a sip. "I can't imagine what you're implying."

"Jayde. You went to her condo and hit on her. What the hell are you doing?"

Xavier shrugged. "Why do you care? You tossed her aside, didn't you? You fired her to boot. In my book, she's fair game."

"That's bull. You knew there was something between us."

"You're right. There was something. Now it's gone. That makes her available. I saw something I wanted, so I went after it." He fixed Devon with a pointed stare. "I suppose asking your permission first would've made it okay. Is that what you're saying?"

"Don't play games, X. You told me you were over Candace, then gave me your blessing to date her. If you had issues with it, you should've said something."

"So I owed you a phone call." He shrugged again. "My mistake."

"You threatened her, too, and when that didn't work, you went back and trashed her condo."

"I didn't threaten her. I merely listed the qualities that made me the better choice. As for breaking and entering her condo, you better have proof to back up your claim."

Devon was across the room in three seconds. Grabbing

Xavier's shirt, Devon lifted him off the floor so that they were eye to eye. "I know it was you, Xavier. I'm not as stupid as you think I am. When you couldn't get her to drop at your feet, you decided to shake her up by destroying her home. I'd bet my life you're behind running her off the road yesterday, too."

"My, my, it seems your girlfriend's had a busy day."

Devon increased his hold. "This isn't a game, Xavier. She could've been seriously hurt—or worse."

"I didn't run anyone off the road. That's not my style, anyway. I love to play bump and grind, but not with cars."

"Then where were you yesterday morning?"

Xavier shoved Devon backward. As Xavier readjusted his shirt, his expression grew dark. "If you must know, I was with my lady friend. If you don't believe me, ask her. I'm sure she'd be happy to go into the details."

"Just—"

"Yes, I know. Stay away from Jayde. I get it."

"Setting your sights on her is a moot point, anyway."

"Really? Don't tell me she took you back." Xavier laughed while massaging his jaw. "Wow. Didn't see that coming."

"Well, now you do. So allow me to spell it out for you. Jayde's mine—she's going to stay that way."

"Until you tire of her?" Xavier sneered.

"Where is this coming from, X? Did I miss something? I don't know when things went south, but I'm warning you. I don't want you within two feet of her again, or things between us will get real bad, real fast. Oh, and I wouldn't leave town just now if I were you. I can assure you the Metropolitan Police Department is going to want to have a few words with you."

"I'm telling you I didn't have anything to do with the condo or the accident. You're really going to let a woman come between us? We've been tight since college. We work together, too. Besides, we've already shared one. What's another?"

In an instant Devon connected his fist with Xavier's stomach. Xavier fell to his knees in a heap on the carpet. Laughing, he rubbed his middle while getting to his feet. "You really are hot for her, aren't you? I don't ever remember us fighting over a woman—even Candace."

"Things change."

"Yes," Xavier said, glaring, "they do."

Striding back to the door, Devon wrenched it open before he turned to glare at his friend. "I'm sorry about what happened with Candace. I really am. But don't let my good nature fool you. If you threaten Jayde again, or if I find out you were responsible for that accident or her condo, I'll beat you within an inch of your life and then have you arrested. Jayde's off the market, so I suggest you find another object for your desire."

Xavier's voice turned venomous. "I suggest you keep a better eye on this girlfriend than you did the last one."

CHAPTER 32

"I don't really think this is necessary," Jayde said worriedly. "Did you even tell them we're coming?"

"Relax." Devon ran his hand over her thigh. "I called them en route. They're expecting us—both of us. When we arrive, a car will be waiting at the airport. From there we'll drop by my place. I need to pick up some clothes, and then we're off."

Jayde nodded. Her hand went to her stomach to quell the queasy feeling. In truth, she was a wreck. She and Devon had just gotten back on the same sheet of music themselves; now he was taking her to Illinois, to his parents' house. After Devon had returned from seeing Xavier, he'd ushered her into the car, and they'd driven straight to the police to report the incident. From there, they headed towards the airport. An hour later Jayde stared anxiously out her window. She was nervous about meeting Devon's family.

She didn't know if she'd be entering the warm, comforting arms of the family he'd been raving about or a lion's den.

Relax, Jayde. No sense thinking it to death. If things don't go well, you can always insist he take you to a hotel, she told herself, as she drifted off to sleep. When she awoke, Jayde could see Chicago looming in the distance. Her eye immediately zeroed in on the Sears Tower. While this wasn't her first time in the Windy City, she was certain it would be her most memorable.

After landing, they took the limousine straight to Devon's condo, which was right across from Navy Pier.

Jayde gasped when she saw his building. "Wow, it's beautiful."

"Yeah, it is. It was the tallest all-residential building in the world until 1993."

Lake Point Tower loomed over Chicago's lakefront. Regal in stature, the curved, black-glass high-rise was specifically designed so that residents wouldn't be able to see in one another's windows.

Her gaze went skyward. "Where do you live? The penthouse?"

He laughed. "No, smarty. There's a restaurant on the top floor. The third floor has a residents-only park that's over two acres."

She arched an eyebrow. "A park?"

"Yes, a park. You know, with trees, grass, and a pond. Typical stuff."

"On the third floor?"

"What? Most people don't have parks on the third floor of their condo buildings?"

She elbowed him with her good arm. Devon winked.

Jayde had never visited Navy Pier, Chicago's lakefront family entertainment park. She'd heard about it and longed to go, but on her last trip, there hadn't been time.

Almost as if he'd read her mind, Devon turned. "Once this nightmare is over, we're going to disappear for a while. Just you . . . me . . . and lots of sunblock."

The limousine dropped them off, and Devon ushered

her into the building. His condo was on the twenty-third floor. It had a magnificent view of Lake Michigan, Navy Pier, and beyond.

From the moment she walked through the door, Jayde was in observation mode. Startlingly, Devon's condo was decidedly masculine. Everything was black, brown, or tan, including the wood furniture. It was a rich, dark wood bordering on black. Apparently, Devon didn't subscribe to the white-walls-are-best theory. Every room was painted a warm, rich color. Jayde loved it.

The kitchen was done in an inviting taupe. The brown, black, and white speckled granite counters and the cherrywood cabinets were stately. Jayde's gaze roamed over leather couches, chenille chairs, and glass tables in the main living areas. Everywhere she went, she saw family pictures.

Picking one up off the sofa table, Jayde saw an older couple. They had to be Devon's parents. The man was distinguished, as handsome as any man she'd ever seen. He had the same complexion, curly hair, and startling gray eyes as Devon. Devon's mother was petite and slightly darker in complexion. Her skin was flawless. She had tender topaz brown eyes. Her ebony, gray-streaked hair was tousled around her small face. His mother looked tranquil and elegant. She exuded confidence in her photograph.

"What a striking couple," she finally said, in awe. "Your mother is breathtaking."

"Don't be fooled. She's a force to be reckoned with. She keeps Dad on his toes."

Jayde couldn't contain her mirth. "Of that I have no doubt." Holding up another picture, Jayde saw exactly what Devon would look like if he were female. The only difference was she had hazel eyes. "This must be Melanie."

As Devon leaned over Jayde's shoulder, his eyes softened. "Yep. That's Mel. She takes after Mom. She's a spitfire, too."

Following Devon into the bedroom, she sat on the bed while he sauntered across the room to a massive closet. The same flawless taste and attention to detail prevailed here. Devon's room was a deep olive color. A burgundy leather love seat sat in the corner. A built-in entertainment center with a big-screen television took up the adjacent wall.

Jayde shook her head at the massive unit. "Do you ever do anything on a small scale?"

Devon poked his head out of the closet, pinning her with a look that set her blood afire. "I don't know, do I?"

Crimson color etched her face. "I walked right into that, didn't I?"

He grinned. "Actually, you ran into it. Or should I say, hurtled, dove, catapulted—"

"I get it," she retorted. Making herself comfortable on the king-size bed, Jayde lounged on her good elbow. She propped a pillow under the other. In a few minutes, Devon reappeared with clothes in one hand, a suitcase in the other.

When she saw the mound of clothes, she looked quizzically at him. "How long are we staying?"

His gaze found hers. "As long as it takes. You aren't stepping foot back there until we get this whole mess sorted out and whoever's responsible is arrested."

"We've gone over this before." She sighed. "I don't think whoever ran me off the road will be back. I'm sure it was meant to frighten me."

"You're right. It was meant to scare you, and Xavier is at the top of the list of possible suspects."

"If it is Xavier, what does he have to do with your gallery?"

As he thought of his friend, Devon's expression turned serious. "I don't know, sweetheart, but I'm not willing to take any more chances with your safety. I contacted my father's friend at the police department. I gave him Xavier's hotel information, and he has your police report and my statement from my run-in earlier with Xavier. He's going to have two of his officers stop by and question Xavier. This will be over soon."

"I hope so. Between the gallery, my condo, and my car, this mystery is getting expensive."

Jayde had meant it to be a lighthearted comment, but to her dismay, she found herself crying.

He laid down the clothes he was packing, came around the bed, and covered her in one swift motion. His left hand grazed over her cheek. He stared down into her tear-filled eyes. "Baby, don't cry. We'll replace everything."

"I've got insurance," she sniffed. "I'm sure it will cover all my losses."

"I'll cover whatever your insurance doesn't. There isn't any amount I wouldn't pay to keep you safe." He ran a thumb under her eyes. "Or to get rid of these."

"What? You don't like the dark circles?"

Devon was silent. His sincerity disturbed her. He was too serious, too believable.

Her throat tightened. "Oh, come on," she joked. "It's not like I'm priceless."

He sat up. "You are to me. Can't you see how wonderful, how unique you are?"

Jayde looked away. "Stop it."

"Why?"

She was off the bed in an instant. Too fast. Her ankle

protested the quick movement. She teetered, trying to regain her balance. He caught her before she fell.

"What's the matter?" he asked.

Jayde pulled out of his arms. Agitated, she faced him, crying in earnest now. "I liked you better when you weren't being nice to me, when we hated each other and argued like cats and dogs. This cease-fire is nerve-racking, Devon. I keep waiting for the bottom to fall out."

"For the record, I never, ever hated you. Jayde, I'm not going anywhere. You're stuck with me. So tell me what's really wrong?"

"I'm . . . scared. This whole thing has me terrified."

Devon reached for her. He buried his head in her neck, and his muffled voice vibrated against her skin. "I know you are, sweetheart. I'm scared, too. One thing I do know is that we will get to the bottom of all this. That's why I'm taking you to my parents' house. You'll be safe there while we figure out our next move."

Overcome with emotion, Jayde just nodded.

Devon tilted her face up to meet his. He used his thumb to wipe more tears away from her eyes. "Tell me you love me."

"I do love you."

"Do you trust me?"

She nodded. "Of course."

He hugged her to him. "Then everything else will fall into place. I promise."

Jayde waited in the living room while Devon finished packing. She walked to the wall of windows. Gazing over the water gave her a chance to calm down. There was so much going on in her life, it was overwhelming.

Warm arms gathered her close. Jayde stifled a yelp.

"Where were you just now?" Devon asked.

She leaned against him, breathing in his scent. "Here."

"No, you were preoccupied with something. I've been watching you for a few minutes." Devon turned her in his arms, his face a mirror of concern. "You still worried?"

Jayde fought for composure. "I guess everything is just catching up to me, is all. It's really draining."

"Let's go. The sooner we get you to Bellehaven, the sooner you'll be able to lie down and rest."

By the time Devon maneuvered his Infiniti SUV out of the parking garage, Jayde's face was pressed against the window. Though she'd denied it, Devon had seen the occasional wince she'd made and the way she'd bitten her lower lip. When he'd administered the little white pill, Jayde had taken it without protest. Now she was asleep, her hand entwined with his. Devon took the opportunity to think over their current situation.

In the span of a few months, his life had become more complicated than he could ever have imagined. Assuming command at the gallery, meeting Jayde, sparring with her every minute until they'd come together, and the subsequent cloud of danger hanging over them had made his mind reel. Keeping track of all the chaos was getting to be problematic. Still, amid all the drama, the doubt, and Xavier's strange behavior, one thing had remained constant—his feelings for Jayde.

A fierce determination to keep her and his gallery from harm consumed him. He loved her and would protect her with all the resources at his disposal. The latest "accident" had only intensified his desire to keep her safe at any cost. Reaching over, Devon ran a finger down her partially hidden cheek. He watched her shift slightly. He hadn't brought her to Illinois just to keep her safe; he wanted to talk with his father, apprise him of the situation, and get his input. He trusted his dad's advice. There was no room for missteps. Jayde's very life might depend on what happened next.

For the rest of the drive, he pondered their situation. He waited until he'd parked the car in his parents' driveway before waking Jayde.

"Time to get up, sleepyhead," Devon whispered in her ear.

Stretching languidly, Jayde blinked. "How long was I out?"

"Long enough to slobber all over my jacket."

Shocked, she stared down at the leather jacket covering her midsection. When she saw it was dry, she poked him. "Shut up. We're here? Already?" she asked in a voice laden with sleep.

"Yep."

"Where are we?"

"We're in Northbrook. It's not too far from my place—just under forty minutes."

Jayde flicked a comb through her hair. She reached into her purse, retrieving a small make-up case and a container of cinnamon Altoids. "Want one?"

Devon scrunched his face. "Heck no. Those things are stronger than straight scotch."

"Maybe so, but I'm hardly meeting your family with bad breath," she observed while reapplying her MAC pressed powder and lipstick.

By the time she'd disengaged herself from his car, he'd taken their luggage to the front door. Jayde walked slowly, giving herself time to take everything in—and there was a lot to take in.

His family's house looked like it needed its own zip code. Jayde stared, awestruck, at the massive brick-and-stone structure in front of her. The French manor home sat majestically in the center of a sprawling front yard and a circular brick-paved driveway, all hidden behind a tall black wrought-iron fence. A stone fountain stood in the middle of the heavily landscaped driveway. The sound of trickling water made it to her ears.

"Wow," Jayde whispered.

Looking back toward the mansion, Jayde tilted her head almost all the way back to take in the arched stone entryway. The large mahogany door featured intricate black iron openwork molded around glass. Two sidelights boasted an identical design.

As Jayde entered the Mitchell home, the family butler, Selby, greeted her. "Welcome to Bellehaven, Miss Seaton." When he extended his hand, telling her to call him Selby, some of her nervousness dissipated. "Shall I place the bags in your suite, sir?"

Devon nodded. "Yes, and Selby?"

The old man turned his weathered gaze to Devon. "Yes, sir?"

"Stop calling me sir."

"Certainly, sir," Selby replied, a twinkle in his eye.

Jayde heard an explosion of footsteps heading toward them. Turning, she looked down the wide marbled hallway to see two children running at breakneck speed right for her.

The girl stopped on a dime in front of her, but her brother wasn't so lucky. He collided with his sister, who would've knocked Jayde over if Devon hadn't thrown his arm across his niece to steady her.

"Careful you two. Jayde's been banged up enough."

"We're sorry, Uncle Devon. Is this Jayde?" they asked excitedly.

"Miss Jayde," Devon corrected. "Jetta, Mitchell, I'd like you to meet Jayde Seaton. Jayde, my niece, Jetta, and my nephew, Mitchell Thomas."

Smiling, Jayde carefully lowered herself to their eye level. Extending her hand, she grasped their fingers. "Pleased to meet you both."

Mitchell gave Jayde the once-over before speaking. "You're gawjus," he breathed.

"Why, thank you. I think you're quite handsome, too," Jayde replied.

"It's *gorgeous*," Jetta corrected. "GiGi, isn't she pretty?"

All eyes turned toward Devon's mother, who had entered the room right behind the kids.

Standing, Jayde walked over to the older woman. Extending her hand, Jayde smiled warmly. "It's wonderful to meet you, Mrs. Mitchell."

"Likewise, Jayde, and please call me Avalon." Devon's mother took Jayde's hand in hers. "Welcome to Bellehaven."

"Where's Dad?" Devon asked, kissing his mother's cheek.

Avalon smiled up at her son. "He's still at the office. He'll be home by dinner. Melanie and her husband will be here later, too. That gives the two of you plenty of time to rest up before everyone arrives. Selby, would you put Jayde in the orchid room?"

"Of course, Mrs. Mitchell," replied Selby.

To her grandchildren's delight, Avalon ushered them to the theater room to watch a movie.

Following Selby and Devon up the long, wide, carpeted staircase, Jayde looked around as she went. The second-floor landing broke off in two directions. Devon's parents and guests occupied one end of the second floor, while the rest of the family and their guests were at the other end.

Entering the guest room, Selby placed Jayde's bags at

the foot of the bed. "If there is anything you need, Miss Seaton, just hit the second speed dial on the telephone."

Jayde looked down at the phone. This was too much. "Thank you, Selby."

The second the butler was through the door, Jayde fixed Devon with a stare. "It's like Southfork."

He laughed. "We don't fight nearly as much as the Ewings."

"I'm talking about the house," Jayde admonished. She unzipped the suitcase Devon had let her borrow. Looking around the room, she spotted the dresser. Walking over, she put away what few clothes she'd borrowed from his sister. "This place is like a dream."

"It's a house," he corrected.

"Uh, no. A house is what my parents have. Besides, the house you've got in D.C. barely made it into the house category, and this place . . . this place is a borderline castle. Oh, good grief!"

Devon stopped. "What?"

"Bellehaven. It's the name of the house! I thought it was the city we were in. For goodness' sakes."

Devon couldn't contain his mirth. "We're in the village of Northbrook. Bellehaven is the name of my parents' home. What can I say? My mother read it somewhere, and the name stuck." Devon slid his arms around her waist. Nuzzling her neck, he whispered into her ear, "Relax. House, castle, or hovel, you'll be safe here."

Keeping a coherent thought in her head with Devon holding her was proving problematic. She shrugged out of his embrace. "Where's your room?"

"Trying to get rid of me, huh?"

"It's the only way I'm going to get unpacked. Speaking of which, at some point I'll need to go shopping. can't keep borrowing clothes the whole time I'm here.

"True. How about we go after you've rested a bit?" Aside from her playfulness, Devon could see she was tired.

"I've got to put away this stuff."

"Save it till later. You should rest." Before she could protest, he had her in bed and snuggled beneath the comforter.

"I'll check on you in a few," he promised. "If you need me—"

"Ah, let me guess." She yawned loudly. "Your extension is labeled on the phone?"

He grinned. "No, smart aleck. Just open the door over there." He pointed across the room. "It's the connecting door to my suite. It isn't locked." Devon gave her a quick peck on the lips before leaving.

After he'd gone, Jayde surveyed her room. She studied it with an artistic but sleepy eye. It was serene and undoubtedly feminine. The walls were painted a pale rose. The rich hardwood floor bore several thick floral area rugs. The drapes were sheer white, with burgundy rope tiebacks. The queen cherrywood four-poster bed was adorned with an orchid-patterned comforter and contrasting pillows. On a table across the room was a large glass vase with fresh multicolored orchids.

Suddenly Jayde remembered she'd forgotten to let her mother and best friend know they'd arrived safely. She got out of the bed and went to retrieve her cell phone. Snuggling under the covers again, Jayde dialed her mother. Ten minutes later Harriette Seaton was assured her daughter was safe and sound. She informed Jayde that she expected regular updates so that she wouldn't worry.

"I promise, Mom. I love you," Jayde told her.

"I love you, too, my sweetie."

"Tell Dad I asked about him."

"Don't tell Devon I asked about him," Harriette joked.

"Mom."

"Just kidding, darling. Say hello, and inform that man he'd better take good care of my only daughter, or he'll answer to me."

"Will do."

"Jayde?"

"Yes?"

"Do you love him?"

"Mom, I love him like crazy."

"Oh dear, that's too bad. The minute they find out they have you hook, line, and sinker, it's all over."

After she got off the phone with her mom, Jayde checked in with Christy. She brought her up to speed on Devon's visit with Xavier and their suspicions that he was behind a lot more than just making a play for her.

"I hope you contacted the police about him," said Christy.

"We did. They are going to question him."

"Good. If he is behind all this, I hope they nail his butt to a jail-cell wall."

"Me, too."

Once she hung up from Christy, she noticed she had new voice-mail messages. Leaning back against the pillows, she dialed her voice mail and waited. There were only two messages. The first was from her mother. Once she heard it, she hit the key to delete it. The second message had been recorded while she'd been on the phone with her mom and Christy. As soon as she heard the voice, her hand shook.

"Sorry I missed you, Jayde, but don't worry. I promise you I'll try again." Xavier chuckled before disconnecting the call.

CHAPTER 33

Devon looked out over the grounds. Usually, his eye swept over the grass, trees, and pool without stopping. This time he zeroed in on the huge maple tree. *His tree.* From the moment he'd been old enough to walk, Devon had claimed the towering giant as his own. Breathing deeply, Devon closed his eyes and listened to the symphony of sounds from nature's inhabitants.

"I know that look."

Hearing his mother's voice, Devon gazed down at his side. "Do you?"

"Of course. It's the one you wear when something's happened that's beyond your control. It's a unique look, a cross between vulnerability and impatience. It must be encoded in the Mitchell DNA—all the men in the family seem to have it."

"A lot's been going on lately. More than I could've imagined."

"I don't know about that. You can imagine quite a bit," his mother joked.

"Mom, this is serious."

"I'm sorry, honey. I know it is. Lately, it seems turmoil has been the norm in your life."

Uncrossing his arms, Devon shoved his hands into his pockets. He stared straight ahead. "By turmoil, do mean Candace's untimely death, strange incidents occurring at my gallery, falling in love with my bullheaded director, her condo getting ransacked, Xavier hitting on her, her getting run off the road, and my supposed best friend possibly at the crux of it? That's just normal, everyday stuff."

Avalon pulled her son's hands out of his pockets. She wrapped her arm around his elbow and proceeded to walk. Devon immediately fell into step beside her. "There's one particular occurrence in that montage that stands out."

"Xavier hitting on Jayde?"

"The one before that."

"Ransacked condo?"

"Actually, I was referring to you falling in love with your bullheaded director."

"Oh." Devon smiled, but it didn't reach his eyes. "Nothing gets past you, does it?"

Avalon continued walking when her son didn't elaborate. "You know, I'm used to waiting you out. Eventually, you and Melanie can't help yourselves. You have to open up of your own accord. Yes, indeed. That's one thing my mother taught me well. Patience. It's a practiced virtue."

Eventually, Devon broke his silence. "It's true. I'm in love with Jayde. I didn't want it to happen. Lord knows, it's the last thing I expected when I went there, yet here it is. Actually, that was the easiest thing I've ever done She's so lovable, Mom—when we aren't fighting." Devon smiled.

"It's about time."

"About time? Weren't you listening to the recap? My life's a mess right now. Actually, it's been upgraded from a mess to an utter disaster. Someone is trying to harm her, Mom, and I just found out Xavier could be behind some or all of this nightmare."

"Xavier! I don't understand. He's your best friend, Devon."

"That's what I thought, but it appears he's been holding a grudge for I don't know how long about Candace."

"Is it just Jayde he's after?"

"I don't know yet. You didn't see the way he looked when I confronted him. It was as if he didn't have a care in the world. I have to keep Jayde away from him until I can figure out what his end game is. I want to protect her, keep her safe. Granted, sometimes Jayde's the most pigheaded woman I've ever known, but I can't let anything happen to her. I can't."

"What are you going to do? Stand guard twenty-four hours a day?"

"If that's what it takes."

"Devon—"

"She was run off the road, Mother. It happened right in front of me." His voice wavered. "Jayde could've died, and I was powerless to stop it—again."

Putting a hand on his shoulder, Avalon stopped him mid-stride. "But she didn't. You can't live in the past forever, sweetheart. I know Candace's death still haunts you. It tears me up inside watching it eat away at you, but Jayde isn't Candace. What happened to that woman was a horrible accident."

"Yeah, and what's happening to Jayde is on purpose. I swear, if I find out Xavier was behind hurting her, I'll kill him. I love her—more than anything. If I lost her now . . . I couldn't survive it."

"You're a strong man, honey."

For a moment Devon tried to imagine life without Jayde. Tormented gray eyes met sympathetic brown ones. "Not that strong."

When Devon and his mother returned, it was to find Jayde sitting in the kitchen, waiting for them.

"Sweetheart, I thought you'd be taking a nap," said Devon.

"So did I. Um, can I speak with you for a second?" replied Jayde.

Devon frowned. "Sure. We'll be back, Mom."

He led Jayde to the library and closed the door. "What's wrong?"

Jayde retrieved her cell phone. After dialing her voice mail, she held the phone up to Devon's ear. He listened intently. After a brief time his expression turned murderous. "That bastard."

The next morning the Mitchells were sitting around the kitchen table.

"Son, are you sure you two have to go back? Can't we take care of everything here?" asked Sterling.

"No, Dad, I've checked. Detective Calvert said that in order for Jayde to file a petition to get a temporary harassment restraining order, she has to do it in person. We were able to call in and have the police fill out a report about Xavier's phone call. Since this is the second documented incident of harassment, Jayde can sign a warrant and have him arrested."

Avalon lowered her coffee cup. "Neither of you will have to go near him, I hope."

"I won't be responsible for what happens if I get near him. Jayde can request the court to appoint a U.S. Marshall or some other office to deliver the summons to him," said Devon.

"What happens if he's not there? He lives in Batavia. How can he be served if he decides to fly back to Illinois?" asked Sterling.

Devon shrugged. "I don't know, Dad. I suppose we'll get our questions answered when we go to the superior court. After we've filed everything, it's my intention to bring Jayde back here."

Jayde turned to Devon. "Are you sure that's necessary? I mean, if we have a restraining order, he can't come near me, right?"

"I'm not banking on him playing nice, Jayde. It's a deterrent, but it's useless if he doesn't adhere to the order," Devon noted.

"We can have him arrested if he disobeys the order," Jayde pointed out.

"Yes, we can, but the police would have to get there first. I'm not willing to chance it, sweetheart. We have to be smart about this." Devon checked his watch. "We have to get going if we're going to meet the jet in time."

Jayde turned to Devon's parents. "It was wonderful meeting all of you. I'm sorry to come here under these circumstances."

Devon's mother reached over and grabbed Jayde's hand. "Nonsense, dear. This isn't your fault. I'm glad you came and that we had a chance to meet you, regardless of the reason. You're welcome here anytime."

Everyone stood up. Jayde walked around the table and embraced Avalon. "Thank you, Mrs. Mitchell."

"None of that. Call me Avalon."

"Okay." Jayde sniffed.

Sterling hugged Jayde to him and whispered in her ear. "Don't worry. We take care of our own in this family—and that now includes you."

Tears streamed down Jayde's cheeks. She was overcome with emotion. "Thank you, Mr. Mitchell."

Devon's father fixed her with an expression that mirrored his son's when he was exasperated.

Jayde laughed despite her tumultuous feelings. "Sterling."

"Much better," Sterling said approvingly.

Melanie and her children arrived minutes later. After many hugs and a few more tears, Devon and Jayde were on the road, headed toward the interstate.

A call from the private investigator his father knew verified what Devon had been dreading: Xavier had already checked out of the hotel, and so far the investigator had been unable to locate him. Devon tried Xavier's home number again, but still no luck. He wasn't answering his cell phone, either. Maneuvering his SUV toward I-294 south, Devon surveyed the traffic. If all went well when he took the I-88 west exit, heading toward Batavia, he wouldn't be sitting in a parking lot. Devon gripped the steering wheel. Deep in thought, he replayed conversations, meetings, scenarios over and over in his head, wondering where things had gone wrong. Each time he came up blank.

He pulled his cell phone out of his pocket and dialed his pilot's number. He told the pilot that he and Jayde would be detained and would need to delay their departure. Hanging up, he turned toward Jayde.

"Sweetheart, I'm sorry, but I have to try something first."

"What?"

"I'm going to go to Xavier's house."

"What?" Jayde practically yelled. "Are you crazy? We're headed back to D.C. to get a restraining order against him, and you want to just drop by his house and say hi?"

"I know it sounds strange—"

"More like insane, Devon. What if he's there? How do you see this playing out? We'll show up, and he just invites us in for a chat?"

"He's not there. I know it."

"Then tell me again why we're going."

"I've been going over this in my head, and I can't figure out why it got to this point. If you'd have told me a few weeks ago that Xavier was capable of this extreme behavior, I would've said you were out of your mind."

"Maybe he's the one who's out of his mind," Jayde countered.

"Possibly, but surely I would've known before now. He was my best friend, Jayde."

Devon hit the steering wheel in frustration. Jayde put a hand on his arm. She watched him struggle with his emotions. "Okay. We'll do it your way," she said reassuringly. "What happens if he's not there?"

He placed his left hand over her fingers and squeezed. "I have a key."

Devon's SUV sidled up to the curb. Turning the engine off, he gave Jayde a quick kiss. "I'll be right back."

"You'd better be. I have my cell phone ready to dial nine-one-one. If you aren't back in five minutes, I'm calling."

He smiled. "Fair enough."

Opening the door, Devon grabbed his cell phone and stuffed it in a pocket of his slacks. Quietly, he closed the door and walked up the driveway. There were no cars in sight, which didn't surprise Devon. Xavier was adamant about parking his cars in the garage. He strode up to the front door, pressed the buzzer, and waited. An eight-tone doorbell chimed inside. The sound was muted, but Devon could still hear the aristocratic melody. He waited. After a minute, he tried again. Still no answer.

Devon dug in his jacket pocket and withdrew a ring of keys. Flipping keys around, he finally found the right one. Inserting it in the lock, he turned it in the tumbler. Cautiously, he pushed the door open. "Hello?" He listened a few seconds to determine if the security system was armed. It wasn't. Once inside, Devon surveyed the foyer and surrounding hallways. He wasn't sure what he expected, but he decided to be on guard, anyway.

It was quiet. Eerily so. "Xavier? It's Devon. Are you here?"

Climbing the stairs, Devon toured the second floor. He opened the double doors that led to the master bedroom. The room was as neat and organized as it always was. Checking Xavier's closet and nightstand, Devon quickly looked through the drawers. Nothing.

He went back downstairs and walked around the entire first floor. He didn't notice anything out of place there, either. He walked in Xavier's study. As he looked around the spotless room, Devon's gaze traveled to the large desk. Noiselessly, Devon ambled over to it. His fingers traveled over the top before coming to rest on one of the drawer knobs. Glancing at the study entrance, he took a deep breath and pulled the knob. The drawer opened easily.

Devon peered into the dark space, his hand moving quickly over its contents. Nothing out of the ordinary drew his attention. He opened a second drawer, then another. Opening the last drawer, Devon came across series of folders. Flipping through the first two, Devon saw the company logo and set aside the work papers. The third folder he opened caused him sit down.

Several newspaper articles about his car accident were neatly clipped together. Removing the metal clip, Devon leafed through the articles. Another stack contained Candace's obituary, old photos of them during college, as well as several business magazine articles highlighting the company. Other clippings from various magazines detailed his family life. A fourth folder contained more information on Devon and his father. Stunned, Devon sat speechless for a few moments. He wiped a hand across his face. Placing the items back into the folders, Devon put everything back the way he'd found it. Crossing the room, he silently let himself out of the house.

Once in the car, Devon sat for a second to compose himself.

"Well? What happened?" asked Jayde.

"I just looked around."

"Did you find anything?"

His instincts told him to tread cautiously where Xavier was concerned. He could no longer be trusted. Jayde was staring at him expectantly. He saw the concern and worry in her eyes. It killed him. He kissed the bridge of her nose and forced himself to give her a reassuring smile. "No, sweetheart. I didn't find anything."

CHAPTER 34

Disarming the alarm, Devon placed their bags on the tiled floor and flipped on the kitchen light. Jayde followed him into the kitchen. She sat on a bar stool and kicked off her shoes. "I'm pooped."

His head popped out of the fridge. "You look it. You want to call Christy, tell her we're back?"

The loud yawn that snuck past Jayde's lips was none too subtle. "I'll call her first thing in the morning—Mom and Dad, too."

"What about your insurance claims?"

"I phoned both agents from Illinois. For the condo, I told him I'd fax over a detailed list of the contents in a day or two. The Jeep was already towed to the dealer, and the adjuster received the police report and has already finished his estimate. "

"Good. We'll head to the courthouse first thing in the morning. There's nothing more we can do tonight, and we're both exhausted. I say we head to bed."

"Are we heading to bed to sleep?" she teased as they climbed the stairs. "Or are we heading to bed to . . ."

Devon grinned lasciviously. "That depends. I was going

to say I'm too tired to ravage your body tonight, but you know, I feel a second wind coming on. I just might be up for the task, after all."

Upstairs, Jayde opened the door to his bedroom. She didn't bother with the lights. In seconds she was devoid of all clothing. "A task, is it?"

Devon took a moment to rake his eyes over her silhouette before sweeping her up into his arms. "Hardly. No body as exquisite as this one should ever be deemed a task. Still, the more pressing question is, do you feel up to it?"

"Aside from the occasional aches and pains, I'm much improved. Besides, we made love the night after my accident, remember?" Jayde turned his face to hers. "We've done nothing but talk about Xavier, my trashed house, my wrecked car, and the threatening phone call for days now. I need a break from it all, Devon. Just for tonight, I don't want any of the nightmares to get in. Please?"

Devon was all too familiar with nightmares. He'd had enough to last a lifetime. His thoughts drifted back to the damaging information in Xavier's study. Tomorrow he would contact his father about his findings. He pushed it all to the back of his mind. Tonight was all about Jayde.

He placed her in the middle of the king-size bed before lying on his side next to her. His face registered his skepticism. "Baby, are you sure?"

Draping her leg over his waist, Jayde undulated her hips suggestively, while her hands teased his body. "Trust me. I'm more than ready for this."

"I don't think that's wise," Devon whispered against her ear, then trailed kisses down her rapidly warming skin. "Considering how much I want you."

Jayde pushed him up so she could pull his shirt over

his head. Next, she unbuttoned his jeans. "So I'll live dangerously."

Devon rolled over to slide off his cumbersome jeans. While he was on his back, Jayde straddled his midsection. Her exultation at feeling his massive body beneath her was absolute. Stroking his hand over her heated skin, Devon leaned up to glide his tongue across her belly. Jayde quivered above him. Unable to contain her feelings, she moaned loudly. When she tossed her head back, her loose tresses skimmed his thighs. When she leaned forward, her dark eyes smoldered with arousal. Need in its truest form enveloped the lovers in a web of desire so strong, it had them shaking.

Devon's touch caused Jayde to writhe in pleasure. If he didn't make love to her soon, she told him, she'd combust. So would he.

"You don't know how much I fantasized about you while at Bellehaven, about what I was going to do to you when I got you alone," he told her.

Jayde skimmed her hand over his hard chest. "No more than I did."

He stroked her bottom lip with his finger. "I don't know about that."

Jayde nipped at his digit before pulling it into her mouth. After she released his finger, she smiled seductively at him. "I do."

The playfulness was at an end. Devon set about showing Jayde just how real his fantasies could be.

Devon placed the steak on the grill, then rotated the corn on the cob. The last week in D.C. had been spent in accident-free bliss. Since returning from Illinois, all had been quiet and uneventful at the gallery. No threats, no Xavier, and no attempts on Jayde's life. Even their relationship had progressed without any bumps in the road.

Since they were getting along so well, Devon had broached the subject of Jayde coming back to work at the gallery. At first she wondered if he'd asked her so that he could keep an eye on her during the day. When he told her he'd asked because that was where she belonged, Jayde told him she'd think about it.

Devon took another swig of his beer. Life was good. So why did he feel like a shoe was about to drop? It had been a Herculean effort, but Jayde's condo had been put back together. She'd purchased all new furniture and home furnishings. Even her wardrobe was brand new. Her vehicle would be ready in a few days, too. From an aesthetic point of view, the break-in was a thing of the past. From an emotional viewpoint, he knew Jayde still had scars. He was far from elated when she insisted on moving back to her condo, but he respected her decision.

For him, her first night back at her place was a sleepless one. Tossing, turning, and eyeing the phone took up his time in equal measure. Waiting until six in the morning before calling her almost killed him. When he finally dialed her number, she picked up on the first ring. Her wide-awake voice made him smile in the darkness. "Couldn't sleep, either?"

"Not really," she admitted. "It feels . . . different."

"Plus, you miss me."

Despite her weariness, she laughed. "Yes, I miss you. It feels weird not having you in the room or in bed next to me."

"Tell me about it. Still, I'm glad your first evening back was quiet and uneventful."

"You forgot exhausting. Thank goodness, I don't

have to go to work. Having to stay awake today is going to prove to be a challenge."

Erotic images danced through his sleep-deprived brain. "I can think of several ways to occupy our time today."

"You've got a one-track mind."

"Most men do."

Seconds later, they hung up. Though it was dark, his eyes were wide open. Hearing Jayde's voice, knowing she was okay, made a huge difference to him. Yet, something he couldn't put a finger on made him uneasy. Since Candace's death, he'd become more aware of his feelings. His intuition was more acute. Rarely did he ever ignore his gut instinct. At the moment, it told him to watch his back—and Jayde's, too.

The police still had no suspects in Jayde's condo ransacking or her car accident. That news had Devon convinced their troubles weren't over. Xavier's strange behavior and fixation with his family bore close watching. Xavier's newly revealed jealousy had caught Devon unaware. Devon vowed he wouldn't be caught off guard again.

A day later, his instinct paid off, but not how he'd expected. Devon was in a meeting when the receptionist buzzed his line.

"I'm in a meeting," Devon said brusquely into the intercom.

"I know," the receptionist replied. "I'm the one who set it up."

"What is it?"

"Your mother is on the line. I told her you were ir

a meeting and not to be disturbed, but she said it was imperative she speak with you."

Devon raised an eyebrow. "Imperative?"

"Those were her exact words."

"Thank you. Put her through."

Excusing himself, Devon walked over to take the call at his desk. He picked up the receiver the moment the phone rang.

"Mom, what's going on?"

"It's Henry, dear."

Instantly, his annoyance fled. "What about him?"

"Oh, Dev, he's collapsed."

Devon tightened his grip on the receiver. His stomach lurched. "When?"

"I don't know exactly—I think sometime yesterday. We received a call this morning. Seems he was able to call his friend at a neighboring farm. Unfortunately, by the time the man got there, Henry was unconscious. The neighbor called for an ambulance immediately."

"How's he doing?"

"He's stable. The doctors think it's exhaustion or dehydration. Your father and I are leaving to head up there now. I'll let you know more when we get there and talk to his physician."

Devon's eyes widened. "Dad's going?"

"Of course. I'd ream him a new one if he didn't. They're family, no matter how much they claim not to get along."

"Keep me posted. Let me know if we need to hop a plane."

"I will, sweetie. How's Jayde, dear? Any new leads?"

"None." Devon grimaced.

"I'm sorry, honey. I have to go. Touch base with Melanie later. She didn't take the news too well."

"Will do." Suddenly the thought of his parents' mortality barreled to the surface. His breath constricted in his throat. "Mom?"

"Yes?"

"I love you—Dad, too."

"We love you, honey." Suddenly Avalon added, "Don't worry. Henry will be fine. He's too crotchety to die anytime soon."

"I pray you're right."

From that moment on, the day went progressively downhill. Problem after problem arose—fires to be put out—and through it all, his uncle never strayed from his thoughts. Devon's worry for him was constant. He'd spoken with Jayde twice that day. The first time was to fill her in on his uncle, and the second was simply because she wanted to tell him she loved him and to offer her support. Devon was moved by her concern for him and his family. When she offered to drop by his house later to cook him dinner, he couldn't refuse. His head was a mess, and Jayde's love offered a sweet reprieve from the turmoil circling him like a ravenous vulture.

"You're going to turn down dessert?" Jayde eyed him, incredulous.

"I can't think of a single spot to put it in. I'm good and stuffed."

Taking the lemon-cranberry bar, Jayde bit down on the end. She closed her eyes in true appreciation. Between chomps, a moan of pleasure escaped her lips. "This is truly incredible."

Devon's eyes turned opaque. "From where I'm sitting, it certainly is."

Jayde was about to retort when the telephone rang.

Excusing himself, Devon went to the kitchen to grab the cordless phone. After finishing her dessert, Jayde began clearing the dishes off the patio table. She was blowing out the candles when Devon returned.

"That was Mel."

"How's your uncle?"

Devon moved to take the dishes out of her hand, but she batted him away and walked into the house. Picking up the iced tea pitcher, he followed her. "He's much better. Turns out he'd overworked himself and was dehydrated. Mom and Dad are there now. Melanie thinks it's likely he'll be coming back to stay with my folks for a while."

"I'm sure that's the best thing for him right now. I just wonder if he'll agree. From what you've told me about your uncle, he's fiercely independent."

"He is, but I'm sure when Mom has her way, there'll be nothing he or my father will be able to do about it. Those two, stubborn as they are, are no match for her machinations. She'll get her way. Of that I have no doubt."

Jayde's cell phone rang. "That'll be Christy. She's downtown, shopping, and I made her promise to call if she found that glass bowl I was looking for." Diving into her purse, Jayde grabbed her phone. She saw it was a local call. Smiling, Jayde hit the talk button. "So, did you find it?"

"Did you miss me, Jayde?"

Jayde's eyes widened at hearing the familiar voice on the line. "Would you be mad if I said no?"

"We didn't exactly start off on the right foot. I'd like a second chance to make a first impression. How about it, Jayde? Give me another shot?"

"I don't know what kind of game you're playing, Xavier, but I'm not interested."

"Devon will let you down when you need him most, Jayde. Candace didn't listen, either, and look what happened to her. That could be you if you're not careful, Jayde."

Devon snatched the phone from Jayde's ear. "Xavier! I know it's me you want, not Jayde. It's always been me, hasn't it? You've got some personal vendetta against me. Admit it."

"Don't worry, Dev. You'll know everything—in time," Xavier growled.

CHAPTER 35

Henry sat forward while Avalon adjusted his pillows. "Are you done now?"

"In a minute," she said merrily. "You'll be more comfortable in your bed than in a chair until we're ready to go."

After his collapse, Henry had been given strict orders to rest and take things slow. Much to Henry's dismay, Avalon had taken those words and a lot more from his doctor to heart. She'd personally made arrangements with his neighbor to temporarily take over the day-to-day operation of Henry's farm. She'd told him to hire any additional help required while Henry was convalescing at their home.

Agitated, Henry fussed and complained the whole time Avalon packed his suitcases. Sterling, sitting in a nearby chair, on this rare occasion took sides with his brother. Nonplussed, Avalon sweetly ignored them both. Her task complete, she went out to the front door and signaled their driver that Henry's bags were prepared.

Returning, Avalon looked at both men. "I'd say we're ready to go. Do you need help getting to the car, Henry?"

"Of course, I don't need help," Henry griped. "Since when haven't I been able to get around under my own steam?"

"That's what I thought, dear. Sterling, help your brother to the car," Avalon ordered.

Stupefied, Sterling looked at his wife. "Darling, he just said he didn't need any help."

The look Avalon gave her husband spoke volumes. Sighing loudly, Sterling helped Henry up off the bed.

Henry fixed his brother with a glassy-eyed stare. "Is she always this pushy?"

"Yes, I am," Avalon called from the other room.

"Well, I don't like it one bit. I'm fine where I am," Henry muttered. "There's no need to be cartin' me off to Bellehardy. I can manage just fine right here. Me and Abigail."

"Quit complaining, Henry," Sterling said impatiently. "It's not going to work. Kiss the damned cow before you leave if you have to, but either way you're coming home with us. And the house isn't named Bellehardy. It's Bellehaven."

"Whatever. I knew it was something stuck up and fancy," Henry replied.

"Ava? I think he's going to need another pill," Sterling called.

"I knew it!" Henry skidded to a halt. "You're tryin' to put me out so I'll shut up."

"The thought had crossed my mind," Sterling mumbled.

"You two, stop arguing," Avalon chided. "This isn't good for Henry's peace of mind."

"Mine either," Sterling grumbled, giving his brother another nudge toward the door.

The drive back to Bellehaven was peacefully silent.

Except for an occasional comment, everyone was left to his or her thoughts. It was late by the time the driver pulled to a stop at the front door. Selby came out and opened the passenger door.

"Welcome back, Mr. and Mrs. Mitchell."

"Thank you, Selby," Avalon replied. "Is everything ready?"

Selby nodded. "Of course, Mrs. Mitchell. I'll help Mr. Henry in and come back to retrieve his luggage."

"That's not necessary. Sterling can see him up," said Avalon.

Sterling cast his wife a look before easing Henry out of the limo. Some time later, after his brother was ensconced in the guest suite down the hall, Sterling went to find his wife.

"Avalon, just how long do you think Henry and I can live under the same roof?"

Placing her washcloth on the marble counter, Avalon faced her husband. "As long as it takes."

"This is absurd. Henry and I don't get along."

"Whose fault is that?"

"Not mine," he argued. "He and I have nothing in common. Since his falling-out with Mother years ago, we've barely been civil to each other. You and the kids are the only ones he seems to care about, and now you expect me to turn the other cheek and forget? It was his decision to put a wedge between us, not mine."

"He had his reasons, dear."

"Bull. He let a woman come between us. A woman! I had nothing to do with my mother's harebrained scheme. I wasn't the one who betrayed him."

"I realize that, darling, but despite the past, he needs us now. He needs *you* now."

"Oh no, he doesn't," Sterling said bitterly. "I remember all too well. He doesn't need me, our mother, or the Mitchell money. For all he cared, we could all go to hell in a handbasket. Those were his exact words, Ava." Sterling's gray eyes darkened. "I'm not letting him back in. He can stay here until time stops. I'll be cordial until it kills me, but I'm never letting him in *here*." Sterling pointed to his heart. "He's done enough damage— a lifetime's worth."

Avalon placed her hands on her husband's shoulders. The pain in his voice belied the air of indifference. "A heart can mend, Sterling."

"It has, and I'll be damned if I let my brother hurt it again."

Sitting back in his chair in his office, Devon stared at the ceiling. Xavier still hadn't resurfaced. Aside from scaring Jayde and angering him, Xavier hadn't done anything that could be considered life threatening. They still hadn't located him, so the restraining order couldn't be served. If they didn't find him soon, it would expire, and they'd have to start all over again.

Picking up the telephone, Devon dialed his father. When the elder Mitchell answered, Devon's eyebrows shot up. "Geez, Dad, what's up with you? You sound as grouchy as a hungry bear."

"Between your mother harping and your uncle eating me out of house and home, I can't get a moment's quiet around this place. I swear, I'm going to rent an apartment in town while he's here."

"There you are!" Jayde barked. "I've been looking all over for you."

Devon frowned. "Dad, I have to call you back."

"I can hear that," said Sterling.

Devon hung up the phone. "You've found me."

"I can't believe you," Jayde said hotly.

"What are you talking about?"

"Of all the underhanded, sneaky, overbearing things you have ever done, Devon Mitchell, this is the worst."

Standing, Devon walked over to Jayde. He placed a hand on her arm. She threw it off.

"You know darn well what I'm talking about. You hired a bodyguard for me," she accused.

Devon sat back against his desk. "Yes, Jayde. I did hire someone to look after you. I just haven't had a chance to tell you yet."

"Why did you think I needed one?"

"In case you haven't noticed, Xavier is nowhere to be found. He's called your cell phone twice. We've blocked the calls from both locations, but there's nothing to stop him from doing it again. He's been playing cat and mouse with us, and I'm damned tired of being one step behind the lunatic! I'm sure when you calm down, you'll realize I did it merely as a safety precaution."

"How can you be sure of anything?"

He went over to her. Rubbing her arm, he asked, "Jayde, what's this really about?"

She yanked her arm free. "This is about you and me. I'm too old to be coddled, Devon. You have this over-powering urge to protect me from everything and everyone. You can't go around shielding me from things. I'm not some fragile china doll that's going to break if I get knocked down."

"That's not what I'm trying to do," Devon insisted.

"What about you sweeping in and shuttling me over to your house after my place got ransacked? How about what happened at Xavier's house? You looked like you'd gotten kicked in the stomach when you came back outside, and then you get in the car and tell me nothing's wrong? I could see you were shaken, Devon. I'm not blind! Now you expect me to rush into your arms because you took care of the big, bad guy by hiring me a bodyguard?"

"The condo looked like an explosion went off inside it. You couldn't have slept there if you tried. Besides, you were in shock, and you know it. As for Xavier's house, I found some files in his study. It looks like he's been keeping close tabs on me and my family for quite some time. He's obsessed about us, and I don't know why. I didn't tell you, because I didn't want to worry you more." He took a deep breath. "I'm supposed to protect you, Jayde. I love you. You're mine, and I want to make sure you stay that way."

"Yours? What am I? Furniture? You're going overboard with the possessive thing," she said, with exasperation. Suddenly her eyes narrowed. "It's because of Candace, isn't it?"

Devon reared back like he'd been shot. "What?"

"This overpowering urge to protect me. You think I'm going to get hurt or worse, and you'll be powerless to stop it. Can't you see it's affecting you—affecting us? You're so worried you won't be there to save me if something bad happens that you're overcompensating."

His gaze turned glacial. "Don't psychoanalyze me."

"I'm just trying to—"

"You don't have a clue what you're talking about. You go off half-cocked more times than not, and you're berating me for trying to keep you in one piece? It's *you* who's overcompensating. You're so worried something's going to happen that's beyond *your* control. It bothers you when you don't have a handle on every aspect of your life. It's like you've got this little book o instructions, and God forbid, something crops up that you can't check off the list."

"Stop it."

"When are you going to realize that life can't always be controlled?" He threw his hands up. "We can't always have things nice and neat. You can't run away every time something happens that you didn't foresee. What happened to you, Jayde? Some guy break your heart and you've never fully recovered? Is that what you're trying to prove? That you can handle yourself no matter what? Or is this little insecurity tied into some power struggle you had with—"

"You don't know what you're talking about!"

"Can't take a little constructive criticism? You can dish it out, but you can't take it, huh?"

"You've got nerve. What happened to you, Devon? You accuse me of always running away, but you did the same thing. Candace died in a freak accident, and you head for the hills for months. Who's the hypocrite now?"

"I left to give my family a break. Reporters were hounding them everywhere. I left to force people to get on with their lives and leave us alone."

"No. You left because you were running away from the pain, from the guilt about what happened. You put your family through hell because you were so involved with your own pain that you didn't think about the pain your leaving caused them."

Devon grabbed her arms and drew her up until they were nose to nose. "I didn't run from the pain or the guilt. They were with me every day for the three months I was gone. I'm not a coward, Jayde. I took responsibility for my actions. Her death . . . tormented me." Devon loosened his hold, dropping his arms to his sides. Anguish ravaged his features. His eyes told the depth of his memories. "Every time I closed my eyes, there it was. There they were. Candace and the child we lost."

"But you weren't living, Devon," Jayde said quietly. "You existed—nothing more. You surrounded yourself with your misery and wouldn't let anyone in."

"You don't let anyone in, either, Jayde. Not when it really counts. You have to solve everything on your own. You're afraid to lean on anyone or ask for help or show that you're scared to death about what's going on around you. Well, I can admit it. I am worried out of my mind, and I don't have all the answers. I've been betrayed by the one person I thought always had my back. The woman I love is being tormented by a man I trusted like a brother, and you want to get upset with me because I hired someone to make sure he doesn't harm you? I'll do whatever it takes to make sure this crazy grudge against me doesn't turn fatal. There is nothing more important to me than your life, Jayde. Nothing. I need you, and I am man enough to admit it. Yet, for some reason, you think your needing someone, truly needing someone, is a sign of weakness. The question is, why?"

Too close. He is delving too deeply. "I . . . I can't deal with this right now," Jayde cried, shoving past him.

"Ah, there it goes, the Seaton backside," Devon yelled after her. "I knew if I stuck around long enough, I'd eventually see you turning tail and running off into the sunset—again. Well, you'd better hurry, Jayde. It's getting late. The sun's almost gone."

Her step faltered momentarily, but she recovered. She didn't say another word as she pulled open his office door and walked out.

CHAPTER 36

Henry leaned his head back against the cushion and sighed. The water swirled in loud, powerful currents around him. Sinking lower into the hot tub, he inhaled the faintly chlorinated air around him. "Aren't you going to ask me how I'm feeling?"

Across the swirling water, Sterling didn't bother to open his eyes. "Why bother? It's apparent you're feeling better. Your appetite has increased exponentially, you're walking around the grounds without assistance twice a day, plus you're in this spa with me, hogging up all the heat. I'd say your health is the least of my problems."

"For someone who doesn't give a fig about me, you sure do pay attention."

Sterling raised his head off the built-in pillow and regarded his brother. "I never said I didn't care about you, Henry. Those were your words, not mine."

"What am I supposed to think? You've barely spoken a handful of words to me since I arrived. It's obvious you can't wait to get me gone."

"Will you stop talking like you grew up in the country? Your English is as polished as mine. I suppose when you turned your back on your family, you forsook the proper vernacular, too. You know, it amazes me how someone who disowns their family gives a crap about how often his estranged brother converses with him."

Henry's jaw flexed. "Forget I mentioned it."

"Done," Sterling snapped back.

After a few moments of tense silence, Sterling stood. Once out of the hot tub, he grabbed a nearby robe and towel. Drying off, he glanced at Henry.

"If I live to be one hundred, Henry, I'll never understand how you could've done it—how you could just write me off. We were more than brothers. We were the best of friends. You cared so little for me that you just believed I was guilty of tampering with your future, of coming between you and the woman you loved? All for the sake of money?"

Henry got out of the water and grabbed a towel. His round stomach heaved with each angry swipe of the towel as he dried off. "You've done plenty of things in your life for the sake of money. Tell me I'm wrong."

Sterling's jaw flexed, and he looked away.

"I didn't think so," Henry said sarcastically. "Besides, I heard you, Sterling . . . both of you, one night by the pool. I know Mother saw her as an outsider. You didn't disagree. Mother said my girlfriend wasn't good enough to be a Mitchell, that she'd never be good enough."

"So what you're saying is my not jumping to your defense that night translates to me siding with Mother?"

"Try to imagine how I felt. Gloria was the love of my life," Henry said brokenly. "She was shunned and unwelcome by the two people who mattered most to me in the world. All I wanted was a happily ever after, Sterling. I wanted what you found with Avalon. I deserved a life, a family, and it was all taken from me, and for what? Mother's paranoia about our family's precious millions?"

Confusion clouded Sterling's gray eyes. "Henry, I didn't shun her. I didn't even know her that well."

"That's not what Mother told me. She said you both felt that way. That you'd gone off to try and talk some sense into Gloria, to show her how a life with me would never work."

Sterling looked incredulous. "I did no such thing. Henry, I never tried to break the two of you up. I don't care what our mother told you. It wasn't true. That's what I tried to get you to understand, but you wouldn't listen. You were so angry with Mother, at what she did, that you wouldn't entertain the idea that I didn't share her lowly opinions and bigoted notions of Gloria. I was merely a sounding board for her, nothing more. You'd have known that if you'd stayed around to hear the rest."

Henry was ashen. His gray eyes clouded with doubt and surprise. "You didn't have anything to do with Mother sending Gloria away?"

Sterling met his brother's uncertain gaze head-on. "No, Henry. I didn't. I told you that then, and I'm telling you now. I didn't betray you. We're brothers. Regardless of what we fight about, we're flesh and blood."

Henry closed his eyes. His breath shuddered. "Why . . . why didn't you keep telling me this until I believed it?"

Sterling shrugged. "Would it have worked? We're both too stubborn for our own good. The Mitchell curse, I guess. Besides, I was too damned mad at you to keep proclaiming my innocence. You weren't the only one caught in the middle of Mother's machinations. It cut deep that you didn't trust me enough to realize I'd never hurt you, Henry—that I'd never lie to you."

By the time Henry made it over to his brother, his eyes were burning with unshed tears. Relatively the same height, both brothers eyed each other speculatively. "Sterling," Henry choked out, "how . . . how can I ever earn your forgiveness?"

Sterling put some distance between them. Looking out over the lawn, he was thoughtful. Finally he shrugged. "I don't know, Henry. We've been at odds so long, I don't think forgiveness is going to come easy for me."

Stricken, Henry simply nodded. "I understand," he finally managed to get out. "For what it's worth, I'm sorry, terribly sorry, for this whole mess." Wrapping his towel around his neck, Henry slipped his feet into his worn flip-flops, then headed slowly toward the house, his shoulders hunched in defeat.

Sterling watched him for a while before yelling after him. "You're just going to give up like that? No wonder that decrepit cow doesn't give you any milk."

Turning, Henry observed his brother as he came forward. "Abigail knows that despite her obstinate behavior or my surly disposition, I love her, no matter what."

"Yeah, well, I don't subscribe to that theory. I'll tell you right now, I'm not rolling over half as fast as that crazy bovine. You've been an ass for a lot of years, Henry, and you've got a lot of kissing up to do."

In that moment, in their own way, both brothers acknowledged the newly erected, fragile truce between them.

"What about you?" Henry countered. "Your countenance hasn't improved with age, either. Honestly, I don' know how Avalon puts up with you."

Sterling shrugged. "Ava loves me."

Henry started to speak, but Sterling stopped him. " you even think about comparing my wife to that damne cow, first I'm going to deck you, and then I'm going to tell her."

Henry started to chuckle. Eventually, Sterling joined in. What started off as lighthearted jocularity quickly turned into full-bellied, all-out roaring laughter.

CHAPTER 37

Looking up at the sun-filled sky, Jayde wiped the sweat from her forehead. It was hot and she was tired. She'd been at her beach house, doing manual labor, since that morning. Glancing down at the dirt and mulch at her knees, she smiled in satisfaction. She'd been pushing, pulling, and twisting the steadfast weeds in her flower beds since eight o'clock that morning. Triumphantly, she yanked the last piece of root up from the dark, rich soil. She pretended it was Devon's head. In the sunlight the sweat glistened on her tanned skin. Working her aggressions out was just what she needed.

Her cell phone rang shrilly, interrupting the peaceful silence. Pulling off a glove, Jayde dug into her shorts pocket to retrieve the phone.

When she looked at the incoming number, she saw it wasn't Devon. Jayde found herself both relieved and annoyed by that. "Hello, Christy."

"Hey. Where've you been, girl? I've been trying to reach you for days. Personally, I thought you and love boy were holed up in your house, crunching noodles."

"We haven't been crunching anything lately. In fact, haven't seen or spoken with him in three days."

"Whoa. Do I detect a trace of annoyance? What's going on, Tree? Lover's spat? I thought the two of you would be picking out his and her towels by now."

Jayde sat back on her haunches. "Actually, Chris, now really isn't a good time to talk about it."

"Nonsense. Now is the perfect time to talk about it," Christy replied. "It's still new, and you're still mad. Now tell me what Captain Charisma is up to."

By the time Jayde ended her call with Christy, she was all worked up again. Deciding a walk along the water would ease her troubled mind, she called Boomer to her and took off for the beach. Finding a rock along the water's edge, she scrambled up and sat down.

Jayde sat for so long, she lost track of time, and her lower extremities went numb. When the wind picked up, she decided it was time to go inside. She eased off the rock. As she turned around, she was brought up short by a tall figure looming over her.

"You're an easy person to follow, Jayde. You don't look behind you much, do you?"

The air left her body like a cannon being shot. Her hand rose to her chest in an effort to silence the deafening beat of her heart. "What are you doing here?" Jayde gasped, taking two steps backward. Her knees came in contact with the rough rock she'd just vacated. Boomer growled menacingly, his teeth bared. With his head level, the dog looked directly at Xavier.

"Call that dog off, or he turns into fish bait."

"Boomer, easy," Jayde commanded. "Come."

Going immediately to his owner's side, Boomer growled low in his throat.

Jayde glanced frantically behind Xavier.

"Don't bother looking for your shadow. I took care of im earlier, so he won't be interrupting. He wasn't a very good bodyguard. If I were Devon—I presume that's who hired the loser—I'd get my money back." His treacherous grin made his icy stare pale in comparison, and it scared the daylights out of her.

Grabbing Jayde's arm, Xavier jerked her to him. Boomer started barking and growling.

Fearing the consequences, Jayde grabbed his collar with her free hand. "Boomer, no!"

Xavier smiled nonchalantly, as if his presence there and his actions weren't out of the ordinary. "Let's go back to the house and have a chat. You and the dog go first. Don't be stupid enough to try and run, Jayde. You won't make it."

Jayde coerced Boomer down the gravel path. Xavier followed. Back at the house, Jayde guided her dog into a bedroom and pulled the door shut behind her. He whined and scratched at the door.

Without warning, Xavier pulled her close and buried his face in her hair. "How I've missed you. I would've come sooner, but I was working on my plan. It had to be perfect."

Her legs buckled. "What . . . what plan?"

Steadying her by grabbing her arm again, Xavier leaned in to whisper into her ear. "You're going to do me a favor, baby—one that will save both you and your lover's life, if you're convincing enough." He handed her the phone. "Your assignment is simple, pet. You'll call Devon and tell him to get here as soon as possible. I suggest you make it convincing."

Jayde bit her lower lip. "I haven't spoken with him in days. We had a big fight. He wouldn't believe me if all of the sudden I ask him to come here. It would never work."

Xavier's grip tightened on her arm. Jayde winced i

pain. "Let me rephrase that, lovebug. If you don't call Devon, I won't hesitate to use this," he said, pulling a gun out from under his shirt at the back of his pants and waving it in her face. "And if you don't think I'll use it, *you've* got another thing coming."

Jayde instinctively took a step back. Shaking, she waited while Xavier dialed the number. It rang four times before Devon's deep voice interrupted the loathsome ringing.

"Mitchell," Devon answered.

"Hi, Devon. It's me," Jayde said stiffly.

A long pause ensued. Jayde gritted her teeth.

"Jayde. I'm surprised to hear from you."

"You're telling me."

Xavier frowned and raised the gun higher.

"What's wrong?" Devon asked. His smooth voice caressed her ear, and Jayde struggled to maintain her composure.

"Nothing. I'm fine. Just a hard day, that's all. How are you?" Jayde said, with forced brightness.

"Let's see. We had a knock-down, drag-out fight a few days ago, and neither of us has been intelligent enough to call the other and settle things—until now. Other than that, I'm great. Thanks for asking." Devon mumbled something under his breath. "Look, Jayde, I think I should go. The last thing I want is another shouting match between us."

"No," Jayde nearly screamed.

"Jayde, what's gotten into you?"

At that moment Xavier twisted her arm up her back, his warning clear. Jayde grimaced in pain. In her opinion, Xavier was certifiably crazy, and that made him treacherous and unstable. It was suicide to risk angering him further, but she had to find a way to forewarn Devon.

"Nothing, sweetie. I just miss you. I don't like it when we fight."

She heard Devon breath loudly into the phone.

"I don't, either, but this ran a lot deeper than just a difference of opinion. We said some harsh things to each other. We need to address them before we go any further."

"I agree. Our conversation got out of hand, didn't it? We both said things I'm sure we didn't mean, right?"

"Jayde, what's going on? You're acting peculiar. Is there something you aren't telling me?"

"Uh, well, I—I would rather you came to the beach house to talk about this. I really need to see you."

"The beach house, huh? Figures," Devon said dryly. "I knew you'd been trying to avoid me. Stupid of me not to realize you'd head there."

"I'm sure I can make it worth your while if you come straight here." Jayde lowered her voice seductively.

"I don't know what's going on with you, but I'll be there shortly."

"I can hardly wait," Jayde breathed. "Don't forget to bring my painting with you. I've got the perfect spot picked out. It's in your study, against the desk."

"Painting? You didn't ask me to pick up a painting, and it's certainly not at my house," Devon replied.

"Baby, that's a great place to hang it. Why didn't I think of that? I'll bet *El Matador* will look fantastic over the fireplace."

Silence came over the line, and Jayde thought her nerves would crack like an eggshell. Suddenly Devon broke the silence. "Jayde." His voice shook. "Is someone with you?"

"Yes, I've already eaten, but I'll save dessert for when you get here."

More silence. "Is the bodyguard there?"

"No, silly, I'm not wearing that."

"Xavier?"

"Yes, I could change into that if you want me to. You really are naughty."

The expletives that followed were numerous and loud. "Jayde, listen to me. Hang on, sweetheart. I'll be there as soon as I can. I promise you."

"I'm sure you will, baby." Jayde chuckled. "Hurry. I can't wait to see you."

The moment Devon hung up, Jayde handed the receiver back to Xavier. He placed it back on the hook. Releasing Jayde's arm, Xavier motioned for her to sit on the couch. Cradling her bruised arm, she sat down. Her loathsome gaze tracked his movements around the room.

"Well done, Jayde. You did a very good job of convincing him to come. I liked the painting thing. Not too original, but I'm sure it warned him all the same. It's great when everything goes according to plan." When he saw her flinch, he laughed. "Come now. You didn't think that little game of drop the clue got past me, did you? A bit elementary, but I'm sure it alerted Devon that you were in danger."

Jayde suddenly felt sick inside. "Xavier, why are you doing this? I think I've earned the right to know."

He sat next to her on the couch. Running a finger along her leg, he leaned back, crossing his legs at the ankle. "Sorry. It's not time for you to know. Not yet. Don't despair, Jayde. You've done well, sweetheart. I think I'll let you live a while longer."

For the next hour, Xavier walked around like he was a guest. He helped himself to a snack, then offered Jayde bottled water, all the while talking to her like they were old friends.

"It wasn't always this way, you know. Devon and I were the best of friends. Aside from a few disagreements, we still are," he told her.

"Are you kidding? You threatened me at my condo, and now you're holding me at gunpoint. You call this normal, everyday behavior?"

"You aren't hurt, or dead, are you? I'd say I've been extremely polite. This will all be over soon."

Trapped and *utterly confused* were words that suddenly came to her mind. She'd played into Xavier's hands. Devon was on his way, and that was exactly what Xavier wanted. What eluded her was *why* one of Devon's closest friends would suddenly want to harm them. Jayde felt like she was putting a puzzle together without all the pieces. There were too many questions, and only Xavier had the answers.

"I'm trying, but I don't understand. What could Devon or I have possibly done to bring you to this point?" Jayde asked her captor.

"Yes, what indeed?" came a cold voice from the door.

Xavier and Jayde turned in unison at the sound of Devon's voice. Jayde's gaze roamed over Devon like she hadn't seen him in years. Xavier's expression turned to granite.

"Devon," Jayde said, sobbing. She moved toward him but Xavier's hand snaked out to restrain her.

"Man," Xavier said, chuckling, "I forgot how stealth you could be. I really didn't hear you come in. I'm truly off my game."

Ignoring Xavier, Devon allowed his eyes to devour Jayde. "Are you all right?"

"Of course, she's all right," Xavier snapped. "She's not dead, is she?"

At the murderous look in Devon's eyes, Jayde spoke up. "I'm fine, Devon. He hasn't hurt me."

Devon inched forward. "This has gone on long enough. What the hell is this about, Xavier?"

Xavier backed up, holding Jayde tight against him. "Not too close, Dev. I might get desperate and snap your girlfriend's pretty neck," Xavier warned, placing an arm around Jayde's neck for emphasis.

Devon stopped where he was.

"That's better. Now sit down on the couch and take her with you," Xavier said, shoving Jayde in Devon's general direction.

Strong arms reached out to steady her, and she smiled thankfully at Devon before they sat down on the couch.

"You know, try as I might, I can't fathom why she'd pick you over me—why anyone would pick you over me. I tried showing Jayde the error of her ways, but she just didn't listen," Xavier reflected.

Jayde's head snapped up. "You call destroying my home teaching me a lesson?"

Xavier put up his hands. "Guilty as charged. I can't say it wasn't fun, either. I mean, the time I had going through your lingerie drawer alone was worth all the work."

Tears ran down her face. "Did you run me off the road, too?"

"Now, that I can't take credit for. Not directly, anyway. I hired two idiots to do that. Don't worry. They weren't local, so you'll never find them."

The curse Devon flung at Xavier hadn't stopped reverberating in everyone's ears before Devon had Xavier on the floor. Rolling around on the floor, Devon sent a jab to Xavier's stomach. Xavier redistributed his weight and rolled Devon over. Retrieving the gun from his pocket, Xavier blindsided Devon with a blow to the side of his head. Stunned, Devon turned on his side.

"Devon," Jayde screamed, diving to the floor at his side.

Standing, Xavier moved back. Blowing air out of his mouth, he ran a hand over his midsection. "Nice punch, but I wouldn't advise trying it again."

"Go to hell," Devon muttered while allowing Jayde to help him to his feet.

"Only if you go first," Xavier growled.

"Whatever this is about, you'll never get away with it," Jayde muttered, helping Devon recline on the couch.

"Now that's where you're wrong, sweetheart," Xavier hissed. "Funny how things work out, isn't it, Dev? I mean, who would've thought my goal would finally be attainable? I've plotted and planned for years how I'd get my revenge. Then you up and disappear without a trace, and that damned family of yours wouldn't tell me where you were. Always so protective, aren't they? At least of their own. Do you know what day tomorrow is, Devon?"

"It's Sunday," Devon replied impatiently. "Why?"

"You forgot," Xavier said, with disgust. "It figures you'd forget. She didn't mean a damn thing to you, did she, Devon? You didn't deserve her. I told her that often enough, but she just wouldn't listen."

"Who is he talking about, Devon?" Jayde whispered. "Oh, he means . . ."

"Candace," Devon replied, glaring at his estranged friend.

"Yes, Candace," Xavier snapped. "Tomorrow is her birthday. She would've been thirty-two had she lived. But she didn't, thanks to you and your damned family. You killed her and then used the Mitchell name to cover it up."

Devon bolted upright, with fists clenched at his side. "Is that what this is all about, Xavier? That's a damned lie, and you know it. I didn't kill Candace. It was an accident. My family didn't cover anything up. They would never have done that. It wasn't my fault she died."

Something snapped inside Xavier. The calm facade he'd erected suddenly broke away to show the anger, pain, and torment that festered beneath. "Everything is your fault," he shouted. "It's always been *your* fault. From the day you were born, you've made my life a living hell that I can't escape from."

"I don't have a clue what you're talking about," said Devon.

Xavier nodded. "You're right. You don't have a clue, but you will. We're taking a ride. The three of us are going back to Bellehaven. I suggest you call and get the company jet flown here to meet us. I can't fly with this gun, but I don't have to. I've got all the guarantees I need. If we don't arrive back in Illinois this evening, things won't go well."

Devon lunged for Xavier. "What have you done?"

Xavier backed up, holding his gun in front of Devon's face. "Nothing . . . yet. Don't cause me to use this. I will, trust me." When Jayde pulled Devon back, Xavier relaxed. "Listen up, if you try to get away or draw attention to us, your precious family will pay the price. A friend is close by, waiting for my call. If he doesn't get it, the Mitchells won't live to see dinnertime—none of them."

CHAPTER 38

Remaining outwardly calm despite the terror she was feeling was one thing. Keeping her hands from trembling was beyond Jayde's control.

"It'll be okay." Devon's warm voice wafted against her ear.

Jayde shrugged. "I hope so. You know, upon further inspection, I've determined I don't have a problem admitting my fears. Take right now, for instance. I'm scared to death, and I have no qualms about divulging it. See, no checklist, no trying to solve everything on my own anymore. I'm an open book—an open, vulnerable, terrified book."

"Jayde?"

Staring out the window, Jayde didn't turn around. "Yes?"

Devon used a finger to tilt her face toward him. When their eyes made contact, his jaw clenched. Jayde wasn' downplaying her feelings. They were written in perfec clarity on her face. She was terrified. "I'm sorry."

She looked confused. "This isn't your fault."

"It is. Something tells me this isn't all about Candace

There's more to Xavier going off the deep end than mourning the death of his ex-girlfriend. For some reason he needs an audience before imparting his endgame, but that's not the only reason I was apologizing."

"Then why?"

"I'm sorry for what happened the other day. The things I said. I was out of line, and I didn't mean to hurt you."

The ice around Jayde's heart had begun thawing the moment he walked through the door of her beach house. The closer they got to Illinois, the more her heart softened. What would happen there was an unknown, but one thing was certain: Jayde didn't want what could possibly be their last hours spent together marred by anger or hard feelings.

"Devon, it's all right. Let's not lie. We both meant the things we said. It's okay to admit the truth. We both have been hurt and have difficulty letting our guards down for different reasons, but we'll get over it. Of that I have no doubt. I guess what I'm trying to say is, I love you, Devon. Despite your overbearing nature, heaven help me, I still love you."

He kissed the bridge of her nose before running a finger over her cheek. "I love you, Jayde. I always have. Despite your being a control freak. I promise you we'll live to fight another day."

Devon drew her close. As he lowered his mouth, Jayde smiled.

"I know," she said breathlessly before losing herself in his kiss.

After landing, Xavier ushered them into an awaiting car. Retrieving a gun from under the seat, he insisted

Devon drive and Jayde sit up front, too, so he could keep an eye on them. During the drive to Devon's parents' estate, Xavier kept up constant chatter. Devon itched to do something to free them, but he squelched the idea. There were more players in this sick, twisted game. Devon wouldn't take a chance on causing his family members or Jayde harm.

When they arrived at Bellehaven, Xavier's eyes were alight with excitement. "Finally, we're here. Now, let's go embrace destiny."

With his hand entwined with hers, Devon pulled Jayde along behind him, keeping her as far away from Xavier as he could. Xavier rang the bell and waited while Selby greeted them.

"Where's everyone, Selby?" Devon asked tightly.

"In the family room, sir. Your sister is here, too," replied Selby.

Jayde's stomach clenched. "Are the children here?"

"I'm afraid not, Miss Seaton. Their father took them to a movie this evening." Selby glanced at Xavier. "Can I take your jacket, Mr. Taggert?"

"No thank you, Selby. I prefer keeping it close. I won't be here very long," said Xavier.

Selby ushered them down the hall toward the family room. Devon wanted to hang back, but Xavier insisted on going last. Devon tried frantically to think of a way to get Xavier alone, but even if he did, Devon didn't know who else was involved. He'd have to wait to see what went down before making a move.

The entire family, save Uncle Henry, was seated on the couch, laughing and talking.

Devon went in first, followed by Jayde.

"Oh, my goodness," Devon's mother exclaimed ex

citedly. "Sweetheart, what are you and Jayde doing here? What a wonderful surprise."

"I'll say it is." Melanie jumped up and ran toward her brother. Wrapping her arms around him, she kissed him on his cheek. "You could've called to let us know you both were coming."

"Sorry. I thought a surprise would be better," said Devon.

"Well, this is certainly a surprise," Sterling said, going to greet his son.

Avalon pushed past everyone to hug her son. "Honey, you sure know how to make an old woman smile." Avalon looked behind Devon. "You, too, Jayde. Welcome back, dear."

"Thank you, Mrs. Mitchell." Jayde's voice quivered.

"Please, dear, call me Avalon."

"What a lovely scene," Xavier observed from the doorway.

"What's he doing here?" Sterling bellowed, advancing toward his son. "What's this about?"

"Sterling, please calm down," Avalon said worriedly.

"Listen to her, old man. She's wise, despite being a home-wrecking bitch," Xavier spat.

Everyone gasped. Sterling's face was mottled with rage. "How dare you!"

"How dare I? How dare I? That's laughable. I'll dare a lot more before this night is through, I promise you. Now sit down." Xavier pointed to Avalon. "You, too. As a matter of fact, all of you sit down. I'm going to tell you all a little story."

Triumphant, Xavier looked over the crowd of shocked people. This was his moment to finally be redeemed. To get what was rightfully his. To take his place in society, as he should have the moment he was born. He looked at

Devon, who was standing by his family. Xavier laughed. "Defiant to the end, aren't you, Devon? It all comes back to you. You and that demanding mother of yours saw to it that everything was taken from me. Things could've been so different if you hadn't been born," Xavier said longingly.

Devon eyed him with contempt. "Stop talking in riddles. It's obvious you want to say something. You've gathered us all here, by hook or by crook. So let's hear it, Xavier. What's this big revelation you'll be going to jail for?"

"Quit the bravado, Dev. I know you're at your wit's end trying to figure out how to get the upper hand. Well, forget it. I've got it, and I intend to keep it. In the end, I'll get everything, and you'll finally get what you've deserved." Xavier's gaze turned to Devon's father. "Tell him, Sterling. Tell him why I'm here."

Everyone looked at Sterling, whose gaze had never left Xavier. "I haven't the foggiest notion what you're talking about. Aside from the fact that you're deranged, I don't know why you're here."

Xavier snorted. "That's not exactly true, Dev. All these years we've shared more than just Candace Monroe. We've shared blood, too. DNA."

Devon shook his head. "What the hell are you talking about?"

Xavier took a deep breath; his eyes glowed with contempt. "Sterling Mitchell is my father, too. I'm his illegitimate son."

Devon's warm bronze complexion suddenly turned ashen. His breath caught in his throat. He felt as if a heavy stone had been thrown into the pit of his stomach. "No . . . it can't be."

Xavier went on. "Your father had an affair with m

mother, but she wasn't good enough to end his precious marriage to your mother. So he paid her off to raise me on her own, but he knew about me. The spineless bastard left me without a name—without a father."

"That's a damned lie. I am not this lunatic's father," Sterling roared.

Devon closed his eyes and struggled within himself. A moment years ago came barreling back to him. He'd overheard his parents arguing. It was a major, heated exchange. His father had been unfaithful to his mother, but Devon had never imagined a child had been born from that affair.

"I never knew I had a brother." Devon's eyes went to Xavier. "You were in front of me the whole time, and I never knew."

"Devon, he isn't your brother. It's not true," Sterling said quickly.

Devon turned to look at his parents, his expression raw and exposed. "But, I heard you. One night I heard you both arguing. I had hidden in your room. I heard you fighting, and Mom was crying. I heard her accuse you of having an affair. You admitted it. I heard it with my own ears. You admitted it."

Melanie gasped, tears in her eyes. "That's not true." She turned to her parents. "Mom, Daddy, say it isn't true."

"Oh, sweetheart," Avalon cried out, looking toward her children with despair. "I'm so sorry. We—"

"It's true." Sterling's voice shook as he took his wife's hand in his. "It was a long time ago. You both were young. I . . . I did have an affair. I betrayed your mother, and she found out. It was my darkest hour, her confronting me about it. I couldn't lie to her. I admitted it, begging her forgiveness. Your mother didn't speak to me for two

weeks, while she pondered the fate of our marriage . . .
of our family. In the end, she agreed to take me back—
to give us another try—under one condition, that I never
see the woman again. I'd embarrassed her, humiliated
myself, and broken the trust she'd placed in me. It was a
time I wished had never occurred. I'm ashamed of what
I did to my family, but I swear to you, Devon and Melanie,
there was no child from that indiscretion."

"You're lying." Xavier shook with fury. "He's only
trying to protect his precious son and the Mitchell
name."

Devon turned to face his friend. "What do you hope
to gain from harming me, Xavier? From harming
Jayde? We aren't the ones causing you pain. It's your
hatred and need for vengeance that's eating you alive."

"You've caused me pain from day one," Xavier declared. "My mother told me everything. I was the first
one born, but you were the heir, the one who would
carry on the Mitchell name and be a son to our father.
It was my mother's quiet suffering that helped me realize that I could bide my time to get what was due me by
birth. Sterling made sure I had the money and means
to make something of myself. He gave me everything
but his name, his love, and recognition, and the bastard actually thought that was good enough."

Xavier laughed, harshly. "Then there was Candace. I
loved her more than I've ever loved anyone. She was
mine. We would've been happy together. Forever. But
you ruined that, too. She took one look at you and saw
all the dollar signs after your name. I couldn't compete
with that—at least not at first—but I waited. I made my
mark on the world, made a name for myself. Eventually,
I was well off in my own right. I was ready to reclaim the
love of my life—but all she wanted was an affair. I gave

her my heart and soul, and all she wanted was sex. It was my child growing inside her when she died."

Devon staggered backward. "What?"

"We'd had an affair while you were gone," Xavier said, with derision. "It was my child she was carrying, not yours. I'd planned for her to run off with me, to tell you the truth, but she wouldn't have it. She only wanted you, your name, and all that came with it. She told me she was going to raise my child as a Mitchell. I made her a promise that if she didn't tell you, I'd tell you myself. I loved her. I would've done anything for her. The night of the party, I'd planned for us to be together, but you got to her first." Xavier's voice broke. He looked down, fighting for composure. "She was supposed to leave with me, not you. Because of you, she's dead. My child is dead. "

A roar of pure rage was ripped from Devon's throat. He lunged at Xavier, knocking him over. The gun slid across the floor. "I'll kill you," Devon promised, tightening his grip. He heard screams behind him, but Devon was undeterred. His only thought was to make Xavier pay for all he'd done. "I was sick inside with guilt, you bastard! I thought it was my child that died, and you were having an affair with Candace?" Devon closed his hands around Xavier's throat. He smiled as he increased the pressure. Hands were behind Devon, trying to pull him off, but he remained focused on the task of squeezing the life out of Xavier.

"You're going to pay for what you did to her . . . to me, to my family, and to Jayde," Devon thundered. "The hell you put us through is going to pale in comparison to what I'm going to do to you. You say you can't live without her? We're going to find out if you mean it."

Jayde moved slowly toward the back of the room.

Turning her body away from the commotion, she pulled her cell phone from her pocket and dialed 911.

Melanie glanced at Jayde. She moved to stand in front of her.

Devon slammed Xavier's head against the floor several times.

"Devon, no!" his mother cried. "Please don't do this!"

"Son, don't go to jail over this lunatic," Sterling implored him.

Xavier tried to pry Devon's hands off his neck. When that didn't work, he took his fists and slammed them on either side of Devon's head. Devon's hold loosened. Xavier used his weight to knock Devon over. Scrambling out from under him, Xavier was up on his feet. Devon grabbed his leg and yanked him back to the floor. Xavier used his other leg to kick Devon in the chest. Momentarily free of him, Xavier went back to retrieve the gun.

CHAPTER 39

"Xavier," Sterling said, slowly extending his hands out in front of him. "This has to stop. I'm not your father. If I were, I would never have turned my back on you. You've made Devon's life a living hell for nothing. It won't bring back Candace or your child back, or change the fact that you aren't my son."

"Stop lying to me!" Xavier held the gun in front of him.

Devon and his father moved in front of the women.

"You did turn your back on me . . . and my mother, Gloria. You deserted both of us when we needed you most. I was born a Taggert, when I should've been a Mitchell," Xavier raged.

"Sterling isn't lying, Xavier. He's not your father," a gravelly voice said from behind Xavier, "but it would appear that I could be."

Whipping around, Xavier stared at Henry. "Henry, what are you doing here?"

"Stop," Sterling said, with contempt. "Don't you dare harm him."

"You said your mother's name was Gloria?" asked Henry.

"Yes," said Xavier.

"What was your mother's maiden name?" asked Henry.

Xavier looked uncomfortable. "Why?"

"Answer me!" Henry roared.

"Bigelow. Her last name was Bigelow," replied Xavier. Henry swayed on his feet.

Not caring about the gun, Devon rushed over and shoved Xavier aside. "Uncle Henry."

Sterling rushed over and helped Devon ease Henry onto the couch. Xavier stood rooted to his spot, staring at the older man in stunned disbelief.

When he'd gathered himself, Henry glanced at Xavier. "My God, Gloria had a son. Our son. I didn't know. I swear to you, I didn't know."

"No. It can't be." Xavier staggered backward, running a hand over his face. "You can't be my father."

"Is . . . is she still alive?" Henry asked. When Xavier didn't answer, Henry roared, "Is she?"

Dumbfounded, Xavier nodded.

"Thank God." Henry's eyes closed. When they opened again, he looked directly at Xavier, taking in every inch of him. "I fell in love with your mother the moment I laid eyes on her. She felt the same. From the first time I touched her hand, we were inseparable. I declared my love for her two weeks later. We were young. I proposed marriage, and she accepted. After college, we were going to be married. When my mother found out I'd proposed to her, she was livid. My mother—your grandmother— wanted more for me. Your mother's family wasn't well off or connected. I didn't care about that, but my mother aspired to be connected with one of Chicago's wealthiest families. I wanted no part of it." Henry's eyes misted. "I just wanted your mother."

Xavier backed up until he was at the doorway. "Why?

Why did you leave her? Why didn't you want me?" It was the cry of a tortured soul, childlike in nature and utterly desolate.

With Sterling's help, Henry got off the couch and walked slowly toward his son, as if Xavier would bolt at any minute. "I always wanted your mother. As for you . . . I didn't know you'd been conceived. After arguing repeatedly with my mother, I went to Gloria. I asked her to run off with me. I didn't care where we went, as long as it was away from my conniving mother. Your mother promised to go away with me. We loved each other that much. That night, before I returned home, we committed to each other . . . in body and soul."

Henry went on. "We were going to leave the next day. When I returned home, my mother and I had a terrible argument. In my anger, I blurted out our plans to elope and that I wanted nothing to do with the Mitchell fortune or her. The price was too high. My happiness— Gloria's happiness—couldn't be bought. I was packing later when she came into my room. She implored me again to consider my life and what I'd be giving up. When I wouldn't be deterred, she threw a letter on my bed and left. It was from Gloria. She wrote . . ." Henry battled to keep his emotions under control. "Her letter said she was leaving me. That by the time I read the letter, she'd be gone. That she'd always love me, but that she realized we'd never be happy if I gave up what I had to be with her. It was ridiculous. I would've given up anything to be with her."

Henry's voice failed, but then he continued. "I rushed to her house, but it was too late. The whole family was gone. Everything was packed up, and the place was deserted. I knew my mother had something to do with the Bigelows leaving. When I confronted her, she didn't even bother denying it. She'd paid them to leave town, never to return. It was more money than Gloria's parents would see in a lifetime. I can't blame them for leaving. It was an opportunity to support their children in a comfortable manner."

Henry looked at Sterling. "I went off the deep end. I had a terrible row with my mother. I accused my brother of being in league with her. I left that night— never to return." Henry's gaze connected with his brother's. "I know now I was wrong. My brother would never have betrayed me."

Xavier's expression was stricken. "You didn't know?"

"No. I swear I didn't. I tried for years to find your mother. At first, I didn't have much money to look. I struggled to make something of myself, to earn a living and become someone in my own right without the Mitchell money. It was hard, but I survived. I went into business for myself, and I prospered. I'd always had a keen business sense—heredity no doubt," Henry said dryly. "Anyway, I opened my own import/export company. When I made my first million, I sold the company. I'd done what I'd set out to do. I'd made something of myself, away from my poisonous, controlling mother.

"Before she died, I made sure I saw her. Little did I know, she'd been keeping tabs on me. She knew of my successes and my failures. I made peace with her, on my own terms, but I never forgave her. She robbed me of a life, of the only woman I have ever loved, for the sake of money. It was a blow I never recovered from. I continued trying to find Gloria, but I never did. After a while, I craved the quiet life—solitude. I bought some land, animals, and eventually started a farm. I've been doing that ever since. Your mother . . . she eventually married?"

Xavier shook his head. "No. She never did."

"But, where'd you get the name Taggert?" asked Henry.

"It was my great-grandmother's last name," Xavier explained.

"I don't understand," said Henry.

"Eventually, she told me my father was a Mitchell. She wouldn't tell me much more, except that she had loved him very much, but that it hadn't worked out. She admitted that she had changed her last name and moved. My grandparents had money, but I didn't know it was bribe money," Xavier said bitterly. "My mom told me my father had left me a nest egg to go to school and make something of myself with. I guess that was just part of my . . . grandmother's legacy, too. She made me think . . . I thought Sterling was my father. She didn't correct my assumptions. All this time . . ." Xavier dropped his head. He couldn't continue.

Henry struggled for composure. "Xavier, I know that I'm not in a position to ask anything of you, but I am your father. In my heart, I'm certain of it. I'll take whatever test I need to prove you're my son, but you've got to let go of this hatred. I would never have willingly given you up had I known you existed. I would never have abandoned you or your mother. Devon and Melanie are your cousins. Avalon and Sterling are your aunt and uncle. Regardless of what happened in the past, or today, we're family. It's time to release the bile that's driven you for so long. Candace is dead, and she's not coming back. Please, give us the gun. You've got to end this before you get in any deeper."

Before anyone had time to react, an officer yelled from the hallway, "This is the Northbrook Police Department. Drop your weapon, and put your hands over your head. Now!"

A flurry of activity ensued as several police officers entered the room and apprehended Xavier.

"Is everyone all right?" one officer asked, looking around the room.

"We're fine," Sterling answered.

The officer approached the small crowd and took their names and statements. "That was remarkable bravery you all displayed, especially you, Miss Seaton."

Jayde looked uncomfortable. "I didn't do anything special."

"I disagree. If it weren't for the call you placed, we might not have arrived in time. It could have been a very different scene when we arrived," said the officer.

All eyes went to Jayde. She blushed. "Melanie helped."

Devon pinned Jayde with an intense stare. "What call?"

"Miss Seaton used her cell phone to call us," explained the officer. "The dispatcher was able to ascertain from Miss Seaton's information that it was a possible hostage situation in progress."

"It wasn't anything special," Jayde protested.

"Yes, it was," Henry said, joining the group.

"Do you need a ride to the police station?" Sterling asked, putting his arm around his brother.

"Thank you. I just pray that he'll be okay . . . that I can help turn his life around. He's done terrible things, and he's hurt people in his quest for vengeance. Despite everything, it was a blessing we found each other, and I'm thankful. I just hope I don't end up losing him before I've really had a chance to know him." Henry's voice wavered as he choked back tears. "I guess we've all learned something today. Not to take anything or anyone for granted, and that life is precious and should be treated wisely. I thank God this terrible situation is over. Let's try to get past the nightmares. I know I'm ready to."

"I think we'd all like that," Avalon said, eyeing her husband pointedly.

Sterling shifted uncomfortably. "Ava, I'm sorry you had to relive that terrible time all over again—in front of everyone."

"We'll discuss everything later, Sterling." Avalon took her husband's hand.

Just then Selby walked into the room, sporting a wide white bandage around his head.

Everyone looked over at the butler in surprise.

"Selby, what happened?" Avalon rushed to his side. "Are you all right?"

"Quite, Mrs. Mitchell. Sporting a bruised head, compliments of Mr. Taggert. I was checked over by the EMT, and I'm fit for duty," replied Selby.

"The only duty you have, Selby, is allowing me to help you upstairs to bed. You won't be waiting on anyone until we've had you cleared by the doctor," Avalon said, guiding him to the door.

Devon took that moment to guide Jayde to a quiet corner of the room. Once there, he looked down at her in undisguised admiration.

Jayde's body tingled from what she saw in his gaze. She blushed all the way to her toes. "What?"

"What do you mean, what?" he said in wonder. "Jayde, you saved our lives. All of us. I'm beyond grateful for what you did for my family—for me." He kissed her solemnly. "You had our back when we needed it most. For that, you have my undying adoration and gratitude."

"Devon, all I did was call the police when I got the

EPILOGUE

Sitting on a window seat, Jayde stared at the water below. She couldn't help but reflect on the numerous changes in her life over the past year. They'd all survived Xavier's need for revenge and his plot to kill them all and take over the Mitchell family business, which he'd confessed to police. Convicted of assault with a deadly weapon and kidnapping charges, it would be a very long time before he was even eligible for parole. It was a terrible tragedy, and one that might have been avoided if Xavier hadn't blamed Devon for not being accepted into the Mitchell family. Jayde said a silent prayer of thanks that everyone was alive and well.

Shaking off her melancholy, she went back to hanging her artwork. Half an hour later, she breathed a sigh of relief at having finished her task. Jayde looked down at the floor by her feet. "What do you think, Boomer?"

"I don't know about him, but I think it looks great," a voice whispered in her ear. "Somehow I knew you'd be exactly where I left you. The paintings are perfect, sweetheart. You've done a tremendous job in here."

"Thank Paolo. He assured me I'd love his choices, and he was right."

"I'm surprised he offered, considering I'm involved," Devon replied.

"I told you he's forgiven you for accusing him of sabotaging the gallery. He doesn't curse you out in Italian nearly as much as he used to." Jayde chuckled, leaning back against her husband.

Devon encircled her in a loose but warm embrace.

"Devon, I'm not going to break." Jayde smiled at her husband's timidity.

"I think pop would be more applicable," Devon joked, looking down at her burgeoning stomach.

Turning, Jayde smiled serenely and punched him in his arm. "Did you come here to insult me, or do you have some higher purpose?"

Devon informed his wife that the Mitchell-Seaton Gallery and Youth Center would be opening the following week, as scheduled, and that his parents and his sister's brood would be arriving the day before.

"Mitchell and Jetta insist they be shown around Annapolis when they arrive," he told her.

"That would be your job," Jayde informed her husband.

"By the way, Mom wanted me to tell you that it would be nice if you could have the baby while everyone's in town for the opening," Devon replied.

"Our baby won't be ready to make an appearance for at least another three weeks. You Mitchells sure are pushy, aren't you?"

"Don't laugh, sweetheart. That observation includes you, too," Devon said, steering them from the nursery to the adjacent master suite.

She went out on the balcony and stared silently a

the water. Devon sensed the change in her mood, but he didn't pressure her. He knew Jayde would speak her mind when ready.

She turned around. "I was thinking earlier that so much has happened over the past year. Life is so fragile, Devon. If we hadn't been able to stop Xavier before he really hurt someone, all this wouldn't be here. *We* wouldn't be here," Jayde said tearfully.

Closing the distance between them, Devon gathered his wife against him. "I know, sweetheart, but I thank God that Henry was able to get through to him. It's sad when you think how things could've turned out so differently if he would've just come out with his suspicions years ago, instead of plotting revenge against our family. I know I shouldn't feel bad for him. His hatred for me cost me the most hellish year of my life and almost destroyed what you and I share." He kissed her neck.

"True, but I'm glad that Henry has come out of this whole experience with the love of the family he never thought he'd have. Now that he and Gloria are reunited, they can finally have their happy ending."

Devon thought about Xavier now being his cousin. It was still a surreal notion. He didn't think he'd ever be able to forgive him. Devon didn't doubt that his uncle and his new aunt, Gloria, would continue to stand by Xavier and give him the family unit he'd so desperately longed for. Nothing was more important than family.

He looked at his wife. "Though Xavier made my life and yours a living hell for a time, I'm glad he is finally at peace and has the father he desperately wanted. I don't know how I feel about him being my cousin, though—especially a mentally unstable cousin who tried to kill me."

"I know." Jayde shuddered. "Maybe things will be

different soon. With professional help, he's bound to get better."

Devon's expression turned possessive. "I don't care. I just don't want him near us. I promise you, if Xavier so much as breathes our way wrong, I'll kill him."

"It'll be fine. I sincerely believe that," Jayde reassured him. "I mean, look at my mom. If she can forgive you for taking her baby's job and firing her, there's hope for us all."

Devon was skeptical. "I suppose our marriage and the impending birth of her first and only grandchild have nothing to do with it?"

"Mmm, probably," Jayde admitted. "Well, at least she's honest about it. Besides, we're business partners now, too, so your standing in her eyes has increased tenfold."

"Oh, joy."

Taking Devon's hand, Jayde guided him through the French doors and toward the hall.

"Where are we going?" He grinned lasciviously, all thoughts of Jayde's mother forgotten.

"Don't get excited, Mr. Mitchell. I'm only taking you to the kitchen. It's time for a snack."

"Oh," Devon said, disappointed. "I thought—"

"I know what you thought."

Taking a bite of her cream-cheese bagel a few minutes later, Jayde sighed dreamily. "How's your dad faring with his new second in command?"

"He's making the best of it. He respects my decision and it's not like I'm completely out of the picture. I'm still on the board. So is Melanie."

"Yeah? You were on the board at the gallery, and look how that turned out," she teased.

"He knows my interests are here"—he kissed th